"GIVE US A BIG HUG..."

Baird's voice was a sigh as he moved restlessly into her arms. "I wanted to call so badly." His chilled palms cupped her jaw, and for a moment their eyes played an intimate melody.

"I've missed you, too," Dawnelle breathed against his descending lips.... Time and anger eddied away. She clung, exciting him, slowly transforming his adulation to a sweet aching passion.

"I planned a hug of greeting—just a hug," he murmured. "But you look so good after so long! How could the feeling between us ever turn to anger?"

She was shivering now, her cheek nestled against his brawny shoulder. "Feeling, Baird? You won't deny it—hide it—fifteen minutes from now?"

No answer.

Dawnelle didn't deny it—she loved him. And minded very much that she couldn't say it aloud.

WELCOME TO...

SUPERROMANCES

A sensational series of modern love stories from Worldwide Library.

Written by masters of the genre, these longer, sensual and dramatic novels are truly in keeping with today's changing life-styles. Full of intriguing conflicts, the heartaches and delights of true love, SUPERROMANCES are absorbing stories—satisfying and sophisticated reading that lovers of romance fiction have long been waiting for.

LOUELLA NELSON

SENTINEL AT DAWN

A SUPERROMANCE FROM
WORLDWIDE

TORONTO • NEW YORK • LONDON • PARIS
AMSTERDAM • STOCKHOLM • HAMBURG
ATHENS • MILAN • TOKYO • SYDNEY

FOR DEAN
And in gratitude to
Luster Productions
—Lou, Steve, Eric—
May the circle remain unbroken

Published January 1984

First printing November 1983

ISBN 0-373-70096-2

Printed in Canada

CHAPTER ONE

DAWNELLE BELANGER'S GAZE trained uneasily on the timber shadows, the corridors of sunlight around her. Like the offshore swell of the Pacific, her emerald eyes revealed a fathomless strength. Yet a watchfulness spoke from the depths of those eyes. . . as if her heart had survived old wounds.

A flick of her wrist silenced the purring Fiat 124 Sport. Her hand remained at the ignition, and as her fingers closed over the latch key to the lighthouse cottage five miles north, her brow creased in worry.

After a moment her spare shoulders rose. The shrug might have said, "I hope I've done the right thing."

Thoughtfully she looked to her right. The passenger seat shuddered as the German shepherd shifted nervously, tapered claws biting into the Naugahyde. Champion blood displayed itself lavishly in this female. Ebony brows arched above splendid brown eyes. Erect silver ears boasted a generous breadth between them. Even her muzzle seemed royally carved and sheathed in black velvet. But the wary flickering of her eyes was no stamp of the proven, confident champion. Rather, the shepherd's plume tucked around her forepaws and her darting looks over one shoulder suggested fear.

Sighing in dismay, Dawnelle withdrew her key ring

and snapped it over a loop in the waistband of her jeans. The dog whirled, crouched, traced her muzzle uncertainly along her mistress's arm. Startled, Dawnelle drew back, her chestnut hair shimmering at the sudden move.

Again the shy nuzzle.

At once compassion deepened the color of Dawnelle's eyes to the rich green of shaded spring grass. *The animal is afraid of the slightest sound,* she thought. Would the dog ever forget her past, trust people not to hurt her? Would visitors to the light station be safe around her? Having bought the dog out of pity, Dawnelle now wondered if she'd sacrificed her job. She hoped not, because city life had lost its allure, and the antiquated facilities and isolation of Trinidad Head Light Station were precious to her. The Trinidad beacon flashing relentlessly through dark blankets of fog; waves purging the boulders nearly two hundred feet below her wood-frame keeper's cottage—these assets uplifted her. Allowed her to think, to plan. Already the gathering-back of her emotions had begun. Surely one year at the station would shore her up enough to tackle the lucrative corporate life again?

And now she had a companion, a gaunt young shepherd who needed all the love and patience Dawnelle was capable of offering. Returning her attention to her pet, she tenderly caressed the animal's back. The silver fur quivered. No. Dawnelle shook her uncertainties away. No, she would not regret rescuing this lovely creature. Having a German shepherd around for protection was smart for a woman alone at a lighthouse. Besides, by the time she'd showered Miss Mo with love and trained her to obey commands, the nervous hatred of children would vanish. She'd simply restore the dog's faith in human kindness.

"Miss Mo Maya of Gerardi," she said softly, suppressing a desire to draw the timid female close, "I'm sorry for the horrible treatment you've endured. No need to cringe. I'm not going to box your ears."

Gently she tugged the chiseled head around so Miss Mo couldn't avoid her gaze. "You're with me now," she said firmly. "Jenkins and his kids will never kick you again. Never choke you with that heavy leash. Let's just forget the unhappiness we've both been through." She leaned close. "Forget it, do you hear me? We're starting over."

But Miss Mo pulled away and poked her tapered muzzle through the partly open window. A low whine sounded in her throat. She sniffed the air, her attention suddenly held by a squirrel scurrying across the cliff trail.

Dawnelle's eyes slid to the sheltering forest, its lush huckleberry patches and high canopy of redwood branches contrasting starkly with her windswept lighthouse rook in Trinidad. Idly her hand scratched the ruff of Miss Mo's chest. *Don't push her,* she thought. *We each need time to get used to freedom.*

And they had plenty of time. Miss Mo was still young. At that thought she felt another ripple of irritation. She wished she'd bought the dog yesterday with her usual business aplomb. But in her hurry to get herself and Miss Mo away from the fat ugly Jenkins outside that Eureka supermarket, she'd forgotten to get the registration papers from him. Perhaps she ought to drive south the thirty miles and see if she could locate

Paul Jenkins. Maybe in a few days, she mused, after Miss Mo adjusts to her new surroundings.

Well, at any rate, the papers Jenkins had briefly shoved under her nose indicated Miss Mo was only eighteen months old. Young enough to forget she'd been chained up her whole life. Chained and tormented by Jenkin's children, on bicycles.

Reminded of the mental cruelty she'd endured herself, Dawnelle pounded the steering wheel in disgust, then jerked open the door of the Fiat. Oblivious to Miss Mo's reactions to this show of temper, Dawnelle let the old memories carry her two swift steps from the car. She stood with hands fisted, the sea breeze whipping brown tendrils across her heated cheeks.

I never should have fallen in love with my boss, she fumed, more disgusted with her own foolishness than the hurt. It wasn't enough to be well-read, attractive, loving and competent at public relations. Jeff Dugan's Harvard M.B.A. and his city-slicker, pin-striped ways demanded she shelve her pride, as well. He'd actually *expected* her to stay on with him, getting the work of the marketing division out on time, expanding the company's success in medical-surgical technology—as if he'd never hung that ceiling over her career. She'd been so blind to his true character! The reckoning had come all in one jolt, she recalled, a brutal slap in the face.

She'd remained seated in the boardroom of Valley Laser, Inc., stunned, while Jeff appointed the boss's daughter director of advertising and promotion, heading the very department Dawnelle had spent three years setting up. She shook her head. *My career dirtied, then thrown away like dishwater in exchange for Jeff's own success. Men!*

"Thank God I never married the creep!" she muttered.

The nervous thud of the dog's tail made her turn in surprise. Miss Mo crouched anxiously in the car.

"Who needs men, anyhow?" Dawnelle smiled ruefully. The dog sat still, as if expecting Dawnelle to erupt again in anger.

She leaned in to ruffle the dog's fur. The fluffy tail thumped in response. Impulsively Dawnelle hugged Miss Mo, burying her face in the thick coat as she forced away the despondency, the bitterness of betrayal. Next time she'd order up straight business, she silently promised. Tell them plainly to hold the pleasure. A bright woman need be taught only once the taboo of mixing the two.

Beneath Dawnelle's cheek, Miss Mo's heart beat wildly for a moment as she struggled to inch away. And then Dawnelle felt a cold nose on her neck and a warm discreet lick on her ear.

She pulled back to look at the dog. "Have I won you so quickly, little one?" she murmured, delighted.

The tail flopped on the cream-tone seat.

"C'mon!" Eager to stretch her legs, Dawnelle urged the animal to the ground and shut the door. "You're going to love my favorite beach!" Instinctively she knew this romp would relax Miss Mo, set a tone of friendship and trust between them.

Beyond her car, the cliff trail tunneled a quarter mile into the redwoods before emerging above the beach. Attuning her hearing to the call of a Stellar's jay and her sight to the dim shadows, Dawnelle headed into the forest, her tennis shoes treading soundlessly over the russet needles. As Miss Mo dashed ahead, her tail a silver plume against the gloom of deep woods, Dawnelle smiled in satisfaction.

Jeff and the city be damned. A beautiful dog at her side, a year in the wilds of the great Northwest—this was the life! For now, she wanted nothing more.

A LONE SITKA SPRUCE stood watch over the craggy inlet, its roots shriveled and tentaclelike, because the fallen logs from which it had once drawn moisture had long ago decayed.

Ignoring the path that branched right along the bluff, Dawnelle stood beneath the spruce boughs for a moment and studied the sea-stacks offshore. Once part of the mainland rock, these ledges stood like squat soldiers surrounded by surging ocean. Sand lace-edged with surf lay like a pale crescent below the cliffs. As usual, Dawnelle noted with pleasure, the intimate cove was deserted. Calling the dog, she began sliding and scrambling down the ragged trail.

Her teal blue cotton blouse was hugging damply to her back when she finally felt her tennis shoes sink into the sand. Collapsing in the shadow of a castle formed by driftwood caught against a shoulder of rock, she looked around. The dank smell of bleaching seaweed rose to her nostrils; heaving waves filled her ears with a muted roar. A ripple of pleasure, a sense of freedom and belonging, drew laughter from deep in her throat, and the sound brought Miss Mo's nose under Dawnelle's chin. Dawnelle closed her eyes and reached for the dog.

"Yes." She laughed, patting the tufted chest. "This is our beach, Lady Mo. It's been here aeons, waiting for us!"

Why did Miss Mo's muscles tense like that? Dawnelle blinked open her eyes.

A low cry rose from within, but she stifled it, innately cautious as a result of her years among wild things. Clamping her teeth shut, she looked at the huge black dog peering down at them from a rock. He was all shoulders, forelegs, lolling pink tongue—and power. His long coat gleamed with health and sunshine. Framed by the sky, the muscular animal held them still with his brown gaze.

"Hello," Dawnelle ventured, weaving her fingers into Miss Mo's chain collar. As if invited, the black dog clambered forward and leaped for the sand.

"Hey!" Dawnelle backed against the rocks, dragging the wriggling Miss Mo with her. She glanced left toward the trail, toward safety. Looking back to the intruder, she saw him standing stiff-legged in the wash of sand. He was grand against the shells and sky, his long black nose arrogant, poised. Then he yawned, a grin of mock boredom revealing ivory canines that lacked the pearly sharpness of Miss Mo's. Something in his eyes...a laughing look. *Why run,* Dawnelle thought with sudden clarity. *This fellow wants to play!*

Relieved, she watched the intruder prance away, silky hair swaying. "Go on, Miss Mo," she urged, nudging her quaking dog toward the waiting male. "You can't refuse the invitation of a good-looking guy like him! Go!"

Dawnelle jogged from the shade of the driftwood castle to watch as the shaggy black tackled Miss Mo, rolling her silver form into the sand. She yelped; he leaped to his feet and stood rigidly above her, every line of his formidable body demanding subservience. But his thickly feathered tail waved minutely, and Dawnelle felt a touching emotion strike like a brass bell inside her.

Then the dogs were running along the surf line, splashing into the water, mouths open, bodies weaving in dolphinlike rhythm. Dawnelle's heart lightened. She began to run with them, calling her dog, relishing the feel of warm bodies pushing against her legs in salty ungainly tumbles.

In minutes her shoes and jeans and blouse were soaked, clinging to her. She knew her hair lay in a chestnut tangle on her shoulders, but she loved the sense of abandon. She splashed thigh-deep into the icy water, the dogs leaping after her, barking and nipping each other.

Eventually Dawnelle's legs grew numb in the cold June surf, and with a rolling wave as impetus, she staggered toward the warm beach. As the wave receded, sucking sand from beneath her shoes, she stiffened.

He seemed a giant of a man, emerging from beneath the arching cliff. He strode toward her, brown-bearded and wearing the lumberjack's garb of jeans, heavy boots and roll-sleeved plaid shirt. An oval of pale face glowed beneath the pelt of brown hair, the beard, the mustache. Unmistakably, he issued an air of no-nonsense—and something else: anger, or merely purposefulness? Dawnelle bit down on her lip.

In this area of friendly fishing families and earthy woodsmen, she would not have felt apprehension—ordinarily. But that broad chest thrust forward above those swinging legs reminded her of a provoked bull elk.

Instinctively Dawnelle murmured Miss Mo's name,

but the dog was wrapped in a gritty heap with the brawny male.

"Miss Mo!" she called sharply, and because her eyes were on the approaching man, she could only sense the dogs' sudden stillness. One of them issued a low warning growl.

"Yurok!" thundered the man, his deep masculine tone, like a stage actor's, carrying easily across thirty feet and the landing waves. "Come!" he commanded. The black dog galloped forward, his pads churning softly in the sand. He bounded against the man's faded jeans.

Seeing Yurok's black tail whip joyously, Dawnelle relaxed.

The man's wavy brown hair glinted as he bent slightly, withdrawing a heavy chain from the back of his waistband. Snapping the catch to the dog's collar, he sent a stinging jerk to Yurok's throat.

Miss Mo whined and lowered her head.

Dawnelle saw the shaggy dog yanked roughly to heel by the woodsman's right side. The magnificent animal crouched as if shot.

Reminded of Jenkins's treatment of Miss Mo, Dawnelle bolted forward. "What the devil are you doing to that dog?" she demanded angrily.

Evidently surprised, the man straightened abruptly. "Who's asking?" He stared at her.

She ignored his question, shocked into silence by the intense blue of his gaze—and by the profound magnetism she felt emanating from him.

Up close he was even more massive. A towering man with heavily muscled shoulders. A man of battle. A wrestler, perhaps? The patch of face above his neatly trimmed beard and mustache was pallid, hardly robust. Rough-hewn cheekbones rose from a strong jaw. His eyes were deeply set beneath a prominent brow, and from the twin arches of that brow, his brown hair sprang thick and soft. Looking at the man's craggy face, Dawnelle had an impression of intelligence warring with an earthy virility.

Nordic eyes probed Dawnelle's wet blouse and jeans. The only soft characteristic about him was his mouth. The lips were sensuously full, and they parted now in wry amusement.

"Who's asking?" he said again in a gently mocking tone.

"I am." She flung her arms carelessly wide. "Your dog was so full of life, having such a great time. Now look at him!"

The rugged man shifted, planting his feet apart, folding his arms across his chest. The chain clinked, causing Miss Mo to whine again deep in her throat. Then his stunning eyes locked with Dawnelle's. "Who was Yurok having a great time with?"

"Miss Mo." She indicated her dog. She sensed the pull of power behind those eyes and boldly returned his stare.

"And?"

"And you've cowed him. He was magnificent on the beach."

"What would you have me do? Reward disobedience with praise, Miss—what was the name?"

"Belanger."

It was almost imperceptible, the narrowing look, the

quick return to guilelessness. "Miss. . . Belanger. Dawn something-or-other Belanger, isn't it?"

He swayed in a self-satisfied manner as Dawnelle's expression flickered from irritation to surprise to curiosity. He shrugged in response. "Small town. *Trinidad News & Views* carried the story of the public-relations executive come to do the town a favor and run its lighthouse."

She paled slightly at his mild sarcasm. "You're editorializing without having all the facts."

"Pardon?"

"The Coast Guard runs the lighthouse. I'm more of a curator who takes visitors on tours."

"By appointment, I believe." He smiled, the mockery more pronounced. "It's surprising—do you mind my saying—to find someone of your corporate experience taking over an antiquated lighthouse."

"Urban exodus. People are always escaping to the quiet countryside. The seashore."

"Yours is hardly an upward career move, is it?"

"You mean—" she matched his baiting smile with a cool one of her own "—among the painters, writers and otherwise talented recluses of Trinidad there are no other former executives?"

His eyes shadowed suddenly as his brows locked. He looked quickly toward the sea.

Dawnelle felt a brief confusion. This man stretching his legs in the sand a few feet away transmitted "boardroom executive" from his polished manner. Yet he looked the woodsman, acted the churl with his dog. And just now, did his turning away mean she'd angered him? Over what?

Miss Mo rose from the beach then and gingerly approached Yurok. The male didn't so much as glance in her direction. Even when Miss Mo sniffed his shoulder, Yurok kept his brown eyes staring at the horizon. Evidently perplexed, the female sat on her haunches again, panting down at her immobile friend.

Dawnelle's mouth turned down. "Look at him." She waved at Yurok. "He's afraid you're going to beat him."

Angling a sharp glance at his dog, the stranger laughed low in his throat. "He's not afraid I'll beat him, Miss Belanger. He's an attack-trained dog. I'd hardly want to beat the spirit out of an animal who protects my life and property."

Dawnelle felt the chill of wind on her spine. She'd been romping with a dog trained to kill! "He seemed so friendly. I was playing with him."

"So I noticed. But I doubt you'd have been met so warmly if you'd been nearer my place—up there." She followed his gesture and deciphered a shard of glass wall. Red brown shingles jutted from an evergreen brake that obscured part of a modern cliff house.

"My humble retreat," he mocked, bowing slightly. "Yurok has extraordinary perceptions about people. He'll admit a friend even if I'm not home. But let that person give off vibes of premeditated burglary or attack...." His shoulders rose expressively. "Yurok's sensory-receiving capabilities are amazing."

Dawnelle had difficulty controlling a shiver. What a pair, she thought dryly: lean, seemingly normal—yet deadly. Still, she felt a tremor of response to the very maleness of the man who owned the attack dog. Raising her gaze, she met his steady look. This time, involuntarily, she shivered.

"You're cold," he said at once, stepping toward her.

Immediately Yurok was on his feet, dark wet hair pressed close to his master's leg.

"Yes," Dawnelle acknowledged. "I should be getting up the cliff."

"How about some tea or cognac?"

"No, thanks. My car's just through the woods."

"Perhaps another time, Miss Belanger."

"Dawnelle," she corrected, stepping toward the rock shoulder hiding the trail.

"Baird Langston." He reached out, clasping Dawnelle's right hand, looking at her as if she should recognize the name.

Glancing at the broad warm palm wrapped around her slim fingers, she felt a stomach-stirring response. His pale fingers lay carved against the creamy pink of her own hand. They were finely molded fingers, the lean flesh tapering from smooth joints. Soft brown hair curled around his wrist. Like the other, this hand was ringless, and hardly the toughened ham of a logger. Dawnelle sought the thrill of his eyes again and was not disappointed.

"Nice to meet you, Baird," she said softly. "I'm hoping I haven't misjudged you, but you were awfully harsh on your dog."

"Does that bother you so much?"

She nodded.

"Then I hope this will balance first impressions." Baird leaned down and unsnapped the leash, tucking it into his belt.

Yurok's tail curled, but he remained where he was, his head centered against the faded blue legging. Baird grinned again. After patting his dog, he swept his arm toward the water.

Instantly Yurok rushed after a startled Miss Mo, chasing her down the beach with every ounce of the energy and spirit he'd shown before. In a thundering arc that sent gulls screaming into the sky, he returned to Baird, slamming into his legs with such enthusiasm the man stumbled back. Chuckling, Baird tussled affectionately with the dog's head for a moment, a rough gesture of love Dawnelle found strangely moving. He straightened finally, and thus fortified, Yurok began zigzagging among the rocks, his shoulder never more than a few feet from his silver companion.

"A matter of obedience training." Baird shrugged conclusively, his eyes crinkling with amusement. "Does that change your mind about me?"

"A little, yes." She grinned.

"I'm very glad it does."

A rush of pleasure flushed her cheeks as Dawnelle turned away and began to ascend the cliff trail. She grasped roots and embedded stones, pulling, steadying, toiling up the slope.

Aware of Baird's low grunts as he climbed behind her, she said over her shoulder, "How's the rock fishing along this section of beach?"

"Nice pool in the lee of the north point. Why? You an angler?"

"Avid. You?"

"All my life."

She wondered if he was one of the fishermen in Trinidad's salmon or crab fleet, although his pale complexion made her hesitate. "Are you a commercial fisherman, Baird?"

"Of sorts. When the weather holds I collect specimens for Humboldt State University—among other pursuits."

"You mean you gather starfish and things?"

"Right," he huffed, sounding surprisingly out of breath for a man with shoulders like Attila. "But I don't like coming home to find the place unguarded and Yurok off gallivanting with the ladies."

"I can barely tolerate the thought of all that happy energy cooped up inside while you enjoy the elements," she countered. "Most people use locks to keep out the criminal element—especially in a rural area like this."

"So the gossip's gotten to you already, has it?"

Strange bitter edge to his voice. "Have you had a break-in?"

When he didn't answer she twisted to glance down, and saw his mouth drawn into a hard angry line as he climbed with undue roughness. His eyes glittered up at her briefly before he tore a tuft of green weeds savagely out of the way. Evidently the subject was closed. Perplexed by his attitude, she turned her back and moved upward.

As he made sounds of exertion on the steep section of trail she's just traversed, her lips curved in satisfaction at her own agility. Four years at San Jose State and four more working in San Francisco's Silicon Valley among the computer wizards hadn't taken the edge off her strength. Since she'd spent her vacations skiing, hiking and fishing, her long legs were as capable of clambering over rocks and logs as they'd been during her years at her father's fish hatchery. Eagerly she scrambled up a spot dusted with loose pebbles.

"Is it surf, lake or stream fishing you like?" Baird interrupted her thoughts, his tone once again conversational.

"Oh, fast cold streams, most definitely," she laughed, pleased beyond reason that his ill humor had passed. "My brother Tommy and I—"

The memory of her kid brother struck her painfully, with the brilliance and speed of the chrome bumper that had crushed him from her life. She shook her head, clearing away the old hurt. "We used to spend summers digging up angle worms and finding new spots on the creek near our home."

"Lucky. To share things like that with your brother. All my brother was interested in was the next new car Granddad Langston might buy him."

She looked down at Baird and noticed a peculiar whorl about the size of a quarter in the beard carpeting his right jaw. Old scar, she speculated, wondering how he'd gotten it. "You're bitter about quite a few things in life, aren't you, Baird?" she said gently, certain she was right.

He paused six feet below her, his bulwark chest heaving slightly as he leaned into the face of the bluff. Again she pondered on his conditioning, since he was built solidly around the shoulders and torso. Then his gaze met hers, and her questions were driven away by the warm rushing sensation in her stomach. She realized he was studying her with a kind of open vulnerable intensity. Almost. . . longing.

"Your eyes remind me of those redwoods sprinkled

through the forest up there," he said gravely, raising his chin without moving his own eyes. "If you've ever noticed, the sun turns the needle tips to translucent green."

Very, very nice, she thought, and smiled her thanks. *Take me fishing with you, Baird Langston, and I'll forget I ever knew that marketing director in San Francisco.*

But she turned away with the thought that her judgment of a man had been too hasty the last time. And too heartbreaking. *I need time,* she said to herself, picking her way along a narrow embankment. *Time to analyze how I could know Jeff for three years and still be surprised by his character.*

"Where's your favorite fishing spot in these parts?" she asked, curling her fingers around a convenient whisk of grass.

"I've taken my share of salmon from the mouth of the Klamath River."

He was a stream man himself, she decided, strangely satisfied. "Lure or bait?"

"Depends what's working."

Of course. She knew that. The mighty Klamath River. She'd heard stories from her father and his cronies—terrible drowning accidents, *Guinness Book* catches of salmon, trout and sturgeon. The Klamath was high on her priority list of planned fishing trips, along with hikes through the redwoods to see some of those twelve-foot-thick trunks and an investigation of the elk herds at Prairie Creek.

She heard the dogs barking and looked out over the cove—thrashed by surf, wild, guarded by those black crags rising against pale sand and blue sky. Gulls scattered from feeding along a dark ribbon of seaweed. Her brief serenity disturbed by their cries, Dawnelle smiled at the excited dives of the dogs and resumed her climb.

Baird's voice carried to her again. "How do you like living at the lighthouse, isolated as you are?"

"It's lonely and I love it. I have plenty to do, setting out flowers and cleaning up the place for the tourists who'll be arriving soon. I'm only taking a few hours off today to let Miss Mo stretch her legs."

"You're not bored yet?"

Had she imagined a brittle edge of sarcasm to his question? Hoisting around a boulder, she said firmly, "I'm definitely not bored. How about yourself, Baird? How long have you been in Trinidad?"

There was a significant pause. "Three months."

"I haven't seen you."

"You've only been here two weeks yourself." His knowledge of her took her by surprise. Until she remembered he'd recognized her from the newspaper account of her arrival.

"It's true—ah!" She was brushed rudely into a bramble by the panting dogs as they scrambled up the trail. "But Trinidad's a tiny place, Baird," she laughed, righting herself. "Do you keep yourself and Yurok locked away like common criminals in that lovely redwood retreat—I mean, when you're not out collecting?"

She heard an angry curse behind her. Then: "Keep your corporate innuendos to yourself, Miss Belanger!"

"Corporate *what*?" Whirling toward the harsh voice, she lost grip of a rotten stump. In moments she was sliding down the path, digging her nails into the moist bank, greens and blues and dank colors a kaleidoscope before her eyes. A stinging pain shot along her arm. She was enveloped by the instant, cold-sweat fear of falling without control.

She yelped as she crashed into something solid. Realizing it was Baird's heavy boot, and that he now held her fiercely by the arms as she lay beneath his arched torso, she flushed. "Damn!"

"Damned lucky I was here," he growled, his aggressive stare making her shrink involuntarily against the rough terrain.

"Lucky!" Dawnelle glowered indignantly at his bearded face. "If you hadn't made that nasty crack I wouldn't be here!"

"But you are, now that's the truth of it."

"Your attitude is galling, Baird. Please get off me!" She twisted and wrenched, her breath shortening in anger.

Baird's blue eyes narrowed. "I'm hardly on you, green eyes, so much as you are under me. But I don't think I should do all the work!" He settled more comfortably against her, only his shoulders and shaggy head held away. His deep laugh sounded mellow with satisfaction.

With a startled cry, Dawnelle drew a breath that mixed tangy sea air with Baird's male scent, a smoky-cinnamon aura, appealing and heady. One Herculean shoulder clad in green-and-black plaid cut out the sky.

"Move so I can get up, will you?" she demanded, trying desperately not to croak the words.

"What?" he taunted, lowering his head. "No executive jargon now? No clever boardroom terms to rectify the impasse in negotiations?"

"What are you muttering about? Negotiations, boardrooms. You're not making sense!" She tried to push him off, but he stiffened, refusing to budge. "Get off me!"

What was he attempting, holding her arms so she couldn't move? And lowering his head still farther....

A flutter of alarm caught inside her like a paper in a draft. Her stomach muscles contracted, propelling a spasm along her arms to her chilled fingers. The feeling of fear was so *familiar*. That other time, so long ago...her brother's healthy freckled face suddenly tortured and white.... He was clutching at her, sputtering, choked by the lake that would have taken him if she hadn't dived into the murky depths to save him....

And now she was the victim. She shook herself mentally, trying to jar loose the panic that linked past with present. Tommy was gone. She was here on this sheer cliff trail, pinned beneath a stranger whose masculinity vibrated through her being in a way totally unfamiliar, totally unsettling. Pride rose within her like a demon, and she quelled the fear. Her brain clicked into high gear, nerves humming while she shaped reason, action.

This man had been furious. Why? Was he still angry, or was he goading her? To what purpose? "What do you want?" she said bluntly.

A flicker of respect brightened his eyes. "Your apology is first on the agenda."

"Apology!"

"You'll say you're sorry like a nice corporate princess," he rumbled, looking decidedly predatory, "or be here all day in those wet clothes."

"Sorry? Is this your idea of a joke? You expect an apology, when all I did was suggest you stayed home a lot with your dog? You're behaving as if you've been chained up for twenty years and starved for human contact!"

The plundering look that flushed his pale face seemed to sweep through her being. Dismayed, she drew in a breath, began to speak.

But he muttered something and took her open mouth with his—moving, hungry and strangely bitter. His beard, soft as it was, seared across her flesh. His kiss sent trepidation racking through her. Yet strangely, she ached to hold this man. To crush him close the way he was crushing her.

Remembered nights with Jeff Dugan ricochetted through her mind, the memories less intense, certainly less thrilling, but maddening in their cruel conclusion. Jeff had used her. He'd taken her love until boardroom politics had warped that love. Then he'd thrown it out with the junk mail. How dared this stranger kiss her with the rough possession of an angry lover? And insult her with cheap innuendos!

She began to squirm, her breath choked, wheezing. The thought rang through her mind that she could be raped. But Baird Langston wouldn't violate her, she told herself. Wouldn't do more than frighten her, with his male bravado showing like a red flag.

Her temper flared at the realization that another stronger individual would toy with her without the slightest real provocation and wield strength to force his will. *Animal,* she thought, and worked one hand free. She hit him, feeling the muscles that arched from his neck to his shoulder. She tried desperately to shift her head away, but the pressure of his mouth held her and she could only beat at him and twist her shoulders. A groan of desperation tore from her.

Suddenly Baird gentled. A floating sensual quality came to his kiss, and she stopped struggling to feel its sweetness. His lips lured, circled, tantalized. His mouth made her lazy with its slow deep caress, while his fingers drew her arms, shoulders, breasts into his body—molding, cherishing, building her laziness to a yearning ache. This was seduction that took her apart limb by limb, without pain. She wrapped her arm around his great shoulders, wishing she could free her other to hold him entirely.

She heard him make an agonized sound in his throat, and he twisted away from her lips, though obviously as reluctant as she to end the glory. His head went to the chasm between her collar and shoulder. She felt the softness of his hair brushing her chin as he breathed.

"Baird!" slipped from her lips.

But when he raised his eyes to take in the surprise on her face, she saw anger in his tight lips and icy glare. He grasped her arm. "How does it feel to be imprisoned, Dawnelle?"

Instantly she shuttered the surprise, buried the pleasure and retorted, "I don't like it!" She wrenched her arm free. "You have no right—what are you going to do, rape the keeper of the lighthouse?"

"Rape?" he muttered.

"They'd find you!" She twisted to avoid the sharp keys jammed beneath her waistband. Unnerved by the new bullish look in his eyes, she wondered if she had been wrong about his intent. "They'd lock you up so you'd never see this lovely cove again!"

Baird Langston roared with anger, clenching his teeth when he said, "You fool! Do you think I'd let anyone—I'd—God, I'd probably kill any fool who tried!"

Her flesh crawled along her arms. Dawnelle felt her eyes widen in spite of the firm grip she had on her emotions. Who was this man? Such power in his body. He must be more than six feet, lots more. Burly shoulders. Blanched hairy face. How would she escape? Never in all her twenty-six years had there been cause to arm herself against this kind of assault.

Reason with him, she commanded herself through rising panic. She forced herself to meet his eyes. "Do you—what made you angry?"

"Save it! You know damned well!"

"What have I done but fallen down a cliff to you?"

"The innocent act won't work. Do you think you can throw out your mean-minded digs, and I'll stand for it? You forget I've been part of your world! I know the games you people play!"

"What world? If I just knew why you're angry!"

"I take little pleasure in having my past thrown in my face!"

"Your past? I don't in heaven's name know what you mean!"

"Don't you?" The glacial gaze narrowed. "Do you enjoy the gossip?"

"No! My business is public relations, not gossip!"

"I'll bet! Don't tell me someone with your pampered past isn't bored, stuck out on that desolate chunk of rock a mile from civilization. Do you breakfast at The

Eatery for company? Humble as it is compared to what you're used to, it's still the proverbial lifeline to local news, isn't it?" Because his hands were occupied, he hunched his shoulders at her. "Do you keep those tiny ears tuned for something exciting, Dawnelle? Something to remind you of the exciting corporate life?"

This was no time to avenge her injured pride, she decided. "I—hate corporate life," she said, disconcerted by the warm weight of the body pressing her down. "Could we have this interview up on the cliff, do you think, Baird? You're hurting my back."

"What's the matter?" he taunted. "Missing the polish of an executive's romantic approach? Ex-con not good enough to touch you?"

Her brows shot up. "Ex-con?"

"Don't pretend innocence!"

"No, no, I won't—I'm not." She angled her head Miss Mo was nowhere in sight. "Please, my back. . . "

Baird grunted with disdain and pulled away.

Before he could remove his weight fully, Dawnelle was twisting and dragging herself up the narrow path.

Get away, her mind screamed. How could she have so misjudged this man? An ex-convict with an attack-trained dog! Like a street fighter, he wore that chain hanging from his waist. Its dull clink told her he was scrambling behind her. She felt her foot slip as Baird's laughter rang up the mountainside. She moaned, pulled higher, cursing the steepness.

Finally she was near the top. Far down the bluff she saw a flash of pearl gray as Miss Mo dived into the underbrush. Dawnelle raised her voice. But the dog's name died beneath the man's plea. "Dawnelle, please. . . ."

CHAPTER TWO

An arabesque of dark spruce roots yawned above Dawnelle's head. She paused.

"Dawnelle...." Baird's low voice cracked, stilling the breath in her throat. "I paid three years of my life while my ex-partner lived like a latter-day sultan on my wealth. A thousand and ninety-five days, while the bastard played around in Hong Kong and Singapore."

"Please, Mr. Langston—Baird." She angled her head so she could see his chalky face. "I know nothing about you."

"Do you think because I'm a Langston I'm immune to the gossip? All the more reason—a Langston brought to his knees when he tried to break tradition, go his own way."

At the terrible anguish in his words, Dawnelle felt her emotional defenses crumbling, exposing the old easily aroused sympathies. *Vulnerable,* came the inner warning. *Used. Betrayed.* Barely in time, she stopped herself from turning to him in understanding. Instead she said crisply, "I've said I never heard of you."

"Everyone knows!"

"I don't!"

"Why lie?"

Her anger now overrode finer feelings, and she

whirled, looking down at him with eyes slitted in fury. "Don't call me a liar!" She scrambled up the bank and stood glaring at him. "You're a brutal man, Langston! If you didn't commit the crime, you're capable of it! Don't come near me again, or I'll charge you with assault!"

She began to pick her way over the gnarled roots of the sentinel spruce, watching him hoist up over the edge. She felt the dogs brush excitedly against her legs. Linking Miss Mo's chain in her fingers, facing the man, Dawnelle inched backward.

Baird now towered over her, shoulders hulking against the sky, face china-white, hands fisted at his sides. Neither of them spoke. Tension strung between them, and by comparison the forest seemed silent. Dawnelle stepped back; Baird followed: panther stalking the long-limbed eland.

The dogs' panting sawed through the stillness. A jay screeched, spinning into the woods.

Dawnelle felt the forest close around her, so that an arbor of greenery framed the broad-shouldered man against that oval of blue sky. Sunlight lanced across her shoulder. A breeze swept in from the ocean, fanning around her the scents of salt, pine and leaf mold.

"Bring your dog to heel," she ordered quietly.

After a moment when Baird seemed to consider her demand, he nodded. Then, "Yurok, heel!" The dog spun into place beside him, and Dawnelle breathed more deeply, releasing Miss Mo. Pausing between them, the female looked from Baird to Dawnelle. She whined softly.

Dawnelle halted. Baird stopped a few paces away. "Your dog is concerned," he said.

"Do you blame her?"

Sighing deeply, Baird drew a hand across the Gothic arches of his imposing forehead. "I suppose I couldn't blame either of you for being on edge," he muttered. "But you should take care what you say to me about the so-called criminal element. My view of the past differs from the majority—for obvious reasons."

"Reasons more obvious to you than me. How was I to know about your past? I just met you."

He shrugged. "I assumed you knew."

"You assumed I knew all the local gossip," she challenged bitterly, "and that I believed it like some mindless company secretary!"

"Secretary, big-shot P.R. director—hell—" his eyes glowed with temper "—is there a difference? Most women are about as faithless as a fire-and-brimstone preacher in a house of joy on Sunday!"

"What insane notion is that?"

She could hear the frustrated whoosh of air as he exhaled. He crossed to a hemlock and stood with his face averted, reaching toward the greenery, obviously striving for control. Then he turned so abruptly, he tore a slender branch from the tree. "Women believe what they want to believe, not what a man's proved by his actions!"

He talks in riddles, she thought, intrigued. "Your girl friend left you when you were sent to prison?"

"Wife!" he shouted. He sent a release signal to Yurok, then strode to Dawnelle and grasped her shoulders. "My *wife*," he said bitterly, "not my girl friend! I tarnished her daddy's name, dishonored her social reputation. It seems I even ruined her standing in the business community. Isn't that reason enough to leave your husband?"

Dawnelle's heart pounded. Though he frightened her with his angry eyes and his strong hold, she sensed his futility, knew that something in his past had hamstrung his sense of justice. These were feelings she understood. Suddenly she fused her own feelings of betrayal into a resolve not to lash out at this unhappy man.

"Baird," she said gently, "stop hurting me. I'm not your wife."

Her rebuke was soft enough to reach him, for he relaxed his grip slightly. But he continued to stare. Almost hungrily his gaze sought her parted lips, her watchful, open-eyed expression, the wisps of chestnut hair lifting around her face.

He released one shoulder and absently ran a thumb over her throat. The touch was gentle, lacking the roughness of their struggle. She shivered, smiled, locked her gaze with his and let the questions flow into her eyes.

"No," he said at last. "You're not Suzanne. That newborn curiosity in your eyes. . . perhaps it would have made a difference." Bitterness compressed his lips, and he half turned toward the bluff.

"What kind of difference were you about to mention?"

"None—forget it. Yurok!" Baird signaled the animal to heel and started away. "Good day, Dawnelle Belanger," he said over his shoulder. "Forgive me for being so rough on you."

Dawnelle stared after his retreating back, watching until he was a miniature—man and his dog in a tunnel of blue. She watched even after he'd turned right along the bluff and disappeared, feeling a strange lightness buzzing through her body.

Thoughtfully she made her way back to the Fiat. Baird Langston jailed. Why? Deserted by his wife, left alone for that deep resentment of women to burn like hot iron into his soul.

Still wondering about him, she admitted Miss Mo to the passenger seat. She brushed away the deposit of leaves and sand, slid in and unhooked her key ring. How had Suzanne Langston contributed to Baird's obvious dislike of corporate women? Had she been an executive? Baird seemed more the macho type who wanted his women in their place—his bedroom, likely. And yet there had been an indefinable sadness in his eyes when he'd hinted his wife had misjudged him. His wife? Or was Suzanne his ex-wife?

It was a mystery. She dismissed Baird Langston, swung the car in a neat U-turn and headed north toward Trinidad. She'd stop in town for the mail, pick up some dog food and groceries, then head for the station and a leisurely bath. By this evening Langston would be a fading memory.

She grinned at the exhausted dog curled in the corner. "We don't need any more men, do we, Lady Mo?"

HENNY CALDWELL hefted the parcel to the marred postal counter, spreading thick fingers across the wrapping. "You'll catch your death in them wet things," he chided. His tone suggested he wouldn't release Dawnelle's package unless she promised to go right home and change her clothes. "Little early for swimmin', ain't it?"

"Only when the breeze picks up," she admitted with a laugh, anxious to get back to the Fiat, where Miss Mo waited unattended. She glanced through the window toward the roly-poly woman she'd greeted before stepping inside to collect the mail—a smiling grandma type who'd been Henny's wife for thirty-seven years. But Sarah Caldwell hadn't drawn Dawnelle's gaze outside. There was a woman with Sarah, a beauty with ebony hair lifting in the breeze and ethereal brown eyes narrowed anxiously on her companion.

Dawnelle frowned at the pair. She'd been certain she'd just overheard Sarah say "Langston" in a derisive tone. And Sarah had given Dawnelle a vague smile, a little absentminded wave as she passed—not Sarah's usual motherly friendliness at all.

Turning to watch Henny rustle papers on the counter, Dawnelle reminded herself that she'd planned to make Langston only a fading memory by nightfall. Now he was lodged in her thoughts again, this time connected with the beautiful dark woman speaking to Sarah.

Someone rapped loudly on the window.

Dawnelle and Henny both swung around to see the woman with the flowing black hair disappearing down the sidewalk and Sarah smiling and waving to the postmaster. "See you tonight," she said, her voice a squeak through the glass.

Chuckling, Henny saluted his wife. "Light of my life," he commented. He eyed Dawnelle humorously. "Now. Where were we?"

But Dawnelle was still wondering about the stranger. "That woman talking to Sarah," she said. "Who is she?"

"Oh, that's Lau. Family's part of the land, practically."

"What do you mean?"

"Half Yurok Indian. Her grandmother was the last medicine woman hereabouts. Her people owned Trinidad before the whites took over." He clucked sympathetically as he shoved a clipboard beneath the counter. "Had a run of bad luck, that one has. Lost her husband at sea; son came down with pneumonia a few years back. Nearly took him outta commission. Then the boy took sick last December, and nobody knew what it was. Mystery. Hell of a woman, too. Shame."

A shrill bark filtered through the old walls, and Dawnelle remembered Miss Mo. Wishing she could mention Baird, find out if he and the woman were connected in some way, she nonetheless forced her attention back to priorities.

"Well," she said, "guess I'd better be going."

Henny's wide veined hand clutched her package proprietarily. "You planning on stickin' around long?" he asked, beginning to stroke his full jowl.

"Where, your post office, Henny? Or Trinidad?"

"Light station," he grunted. "One fella kept the light on day and night for nearly thirty years, ending back in 'sixteen."

"That would be Fred Harrington," she said. "I hear his grandson, Ralph Hunter, drops by all the time."

"Yeah. So you know about ol' Cap Harrington."

She wedged her father's latest letter into her back pocket and, thinking of Miss Mo, hurriedly handed Henny the parcel notice. But he and his wife Sarah were practically her only acquaintances in Trinidad, she reasoned. Shouldn't their warmth be returned by a few minutes of politeness?

She smiled. "I bought several books on lighthouses before I arrived here," she went on. "Almost every one of them recounts Harrington's journal entry about the big wave that hit Trinidad Head three winters before he retired."

"That'd be him, all right. Two-hundred footer came clean up over the bluff and put the light out." He studied her shrewdly for a moment. "Don't imagine you'll be staying out there for anywhere near thirty years, though."

"Who knows what'll happen when my contract runs out? That's a whole year away, Henny. I'll be around at least till then."

"I hope the star-spangled blue blazes you mean it, missy. This town's had its bellyfulla sunny-weather keepers. Last fella said his wife complained she got dizzy—*dizzy*—with the light goin' round day 'n' night. Buncha lightweights!"

Knowing Mayor Henny Caldwell and his council members had strong-armed the Coast Guard into hiring her, she politely controlled her smile of amusement. Instead she sent him a level appreciative look. "I was raised to believe my word counted for something."

"Thought so. 'Magine there's more than a little gumption behind those steady eyes of yours." A wry smile played around his lips. "Well, you get tired of the wind for company, missy, you just come on over to Sarah 'n' me—spend some time in town. Sarah always has coffee on."

And plenty of the "news" Baird Langston was so

concerned about. Gossip, free and on tap, twenty-four hours a day. She'd met Henny's heavy-set, talkative wife the last time she'd stopped by for the mail. She liked Sarah, liked her clucking and fussing over Dawnelle's needs at the light station. Perhaps it would be a nice break to stop by for coffee. It would be interesting to hear what Sarah had to say about Baird Langston. Dawnelle smiled and assured Henny she'd take him up on the offer.

"I've got to run," she added, hauling the package into her arms. "Left my dog in the car. We'll compare notes on Harrington another day. I'll bring over some of my books on lighthouses. How about—" The dog's barking was an aggravated yodel now. Dawnelle backed toward the door, the package sagging. "Couple of weeks? Sarah's coffee and a good bull session on Fresnel lenses."

"Fine," Henny said, looking disappointed at losing his leverage for conversation. "You best be gettin' out of them wet clothes, anyhow. Sarah would scream six ways to Sunday if she thought I'd kept you gabbin' while you caught your death of cold...." His words died away as Dawnelle nodded, eased out into the crisp air. She hurried along the chipped sidewalk.

Barking and the hoots of children drifted to her. What was Miss Mo up to, she wondered as her car came into view. Then she stopped as if a fence had suddenly sprung up to block her way.

Teeth bared, snarling and barking, Miss Mo parried the taunts of a chunky boy about twelve and a reed-thin girl barely into her teens. The boy reached a heavy arm around the front of the Fiat and plucked the wiper blade from the windshield, letting it slap against the glass. As Miss Mo snarled at the offending sound, the children fell against each other in laughter.

Miss Mo began surging from side to side as if tethered on the hated leash. The girl pounded a fist against the slightly rolled-down window, leaping back when Miss Mo lunged against the glass.

Then reality penetrated. Dawnelle lurched forward, the package swaying awkwardly. "You monsters!" she yelled. "Get away from there!"

Reflexively the girl jerked her hand behind her white T-shirt. "We were just playing with him," she wailed. She backed away, glancing guiltily at her companion in the baggy jeans. "Billy wanted to play with him."

"You did," the boy retorted, full freckled cheeks reddening beneath his thatch of brown hair. "Don't blame it on me!"

"I ought to call the sheriff," Dawnelle said harshly, filled with rage. She thumped the package on the canvas roof and snapped around to face the retreating children. "You're lucky this animal didn't go through the glass and take a chunk out of your mean little hands!"

A quick look inside the car told her that Miss Mo was cowering. Dawnelle's heart went out to her pet for the terrible habits she'd had to learn in self-defense. "You were lucky this time," she called sternly to the children. "Don't let me catch you at your nasty tricks again, or the sheriff will have you!"

"We won't," piped the skinny girl, tugging her companion by his shirt-sleeve. "We were only trying to play with him. Weren't we, Billy?"

"Yeah, I guess." Billy jerked his arm free.

Disgusted, shaken, Dawnelle stowed her father's crudely wrapped box and climbed in beside Miss Mo. The dog's tongue lolled as she panted, the whites of her eyes showing red veins when she looked balefully at Dawnelle. *She thinks I'm going to beat her,* Dawnelle thought. She groaned, briefly touched the silken head and started the engine.

Her planned quick stop by the grocery store was out of the question, for the second time, she grumbled silently. First, yesterday, she'd paused to look pityingly at the poor dog being half choked by Jenkins outside the store in Eureka, and ended up buying the dog and making a quick exit to avoid the fat man's threatening presence. Today she couldn't risk another incident with Miss Mo sitting in the car while she shopped for groceries. Well, there was that last can of mushroom soup, she supposed. The leftover casserole Miss Mo could finish up. They'd get by.

"What am I going to do with you?" she chided, and Miss Mo sheepishly lowered her muzzle.

As Dawnelle pulled away from the curb, she wished she felt comfortable enough around Baird Langston to ask for a few pointers on obedience training. Surely with some work Miss Mo could be reliable around children? It was chilling to think what those sharp new teeth could do to a child's arms and legs.

Baird. A flashing warmth accompanied the memory of him. But calling him even on a reasonable excuse like Miss Mo's need for training was out of the question. Risky business, getting tangled up with a man fresh out of prison. Especially a man who made her blood race like Baird had not half an hour ago. No matter that her instincts told her he was a decent man with circumstances thrown against him. She just couldn't trust her instincts anymore. Besides, a chemistry existed between them that was definitely explosive. All the more reason to stay away from him. *I need time to think, plan for the future,* she repeated to herself, fighting the appeal of asking for his help. *If I'm going to learn to handle men I need to repair my emotional fences, and I can't do that staring into those bottomless blue eyes of his!*

She would read a book on how to train a dog, and resolved to visit the tiny library tomorrow when Miss Mo was safely home. She left the loose grill of streets that comprised Trinidad, heading for the bluff on the south edge of town.

An old fog bell set like the Liberty in its square collar, whitewashed to match a miniature memorial lighthouse nearby, perched above the rock-strewn bay. Her gaze skimmed the water in a brief inventory of the harbor, a habit she'd quickly developed. The fishing fleet was out. Only a dozen small boats lay at anchor; a few skiffs hugged the dock. And protecting these toylike bits of wood was the great rounded headland.

Trinidad Head rose from the northwest edge of the harbor like a mighty fist threatening defeat to the raging winds and surf she'd read so much about. The knot of land was connected to the mainland by only a sandy spit laced with the narrow dirt track she now drove over. Passing a boat launch and the tiny Seascape Restaurant nestled against the foot of the dock, she began the climb into the headland.

Dawnelle's eyes narrowed slightly at the feeling that enveloped her now, the pride and anticipation spreading through her like the effects of a fine wine. *Charts, bells, beacons and man's wily mind,* she mused. Each link in the navigational system kept him from a fateful clash with the land. Land, the seaman's dreaded enemy, hovering far beneath the fragile planks of his craft. Dark jaws opening like saw blades to hack away at teak and fiberglass and metal.

She was proud, she reasoned as the car shuddered in the buffeting wind, simply because she was playing a role in this centuries-old lifesaving system. If the beacon went out unaccountably, she could always call the Coast Guard. She'd been briefed about that the first day she arrived.

"Call us if anything goes awry," gray-haired Captain Kern had said smugly. "Not that you'll have any worries about the system on the Head—we're automated these days. Everything's monitored by computer."

Rounding the last bend and pulling up outside a high gate bordered by tangled blackberry bushes, she wondered if Kern or one of his staff had left any messages on the telephone-answering machine in her living room. He'd promised to let her know twenty-four hours in advance if someone wanted to tour the station. So far—to her relief—there had been no messages, no visitors to disrupt her cathartic isolation.

Dawnelle climbed out, unlocked the heavy padlock and swung open the gate, clearing the way to drive through. At least she didn't have to worry that Miss Mo might get off the station, she thought, returning to lock the gate. The fence arched across the headland for half a mile, to the very lip of jagged cliffs on either side.

Moments later she parked in the shade of an immense

gray boulder and killed the engine. Soothed by the bouquet of fresh sea air and spicy chaparral, by the very desolation of the station, she eagerly wrestled her package into her arms. Miss Mo circled around her legs, her panting barely audible above the bar-ro-o-o-m, hiss-s-s of the waves two hundred feet below.

Only natural sounds, she noted with satisfaction, gazing down over a bank of brush and vines in the direction of the foghorn, hidden from view below the tip of the bluff. She knew well the irritating toot that could emanate from that small white structure.

Beyond a pair of jack pines, she could see the Pacific as it chopped against Pilot Rock, wreathing the blunt islet in creamy suds, then flattening to pale azure at the skyline. *Mine,* she thought suddenly, possessively. *Mine for one year. Every scraggly tree, every inch of this windy bluff. Except the foghorn. That belongs to the Coast Guard!* At that moment, Miss Mo darted through a thicket of dark green Indian soap bush, the purple blossoms shivering as she escorted Dawnelle to the white picket gate of their tiny yard.

Nestled in the embrace of large rocks whose contours had been softened by wind, the two-story white clapboard cottage faced south toward Mexico. Flowering shrubs formed steps of color beneath wooden grid windows. Crimson begonias banked the miniscule front porch.

The white hackles of the fence drew Dawnelle's gaze along an undulating boardwalk, past banks of marigolds blooming in the rock garden, beyond the sheds, the water tank, to where the path was literally carved from solid rock and overhung with greenery. This was the graceful setting against which she loved to view the stark lighthouse.

Trinidad Head Light stood alone on a concrete pad, the base at one point only ten feet from a sheer, one-hundred-ninety-six-foot drop to the water. The beacon looked like a square white candle, its tapered, twenty-four-foot mortar framework dwarfed on the north side by enormous rock formations, its strobe burning over the sea—an almost *living* thing that pulsed silently through every hour. Even now, while Dawnelle watched, its signal slashed pale-bright through the golden afternoon.

Humble in size but mighty in purpose, she thought with an affectionate shake of her head. Drawing deeply of the breeze, she climbed the two plank steps to her front porch and slipped her brass key into the latch. With great relief she pushed open the wooden door.

Setting her package on a narrow table inside, Dawnelle hung her key ring above it on a stressed-wood key rack.

Worn flooring met her at the entry. An oak hall tree on her right stood near the doorway to an empty dining room. A blue chintz couch on her left served as a divider between the hall and the living room. Ahead, the hallway ended abruptly in a stairwell leading to the upstairs bedrooms. That dark niche was flanked by the kitchen and the bathroom with its chipped brown tiles and creaky plumbing.

Her kingdom for a bath! She relished the idea of reading her father's letter while she soaked the salt from her skin. And later, while the canned soup heated, she'd light some driftwood in the fireplace, feed Miss Mo and settle by the fire to open the package from her father. Altogether it would be a hermit's delight, this afternoon blending into golden evening, with the muffled thunder of waves and the silent companionship of a beautiful shepherd dog.

A huge braided rug in faded blues, reds and yellows centered the eye directly in front of the fieldstone fireplace. Stacked firewood occupied the corner between the hearth and the west window, and a comfortable blue fabric chair with painted wooden armrests faced this window, its companion hassock caved in at the middle from heavy use. Save for bookshelves bracing the fireplace, the rest of the walls were white, pristine looking with the sun shining through wood-frame windows.

It was the gleam of plastic that finally broke her almost reverent review. She detoured around the chintz divan and crossed to an end table next to a worn leather chesterfield. Chilled despite the sunlight streaming from the southern window, she bent to peer at the answering machine. Blast! A white flag showed through the smoke-tone face plate. It seemed the summer season was upon her. Unless—slim hope—it was only Sarah Caldwell asking again to list Dawnelle among the member of the Civic Club. She twisted a silver knob, rewinding the tape, and turned on the speaker.

"Miss Belanger, ah, this is Bos'n's Mate Charlie Mathews callin'," boomed an unfamiliar voice, sounding slightly metallic but with a Southern twang. "Ah, ma'am, you've got Ben Fallon comin' by tomorrow to take some samples outta the face of the bluff. Says he'll be by about seven-thirty Thursday mornin'."

To her chagrin the sage voice chuckled, then added,

"Ben says he won't be botherin' you till he's done takin' the cores, case you won't be up and about first thing in the mornin'. But he'll stop by to say hello when he's done, though. Pleasant kinda guy, Ben. Nothin' else on the books but him, so far, ma'am, so I'll be sayin' good day."

In case I won't be up and about! Dawnelle simmered as she heard the dial tone hum discordantly in her ear. Who did Fallon imagine would open the station gate? Did he think because a woman was keeping the station she'd lie in bed and let the day go on around her? There were boardwalks to sweep, gardens to prune and plant, minor repairs, painting, polishing, cleaning the shed, dozens of tasks she'd agreed to conduct for the Coast Guard. Exhaling in disgust, she resolved to be engaged in those tasks when Ben Fallon arrived at the big boulder parking area.

She was reaching to rewind the tape when a second message beep sounded. But her close attention picked up only raspy breathing, then the dial tone. Whoever it was left no message. Pursing her lips in mild frustration, she turned the machine off and set out for the bathroom.

PERFUMED STEAM ROSE in the cool room, drifting across Miss Mo's silver-and-black body as she lay stretched across the brown bath mat, one hind foot propped comfortably against the open door. At a muffled sound from Dawnelle, the dog raised her head to glance at the bathtub, then eased back to the pile rug and closed her eyes.

Her father's scrawling blue writing began to blur

again as Dawnelle finished his letter through tear-filmed eyes:

I went through your brother's room after all these years and removed his things. That tattered red baseball uniform, his Keds with the rawhide laces—you remember.

Afterward, out at the ponds, I climbed on Mitch pretty hard for dumping our new batch of silver smolt into the wrong holding tank. He didn't say much, though. Just tucked that grimy gray felt hat down over his eyes and lighted a cigarette. Guess he knew what I'd been up to, seeing the back of the pickup piled with Tommy's gear.

I stuck Tommy's fishing kreel into that package I sent you. Nobody but us would know how many trout that little tyke could pack into the basket, huh?

Well, pet, with your mother and the boy both gone, we've got to hang on to each other. It's bad enough, you being halfway across the state and wading waist deep in the Klamath without my sage advice! Take care out on that light station, hear? Try to get home for Christmas.

Mitch and Nancy send their love along with mine.

Dad

Dawnelle's arm drooped over the side of the tub, and her head sank against the cool porcelain. She'd hoped that letter to her father would make him understand. About Jeff. About needing time alone to figure out what was important to her. She knew he'd be hurt because she'd moved here instead of returning to the fish hatchery, but that couldn't be helped. Her father was the last person in the world who'd want to see her woven into this spider's web of self-pity. Coming home needed to be a strong act, a time for giving back some of the love André Belanger had given her. Anything less would be selfish and weak.

Rubbing the scratch on her left forearm, that remnant of her struggle with Baird Langston, she decided she'd have to explain again in her next letter. She sighed, tossing the buff pages to the sink ledge. The dog rose from the rug and approached, her brown eyes bright with curiosity.

Vaguely glad she'd taken the time to brush the thick hair free of sand, Dawnelle leaned out of the bath to pat Miss Mo's head. It was almost as if the dog sensed her sadness. Strange, to see sympathy in an animal who'd endured mostly cruelty. Scrunching down, feeling the hot water wash over her breasts, she stared into those somber eyes.

In a moment elation began to eddy over her depression. Of course! For the time being she couldn't do anything about her father's loneliness. But he was concerned for her safety, too, wasn't he?

"Lady Mo," she laughed, hugging the dog's neck, "we'll end at least part of his worries. We'll tell him about you!"

Sensing Dawnelle's return to good humor, the dog squirmed out of her arms and stood back from the tub. She sneezed—a move less forceful than a bark but equally demanding—and wagged her tail. She side-stepped out of the bathroom, returned to sneeze again and stared askance at Dawnelle. She's hungry, Dawnelle guessed, giggling. She was a terrible keeper, feeding Miss Mo scraps both days the dog had been with her. Rising dripping from the tub, she reached for a towel and wrapped herself, dabbing at her wet hair as she stepped onto the bath mat.

The slender shepherd suddenly tensed, cocking her head toward the kitchen across the hall.

"I swear you're reading my mind, you crazy puppy! Just a few more minutes. . . ." Dawnelle reached behind the door, groping for her green satin wrapper. The fabric flowed like cool water over her warm skin. Working and living in the city among affluent sophisticated colleagues had provided at least one good influence, she thought. She had discovered a knack for selecting a wardrobe Diane von Furstenberg herself would be proud to own.

Her musings dissolved in a ripple of shock as a growl rumbled from Miss Mo's throat. Dawnelle pivoted around the door. She saw Miss Mo rush into the kitchen, pause with her nose pointed at the kitchen window, then whirl and race down the hall toward the front door. Another ominous growl raised the hair on Dawnelle's arms.

Good heavens, who was here? Dawnelle racked her mind for possibilities and came up with nothing as she hurried into the emerald dressing gown. She knew she'd locked the station gate. And Kern had been emphatic about calling before he or his staff came aboard the station. Who, then?

Miss Mo issued a long howl. The series of hair-raising, snarling barks that followed brought Dawnelle running barefoot down the oak hall. She was hardly dressed! Yet she was too cautious to run upstairs and put on jeans and a sweater. The dog pressed against her for an instant, then rushed the door with such shrill barks, Dawnelle could think of nothing but the rising panic in her throat.

A grating sound—that would be the white gate out front; the hinges needed oil. "Ludicrous thought," she muttered.

Heavy-sounding steps approached. Whose? Who else had a key to the chain-link gate?

The dog's barking because a wail, and Dawnelle suddenly raced for the chesterfield, crouched low and peered surreptitiously out a corner of the window. Too dusky to see anything! Red murk in the sky, and whoever it was had already gained the front porch. Three raps sounded against the door, rattling it and stiffening Dawnelle's spine.

Miss Mo's reaction was a slashing menacing attack on the wooden barrier that unnerved Dawnelle more than the fact that someone was outside. *Control,* her mind screamed.

Stealthily she went to the stone hearth. *This will all seem silly afterward,* a part of her reasoned. Nevertheless, she grasped a heavy wrought-iron poker, its handle feeling cold and lethal in her palm, and returned to stand close to the door. A stream of chilly air slipped between the door and the frame, brushing against her cheek as she listened.

The suddenness of the second summons against the door snapped her head back. Steeling her nerves, she grasped Miss Mo's muzzle to quiet her and said crisply, "Who is it?"

"Baird Langston!" was the response. "I've brought—"

The rest was buried beneath another cascade of Miss Mo's strident warnings.

CHAPTER THREE

A FIERCE HAMMERING began in Dawnelle's chest. She couldn't breathe for a moment. Langston, here? What had he done, rammed the ten-foot-high chain-link fence with that bulwark chest of his?

Shadows suddenly leaped across the living room, swept ahead of the timed strobe of the beacon. Then the room fell into evening hues. A yellowish twilight pooled beneath the dim bulb down the hall, and dusk-rose glowed at the windows.

As Miss Mo snapped and snarled at the plank door, Dawnelle, crouched beside the dog, trembled slightly with each attack. She licked her dry lips. Clenching her hands, she sought to contain her surging emotions. There had been that brief piercing gladness at hearing the rumble of Baird's voice—quickly submerged in a knee-weakening apprehension. Why was he here?

"Dawnelle?" muffled through the portal.

"Baird?" she queried, stalling for time. Would Miss Mo protect her? "I—I'm just settling in for the evening...." Had that been *his* wheezy breathing on her message recorder? She grasped the dog's muzzle while she spoke with a strained rasp. "What did you want?"

"I've brought something—a peace offering, you could call it. Is it so late you can't have a word with me?"

Damn the man for sounding passably honorable! She sighed and released the furry nose, instead grasping Miss Mo's collar. The thought crept in that she was keeper of a public place, and so the man had every right to be here, albeit unannounced. That she was vulnerable to this kind of intrusion spread a red glow of anger over her throat and face.

Awkwardly she fumbled with the doorknob, clanging the poker against the wood, banging Miss Mo's foreleg and wincing herself at the pained yelp. Muttering an apology, Dawnelle swung open the door and stepped back. Miss Mo slipped from her fingers, barking furiously.

Baird's left side froze in white relief as the beacon flashed one revolution. She saw his nose, intelligent brow, bearded jaw—every detail in the rugged face—etched boldly against that powerful strobe. The sight should not have thrilled her, yet against her will she felt the nerves in her legs tingle, as if she'd just stepped into a hot bath. Then the magenta sunset enfolded him in mysterious shadows.

"Sorry I couldn't reach you by phone," Baird offered as he stepped past Miss Mo's gnashing white fangs and into the small entry, dwarfing even the oak hall tree. "I tried—"

"The station is open by appointment, if you'd taken the time to do things by the book!" she cut in shakily, resurrecting her protective armor while she wielded the black iron rod in an effort to recapture the dog.

Baird puckered his lips and pierced the room with a short shrill whistle. Miss Mo plunged to a skidding stop at the toes of his leather loafers. Hugging a heavy-looking package to one side of his body, Baird placed a series of slow calming caresses on Miss Mo's head. As if mesmerized, the animal sat down, then crumpled to the floor and presented her arched chest.

Traitor, Dawnelle thought. Her breath sighed tersely through her lips. Even Baird's command of her seemingly uncontrollable animal got under her skin.

Reluctantly she wedged the door shut with her bare toe and pulled the green collar tighter to her throat. This was hardly the attire she'd have chosen to wear for the hot-blooded Baird Langston. However, he seemed more intent on pleasuring Miss Mo with a hearty scratch on the chest than ogling her plunging neckline. That was some consolation! For some reason, seeing him reduced the fearful shivering, yet she could not dispel her resentment. He'd invaded her cozy nest.

As Baird bent over Miss Mo, his brown hair gleamed with a damp luster, drawing Dawnelle's gaze, inviting her to run her fingers through the lush waves. She quickly thrust the ridiculous notion aside. The rumpled brown paper of his package protruded from the crook of his left arm, intriguing her further. Perhaps he truly intended a harmless visit?

Across the living room, the windows reflected silver as the beacon revolved its face to the surrounding sea. Then the light faded, etching Dawnelle's willowy shadow on the front door. Reminded of her scant clothing, she sighed and sat on the back of the divan.

"Surely you didn't come all this way and break into the light station," she challenged in low tones, angling the poker at the dog, "just to scratch my dog silly."

Baird appeared unmoved by her rudeness as he

glanced up with a wide smile. "Matter of fact, I didn't." Slapping Miss Mo's ribs a few times, he slowly unfolded his long limbs and took a calm stance a few feet away. "But if you'd like similar treatment I could oblige. . . to the greater benefit of both of us."

An amazed rebuttal choked from her. "I'm afraid you'll have to master a more refined approach if you expect me to fall over backward at your feet!"

"Perhaps you'll enlighten me on the details so I can work at improving my technique."

"That, Mr. Langston, would be a total waste of time!"

With a slow burning gaze he seared every available patch of her skin, including the length of calf gleaming beneath the opening of her robe. "I'd hardly be wasting my time." He grinned.

Dismayed by her body's tingling response to that challenge, she swung to her feet, her cheeks flushed.

His laugh came low and taunting to her ears.

"Why are you here?" she demanded. "How did you get onto the station?"

"It seems I'll have to bring you something else tomorrow for angering you tonight," he remarked with a smile, bringing forth the crackling paper parcel. "I guess with you a man can only hope to tread water." He'd avoided her questions outright, and her ire rose. She searched for an appropriate retort.

Miss Mo chose that moment to rear up on her hind legs and bury her nose in the tan wrapping. "Down!" Dawnelle commanded irritably, and was answered by a brief look from the dog, who again rose on her haunches to investigate.

Testily Dawnelle moved forward. She grasped Miss Mo's throat latch, forgetting that when she leaned forward the gown's lapels gaped halfway to her waist, revealing full firm breasts, a tempting valley paved in ivory satin.

The sound of Baird's tightly indrawn breath sent Dawnelle's face angling up to his, her eyes narrowed in suspicion. As she watched his eyes make a deliberate journey along the curves of her bosom to her shadowed throat, embarrassment stained her cheeks, the color deepening when he paused, lingering on her mouth. His blue eyes seemed to smoke.

Her lips parted to deny his hungry progress, but a heavy warmth invaded the pit of her stomach, crippling her earlier fury. Her own gaze dropped suddenly to his lips. Even while an odor reminiscent of the moss-hung banks of a river floated up from his parcel, and even after Miss Mo tugged gently against her chain, Dawnelle gazed at the ruddy fullness of a mouth that promised passion. With a clarity that amazed her, she recalled the potency of his kiss.

The iron clang of the poker as it fell to the floor shattered the moment. A mixture of relief and shock mingled in Dawnelle's mind as she tried to fathom what had traveled so intensely between them. Her heart drumming against her ribs, she pulled abruptly away, dragging the dog to her side.

"I—I was just about to fix tea while I heated soup for dinner," she faltered. Her gaze shifted back and forth for a moment while she pondered her mysteriously deflated anger. Where had it gone? Why such shimmering heat in her bones? Almost painfully aware of his immense frame and his probing gaze, she finally braved a look at his face. The craving she'd seen had vanished, replaced by an expectant interest in hearing the rest of her statement. Her invitation was soft with uncertainty. "Would you like a cup of almond herb tea?"

"Then you've already planned dinner?" He sounded disappointed.

"Yes, I—but I was just getting the ocean out of my hair first. Just... finishing my bath."

"I couldn't have dressed you more perfectly if I'd given my imagination free rein." He chuckled to lighten the comment, but his eyes burned with appreciation.

"But you always catch me when I'm drenched," she objected, raising her hand to damp tangled hair. "I'm beginning to think I've lost my sense of timing."

"No, now don't fret your feminine ego." He ran a fingertip lightly along her satin sleeve, smoothed a fold in her lapel... inflaming her senses with his familiarity. Shaking his head as if unable to believe his own inner reactions, he murmured, "Recently the natural look has stimulated my male instincts more than I care to admit."

She read a deeper meaning in that comment, and wondered if he was referring to their encounter on the cliff. Why did the thought please her?

But caution born of old hurts made her stiffen her shoulders. "Baird," she said quietly, "how did you get through the station gate?"

"Better rest our weapons before we discuss that subject. When you opened the door tonight you reminded me of a she-bear protecting her winter cave—and your little silver cub here." He chucked Miss Mo under her chin. "I pity the unwary!" She laughed uncomfortably. If she was a mother bear, he was a brawny buck.

Sliding the poker from her hand, he disappeared into the darkness of the living room. She heard iron strike stone. Then he was beside her again, putting a casual arm around her shoulders. "I'll have that cup of tea and explain myself, okay?"

She walked slightly ahead of him, feeling his arm warm and heavy against the satin and her tingling skin. *His touch is a comfort I could get used to,* she thought with nagging unease. She worried her lower lip. He made her keenly aware of her nakedness beneath the revealing emerald gown.

As she crossed to the sink to fill her teakettle, his warmth fell away, leaving her feeling edgy and vulnerable. Baird scraped back a chair and seated himself at the sturdy wooden table draped in green-flowered oilcloth. On the floor, an empty green dish reminded her of Miss Mo's overdue meal.

The dog pushed against her, elliciting a caress and a soothing, "Soon, Lady—any time now."

While the water hissed into the copper kettle, Dawnelle pulled the cotton café curtains closed, a habit she supposed she'd acquired from her mother. A private woman, Ellen Walker Belanger had spent most of her married years silently mourning the loss of her elite pampered life on Long Island, where she'd been raised. Marrying André Belanger, a proud independent man who'd grown up on a farm in Maine with his French parents, had cost Ellen too much. She'd grown querulous toward the man who adored her from a stoic distance. Eventually she'd only taken pride in her well-dressed children, her collection of mantle figurines and her bent for baking exotic breads. Dawnelle realized the bleakness of the marriage now, years after her mother's death. Among vague impressions of her beauty were recollections of tense evenings at home, and Ellen's severely enforced rules of etiquette. Dawnelle smiled. She and Tommy had been certain, back then, that keeping elbows off the table was a form of punishment. The thought made her lonely for the patience and sage advice she'd never known.

How would her mother have handled a man like Baird Langston, Dawnelle wondered. Feeling his gaze as the water bubbled into the spout, she brought the kettle to the gas stove, ignited a flame and watched beads of water zap on the gleaming metal. Would mother have felt the same tightening in her stomach? A nervous whir in every nerve ending? A feeling of invasion, a premonition that events were about to career out of control?

But Dawnelle only remembered a very careful woman with lovely green gold eyes and short-cropped chestnut hair. She had no inkling of what opinions might have been given on tonight's situation, nor had she dwelt much on the idea in her relationships with other men.

But Baird was. . . upsetting. Should she remain impervious to his disturbing charm while she licked her San Francisco wounds? Or welcome his attentions as a distraction from self-pity? Truth admitted, she felt inclined to bolt for the front door and slam it behind her. Instead, raising a hand to the drying tendrils around her face, Dawnelle turned abruptly to Baird.

His package lay shoved against the wall in the middle of the table. One of his large hands curled around an open issue of *Advertising Age*. He closed the pages and looked up, studying her with a quizzical smile.

"Do I make you nervous?" he asked.

"No—well, actually, yes. A little. Will you excuse me? I'll be back to fix tea as soon as I finish dressing."

"I've upset you?"

Her pert glance was designed to let him know she was wise to his smug questions. "Unexpected interruptions make me nervous."

"Now you know *what* to expect when a Scotsman loses his temper. Especially when he feels he should apologize for it."

"Huh," she mumbled doubtfully, glancing at the bag on the table. "This whole scene reminds me of the old Mafia movies I used to watch as a kid. Some big hit man was always leaving a threatening package on some poor sucker's doorstep. A fish head or something awful like that."

"A Scot doesn't warn his victims with a dead fish, Dawnelle. That would be a waste of good food."

"So now I'm a victim!" she scoffed teasingly, making light of the uncomfortable exchange. "Well, what does a Scotsman do? Play the pipes on a lonely moor until the bewitched victim wanders into his clutches?"

"Uh-uh."

"No, he probably steals their kilt. Something low like that."

He laughed heartily, obviously amused. "And bring the entire clan down on his head? No way. No, lass, we're talking subtlety when it comes to a Scot's revenge."

She thought it strange he should mention revenge, when they'd been laughing about clichéd Italian movies. But she grinned because he seemed to be having such a good time with the whole theme. His pleasure endeared him to her in a profound way, but she put the thought aside in favor of finding out just what a Scot's warning entailed.

He was shaking his head. "A true Highlander would steal the guy's prize breeding heifer," he explained between chuckles, "then return it a month or two later pregnant with inferior get. Now that's revenge!"

"Baird," she said carefully, growing concerned, "that was a funny thing to do."

"What?" The dazzling smile faded slightly. "What was funny?"

"You kept saying—mentioning revenge. We weren't really talking about that, per se. Threat, perhaps. But not specifically revenge."

He seemed momentarily puzzled, but his easy smile reappeared almost immediately. "Revenge was the motivation in those old movies, nine times out of ten. Sure we were talking revenge. Anyway—" he glanced at his watch, heavy with dials and metal push buttons "—no need to interrupt your schedule, Dawnelle. I'll only be staying a few minutes. I've got to set up some rebuilt saltwater tanks tonight. The filtering systems have to be checked out before I add any live specimens."

Suddenly it mattered that she be groomed no matter how briefly he stayed. Resolutely she moved to the doorway. "I'll at least comb my hair. Make yourself at home."

"Can I help with something? The tea, perhaps?"

She considered his offer a moment. She could have him feed the dog, but he'd probably think she was a cheapskate, making Miss Mo eat leftover macaroni and cheese. "You could build a fire, if you like. There's kindling on the hearth and some pine logs in the corner by the window. Would you mind?"

His long legs moved with lithe ease as he stood up, making the room seem small. "Not at all." He bent to grasp the rolled paper bag. "But this ought to go into the refrigerator if you've got other plans for dinner."

She came to him and took the package, struggled with the weight until he retrieved it and slid it easily to the sink drainboard. Her gift smelled suspiciously like fertilizer. Smiling up at him, she wondered how something so pungent could serve as dinner. Unless.... But it was impossible. He'd told her he wasn't a commercial fisherman by trade. "What on earth have you got in here, Baird?"

"Open it," he urged.

She slipped off the brown sacking, followed by layer after layer of last week's *San Francisco Chronicle*. Distractingly, his chest brushed her back and his breath stirred her hair. Eyes bright, nose twitching, Miss Mo sidled up, pressing against Dawnelle's hip, angling for a better look.

At last, pulling away the front page, Dawnelle let out a squeal of delight. "Oh, Baird, what do you suppose it weighs?" She hefted the plastic bag containing the fresh silver salmon. "It's a beauty!"

He laughed pleasurably. "I'd say nearly twelve pounds. What do you think?"

"At least! Where did you get this?"

"Off one of the boats as I was passing the dock on my way up here. Friend of mine runs her thirty-six-foot troller with the Trinidad fleet."

"Her? She fishes for a living?" Dawnelle imagined

chapped red hands and layers of men's wool shirts over strong shoulders.

"Yes, *her*," he chided.

"Sorry. I'd be the last one to criticize a fisherwoman when I'm minding a light station."

"Good point. I don't take anything away from a woman making a living with her hands. However—" he gave her a closed look "—I've had experience with city women who get their hooks into the business world. That's another matter." He began wrapping the fish. "I'll put this into the fridge if you want to get combed."

"Wrong on both counts," she said firmly.

He'd neatly cut off whatever retort she'd had in mind. Obviously he was used to having his opinion taken as fact. It was a ploy she'd seen daily on the job in San Francisco, a strategy that deserved a small power play on her part to set their relationship on the right track. Nudging his hands away from the salmon, she turned on the tap, rinsing slime from her fingers.

"I know you expect me to fling back in your face some terse hackneyed phrase like, 'You're just being macho,' which, of course you are. But why waste my breath? Suffice it to say, your attitude fits right in with that of eighty percent of the men in this country. I imagine you love being one of the boys." She smiled inwardly at his growled response. "The other twenty percent of the male population knows better. They're reaping the benefits of women's brilliance as both colleagues and competitors in the highest echelons of business. As for the fish—" she grinned at him, liking the slight scowl that drew his eyebrows together "—that's our dinner you're trying to put away. Do you prefer your salmon poached, broiled or pan fried?"

"No, now let's finish this." He leaned against the counter and folded his arms. "There are exceptions to every rule, Dawnelle, but it's been my experience that women think corporate life is a glorified version of college sorority days. They spend more time politicking and worrying about appearances than in keeping up production."

Without knowing it, he'd just nailed Jeff Dugan on his blond head. "Of course, men are different."

"I think so, yes. We've had centuries of practice in leadership."

"I know," she said with a pretense at despair. "That's why only a handful of you are enlightened enough to appreciate the *entire* work force of this country. The rest of you are too blinded by your role in history to realize that more than fifty percent of the work force is women. And the number grows every day."

He laughed. "You're a libber!"

"No, Baird. I'm a businesswoman."

"By your own admission, you're a lighthouse keeper."

"Temporarily."

"Oh? Still in the job market, are you?"

"Not for a year, but I'll be back."

"Why did you leave it? That's what puzzles me. The city life, the parties—" he gestured "—your burgeoning career. Why?"

"I plead the fifth. You wouldn't like my answer."

"I'll reserve judgment."

Suddenly their easy banter was a revealing discussion. Something about Baird's interested but half-doubtful expression made her want to prove herself. Yet it was an effort to delve into her painful experiences with Jeff. Her mouth turned down in distaste. "Very well. I worked for a man who—" She turned away. It was still difficult to talk about, she realized. Still embarrassing. "Jeff was a man who cared more about politicking, as you so aptly put it, than production."

"Ah.... The temperature just dropped ten degrees."

She gave him an uncomfortable frown. "Do you really want to hear this? It's decidedly...trite."

"Every human emotion we experience has been repeated endlessly through time, Dawnelle—love, hate, jealousy. But the way our emotions drive us in different circumstances makes each story unique. What happened to make you so bitter?"

Surprised at his insight, she glanced sharply at him. Did he realized they were taking the first steps toward a relationship? She wondered if it frightened him as much as it did her. She sighed and glanced at the sink. All right. She would give him a hidden serious part of herself, something not even her father knew.

"I'd built my department from a two-hundred-thousand-a-year blue-sky operation, Baird—to a well-oiled machine with a one-point-three-million-dollar ad budget. Even with the simplest hand-held computer, someone could trace the company's after-sales profits directly to my programs. Then one day the boss's daughter strolled into Jeff's office, her spanking-new master's in communication poking tastefully out of her Gucci bag. She asked for my job. Jeff was marketing director, you see, and he had the power to effect changes within my department." The words cut into the stillness of the kitchen, reflecting a bitterness that twisted through her stomach. Suddenly Dawnelle laughed derisively and looked at Baird. "He gave her everything I'd worked three years to create."

"And she didn't deserve it."

"Deserve it! That woman hadn't seen the inside of an office in her entire life, other than her father's executive suite, and then only when she sashayed in on semester breaks to sweet-talk him out of a few thousand in spending money. With her father's blessing, Jeff just handed her everything."

"Why didn't you fight them?"

"Fight them? Simple. Jeff brought her into one of our board meetings and introduced her as the new director of advertising and promotion. No discussion, no warning. That was the title promised to me, by the way, only I'd been so busy earning the title I hadn't taken time to have it made official. I wasn't actually supposed to attend board meetings, you understand. I was only a lowly promotion manager. But Jeff knew that if I didn't sit in on the strategy sessions, he wouldn't have the slightest idea how his marketing department's goals and budget dovetailed into the company's master plan. We had a great partnership," she said savagely, eyes blazing. "I ran the department, and he took care of the politics. 'I'll take on the brass,' he used to say. 'You just get me the ammunition.' The creep thought I'd sit still and work for that University of Southern California greenling he brought in over my head!"

"What happened to end it?"

"We—that is, I walked out."

He reached over and smoothed an unruly strand of hair. "Why do I get the feeling it was more than the job at stake?"

"I find I keep underestimating you," she said dryly, ducking away to crush the newspapers into a ball. "Perhaps you're more enlightened than I guessed."

"I'm sorry about the job."

"Forget it." She flung the wad into the trash, then turned to him, telling herself to calm down. "Let's not debate the business issue endlessly. I repeat, about the fish. . . ."

Opening the cupboard beneath the sink, she withdrew a large cutting block and slid it onto the drainboard. She maneuvered the bagged salmon to the wooden surface, then smiled briefly at Baird. "I'll take fresh salmon over canned mushroom soup any day. How about you? I think I've even got some rice in the cupboard, which should go nicely. With all this fish, there's enough for us and Miss Mo, as well as plenty left over to freeze. What do you say?"

He made a big production of studying her facial features before saying heartily, "Done!"

As he washed his hands and dried them on the russet terry towel near his elbow, he chuckled. "I suggest we broil the beast with lemon and pepper." Under the influence of his easy manner, she felt her anger dwindling. Smiling indulgently, Baird tossed her the cloth. "You get combed, and I'll start the fire. Dinner can be a community project if you don't object to a male presence in your female domain."

"On the contrary," she said with an arch grin, heading for the bathroom. "Men should be liberated, too. Be right back!"

Dawnelle found herself humming as she held the blow dryer to her hair, running the long strands through her fingers until they felt like flowing silk. Even with the drying, her chestnut tendrils curled at the edges of a full, below-the-shoulder style. Pleased by the healthy blush in her cheeks and the slight slant to her green eyes, she ran a moistened fingertip over the dark brows and smiled at her reflection in the mirror. *That man has a way with gifts,* she thought. *A fish! I love it! Why couldn't he have brought me a box of candy like any normal man out to impress a woman?* Because then it would have been easy to toss him out the minute the tea was drained from his cup. Now...dinner, the fireplace....

She heard the rattle of iron implements in the living room, felt a rush of pleasure at the evening's prospects. It had been five months since she'd last seen Jeff Dugan, since she'd last spent an evening in the company of a challenging appealing man. Could she protect herself this time? The answer was buried somewhere between common sense and newly fired emotions, and she shook her head ruefully.

Before the mood of anticipation waned she was hurrying up the steep carpeted stairs to change, her youthful eagerness finally unbound.

SOFT COUNTRY BALLADS poured from the compact stereo system hidden on the second shelf of the end table. Her hair burnished by the flickering orange flames of the fire, Dawnelle sprawled comfortably in the center of the braided rug. Red, blue and white poker chips were stacked near her right hand, and due to Dawnelle's clever maneuvering, a smaller collection lay scattered by Baird's knee. Miss Mo slept soundly nearby, belly bulging with salmon, rice and macaroni, head tucked beneath the blue lounge chair. One foot was slung out, as usual, resting against Baird's back.

With seasoned agility Dawnelle shuffled a deck of playing cards, splitting the deck, packing each half on the rug, fanning them smoothly together. Again she split the stack and watched them drift down into her left palm, the cards fluttering like tiny wings until they were reversed exactly from the original order.

They played for a while. Cards were dealt between rounds of friendly betting. Chips began to mound on the rug between them. It was their ninth hand.

"Everyone deserves a night off now and then," Dawnelle was saying as she dealt an ace to Baird, who'd mentioned he still had work to do tonight.

"Finally!" Baird muttered.

Smiling, she dealt herself a queen. She could afford to smile. She'd won the last five hands. The queen she'd earned made a pair with the other in her hand—hardly cause for celebration, but she considered herself a consummate bluffer. Better than all her old college mates in the dorm, at any rate.

Since his ace took precedence over her queen, he would open the next round of betting. She gave him time to consider the two cards he held, plus the four cards spread near his chips. A possible royal flush, she noted, looking at the ace-king-jack of diamonds snugged against his three of clubs. She wondered if his hidden hand filled out that high straight. After so many losses, she thought, if he didn't have the cards he would fold easily. She'd bluff this hand, take it easy on the first round, then see if she could bump him into a quick fold by tripling the stakes after she dealt the two last cards. While she waited patiently for his betting decision, she watched Baird through dusky lashes, reviewing what she'd learned about him.

During dinner and a session of washing dishes, Baird had explained how he'd gotten through the station gate. It had partly to do with his work in marine collections, the influence of his contacts at Humboldt State University. But the real pull had been the Langston name, the fact that he was the grandson of a lumber baron from the Eureka area. Despite the fact that his reputation was tainted by the trial and his prison term—this offered with such bitterness that Dawnelle's insides lurched—he had been handed a key to the gate. The Coast Guard had granted him unlimited access to the wealth of marine life to be found among the rocks and tidepools edging Trinidad Head. He planned to use the locale for collections, but only at some point far in the future.

She'd wondered why the delay.

He hadn't yet begun collecting around the station, he said, because special pulleys and harnesses were needed to scale the precipitous cliffs. When questioned about the equipment, Baird seemed evasive, mentioning that other priorities were taking a toll on his cash flow. There had been a bad-tempered pull to his mouth when he'd muttered, "Old debts.... Another two or three years.... Still trying to locate my ex-partner...." His tacit refusal to amplify thwarted her curiosity.

Other than Baird's brief grumbling, the evening had been superb, tension free—as if they'd been cooking and eating and chatting together for decades. He'd complimented her on her creamy silk tailored blouse and fine wool slacks and joked about the unruly tendencies of her pet.

Earlier, he'd hung his jean jacket next to her green Windbreaker on the hall tree, and Dawnelle had gotten a good look at his wide shoulders as she closed the drapes and turned on the lamp near the easy chair. *Rock of Gibraltar*, she'd thought, watching his muscles arch beneath the brown plaid shirt, causing the cotton to hoop and ripple and dip. Then he'd turned around and caught her staring at him. But he'd only grinned and said, "Thought you were starved? Let's go fix dinner."

Now Dawnelle glanced up to find Baird studying her solemnly. "Thought you were starved," she mimicked good-naturedly.

"With a full stomach and a warm fire at my back, there's only one hunger left unsatisfied." He smiled provocatively. "Do you read minds as cleverly as you beat men at poker?"

"I've learned to stay one up in most games. Your bet."

He arched a brow and bent to toss a red chip into the pot. "I'll go another five, thanks to your ace. It's on you."

"Mitch would have said, 'You're stating the obvious.' See your five—" flipping a chip onto the pile, she glanced at her hand, hesitated for effect, then flung a blue disk in after it "—and raise you ten."

He called the bet, so she dealt the last two cards and

let him think in silence. After a moment he said casually, "Mitch? Who's he?"

"Best poker face in Northern California." She studied her cards, keeping her face impassive as she looked at the ace, deuce, three and queen on the rug by her chips. Baird would be worried that she had a low straight going. But the nine she'd just slipped between the ten and queen in her hand still only added up to a pair of queens. In comparison, the sheaf of diamonds he was showing looked mighty strong.

She arranged her features in the bored expression she'd learned from Mitch, and perfected in the dorm at college, saying, "Fire could be raging in the next room—Mitch would just sit here letting the smoke from his cigarette drift over the cards while he figured the odds in his favor."

"Always in his favor?" He tossed in a ten chip.

"Always. He's a positive thinker. Raise you twenty-five."

"Gutsy bet, considering I'm sitting on a possible royal. This Mitch...." He threw in five blue chips, doubling her bet, and she sighed inwardly. He wouldn't be railroaded. "Is he special?"

His tone was quiet, off-hand. But something stirred inside Dawnelle, and she felt her pulse quicken. She tossed in five blues, seven reds, a handful of whites.

"Mitch taught me everything I know." She grinned, feeling the old excitement of a gamble tighten her stomach. "About poker, anyway. The bet's to you, Baird."

"Right, right." He studied his hand, dragging out the inevitable. "How much did you throw in there?"

"Sixty-six."

His fingers passed through the meager scattering of chips at his knee. "I can't make it." He looked up, his eyes innocent. "You have something in mind for me to pay you with?"

She blushed at the greed that had replaced her normally considerate manner. Something about Baird had made her want to prove herself again. But this was a friendly game. When a player ran out of chips, the polite thing to do was award the pot to the winning hand. Perhaps she ought to suggest they show their cards.

"Maybe I should reassess your intentions here tonight, Dawnelle," Baird was saying as she tried to form her apology. "But aren't the roles a little reversed?"

"Meaning it's okay for you to scheme on me, but not the other way around?" Her voice was sharper than she'd intended, but he certainly didn't have to get his macho blood boiling! She forgot all about her half-formed intention to show the cards and call it a night. "You're sounding a lot like a poor loser."

"I haven't made my final bet, now, have I?"

She pointed to his chips. "You're broke, Baird. Why not concede like a gentleman?"

"Surely there's *something* I can bid...." He spread his arms like a great hawk's wings and craned his neck to look down at his body.

"Don't be crass!" she snapped, suddenly too threatened by his sexual innuendo to be reasonable. "I'll take the pot and forget the difference you owe."

He grasped her wrist as she was reaching to haul in her winnings. "How'd you ever make it in the big city, green eyes? Backing away from a challenge like that."

She twisted out of his grip, her spine suddenly as stiff as the black iron poker. "What do you mean, back away? I haven't backed away—I've won. You're the one who's trying to finagle out!"

"Afraid of the collateral I might offer?"

"Dreamer! You have nothing I want!"

"Ouch!" He ducked his head. "Mitch teach you this rough stuff?"

She angled her head slightly. Mitch wouldn't speak to her for a week if he found out she'd let someone off her bet. "Women are too soft to play a man's game of poker, kid," he'd say, talking with the cigarette dangling from his lips. "They don't have the guts to be tough. Always thinkin' with their hearts instead of their heads. Now deal the cards and let's see if we can make a real poker player outta André's pet."

"What'll you bet?" she asked Baird through tight lips.

"You prepared to pay up if I win?"

She couldn't help it; she looked at her chips, nearly gone, and then her cards, revealing her uncertainty. Mitch would have been furious. Quickly she looked up, working on an icy glare. "I've got an idea," she said, half afraid Baird would trick her into commencing a relationship, and wanting to control the terms.

"Mitch teach you that look? Doesn't do much for your eyes. What's your plan?"

She ignored his mild insult. "We tell each other what we want. But no physical stuff, no spin-the-bottle stakes."

"You take all the fun out of it! But...since we're

operating outside the book at this point, who goes first?"

"I will."

He leaned back to rest his elbows against the rag rug, spreading his palms in an invitation for her to speak.

"Okay." She uncrossed her legs, wondering if he'd put together the flush, watching his eyes travel up the length of her leg. Perhaps her request would steer him away from the lusty thoughts he seemed to carry around like pocket change. "I win, you teach me to obedience-train Miss Mo."

At the sound of her name, the shepherd raised her head, then stretched and went back to sleep. With a thoughtful glance at the dog, Baird rose and slung a log into the fire, jolting Miss Mo again. She groaned in protest. Standing with his legs apart, tall and rugged against the reaching flames, Baird looked down at Dawnelle, his expression wary.

She held her breath, expecting the worst.

"If I win—" he spoke in a low rumble "—you go to work for me."

She jumped to her feet, surprised he hadn't demanded the obvious. Still, the stakes were impossibly high.

"I can't do that," she said firmly. "I've got a contract with the Coast Guard."

"Who said you had to quit your job here?"

"I wouldn't, of course."

"You don't spend every minute of every day slaving around the station."

"I'll be busier," she argued, smoothing her palms over her light wool slacks. "When the tourists arrive, I'll have my hands full."

"Part-time is all you'll work for me. A few hours a week. Let's make it two hours a week for six weeks—the same time it would take me to teach you about obedience training." He came to stand by his cards, one hand on his hip, the other stroking his beard. "Didn't you call the stakes—we say what we want? Didn't Mitch tell you your word is supposed to be as good as a legal contract?"

"That's my dad's line," she said, ruminating on his proposition. "What would I have to do for you?"

"P.R."

She looked at him in wonder. "Surely you don't expect me to repair your reputation for being...for your...."

"My criminal record?" He laughed shortly. "I've my own plan to set that right. Meanwhile, my business interests might do something to polish up that reputation you seem so touchy about—with your help."

"I'm not touchy about it!" She wished he's sit down, get to the point. "Which business interests, anyway? I got the feeling you had several."

"My marine business, Dawnelle. I'm starting over, here in Trinidad for the time being. In San Francisco, I had hundreds working for me—laboratories, hatcheries and water farms, export offices in Singapore, Brazil, Japan—all over the hemisphere." His eyes seemed to glow with blue energy as he paced away, pivoted, returned. "I want it back, all of it. It may be two, three years before I can put big money into the business for expansion. Meanwhile, I'll build."

For the first time since she'd met Baird, Dawnelle felt a keen respect for him. *Not just a pretty face,* she thought wryly, although he wasn't handsome in the aristocratic sense. Magnificent, perhaps, in a carved-granite way. But he was filled with zeal. As she'd been, four years ago in San Francisco.

She glanced down at the cards and chips. "Six weeks?"

"Six."

Looking into his craggy face, she remembered his insults earlier that morning. "Before, you seemed in a big rush to tell me I was only interested in gossip—like all women. Now you want my skill. Did the wind change direction or something?"

"You're trained in P.R." He shrugged, his manner flippant. "I've got a new business that desperately needs image and promotion."

"That doesn't answer my question."

Fleetingly he looked at his hands. "Against all my instincts," he growled softly, "I want to trust you, Dawnelle. I've got to start somewhere."

A plea. So much was left unsaid—about his background, his scruples, his wife, Suzanne. So much quicksand beneath Dawnelle's heels if she lost the bet. "I don't know...."

Suddenly he took her hand, creating ripples of awareness along her arm and down her back. "I got to know *you*." His intensity softened a bit as he offered her a boyish grin. "And I brought you that salmon to say I was wrong about you."

She smiled. "You did bring the fish. But no more insults about my professionalism—or my sex. Deal?"

"Done! I believe it's my move, Dawny girl. I call. Let's see the color of your cards!"

CHAPTER FOUR

NEXT MORNING AT SEVEN, Dawnelle's step was springy as she went to the hall tree and slipped on her green Windbreaker, preparing to go out and open the station gate. Not even the prospect of her first official visitor, Ben Fallon, could crush her enthusiasm.

She pulled the zipper up beneath the heavy cowl of her seafoam-green sweater, thinking about the poker game. Mitch wouldn't have been too proud of her. But then, losing wasn't embarrassing when the winner was Baird Langston, who'd traveled and conducted business all over the world. Who'd played a good many more rounds of poker than she had. *Who'd spent time behind bars,* a waspish part of her brain pointed out. But that didn't make him a creep, she argued. Just a clever poker player. And with any luck of her own, she'd find out he was a good businessman, too. Since she was going to work for him, she hoped he was more astute than Jeff Dugan had been when she met him. She was realistic enough about herself to admit she had a weakness for people who needed her.

She'd fallen for the "join my team" routine once before when Jeff had hired her to bail out his failing marketing department. And when the team won, another woman had taken home Dawnelle's trophy. Her mouth thinned. She'd be damned if history would repeat that nasty score! In this new game with Baird Langston, there would be no trade-offs—and no trophy to win. Baird had already learned to keep his distance, it seemed. Hadn't he kept to his side of the braided rug all evening?

Besides, her design and copywriting skills were bound to get rusty if she did nothing but gardening, sweeping and walking tours for a year. Wasn't she planning to look for another P.R. job when her contract with the Coast Guard was up? It made good sense to help Langston out for a few weeks, didn't it?

As she studied her image in the shell-crusted mirror near the hall tree, she waved away minor doubts. The fact that Baird had generously agreed to throw Miss Mo's obedience training into the bargain made the deal even better for her. It was very simple, really. All she had to do was curb her feminine reactions to his powerful presence. A few reminders of the shambles she'd made of her life before would keep her emotions in line.

Smiling catlike into the mirror, she patted her hair and turned to the door, where she'd leaned the trout and salmon poles her father had included in his care package. Briefly she felt a pang for her father's loneliness, but when Miss Mo trotted expectantly to her side, obviously intending to follow her to the front gate, Dawnelle grinned. She'd write that letter tonight about the German shepherd who protected her every step.

"Some protector you were last night," she admonished, ruffling the dog's ears. "I let in practically a stranger, and you collapse at his feet!" Yet Baird was no longer a stranger, and she had the sudden uneasy premonition that her feelings for him would not be controlled.

Miss Mo nudged the black doorknob, her tail whipping excitedly. "All right, pushy! We're going!" Dawnelle grabbed her keys, pulled open the plank door and ran down the boardwalk to the picket gate. When the dog rammed through at full speed, Dawnelle was shoved against the sharp points of the fence. Her retort was ignored as they both raced to the chain-link enclosure.

Almost immediately after she'd opened the gate, the hum of an engine sounded around the bend. Dawnelle faced the road and saw a blue Jeep with a black steel bumper. Glancing at the dog, she found Miss Mo poised with one paw in the air, her nose raised to the wind, her eyes trained on the approaching vehicle.

Quickly Dawnelle crossed to the dog and grasped her collar. "Try to behave yourself," she muttered, fixing a smile of greeting on her lips.

Ben Fallon was not what she'd expected, if in fact he was the one leaning out of the cockpit of the Jeep. Dawnelle guessed he looked thirty, perhaps less, with that clean, line-free face. Straight sandy hair formed an unruly shelf above level brows and gray blue eyes. The eyes crinkled at the corners as a smile lighted his face, softening his rather blunt jaw.

He leaned farther out the door as Dawnelle was nearly dragged in front of him by the dog. Glancing uncertainly at Miss Mo, he quickly looked up. "Dawnelle?"

"Hi, yes. You must be Ben," she said, selecting his first name, since he'd used hers. She was jerked unceremoniously forward as Miss Mo lunged at the blue door, setting up a cacophony of barking comparable to last night. "Miss Mo, no! He's supposed to be here!"

It was an effort to maintain her grip on the dog while she directed Ben to park up ahead, near the gray boulder and her Fiat. "The dog's going into training tomorrow," she began apologetically when the geologist climbed to the ground.

But the tall man who looked as if he'd stepped out of a romantic version of *Sports Afield* only smiled. He grasped her hand in a warm firm handshake, cutting the gesture short when Miss Mo struggled toward him.

"Best reception I've ever had out here. In fact—" his eyes traveled over her face, stopping politely short of a complete inventory of her body "—best reception I've had anywhere for a good long while. Sorry to get you out to open the gate so early, but I'm working on a deadline. Got to have samples to the lab by four o'clock."

"No problem." She waved airily. "No inconvenience at all." Releasing Miss Mo, she sighed in relief as the dog sniffed at Ben's denim work pants, then trotted into the brush beside the road. "About this hour I'm usually elbow deep in some chore or other, anyhow. Why are you taking samples? Something wrong around the station?"

"No. Coast Guard's asked my company to test the stability of the rock under the lighthouse," he said, leaning across the driver's seat to extract a khaki knapsack, a hand pick and other small tools. "Just routine, really. Winds and surf are bound to wear away the formations, no matter how solid the bluff seems to you and me. And those earth tremors you get out here off the point— Well, the importance of the lighthouse warrants preventive checking."

Ben's work implements clattered as he chucked them to the ground. He straightened, looked at her. "I'm curious. You're an attractive woman—beautiful, in fact. And from what I've read you're sharp enough to be running *The Wall Street Journal*. What intrigues you about this light station?"

"The town needed a keeper."

He dusted his hands, then leaned indolently against the Jeep, his expression one of narrow-eyed speculation. "Trinidad always needs a keeper, Dawnelle. You're highly trained, if that story about you was honest." He ticked off on his fingers accomplishments Dawnelle took for granted. "Developed an award-winning campaign for the lung association while you were still in college. Headed up some program or other for an environmentalist group. Worked your way up the corporate ladder at that laser company—"

"Everyone, it seems," she commented wryly, "reads Trinidad's newspaper. The circulation must be enormous."

"The fishbowl is bigger than Trinidad, I'm afraid. The Arcata and Eureka papers ran a version of the story, too. It's no small item when a young woman takes over a light station by herself."

Don't I know it, she thought, remembering Captain Kern's displeasure at having to explain lighthouse maintenance to a woman.

Ben scratched his head in a thoughtful way, looking over at her expectantly. "So...what made the pretty woman give up success in the city to brave earthquakes and loneliness? Why Trinidad?"

"Bingo." She laughed. "What people in my trade call 'the bottom-line zinger'"

"Zinger, question—I'm still curious."

"Right. Well, I suppose I don't mind telling you."

She grew serious as she studied the way Ben's tools lay scattered on the hard-packed ground. There were some things she wouldn't be telling Ben Fallon, personal painful things she was amazed she'd shared with Baird. But Ben's curiosity was a reflection of the questions all of Trinidad would be asking. The thought was wearying. She looked into his friendly eyes.

"I'd quit that job in the San Francisco area," she began. "I was looking around for a good replacement when I read about Trinidad and the lighthouse. The article appeared as a human-interest piece in the *Chronicle*. Spelled out the decline of lighthouses all over the country, and the fact that Trinidad was one of the few communities concerned about preserving theirs—not just handing it completely over to the Coast Guard and seeing it run by remote control. It was the kind of goal I thought I'd like to get behind, Ben."

"What about the earthquakes?"

She shrugged. "There had been a couple of serious tremors over time, according to the article, but the lighthouse has never been damaged in all its one hundred thirteen years. Still standing, still reliable. Record enough to put my trust in, wouldn't you agree?"

"Sure—and don't get me wrong. I'm as grateful as the next guy to see you out here—maybe more so, now I've met you." He winked.

Ben Fallon was as refreshing as the cool wind she felt against her face, a pleasant diversion from the serious-minded Baird, and suddenly Dawnelle knew their awkward introduction would blossom into friendship. She sensed Ben was drawn to her.

"Thanks." She inclined her head. "But grateful? What makes you chose that word?"

"She's been through a lot, the old beacon. Deserves a graceful retirement."

"Like an old horse, you mean? Put her out to pasture because she's served her time and deserves a gentle death?"

"No." He laughed at her slight bridling. He drew a boot tip through the dust, kicked at a pebble and looked at her again. "Truth is, Trinidad Light is still very important to the economy of this area. The salmon and crab taken from these waters bring many of the people around here the clothes on their backs, the food in their pantries. Plus, with the aid of Trinidad Light, the charter services get the tourists out into the sunshine and clean air of this rocky coastline, then back safely to their motor homes. Satisfied visitors just keep coming back for more every year. I'm no exception."

"You don't live here?"

He shook his head, pointing toward the southern coastline. "Arcata, down the freeway."

"Strange. You sound like a local. I wouldn't think an out-of-towner would defend the lighthouse as you do."

"Ah. . . ." He studied the distant mainland shore, a greenish gray caterpillar blending in hazy lines with the soft blue of the Pacific. "Funny how a place gets in your blood. Ever since I transplanted from the Midwest and came up this way on my first job. . . .''

''Why did you transplant?'' she said softly, sharing Ben's feelings about Trinidad.

''For the redwoods, I guess. And the way those offshore rocks jut up as if they were the first land on earth. Because of the legends of yellow gold I heard as a kid, maybe.''

He turned to stare at the sky and stretching sea, his gray blue eyes looking very appealing, very sensitive. ''During the gold-rush years,'' he added, ''miners back in the hills relied on the Trinidad shipping trade for their supplies. Trinidad was a whaling town once, too. I'm told the little harbor used to see big clipper ships in her waters on a daily basis.'' He chuckled as he returned his gaze to her, the misty expression swiftly changing to sparkling humor. ''Had my fill of flat land and the feast or famine of the grain belt. The ocean, the great Pacific Northwest—no place like it on earth. I guess that's why this light station is important to me.''

''Because it symbolizes everything the Midwest is not?'' She frowned, attempting to follow his reasoning.

''No. Symbolism isn't worth the powder to blow it to here and gone. I just mean the lighthouse keeps a place like Trinidad alive. I want this little town that calls itself a city—second oldest incorporated city in California, I'm told—well, I don't want it to go away, that's the plain truth. Like it just how it is.''

''It seems to me, loving this place as you do, you ought to move here. I mean, why not?''

''Economics,'' he returned. ''Most of our company's clients are down around Eureka and on south for eighty miles or more. Be an awful commute from Trinidad. But I've been thinking of a scheme that'll get me up here on a permanent basis." His eyes twinkled, and she laughed, liking him.

"Duty first, though." He peered at his tools. "Care to venture to the edge of the world with me while I get those samples and take some measurements?"

"I really can't, Ben. Here, let me help you with your gear." She stooped to gather up the pick and some metal containers, handing them to him. "If I finish checking the paper in the seismograph and seeing to the foghorn mechanism that got stuck a few days ago, plus a few other chores, I'll come and look over your shoulder."

"I'll try to scrape through without you, then. Bring a sandwich, and I'll share my thermos of coffee over lunch."

Amused, she shook her head. "You never give up, do you?" She watched him adjust the tan backpack over his wide shoulders. "I'll see how my chores go, but I'm not promising I'll be through in time. Don't starve yourself on my account."

"I implore you, maiden, join me—" he struck a stage pose, his arm sweeping toward the sky—"lest the bargain should catch cold and starve—is that how the line goes?"

"Not exactly, and was it Shakespeare or shale you studied? Anyway, your offer's tempting enough without the blackmail. Go thee about thy work, and I'll join you if I can."

Feeling coltish in the warmth of Ben's gaze, she chuckled as she turned away. This man could prove to be a pleasant diversion from Baird Langston and the dangerous emotions he had aroused in her, she decided. A backward glance told her the geologist was staring after her. Waving, she rounded the granite boulder. Yes, definitely, she looked forward to seeing more of Ben Fallon.

CHAPTER FIVE

FIFTEEN FEET. Just a measly fifteen or twenty feet more to put away. Arms aching from the strain of lifting the heavy rope, Dawnelle untangled a grimy knot, shook out the dust, wound the last length of hemp onto the pile. The task had stolen an hour out of the middle of her shed-cleaning project, and she was hot, tired and resentful.

Wearily she sank against the waist-high coil, dragging the back of her hand across her sweaty cheek. "Terrific!" she muttered. In all likelihood she'd just smudged filth over the only patch of clean skin on her body. She surely must be wearing most of the dirt she'd tried to clean away.

That was impossible, of course. She'd sent some of it outside. She had wheeled out at least nine barrowsful of sand, oily rags, broken boards and hardened paint rollers, to say nothing of the rusty nest of wire, the splintered broom and the dried pool of white paint she'd scraped off the floor. Plucking at her moss green T-shirt, she sifted musty dust onto her jeans. She sneezed. Forgetting her earlier mistake, she ducked her face against her long sleeve. Silt came away on her lips. "Great, now I'm eating the stuff!"

She wryly shook her head. It hadn't been so bad, really

Not once had she dwelled on personal problems, and only briefly had she thought about Baird Langston. She'd been too buried beneath trash, too concerned with proving she could see this job through.

Evidently the dog had decided to let their visitor coexist in relative peace, too. Ben's drilling machine clattered faintly, sounding like a jackhammer muffled by feather pillows. The wind on the bluff blanketed sound, she realized. Made you feel you had cotton candy in your ears all the time.

She'd left Ben at the gate hours ago. Now the drone of his equipment triggered her own sense of industry, so Dawnelle heaved herself from the lumpy pile of rope.

As she rocked the rickety stepladder against a rack of shelves loaded down with yet another snarl of lumber and rusty pipes, she boosted her spirits with the memory of that grand tour the Coast Guard official had given her two weeks ago. Captain Kern had made his doubts about her ability very clear, so that she suspected the Coast Guard had been pressured to go along with Trinidad's choice in order to help erase that Big Brother reputation the government was earning itself along the coast. She'd read about the legal skirmishes between small-town residents whose families had owned valuable coastal property for generations and agencies desperate to convert parts of California's majestic coastline to public domain.

She wondered vaguely how the dark beauty, Lau, felt about property rights. The coastal Indians had once owned all the land hereabouts, Henny had said. And now the descendants of American pioneers were squabbling with bureaucrats over the same land, land taken in bloody skirmishes from the Indians. Would Sarah's friend Lau feel bitter about the past?

Dawnelle dragged another board over the edge of the shelf and watched it bounce off the rubble skirting the ladder. But after all, Lau was only part Yurok. Perhaps her Indian culture had been diluted or forgotten. Dawnelle shrugged, putting the mysterious woman she'd only seen once from her mind, and heaved a heavy pine box to the floor. Dust rose from the clutter. She coughed in the floating grit.

Then, ever on the lookout for black-widow spiders, she gingerly shoved aside some four-by-four posts, in the process pricking her finger on an unseen nail. She winced and jerked away. Lead pipes clanged, dust swirled and Dawnelle's legs wavered on the creaking ladder. Bending her head, she let the wash of vertigo evaporate. She was tired. She ought to—

"Dawnelle...?"

Reaching blindly for the shelf to steady herself, she glanced sharply around. Particles of dust shimmered around the silhouette in the doorway. "You!"

Her tennis shoes shuffled on the narrow steps as she tried to compensate for the weaving ladder. Groping wildly for the nearest upright post, she felt the ladder jolt beneath her. Her legs buckled. She missed her grip.

Automatically she braced herself for the short descent to the rusty nails and pipes below. Pain shot along her elbow as her arm jammed into a metal brace. Falling! Curl up. Pull in arms, legs. She squeezed her eyes shut and felt the rush of air as she descended. Thump! She landed in warm protective arms. No pain. She blinked.

Baird's blue eyes bored into her. "I thought I

wouldn't make it in time. Are you—anything broken? Sprained?"

"No, thank God!" she whispered, drawing a shaky breath. She glanced down over the taut muscles of his supporting arms. Weapons surrounded them: lead pipes poking up like bamboo spikes in a jungle battlefield, nails thrusting crusted points toward her vulnerable flesh. When she realized she might have been disfigured, shock washed through her.

Then she felt a heartbeat thudding strongly against her pinioned arm. Breath warmed her half-turned face. Slowly, as if awakening in a meadow of sensuality, she brought her eyes to his. Unreasonable joy kindled through her, reminding her, strangely, of a childhood moment—the pleasure of gazing as deeply as she could into the bugle throat of a bluebell in that field behind the hatchery in Bishop, California, where her father had been stationed at the time.

His pale face bent closer, his beard tickling her cheek. "You're all right?"

She nodded, regarding his features with an artist's appreciation for fine sculpture. Never, during other encounters with him, had she been able to dismiss the sheer granite power of this face. She marveled at the natural mauve line shaping his lips, the mustache, the smooth texture of his skin. She absorbed him through the very pores of her own skin.

His brow was as prominent and contemplative as Rodin's thinking man's. A concentration reminiscent of that hundred-year-old bronze was now trained on her, inspiring awe and curiosity, eliciting the warmth of kinship and attraction. He seemed to transfer thoughts through the senses, so that feelings, not inadequate words, flowed between them. He asked mute questions as fundamental as earth-bound metal. Yet she understood he asked these things of himself as much as of her.

Inevitably, he stirred physical heat within her. A growing fire leaped from the cerulean eyes. A vague cinnamon-earth scent stimulated her memory. The curve of pressing muscles forced the awareness that he was not cast of bronze, but of flesh and blood, with desires no casting could express to a woman.

A question formed in some deep recess of her mind, just out of reach, then was lost entirely when his lips touched hers.

He kissed her gently. That familiar pressure of his lips warmed her blood like a living flame. He drew her into his kiss not by crushing her in his arms, but through a deep native passion, and she met his ardor with slow movements of her tongue and the soft yielding of her body.

She wrapped her arms around his strong neck, doubling them over his shoulders, not thinking rationally for the moment, only reacting. He was drawing forth new emotions from her, feelings far more urgent than any she'd felt with Jeff, sensations, driving, unfulfilled needs.... Fragments of doubt began to drift into the fire she felt...a memory of her parents, their lost dreams.... As he kissed her with mounting sensuality, her fingers moved rhythmically over his cotton shirt, ever more rapid and insistent.

He shifted slightly. A board grated. He curved his body and settled her lower against his torso. Feeling him already aroused, her breath quickened at the hardness of him, and as her breathing grew audible, he reacted with a low groan. Her heart tripped, racing to beat with that other life, so that one pulse hammered through their veins, sinews, skin.

And then he was touching her breast, his palm grazing the sensitized nipple, delicately circling until her flesh peaked, firmed, molded to the tentatively caressing hand. But the light touch was not enough, not for either of them, and with a muffled sound he crushed her closer, his hand caught between them.

The movement triggered an emotion she strove to fathom. She felt split in two, the rightness of this moment warring with some foreign, half-remembered fear. The fear and the rightness together were almost a physical pain.

She murmured incoherently. He left her softened mouth and trailed lingering kisses across her face. He bent his head, and she could feel his hair feathering her chin. His lips sought the sensitive hollow between her throat and shoulder.

"Baird," she whispered, her voice keening.

"You have the essense of rare antiques," he whispered, nudging aside the collar of her T-shirt to kiss the curve of her shoulder. He bit her gently.

A bold current jagged through her, down into the nerves in her thighs. She parted her lips and took a corded muscle of his neck in her teeth, tenderly tasting, instinctively wanting more of him. She'd never tasted a man before, not with such sensual hunger. His skin was slightly salty, warm and smooth. She nuzzled there a moment, then eased up the column of his neck, kissing him below the ear, closing her lips over the lobe. Finally, shakily, she drew away. Strangely fulfilled, she buried her face against his chest and sighed.

He chuckled.

"What?" she asked huskily.

"You tasted me. Enjoyed me."

She nodded into his shirt. "And you?"

"Mmm. . . ."

"Oh, dear. . . ."

"Yes?"

"No, silly, that's not what I meant. I meant this is crazy. Impossible."

He tensed, exhaled regretfully. "Yes."

The white-hot pain returned to twist her heart. How could this *feel* so right and be so wrong? For both of them. Dear God, he had agreed with her. Damn him. She swallowed, letting her emotions cool as she asked the inane question, "Aren't your arms tired?"

"What?" He stirred as if waking from a reverie. "Tired?"

"Your arms. How can you hold me so long?"

Absently he rubbed his jaw along the top of her head. "It was. . . ."

She waited, breath held.

"Easy."

"Yes." So right and so easy. Was she absolutely insane, knowing this man for two days, yet feeling their time together had been ordained by immortal Judgment?

She felt him shift, looking for a place to put her down.

"Too damned easy," he muttered. "Nothing but trouble. I could lose everything."

"Let me go," she cried, hurt by the distance in his voice, the cruel words, feeling suffocated by rejection. "Put me down *now*!"

"Take it easy, Dawnelle. God, you're always demanding I unhand you." Muscles rippled against her breast as he swung her around, searching for a clean patch of floor, a way out of the clutter. He stumbled slightly, took a giant step and set her gently on the floor. Standing back, he irritatedly pulled at the whorl in his beard.

"I won't apologize this time," he said. "We were both at fault."

"Did I ask for an apology?" she flung out.

"No, but I realized, as you did, that intimacy between us would mean disaster. My energies are diverted enough as it is."

"I suppose now is the moment in your repertoire that I learn the awful truth? Well, let's have it. Or are you the type to walk off into the sunset wearing that deadpan expression and leaving me guessing?"

He let out an impatient sigh. "What truth, Dawnelle?"

"You're still married, of course. Or you've got a child hidden in the closet, and you're trying to set a good example. How do I know what you're going to throw at me?" She knew she was being far too emotional, but she'd come perilously close to opening her heart to his complicated man, and her vulnerability terrified her. She waved angrily, dismissing any argument he might present. "What does it matter, anyway? I need a sabbatical from men who play with women as if they're simpering idiots who have nothing better to do than be turned off and on like some bloody kitchen stove! I need a sabbatical from men, period! Why did you come here today, anyway?"

"I'm not married."

She looked at him for a long full minute. She began to speak, then stared again, resenting the elation that raced through her like water over a washed-out dam. *Stop it!* She plugged the torrent of feeling, turning to look beyond him into the sunshine blazoned across the barn door.

"And no child in the closet," he said roughly. "I've put that life behind me. I've got to organize my business, get my stockholders paid back—long hours, concentration.... And I've got to find Vee. My ex-partner owes me—godammit, where did this conversation *come* from?"

Inwardly she winced at his bitterness, his trampled pride. *No. No pity.* Her fingers curled into her palms. "I can't possibly work for you now."

Again the impatient breath. "Why not? For God's sake, are you the kind of impetuous woman who falls in love in two days' time?" Sarcasm sharpened his words to razor strokes. "Would things be too 'difficult' for someone with your tender sensibilities?"

Yes. For the first time in my life, she thought, sick with embarrassment that she'd been so transparent. But she hated him for his smug shield. "Of course not," she said finally, her chin jutting up. "That was silly on my part. What happened between us won't make the slightest difference. How could it, when neither of us has anything invested?"

"Absolutely. Nothing happened between us. It was a

minor accident in judgment, nothing more. Shall we discuss the reason I'm here?"

"Certainly." The word ripped the air between them. She glanced at her smudged hands and yanked them angrily behind her. Oh, she was mixed up. Pulled this way and that like a steak between two starved dogs. She was furious with herself for lowering her emotional guard. Furious with him for callously rejecting her.

For a few moments he'd seduced her into believing she'd finally met someone tailor-made for her life. And then to have him deny the beauty, the perfection of the feelings between them! She cringed inside to think she'd agreed with his denial just to save face. How was it possible that only she felt the bonding? "Intimacy would mean disaster," he'd said. As if she were some siren luring him away from his duties! Even if you were up to your eyebrows in work and troubles, you made time for someone you were drawn to. Sure, you worried about the consequences of a poor match, as she had done, but normal people took a chance, gave the relationship at least a few weeks. Her fury was evident, sending sparks of resentment toward the man who stood silently by, his face a mask of reserve. Well, silence was sometimes a woman's only weapon. The next move was his.

Walking to the coil of ropes in the corner beyond the door, she arranged herself on the uncomfortable lumps, every move falsely indifferent. With a disdainful side-glance, she noted his stiff attitude in the middle of the cluttered shed. He could sit on the floor for all she cared.

He'd turned to watch her. Now he moved to the wall

nearby and propped one hand against a horizontal stud. He cleared his throat, and she relished his evident unease. "I brought some catalogs for you to look over."

She laughed harshly, but he forestalled a retort with his raised palm. "Dawnelle, hear me out. I want to pay you for any time you can afford me, any hours you'd be willing to work—beyond our initial two-hour-per-week agreement, that is. These are not the circumstances under which I'd hoped to discuss this matter, but will you do it?"

Anger seethed within her despite the iron grip she maintained on her temper. "Exactly what circumstances had you hoped to see develop here today, Baird? A love nest in which to ply me for favors? That trick died out with feudal lords."

His thick brows darted together. "No favors, Dawnelle. Business. I'll pay."

"You bet you will. You have no idea what a good bargain you got when I lost that poker hand!"

"Keep in mind I'm barely into my first quarter-year of business, will you? Try not to be too bloodthirsty."

She could guess at the neophyte state of his firm, and that was precisely why she chose a figure that would put her out of his reach "Sixty dollars an hour," she stated coldly.

"Damn you, I'm just starting out!" She smiled to herself when he bolted away from the wall and began to pace. "In a few months, perhaps, but not now. Good Lord, with you as a business partner, I'd be broke before I opened the doors!"

"I doubt we'd ever be partners, Baird. I have a hankering to run my own world, and we both know with you breathing down my neck, that would be impossible. Besides, I seem to recall your intimation that women in business spell disaster." She shook her head in mock disbelief, then added sweetly, "I'm surprised. Really surprised, Baird. You must think me better than the average woman if you'd even mention partnership in the same breath."

Lithely he moved to stand before her, taking a wide posture, his eyes shadowed. "I do think you better than average."

Despite the restraint she had imposed on herself, her heart skipped unsteadily. *In what way,* she wanted to ask. Immediately she despised herself for groveling even inwardly for his gold-plated affections.

"Obviously you have a good track record," he said, jabbing his thumb up as if to list supporting data. "Command of your craft, a capacity for bright moves at fortuitous moments, a clever hand at promotional strategies." Abruptly he bent and stared at her, his eyes narrowed. "But that doesn't mean I won't kick you out on your ear at the slightest hint of a power play, the barest breach of loyalty. I've been burned, Dawnelle, and you were right about me yesterday. I can be brutal in business matters when I have to be."

The elation died in her. But something remained. Fear? No. Not when he'd held her so lovingly minutes ago. Respect? She sighed, giving in to her heart. "Twenty-five an hour. It's a bargain in any city in the country. Take it or leave it."

He straightened. "Thank you. Let me know when you've hit the forty-hour mark, will you? If it's agreeable to you, I'll pay in increments of forty hours. Log your hours and itemize them, present your bill, and I'll pay it within thirty days."

"I know the standard procedure, Baird," she replied peevishly.

"I know you do. It's just good business to spell out the terms, although even the most carefully laid plans...." He smiled wryly. "Well, you know what I mean. In any event, I put a note with the catalogs. It will explain what I want."

She looked around but found no hint of the materials he wanted her to go through.

"They're on your front porch. I knocked, but no one answered. There was a truck beside your car so I figured...you had company."

"A man is taking rock samples out by the lighthouse," she said stiffly, explaining about Ben and wondering why she bothered. Outside, the wind gusted, but no equipment rattled. She realized Ben might be searching for her, and suddenly she wanted his friendly face to appear and interrupt the confrontation between herself and Baird. She rose, slipping past her antagonist to stand in the shadow of the door. "I'm surprised you didn't hear the drilling," she added. "He's been working steadily for hours."

"I was headed in that direction when I heard the turmoil in here." Following her to the door, he scrutinized her appearance. "Ambitious project you've got going."

"You'll have to remember the lighthouse is my first priority. Your work will have to wait behind any duty I have around the station."

"I would worry about who I'd hired if you'd said it any other way."

She smiled a small smile. "Well. . . anything else?"

He looked outside for an interminable moment, seeming to consider his words. When he finally confronted her, she felt a tiny pull in the pit of her stomach. He stared through her, his eyes sparkling like blue quartz in the bright sunlight.

"I lied to you," he said in a hushed voice. "Or at least—didn't express myself honestly."

"Oh?"

"You are special. It's odd, but sometimes when I look at you, I feel as though somebody's tightening a rope around my ribs. I feel it inside—" There was a soft thud as his hand hit his chest. "But you can relax about 'complications' in our relationship, Dawnelle. I *will* keep my distance. Damned, but I will."

Forgetting her own need for impunity, she began to form the word *why*. But he'd touched his temple in a loose salute and turned away. He walked out the door, his silhouette brief and black against the harsh yellow light.

CHAPTER SIX

"YOU LOOK GORGEOUS!" Ben grinned as she admitted him to the cottage. "And I'd planned to talk business tonight! It'll be impossible now."

"Business?" Smiling, she placed a chilled glass of California Riesling in his hand as she led him past the entry table where she'd placed the tray. She thought briefly of Baird, wished they could share laughter and fun along with the work. But he'd been as distant as the offshore island she could see every time she closed her cottage door. Ben had sought her company for two dinner-dates, tonight being the second, and she'd been relieved in one way: their dates made her feel safe, made her remember her common sense, not her feelings for Baird. Ben was earthy; he kept her feet on the ground.

Smiling at him over the rim of her wineglass, she felt glad about her decision to see him again. "At five minutes to seven Wednesday evening," she admonished Ben now, gaily, "with the prospect of nothing but fun, good food and our usual share of giggling, you announce plans to talk business? Forgive me, but I thought our thing was friendship?"

"Well...." Stepping close so he could put an arm around her back, Ben kissed her. His brisk cologne tickled her nose. His lips felt cool and smooth, expert.

But she felt no explosion of sexual attraction. The revelation depressed her slightly as she returned his kiss, for she'd been half hoping warmth would eventually blossom between them. Still, it was too early in their relationship to know what they might mean to each other, she told herself.

Ben ended the kiss with a murmur. "Funny...you don't taste anything like friendship."

Smiling gently, she slid away, uncertain why she did.

"Only friends?" he said, following her around the chintz couch against the hall. He sat down, pulling her beside him. *He looks clean-cut in gray,* she decided, appreciating his V-neck sweater and the pearl blue dress shirt beneath. Together, the colors matched his eyes perfectly. After the three-piece suits of the Silicon Valley crowd, it relaxed her to see the more casual dinner attire of a small town again. But the gleam in his eyes was far from relaxing. When he'd sipped his wine, he continued, "Uh...why must we be only friends, Dawnelle?"

"Is that impossible?"

"Nothing about us is impossible. But don't throw me out for saying I was hoping for more."

"Ben...." She tugged at the wide belt cinching her silk shirtwaist dress. The silk clung to her trim torso, then fell in soft waves, like a blue green sea rippling over pale reefs. She knew her eyes picked up the moody hues of this dress, knew it was a simple beautiful creation she'd wanted to wear for Baird. But, disappointingly, he seemed to consider her about as appealing as one of the fish in his saltwater holding tanks. She had to keep telling herself it was she who shunned commitment. She needed this evening with Ben. She needed to laugh, to distract her mind from the compelling feelings she felt for Baird—feelings he evidently couldn't return. She smiled engagingly at her date. "We stand to gain so much from friendship, Ben. I—I'm afraid that's all I can offer right now. Let it be enough, please."

He studied her carefully, trailing a finger along the hollow of her cheek, twining a wisp of her upswept hair. "Ready for a friendly compliment?" he asked gently.

Ruefully she nodded.

"I like your hair up. And another thing, friendship with you holds more promise than most of the 'I love yous' floating around the globe. Of course I'll let it be enough. For now." He toasted her and drank deeply of his wine.

Liberated suddenly, she stood up and grinned, holding her own goblet high. "*Salud* to friendship, Ben. For now."

THE RESTAURANT was set among big trees, with a small café at one end, a pub at the other, and out back a collection of white cottages snuggled beneath the greenery.

Seated in deep, red leather booths near the bar, they ordered from a slim waitress with a generous smile. Ben selected succulent roasted pork, Dawnelle a platter of scallops, prawns and sea bass. After consuming bowls of thick, parsley-sprinkled clam chowder, they were finishing the entrées, accompanied by enormous side portions of crisp French fries, green beans sautéed in a butter-wine sauce and dark coffee. Dawnelle thought the fare as tasty as her mother's finest Sunday-night dinners. She said so to Ben.

"So your mother's a fancy cook," he said, bringing the linen napkin to his lips.

"Was. My mother died when I was eleven."

"Was she lovely like you?"

"Now where do you think I get my looks?" she teased.

"I knew it! Her legacy was all those fine things I admire in you, am I right?" He signaled the waitress, ordered a glass of wine for himself, then paused. "Dawnelle? Something from the bar?"

"A Harvey's sherry, thanks. No ice."

When they were alone, Ben looked thoughtful for a moment. "I did want to mention something...if you don't mind a change of subject?"

"Not at all. Business?"

"Yes. That is, I want to put down roots here in Trinidad. I have an idea as to how I might do that."

"Oh, yes. The 'scheme' you mentioned the first time we met. You mean you're permanently abandoning the Midwest?"

His nod contained certainty. "Naturally I'll want to visit the family now and then—in fact, I plan to fly home for Thanksgiving."

"That's months away, and yet you still call it home."

"If you knew my family you'd understand why." He chuckled, running his fingers over the turned-up edge of the napkin. "My sis, Betty, has the neatest passel of kids you've ever seen. All cheruby and curly locked. Nothing like me at all, with my straight-as-a-stick hair. They're something!" He sighed heavily, arousing Dawnelle's sympathy, for she felt a tug, remembering Tommy. "But I like Trinidad, its small-town friendliness, the fact that you can feel nature all around you. And I think a man can make a good life here, in spite of the fact that there's not a heck of a lot of money floating around."

"What a strange coincidence, really."

"What do you mean?"

She hesitated for a minute. Hadn't she, too, put down roots here? She'd been thinking that history always repeated itself in her life, that she was always helping someone else put zest into his or her business. Why not go into P.R. herself, right here in Trinidad? Yes, a small clientele, reasonable prices, perhaps eventually one or two city clients to keep her in touch with the elegant side of life—

"My," Ben interrupted. "I had no idea the thought of my opening a business could bring such deep furrows to your brow. C'mon, fess up. What coincidence?"

"Several, actually. But the one at the top of the list is that I've thought about hanging out a shingle of my own. After my Coast Guard contract is up, I mean."

"Well, now—" Ben gazed at her with more sparkle "—since I opened the topic, you ought to hear me out first. Just on the off chance we're thinking along the same lines."

She leaned forward slightly, then straightened to let the waitress set their drinks down.

"Anything else?" The woman smiled, pulling her long dark braid becomingly over her right shoulder, reminding Dawnelle vaguely of Sarah's friend Lau. Uncanny how the woman had made such a lasting impression. . . .

Ben looked inquiringly at Dawnelle. When she shook

her head, complimenting the restaurant's delicious food, the young woman slid their plates to her arm and withdrew.

"Okay." Dawnelle held her glass up once again in a toast. "To success in Trinidad."

They sipped quickly. Ben returned immediately to their conversation. "Actually, I'm going to surprise you. I haven't a drop of experience in my newly chosen field, but I have a modicum of cash put by, and I'm as eager as a boy who's been pitching hay all day and just seen his first glimpse of the pond."

"Go on. . . ."

"I want to open a charter business."

"You mean with boats?"

"With a boat, for starters. Now how about it? Are we going to be in competition with each other?"

"No." She laughed, tickled at his mock frown. "I was thinking of P.R.—something small. Oh, Ben, a charter business! How absolutely intriguing. I know nothing about it!"

"Neither do I, but I sure have a hankering to live by the sea—literally. Will you give me a hand? Not in the business or anything right now, just with a few contacts to start me off."

"Contacts? The only people with boats I know about are in service for the government. What can I do?"

"Just listen up for information—someone looking to sell a boat, a guy who wants a partner—anything. Even someone who would be willing to let me work a commercial boat on the weekends to earn my fins, so to speak." He laughed excitedly and took a sip of his wine, choking slightly in his eagerness. "I don't think I'll have any luck with someone who already has a charter service going or anything. But who knows, one of those guys might want to sell in a year or two, and meanwhile I can start learning the ropes with a commercial trolling outfit. With your contacts, Dawnelle, I thought maybe you'd be willing to scout around for me. Introduce me to a few people out at the fish fry next weekend."

"Ah, so you really wanted to escort me in order to take advantage of my connections!"

"Absolutely not!" He looked chagrined, though she was teasing. "I want to dance with you and laugh and—and—"

"And meet my friends." She giggled, enchanted by his evident discomfort. "Oh, you men! Always playing the angles!"

"No, now, Dawnelle, I'm not like that! Really, I have a sincere personal interest in you. It has nothing to do with my business plans. Not exactly—I mean, not entirely. Now see what you've done!" He sopped up wine with his napkin. "You'll have to go with me to make up for this!"

"I'll be glad to go with you next Saturday." She grinned, setting his glass aside so she could help daub at the soiled tablecloth. "There, now, you're clever, after all. You've tricked me into accepting!"

His chagrin vanished. He smiled innocently. "What are friends for?"

SARAH CALDWELL grumbled in protest as she heaved her ample body from the maple dining-room chair, an Early American bentwood. It matched the oval table recently laden with an enormous New England corned-beef-and-cabbage dinner.

"I'll get us some fresh coffee," Sarah said, her hand automatically checking the gray permanented curls hugging her head. "You two sit tight and enjoy your books."

"You're the light of my life, m'dear," Henny responded, sneaking a quick pat on his wife's calico-draped bottom. "But you're about to miss the best part. Dawnelle's goin' to show us the pictorial next."

Squinting at him, Sarah reached around to the spot where he'd tapped her and shook her head. "You know I can't sit still this long. Today was my day to relieve Greer at the library. All that sitting just about wore my sitter flat."

"Impossible." Grinning, Henny handed up the three coffee cups, one of which had a brown crack marring its feminine spring-flowers pattern.

"I can't stay but a few minutes more, anyway," Dawnelle offered, closing *Lighthouses of the North Pacific* and reaching for the oversized blue volume on California lights.

Henny and Sarah both looked disappointed.

"What in the star-spangled blue blazes is so pressin' you've got to run off before our third cup of java?" Henny demanded. "Sarah? Maybe it's your coffee." Sarah batted his neck with the flat of her hand. He flinched, teheeing in delight.

"I've been here hours," Dawnelle laughingly pointed out. "It's not as though I bolted out the door the minute we finished dinner."

"Supper! We've just had supper, dear," Sarah corrected, pausing by the doorway to straighten a floral needlepoint before she headed for the kitchen. "Back in New Hampshire we called lunch dinner and dinner supper. Anyway, Henny doesn't have to work tomorrow, and Greer Sking has the library duty on Sundays, thank goodness. We're both free as birds! How about you?" Satisfied she'd leveled off the rose-patterned hanging to perfection, she went through the door, then peeked around the molding. "Got visitors tomorrow?"

Dawnelle grinned. Sarah reminded her of one of the porcelains her mother used to line up on the mantel. The knitting-needle lady, Dawnelle used to call the grandma figurine. Draped in a lace shawl, she sat knitting in her rocker, peeping out from her white scullery cap with an impish smile that said she knew something exciting and secret. Sarah even wore the same silver-rimmed glasses.

"I haven't got one visitor." Dawnelle shook her head in relief. "That photographer who came out today was equal to ten guests. He had me clipping bushes and closing doors for hours so he could get what he called 'display-quality' pictures. But I did want to ask a favor before I leave." Pleased that Sarah had forgotten all about coffee and was leaning forward to catch every word, Dawnelle explained Ben's interest in working aboard some kind of fishing vessel.

Henny and Sarah looked thoughtfully at each other. "What about Lau?" Sarah asked him.

Dawnelle's eyes widened at this mention of the lovely Indian woman she'd seen outside the post office. Baird's name had been mentioned then, too....

"Yeah," Henny said musingly. "But you know how

she is about that tribal-curse business. Thinks she's doomed or something."

"Exactly!" Sarah slapped her thigh. "If I could talk her into helping Dawnelle's friend for a while—just till he knows the ropes—maybe he would be the ticket to breaking that awful spell she's wrapped around herself. Lord knows she's suffered enough. Ought to be married again by this time. Henny?"

Henny Caldwell stood up and took the coffee cups from Sarah's crooked index finger. She gave him a "what on earth are you doing" look as he guided her back to the table.

"Sit," he said. "We'll never get the java if you keep askin' questions. Ask, ask! I'll get the coffee! If you think Lau Maki will agree to taking on a stranger, fine. But if you ask me, she'll turn down the idea as quick as she did that Civic Club invite you gave her. Speaking of which—" he paused, nodded toward Dawnelle, then turned to Sarah "—weren't you going to do a little recruitin' tonight?" And with that, Henny whistled his way to the kitchen.

"Well—" Sarah smiled, smoothing her dress over her knees "—give us a few days to ask around, dear. If Lau won't help your friend, somebody will."

Dawnelle longed to hear more about Lau, to ask about the connection between her and Baird, but Sarah was fiddling with the china sugar bowl, saying eagerly, "What's happening tomorrow that you have to rush off tonight?"

Evidently the Civic Club idea was momentarily forgotten. Keenly interested in any pearl of information she could glean about the man who dominated her thoughts, Dawnelle answered cautiously, "I've seen so little of the countryside. I've managed to convince a friend to take me to Prairie Creek to see the elk, as long as I don't get in his way. I have to be ready by four-thirty in the morning."

"My good Savior, that's awful!" Sarah glanced at the ornate porcelain clock on her china hutch. "Barely eight hours away. You'll have hay under your eyelids when you answer the door. Who's taking you out so early?"

"A collector of marine specimens. He lives out around Luffenholtz Beach in that fantastic redwood home hanging over the cliff. Perhaps you know Baird Langston?"

Sarah's eyes grew round and unblinking. "Not that criminal with the vicious dog! Dawnelle, let me warn you—stay away from him!"

"For heaven's sake, Sarah, it's not as if he's murdered anyone or anything. He claims he's innocent. I understand he was framed, deprived of his hard-earned money just like his stockholders. Several times he's referred to—"

"*Several* times? Are you seeing him?"

No, she was sighting elk with him because she needed to know more about his work, she kept telling herself. And he had grudgingly agreed, although now she wondered why, since filming elk hadn't anything to do with marine collections. The dull color rising in her cheeks, Dawnelle blurted, "No—that is, not the way you mean. He's not interested in romantic ties. Avoids them, in fact." Her voice trailed off to silence. She'd been bruised countless times by Baird's reserve. Sometimes it was agonizing to have him look over her shoulder at print ads she'd sketched for his business. Her mind was always betraying her with sensuous memories, while Baird kept his promise to remain businesslike—austere was a better word. The sweet-spicy aroma of that imported pipe tobacco he smoked at home nearly drove her crazy. It reminded her too keenly of that first encounter on the cliff near his house.

But if she was to compare her life to a painting, bright splashes of color would depict the hours she spent with Baird, while muted pastels characterized her visits with Ben and other new friends. Shaded somewhere in between were her fulfilling days caring for the lighthouse and grounds. Her perspective had changed dramatically in a few weeks. New feelings and half-formed dreams had evolved from eight evenings and one Sunday afternoon spent with a complex man who scrounged a living from the California coast.

Sarah's chair squeaked as the woman twisted impatiently, and Dawnelle found herself explaining, "To be frank, Sarah, I've been writing some advertising copy for his marine-specimen business. It stretches my salary a little."

"Dawnelle," Sarah began firmly, her hands clenched on the table top, "you must remember my work with the Civic Club. Believe me, those women have devoted more than one social hour to a thorough discussion of that man. They all know he comes from a solid Eureka lumber family, people who worked hard and came to wealth right here among us. They're all gone now except him and his brother, who's making a name for himself in the real-estate business somewhere near Las Vegas, I hear. Neither of the boys had the gumption to take over where their grandfather began. I think the old Scotsman died of a broken heart, to tell you the truth."

"What happened?"

"I heard he died in his office one night. Your Langston friend was still in that prison down south. Imagine leaving an old man like that to worry about running a big lumber business all by himself! Does that sound like the callous type you should get mixed up with?"

"My God," Dawnelle sighed, her heart constricting for Baird's loss. Several times she'd found him standing under that fireplace portrait in his living room, looking up at his grandfather as if the old man might respond to the sheer reverence and loneliness of the grandson before him. "It must have been terrible for him," she murmured.

"It killed him," Sarah said simply, misunderstanding Dawnelle's sympathy. "The women in my club were outraged. Raking Baird Langston over the coals doesn't quite describe what they did to him."

"Do you think that's fair, Sarah? To condemn him without knowing the whole story?"

"And you know all about him?"

"Well, no, but—Sarah, I learned from my father to judge a man by what he is to *me*. No matter what happened in San Francisco three years ago, Baird Langston has been good to me up to this point."

Sarah's hazel eyes glittered with eagerness. "How has he been good to you? What proof do you have that he's good?"

"He's a fair employer, bright, energetic, considerate—if a bit too hard-driving at times. And he's good to my dog, actually. Sarah, don't laugh, he is. He's helping me train her. I told you about Miss Mo, didn't I?"

"Poor darling thing. Yes, you mentioned her, but I wouldn't fall for the 'good to children and animals' routine. He's got a wife, I hear, though we never caught her wasting her life and beauty on a little outpost like Trinidad! Too good for us, the gracious lady was. Eugenia Forester used to clean up the place when Langston vacationed here years ago. Genia said his wife used to phone Langston up—and let me tell you, there was no love coming over the telephone lines from that lady. Likely she saw the writing on the wall about his character right from the start."

"She left him and they divorced while he was in prison."

"There, you see? No wonder she left him, stealing all those millions from innocent investors! I'd have left him, too!"

Hearing Henny's faint domestic rattlings in the kitchen, Dawnelle asked softly, "Would you?"

Sarah looked taken aback. "What kind of question is that?"

"What if someone stole some mail from the post office and set it up to look as though Henny had taken it? Would you leave him because of the scandal?"

"Of course not!" Sarah insisted breathlessly, as if the possibility existed and was only kept at bay by her earnest opinion. "I know his character and so do all the people he's served these many years. They'd stick by him like I would."

"Are you sure, Sarah? Isn't it possible a shred of

doubt might lodge in some people's minds and turn them against him—if he were terribly incriminated? I know you'd stick by him through anything. But what if the scheme were so airtight that Henny got sent to prison in spite of your belief in his innocence?"

Frowning, Sarah turned the sugar bowl in circles, obviously thinking deeply. "Henny would never put himself in a position to be hoodwinked like that. He keeps a tight rein on things entrusted to him. Like the mail, and the town's best interests where his council work is concerned, you know. I just don't think what you're talking about could ever happen to my husband. Not in a million years."

"I hope you're right, Sarah. And I'm not saying I understand Baird Langston yet, but I feel a degree of sympathy for his ordeal. I really believe he's innocent. He seems extremely honest."

Pensive for a moment, Sarah slowly shook her head. "I think he could do you more harm than good," she said finally. "You're new here, and the town has nothing but positive things to say about you so far. The wrong crowd...a mistake in judgment...."

"I have to live my own life, Sarah. If I'd wanted to shut myself away from reality totally, I'd have returned to my father's fish hatchery, let him take me under his protective wing." Her gaze turned contemplative for a moment. "I admit to coming here partly to hide away. A light station is perfect for that, isn't it? But I'm not needing seclusion as much as I thought I would. I'm beginning to feel eager about things again—my work, my new life here. I don't intend to shock the good people of Trinidad with my life-style, Sarah—but I won't hide behind anyone's idea of what they think I should be."

"You've been hurt badly, haven't you, child?"

"Yes, but that's past." Dawnelle smiled. "And I've learned to be careful."

"Good. I hope you keep that in mind where Langston is concerned."

Somewhere in the back of the small house Dawnelle heard dishes clatter again. Henny must be making a grand production of serving coffee. Or perhaps he'd overheard something and withdrawn to allow them a few extra minutes of privacy.

"Sarah?"

"What is it, dear?"

Dawnelle took her hand, noting the delicate skin, the tracing of veins. "I know you'll want to discuss our conversation with Henny."

Sarah opened her mouth to protest, but Dawnelle shook her head. "No, now I understand your closeness, Sarah. I envy what you and Henny have, believe me. It's rare. But will you find a time when the two of you are alone? Entirely alone?"

Sarah hesitated, and Dawnelle realized her friend was fighting an internal battle over this sudden request for confidentiality.

"You have every right to ask it of me, and it may well strain my friendship with Greer and a few others...." Suddenly she winked secretively. "But for now what's your business is your business."

For now. Nodding her thanks, Dawnelle squeezed Sarah's hand and released it.

"So why's Langston so interested in elk?" Sarah asked, her mouth firming with disapproval.

"He put in a bid to supply Humboldt State University with film footage. He won the contract."

"I thought he was in marine work?"

"He is. Film is evidently a sideline, as my writing for him is for me."

"Well, just be careful, dear. You're in the public eye, and justified or not, your friend is still considered an enemy of the people. He may be a local boy, but most folks around here wouldn't claim him as their own."

YELLOW ORANGE NUMBERS glowed in the dark: 3:34 A.M. Baird would arrive in an hour, and then they'd head for Prairie Creek and the elk. She switched on the lamp. Miss Mo's chain collar clinked on the floor beside the bed as Dawnelle settled a writing pad on her lap. Sitting cross-legged in the predawn dark, she began to scribble hasty notes.

> Company name critical to promo campaign. Nix current title. Too cumbersome. Go for simplicity.

Her eyelids indeed felt like wraps for hay bales, as Sarah had warned her, but she dared not disturb her fragile thought process by going for a cool cloth. She willed herself to concentrate.

What does Baird want from his work? Money? Revenge on Vee and Suzanne? Or something humanitarian? What had he said about education? Oh, yes. "Students deserve a chance to decide for themselves whether they'll destroy their world or use it to enchance life. Ecologically speaking."

They'd been discussing marketing strategies in

Baird's library. "If that's your philosophy," she responded, thinking of the young Spanish student who'd written Baird asking to work with him through Humboldt's postgraduate program, "shouldn't you give Serano the chance he deserves? His letter was very persuasive."

"It's not up to me to play nursemaid to one of Dr. Warren's students," Baird argued, pivoting to the redwood bookcase opposite his desk, obviously avoiding her eyes. "My job is to supply certain lab samples Warren can use in his classes. Samples he can't get anywhere else."

"But you said Serano was talented. Showed promise. Don't you think—"

"Look—" his voice was flat "—Serano also intends to return to Spain after his thesis work and open his own marine-studies lab."

"A future client, Baird."

"If he doesn't take half my business with him!" Abruptly he turned to glare at her. "Dammit, Dawnelle! Don't you think I *want* to help this kid? Let it alone, will you? I haven't made my final decision yet, and I won't be pressured by anyone to reach that decision! Just pretend you never found that letter on my desk, and let's get back to the problem at hand."

"All right." Biting back her irritation, she had glanced at her yellow pad full of notes. "Let's be specific. What's your immediate marketing goal?"

"I'm going after schools. At all levels. We've got to study what the professors are already being offered by the huge biological supply houses." Which explained the importance of the catalogs he'd brought to her cottage. "Then we'll sell what isn't being offered. Build a reputation for service, stress service. They eventually begin to trust you to send them unusual, hard-to-get stuff."

Smart, she thought now, keeping a fingertip pressed to her current notes. Service themes were universally successful. But Baird's scars were deep. He was having trouble bouncing back from that past betrayal, even refusing to trust a potentially valuable assistant. What was his hidden motive in business? Reputation, of course, as they had discussed. The recollection sent shivers down her spine, and she wrote:

> Use "Langston" in company name. Sounds stable; his reliability will eventually erase stigma of prison record. Also use "specimens"—perfect—targets the market; doesn't limit to live or preserved specimens. Langston Marine Specimens, Inc. Great!
>
> What about image?
>
> Competition uses very slick stuff. Baird low on cash. Cash and patience. Wants to supply unusual specimens. First-order marine life. Corals, sea anemones, hydroids—stuff like that.
>
> Unique.
>
> See old Bechtel ads in *Time magazine*. Glowing lightbulb in beaker of water, and no electrical hookup. Suggests invention ahead of its time.

But how do I tie that concept to marine studies?

Frustrated, Dawnelle tugged the coverlet closer around her, huddling over her tablet as if it were a warming campfire. The thoughts had been clarion in sleep, yet now they grew hazy, illusive. These rare nighttime inspirations generally lasted only a short while, so it was critical quickly to scrape together every detail that had swirled through her brain. Determinedly she tightened her grip on the pen.

Baird's product is unique.

Underwater. Under microscope. Under study.

"Gearing today's students for tomorrow's challenges." Nice ring, but too general.

"Making a difference to the future of marine biology." Has possibilities. Close, but not perfect. Have another interview with Baird. He's the expert. He *knows*. Drag it out of him.

She reached over, dropped the pen and tablet on the nightstand. Her creative juices were drained, at least for tonight—this morning, she amended. Just a little more than an hour until Baird would pound on her door. Thank goodness he had his own key to the outside gate; she didn't relish making her way to the fence in the dark. *Dark edge of the world,* she thought, hating the sting of cold oak on her bare feet as she slipped out of bed and made her way to the closet.

She really ought to invest some of the eleven thousand dollars she'd saved in throw rugs. It was a cinch her lighthouse salary wouldn't stretch for such comforts. She shook her head, remembering the struggles she'd learned about last night from Henny and Sarah, the "auctions and such" Trinidad had held to pay a keeper's salary. No wonder the contract wasn't always filled. Her salary barely met federal minimum-wage standards. Yet the town's sacrifices made her doubly glad she'd taken the job.

Sarah. Dawnelle grinned ruefully. Clever manipulator with a motherly smile. Sarah had announced late last night that Dawnelle was unofficially called Señorita de la Luz—Lady of the Light—by the members of the Civic Club.

"Trinidad was discovered by the Spanish," Sarah had explained. "They erected a wooden cross on a hill out on the Head. When it deteriorated, the club sponsored the raising of a concrete cross to replace the original." This interest in history had led several women, at Sarah's urging, to study Spanish. Dawnelle's new nickname had evolved during a practice session and was now in frequent use.

The postmaster's wife had promptly taken advantage of Dawnelle's pleasure in this news to gain her commitment to join the group. Next Thursday was to be her induction, and she frowned now, wondering how she would deal with negative comments about Baird. Not very well, she knew, feeling a growing protectiveness toward him. He'd suffered enough.

She pulled on thermal leggings, jeans, a rose pink T-shirt and a burgundy-and-pink tweed sweater that heightened the warm hues of her skin, then went down to the bathroom to put the finishing touches on her appearance. *How involved I am in this town,* she mused. Which was absurd, because the implied solitude had drawn her here. But that requirement was losing importance. With Ben's subtle courting, her internal struggles over Baird and Sarah's recruiting, little time remained for wallowing in self-pity. Dawnelle had to admit her emerging freshness of attitude was a welcome change.

Still, it was going to take some stout self-esteem to weather Baird's indignation when she suggested he change the name of his company. *That* wouldn't be welcome, she realized as she smoothed on wine lip gloss.

She *was* attractive, she decided, enjoying the way her brown hair, straight and sheened this morning, fanned around her shoulders, framing her slender throat. Her father persisted in describing her as "gaunt," though he couldn't fault her wide-set, "startling" green eyes.

Suddenly she giggled, imagining Baird itemizing his assets with such curiosity, such pride. Men preened, too, she knew. She and her dorm sisters at San Jose State had thoroughly discussed every aspect of the male person, and there had been plenty of case studies presented to substantiate men's vanity. But Baird.... She suspected he was more arrogant about his intellect than his looks. *Old granite face,* she thought, surprised by the depth of affection she felt for him. Then she made a skeptical face of her own. *Don't be a fool. Strictly business! Remember to talk him into changing the name of his company.*

After tucking her jeans into waterproof oxblood boots, Dawnelle stood up and smoothed the burgundy sweater over one softly curved hip. Idly her hand traced a long firm thigh. Her appearance would do, she supposed, but her mind insisted on wandering back to Baird. When he slept did he dwell on business problems and getting even with his ex-partner, Vee? Or did he dream of women? Was his fantasy-woman buxom with full thighs—or willowy like her?

Jeff had liked her looks well enough. In fact, he'd

often introduced her rather smugly at parties, as if he personally took credit for her attractiveness. But women only really thrilled him in relation to his work. Strangely, she felt only a slight twinge of regret now, reviewing that first deceptive love.

She'd come to Trinidad to heal and been astonished to feel the betrayal, the hurt evaporate so painlessly. Barely five months after she'd walked out on Jeff in that board meeting she stood here dry-eyed and calm of heart, thinking objectively about their relationship.

Maybe I haven't given myself enough credit. Perhaps I'm better at judging people than I imagine. There had always been something keeping her and Jeff apart. Something shadowy and philosophical. Elated that she could think of him without cringing, Dawnelle tried to pinpoint why she hadn't been permanently devastated by his betrayal.

How he had loved office brainstorming sessions! Blue eyes sparkling, he'd drag his fingers through that golden hair and demand to know what could be done about promoting the new laser medical line. She'd been drawn to that kind of energy. On the positive side, appreciating her brains had been Jeff's best asset. Physical attraction between them had become a secondary consideration, though, and that had probably prevented her from committing herself to a wedding date. She'd put him off for eight months.

Although she had thought she loved him, all too often when he kissed her she'd felt used. Jeff was always interrupting their romantic moments with questions he'd dreamed up about the department. Their chemistry had lacked the triphammer passion of those moments she'd already shared with Baird, and in those days the desire for that intensity had always sparked doubts about her relationship with Jeff. Perhaps it was idealistic, but marriage should offer intimately sublime elements along with intellectual compatibility. Why enter into a long commitment with someone if only half your expectations, physical or emotional, could be realized?

Her mother and father had compromised their dreams, and those tense evenings when she could feel their palpable unhappiness had forged her own resolve for a better marriage.

That she had sensed Jeff would fail her—and she him, for that matter—had saved her from misery. His deception had forced her to review her needs. Trinidad had provided the new faces, the fresh problems from which she would learn to shape her happiness.

And Baird? She pursed her wide mouth. Did he figure in her personal future? Probably not. True, he'd called upon her intellect, and unwittingly fired an unexpected set of emotions. But his briary nature had scratched her deepest insecurities, as well. More than any other man she'd ever met, Baird Langston was capable of exploding that lofty bridge of self-confidence she'd just begun to rebuild. It would be foolish and self-destructive to set herself up for rejection again so soon. Yet sometimes when he looked at her, touched her, the old dreams smoldered anew, and she found herself struggling to kill the longing....

Miss Mo's shrill wail from the living room announced Baird's arrival, cutting short her reflections, putting a wild anticipation in the midst of her sane resolutions. Dawnelle was barely able to maintain a dignified elegant stroll to the front door.

CHAPTER SEVEN

PULLING OPEN THE DOOR, Dawnelle peered into the darkness until she saw Baird's broad-shouldered form outlined by the lighthouse strobe. His swinging stride carried him through the picket gate and into the warm halo shining from the peak-roofed porch.

An exuberant Miss Mo flung herself against his legs as if she couldn't live another moment without his caress. He bent to roughhouse with her.

"Morning," he said matter-of-factly to Dawnelle, who leaned casually against a pillar, her heart jolting so badly she could only smile and nod. Baird pried the shepherd's sharp teeth off his wrist. "Don't you ever feed this she-bear?"

"Would you believe two cans this morning? One tin of dog food doesn't even dent her appetite!"

"She's still teething, I think. Try letting her chew on one of those rawhide bones."

"Anything to keep her from ruining the braided rug," she returned, enjoying his interest in her dog. "She seems to think it's lying on the living-room floor expressly to lure her into a tug-of-war."

While he entertained himself wrestling with Miss Mo, Dawnelle studied him closely. The collar of his red-and-black cotton shirt poked out above his cable-knit sweater and sailcloth jacket, both formerly white but now gray with stains and washings. White socks protruded from the tops of his leather jackboots. Even the mustache and that beard trimmed to the shape of his square jaw did nothing to refine his roughcast image. His size, his aggressive manner of moving, his sharp-eyed blue gaze—these qualities would incline an ordinary man to look away. But not a woman.

He was the kind of man to stir women's fantasies: rugged, masculine, sexually attractive but enticingly aloof, with a hint of vulnerability hidden inside him like a winter acorn. Looking at him, she realized he possessed tremendous physical strength. Yet his brooding nature was tempered by sensitive gestures and lightning-quick moments of warmth.

In her mind she saw him standing broodingly on the misty shore of a loch in his grandfather's homeland; watched him tramp across crags and through dells, stopping to gaze at wild roaming creatures. She imagined him kilted, his muscled thighs bared to the chill Scotland winter as he returned to a thatched cottage, a crackling peat fire and the loving arms of a dark-haired woman. She stopped herself abruptly, running her hands up her arms as if to ward off the sudden dampness of the Pacific-cooled breeze.

Baird, the self-proclaimed bachelor. He carried a romantic ideal cloaked about his person. His looks, his rare burning gazes, even his deeply felt resentment of Suzanne's betrayal said as much. Yet he had denied with terse words any affinity to such ideals. He'd put domestic life behind him, he'd said that afternoon in the work shed. She'd better get a grip on herself, forget about dead-end delusions. Otherwise she faced more heartache, and she'd had her fill of that. Well—she looked at him with an expression of finality—she would learn from him about setting up a business, enjoy his male sexuality from a distance. Period.

"Are we taking the dogs with us?" she asked a bit impatiently.

"No way. With any luck the truck will be downwind from the blind I've constructed, but one bark might ruin a good shot." Straightening, shoving a boot onto the step below her, he appraised her attire. "Better bring a coat. It'll be wet in the brush. And cold."

"Aye-aye, sir. By the way, I fixed ham sandwiches." She turned into the house, retrieved her khaki all-weather coat, then came back, holding up her maroon satchel. "Thought we might get hungry."

"Fine, fine." He smiled indulgently.

Dawnelle slipped out beside him, thrilled by the momentary press of his body against her back as she turned to bolt the door, trapping Miss Mo inside. "Bye," she said through the heavy planks. Grimacing when the dog began to whine and scratch on the wood, Dawnelle followed Baird off the porch. "When I shut her in, Miss Mo tears the place to pieces."

"I keep telling you that firmness is essential in retraining her. Those half-hearted attempts of yours to bring her under control destroy any chance of breaking her bad habits."

"But all I get is slinking looks and a tangled leash. I always end up trying to bolster Miss Mo's crushed spirit."

He tsked to the night. "Praise her for responding to a command, not for eliciting your sympathy."

"What should I do when she tears things up while I'm gone? I can't leave her outside until she's trained in case one of the guys from the Guard comes by, and I don't have the faintest idea how to 'command' her not to wreck the house."

"Scold her when you get home. It's all you can do for now. Young ones always tear things up when they're bored."

She murmured assent, thinking his advice easier given than taken, then concentrated on traversing the rough ground.

In the starlit, blue black darkness, the bluff had a wild aspect to it. The salty nip in the wind felt clean, left one slightly breathless. As it swept around, the beacon carved giants of the boulders to their left, then cast them magically into the inky blackness again. No foghorn moaned, but the faint tinkle of bell buoys down in the water lent a Hemingway loneliness to the ocean.

"Sheep playing out there," Baird said in a low voice.

Dawnelle chanced a digression from the gravel path to peer at him. She was certain he had the night sight of a cat, so sure was his footing. "Sheep?"

"White caps." The light swept by just as he pointed to the water. "Pete used to call them sheep."

"Who's Pete?"

"Careful," he said then, taking her arm as they came around the parking-lot boulder, making her grit her teeth at the sudden jolt to her senses. "Wait a sec." Keys jingled. The passenger door of his baby-blue Ford pickup creaked and popped as he wrestled it open. He handed her in, then came around and slid behind the wheel to start the old engine. Gears grinding, the truck bumped out of the lot.

Baird paused only to lock the gate, and then they were winding through the sandy lane, the dash lights softening his cut-stone features as he drove. His casual manner relaxed Dawnelle, so that she began to think his steely reserve of past weeks had vanished.

"Where'd you get this truck?" She laughed, feeling like a farm girl on her first hayride. The vehicle was tinking and clanking like an old washing machine.

"Thought you wanted to hear about Pete?"

"Okay, who's Pete?"

"Yurok Indian from up the Klamath River. Good man, Pete. Dragged me out of the river one September afternoon when I was fourteen. I was fishing. He saved my life."

"Were you playing hooky?"

"My father had just been killed in a heavy-equipment accident at the main lumberyard," he answered, assuming she was following his reasoning. "My grandfather came out of retirement to take over the family business again. Both were losses I couldn't handle, so I took myself into the woods for a while."

"I don't quite follow."

"What—that I went into the woods?"

"Well, *both* were losses, you said."

He nodded. "I spent a lot of time with granddad in those days, but when he went back to the lumber business, our fishing days were over. He broke it to me as gently as he could, but I guess I was pretty mixed up then. I took off for a while. A few weeks. Pete taught me to live in the woods."

"Pete took the place of your grandfather," she clarified, uneasy about the melancholy quality that had crept into his voice.

"Something like that."

"And you would have drowned?"

"That I would." He ran one large hand over his jaw, cradling it thoughtfully. Raising his chin, he pointed to the strange whorl in his beard. "My face was a bloody mess when Pete fished me out of the water and slung me into his skiff like a gunnysack full of stones. When I was feeling a little more chipper, I told him he ought to go down to San Diego and crew on one of those tuna boats. He laughed like hell." Baird's tone softened. "He could've pulled tuna, all right. Old Pete had arms like a bear. Even at fifty-one."

"Is he gone now? Pete, I mean."

"Yeah. They're both gone."

"I'm sorry."

He shrugged, tightening his grip on the wheel. Suspecting his gruff dismissal hid his pain, Dawnelle rode for a time in silence.

Emerging from the tunnel of greenery to the north slope of Trinidad Head, Baird slowed as he drove through a rusting fence, the original boundary of the light station. The dark hump of Little Trinidad Head rose on their right, sheltering the boat launch and the dock. Flashlights arced here and there as fishermen left parked cars, heading for small motor skiffs that would take them to trollers anchored in the harbor. Baird's lengthy inspection of the moving figures reminded Dawnelle of the fisherwoman who'd provided her and Baird with that tasty meal of salmon. Lau?

"Do you know Lau Maki?" she asked, determined to open the subject that had been plaguing her.

Baird sent her a questioning look. "I know her."

But will you talk about her, Dawnelle thought, put off by his cryptic answer.

"I understand she fishes for a living," she went on awkwardly.

"She does. Where did you meet Lau?"

"Well, I haven't exactly. I've only heard about her. Something about feeling doomed—I don't know."

"Oh?" He released a short derisive snort. "People haven't got enough to do. They have to chew up someone's reputation for kicks. I'll tell you, Dawnelle, Lau's a damn fine woman who's had a run of bad luck, that's all. You won't get one word out of me beyond that."

"Baird, no one said anything bad about her," she replied defensively. "Just that she's...well, got some beliefs that keep her out of the mainstream of things."

"And folks condemn her for being different, is that it?"

"Folks? No, I didn't get that impression at all. I certainly don't condemn her. I haven't even met her. I was just asking you—"

"Forget it," he interrupted flatly. "Lau can make her own impressions on people without my comments. I detest gossip."

Dawnelle's emotions waged an inner battle. Hurt by his assumption that she wished to drag someone's character through the mud, she stared silently out at moonlit Trinidad. The barnlike Smoke House slid by. Single-story cottages made a canyon of the silvered road through town.

Dawnelle found herself longing more than ever to understand Lau's relationship with Baird. Was he protecting the woman because he was romantically involved, or simply because he resented any reminder of his wife's condemnation and betrayal? Baird had assumed she was judgmental, like Suzanne. To even be classed with that disloyal woman made her burn with anger. And yet, she *had* asked about Lau to help ease the nagging jealousy she felt, jealousy when there was no proof of a relationship between Baird and Lau. Ridiculous! She had no intention of getting tied up with Baird, anyway. What did she care if he loved someone else, a woman with superstitions shadowing her life?

She gazed at the stark outlines of Trinidad, knowing she was lying to herself. If she had no romantic intentions, why was she with Baird today—and feeling sick inside because he was angry?

She glanced at him, wanting to resurrect the companionable mood of only minutes before. "I love this place," she began. "I came here for peace, and for the most part I've found it. Let's not ruin what promises to be a beautiful day, Baird."

"Wait till one of those big storms hits this winter," he responded in a cool tone that crushed her. "You won't think it's such a grand and beautiful place then. The rain will drive so hard into your face, it'll feel like steel whips on your skin—blinding you, freezing you. The wind'll rock that old house on its foundations. With the configuration of those boulders out there, the gusts can whip around and sling you into something mighty hard—or worse, send you screaming over the edge."

She shuddered inwardly at the picture he painted. Hurt by his callousness, she retorted, "Sounds like a place only a keeper could love."

"City life never prepared you for that, did it?"

"Did *your* secluded past toughen you up for the storms ahead?"

Conveniently, at that moment he swung the truck into the town's only gas station, parked and rushed out without closing the door. He dragged over a thin green hose, yanked open the hood, began filling the radiator with water. Across the street, headlights cut through the night as a truck pulled in and parked near a small red building, Trinidad's sporting-goods store.

Still simmering over Baird's harshness, hoping to diffuse her anger before their entire day was ruined, Dawnelle rolled down her window and leaned out. A woman's shape was outlined in the red doorway of the store, blond hair shot through with light, a dark skirt flowing around legs like telephone poles. The middle-aged woman was no less interested in Dawnelle, evidently. She stared with some intensity toward the Ford. Only when the burly truck driver shouldered his way toward her did the woman take a final thorough look at Dawnelle before disappearing into the bait shop.

"You have the greatest timing," Dawnelle remarked when Baird returned to the cab and headed north on Highway 101.

He cocked his head in surprise.

"You're always exiting when things get hot."

"Controlling board meetings taught me when to attack, parry or withdraw fortuitously," he replied distantly. "I'm sure you're equally well versed in the art of corporate fencing."

"I've learned enough to know when someone can't take the heat. When he runs to the water cooler to regain his composure."

"My, my. Got corporate protocol down pat, haven't we?"

"Baird, what in heaven's name are you doing?" His cool sarcasm was unnerving. Though she fought to remain calm, her pride rose to the surface as it had the first day she met him on that cliff at Luffenholtz. "Where is the levelheaded businessman of the past two weeks? For that matter, where's the human being I was talking to about Pete?"

"Forget Pete! What are you doing here, that's what I want to know!" He gestured wildly. "You worm your way into my life with those soft looks and that way you have of eating into a man's common sense. What do you expect me to do—forget the fact that you're living on that godforsaken chunk of rock by yourself?"

"Do you think I spent my life being pampered in the city? Or do you think I'm like your—" She paused. But anger swiftly overrode her prudence, and she choked out, "Your *wife*? Is that what you're worried about? That I'll drop off the face of the earth and leave you in the lurch? Or perhaps you're still expecting a nasty power play just because I'm working for you now and then!"

"I didn't say that!"

"You implied it!"

"I wasn't even thinking that. You're just paranoid."

"The whole topic's ridiculous! What are you afraid

of, Baird? Tell me, so we can get past this ugly snarl that always crops up in our relationship."

"We haven't got a *relationship*!" he exhaled in disgust. "Hell, I can't even talk to you!"

"Can't? Or won't? You've thrown so many accusations my way since I've known you, I'm beginning to think you're nothing but a mass of scar tissue and hate. Speak plainly, Baird. Why were you suddenly so rude?"

"It's not just today," he said roughly. "It's—something that's developing."

"Nice start." She breathed deeply, brushed her forehead with a calming hand. "I think it's destructive to bottle up your thoughts and feelings, Baird—ranting and raving instead of saying what's on your mind. It's best to get things out in the open, even if it's difficult. Even if it hurts."

"Communicator through and through, huh?" His attempt to lighten the moment failed badly. In the diffused yellow dash light, his face looked twisted. Emotions struggled to erupt through his reserve. He sighed and fell silent.

"Try, Baird," she said softly, giddy with the realization that he might be admitting he cared about her. "Why is it so terrible that I live at the lighthouse?"

Cursing softly, he glanced at her, an uneasy smile slackening his taut facial muscles. "Guess I've been working too hard. My own paranoia must have gotten the best of me."

"Cop-out."

It was his third sigh and it was a big one, full of frustration. "Dawnelle, why did you come here?"

"Why did I— Baird, it's your feelings we're talking about."

"I have the right to ask—as your employer."

"It's a little late for interviews, don't you think?"

"I'm asking."

Glancing briefly at the silver black surface of a lagoon they sped by, she decided she'd better swallow her own medicine. She raked her hands through her hair as she turned to him. He trained his gaze on the road. The intensity of his attention thus diverted, she felt it was somehow easier to expose the old hurts.

"I was in love with my boss, Baird. You'd already guessed as much, I think. He gave my job to the president's daughter, as I told you, then expected me to remain engaged to him. He tried to hand me the old routine about not wanting his wife to work too hard. From most people, I'd believe they meant it. From him, it was nothing but betrayal gilded to look like spousal indulgence. I was sick at heart, disillusioned, not fit company for anyone. The lighthouse was my...."

"Hideout?"

She smiled, nodded. "Baird...." She edged along the bench seat to touch his jacket sleeve. "I was hurt, too. I thought I would die with the agony of Jeff's deception. I know how you felt when they—when she betrayed you."

Suddenly she was crushed against his rough wool sweater in a hug so fierce she gasped. He pressed his face into her hair, and she could feel the soft scratch of his beard. "Don't ask too much of me, Dawnelle."

She nodded again, too stunned to answer.

"Ah, Dawny, I think I need you," he muttered. "I

What made Marge burn the toast and miss her favorite soap opera?

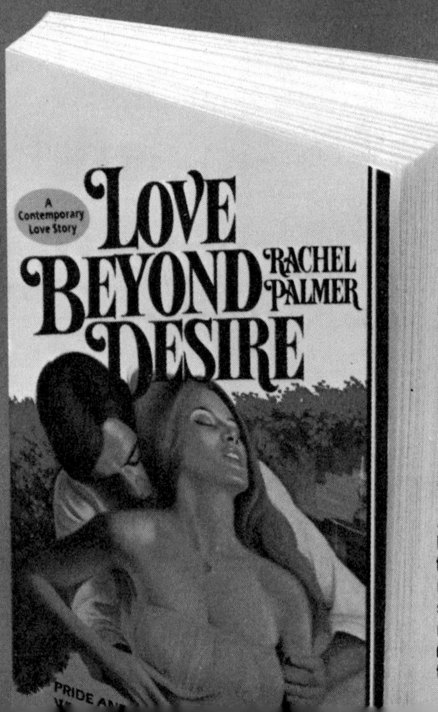

A Contemporary Love Story
LOVE BEYOND DESIRE
RACHEL PALMER

...At his touch, her body felt a familiar wild stirring, but she struggled to resist it. This is not love, she thought bitterly.

EXTRA BONUS
MAIL YOUR ORDER TODAY AND GET A FREE TOTE BAG FROM SUPERROMANCE.

Mail this card today for your FREE gifts.

Business
Reply Card
No Postage Stamp
Necessary if Mailed
in Canada
Postage will be paid by

SUPERROMANCE™
649 Ontario Street
Stratford, Ontario N5A 9Z9

need a friend, someone bright who understands where I've been, what I'm trying to do."

Her heart leaped as if they'd raced blindly down a whoop-dee-do in the road. She wrapped her arm around Baird's. "Need me," she repeated incredulously. "Boy. When you finally decide to communicate, you say it all!"

"Don't...." He wove his fingers into the thick mass of her hair, his emotions seeming to burn through his fingers to her flesh. "Don't read more into it than I meant."

When happiness faded and the ice of rejection curled around her heart, she tried to pull away. But he held her still, pressing his lips to her forehead in a warm, latently passionate kiss.

"And don't get angry," he grumbled. "I'm not used to this baring-of-the-soul business, this private-confession stuff you think is so good for me. Are you listening?"

"Yes," she said with restraint, still reacting to his male warmth. Fire stirred within her. His caress and the threading of his fingers through her hair made her yearn to arch against him and beg him to fill the void of her own loneliness.

As he drove silently, holding her loosely in the circle of his arm, she worried about her reaction to him, so soon after she'd crossed him out of her future. A man of troubled heart. And what about her, afraid of her weak will and unable to blame him for cracking the shell of her resistance.

Yet she realized Baird was not consciously asking more of her than friendship. She should be grateful for even that small capitulation, but she wasn't. Greed leaped ahead of all her other tumbling emotions. She wanted more from this man than simple friendship, she knew with sudden compelling clarity. It might tear her apart to have less.

"I'm listening," she reminded him, a mournful edge to her voice. "What do you want to tell me?"

He squeezed her shoulders, pumping liquid-silver desire through her veins. "I spend many hours each day thinking of what I'll do to Vee when I find him." He tipped her head back and sought her eyes, held the gaze for a long moment while a kind of heat arced between them. Then, as if the physical response scorched him, he dropped a shield over his eyes, even as he pulled her against him again and resumed driving.

"I find it difficult to separate one fact, one emotion from another," his voice came vaguely after a moment. "I want us to work together, Dawnelle. I suspect you're very good for me, both in business and personally. God help me, I don't even know what the latter part means, it's so mixed up with the ugly feelings I have—the anger, the hatred. I don't know who to trust anymore!" Bitterness had hardened his tone again. "Me, the man of the world, the crack businessman, worried about hiring a graduate student who wants nothing more than to learn from me, so he can go home to Spain and share what he knows! Hell of a diplomat for the U.S., aren't I?"

"You dwell too much on the past, Baird. Think what you could accomplish with Serano helping you. At the same time, he'd be learning. That's the whole point of this kind of exchange between student and businessman."

"I know, I know. But then the years roll back...all the years I paid. I can't forget."

"You've only had three months of freedom. Things are too fresh, too complicated. In time you'll see things differently. With less anger."

"It seems so easy to hear you say it. I don't know...."

Leaning back, she studied his profile, surprised to note he had graying temples. Threads of silver wove through the thick brown hair above his ears. "You were going to tell me why you got angry, remember?" she prompted softly.

He gave her a wry grin. "The winters get mighty harsh out on the Head, kid."

"Why don't you just say it?" She shook her head, exasperated but smiling. "You're worried about me. You're afraid you'll lose your P.R. director before we can even get the first sales campaign put together."

"By golly, I picked me a smart one, didn't I?"

It wasn't what she wanted to hear, and Lau hadn't been mentioned again, but wasn't friendship a good basis for more permanent relations? She snuggled against him. "I think you should rename your business," she blurted out from the safety of his warm body.

"What?" He pushed her way to see her face. "Hell, woman, haven't you even been listening?"

"Oh, Baird," she sighed. "You bluster and say I'm trying to undermine your work, but you know damned well I'm only thinking of your best interests."

"No, I don't know any such thing. Not for sure."

"You paranoid old bear!" She punched him lightly

on the arm. "You just practically told me you trusted me! International Marine Laboratory Specimens and Collections—" a deep exaggerated breath emphasized her point "—Services Company. I can't even get my tongue around it. What busy professor could remember a name like that?"

"It's supposed to sound conservative. Reliable."

"It sounds stuffy!"

"It's the name I chose."

"I have a better one."

He looked at her dubiously. "Yeah? What?"

"Langston Marine Specimens, Inc. Nice ring, don't you think? And since you're still using blank billing statements, the change won't cost you a dime!"

His mouth remained firm for a moment, his eyes accusing. Then he said briefly, "I'll think on it."

She thought she recognized a private smile at the corners of his mouth.

Feeling her own lips curve in a smile at her success, she turned her face toward the gray-on-black shapes of the forest outside. One point was won, at least. But he didn't have a heck of a lot of time to discover the wisdom of all her suggestions. He was cash poor, and he desperately needed the orders her promotion campaign would draw.

And Lau? Lau couldn't possibly be all Baird sought from a woman if he still needed a friend.

"FOLLOW ME and step lightly," Baird cautioned in a brusque whisper.

"I'll be right behind you," she returned, her voice low and resonant with contained excitement. "Wait—my flashlight doesn't work— Oh—there. Ready."

Her exuberant indrawn breath brought with it the damp fodder smell of grass, the sharp pungency of evergreens. The muted charcoal glow of approaching dawn barely revealed the knee-high grass and thick brush tumbling over the hill near the road. Mist wreathed the hill; the slate sky seemed spiked by hundreds of black, jagged-edged trees held *en garde* by ghosts.

Baird locked the truck and slid the keys into a snug hip pocket, then lifted the backpack of camera gear to his shoulders. A tripod weighted with a ground steel mounting base and a bubble level now swung from his right hand. Rising from his shoulder like a warrior's lance was the gleaming barrel of his 7mm Remington deer rifle. At her small gasp of surprise he said quietly, "You never know. One of those bulls might get nasty when we sneak into their rutting territory."

He aimed the beam of a small red flashlight into the brush and moved catlike up the incline.

Loaded down with Baird's extra equipment bag, Dawnelle cast the amber glow of her own light on the pebbles underfoot and quickened her pace to match his. Within five minutes her breath steamed into the air. All but her nose and fingertips felt comfortably warm. Mutely she thanked Baird for reminding her to bring a heavy coat.

Knowing she had to be silent, she let memories of her youth settle like a comforting blanket over her nervous excitement. It had been so long since she'd tramped the woods. . . since she and her brother had explored the natural caverns beneath felled trees or marveled at the fluted tans and golds of wild mushrooms. She inhaled the musky familiar scents, thrilled to hear the shriek of a bird that survived by hunting at dawn. Loving this life, why had she chosen corporate communications as her life's work? When she felt so complete in the country, why suffer the carbon monoxide and clatter of the city? Admittedly, the best money could be made there. But could success in the mainstream of a multinational company compare to the fulfillment of fishing waist deep in a swift cold stream? Or lying hidden in a blind, while twenty or thirty magnificent elk munched grass a few feet away?

She was inclined to think here lay her destiny—her destiny and satisfaction. Yet, she rationalized, feeling the slight sting of branches as Baird waded ahead of her, she'd always loved the wilderness as a shared experience. She'd always had either her father or Tommy as tramping companions, and later, the girl-scout troops she'd led during her high-school years. And now Baird. Always with someone else. Never alone. Why?

It wasn't fear of the woods. She'd coddled and praised ten-year-olds through the wilds of the Trinity River. The majestic ski slopes of Mount Shasta had echoed with the happy squeals of the young teens she'd chaperoned on YMCA-sponsored ski trips. Yet she'd migrated to the city, even planned to return in a year, lured by the fast pace and the primeval forces beneath the glitter. She was a "people person," she decided with new insight. Either world suited her as long as she felt needed and loved by those around her.

A dry branch crackled beneath her boot, drawing Dawnelle's attention back to Prairie Creek. Baird's head came around sharply.

"Sorry," she murmured under her breath, easing past the immense trunk of a redwood.

They emerged from the stand of trees on a downhill descent much like the stubby field near the truck. A bird's eerie trill rippled through the wafting mists. They trudged on until the ground leveled to a valley.

Halfway across a meadow, instead of circling a looming copse of trees, Baird bent and slipped through an opening in the branches. Dawnelle ducked in behind him.

Her boots slid over flooring of some kind, the sound reminding her of wind moaning over granite. The beam of her flashlight revealed a canvas tarp neatly fitted to a six-foot-wide clearing surrounded by trees. Willowlike trunks fanned upward to a canopy of leaves. While Baird stealthily lowered his pack and began fitting equipment together, Dawnelle held the light for him.

Their rapid breathing and body heat soon filled the cave with a comfortable warmth, and she unzipped her coat. An intimate lair, she thought. Awareness slithered through her body. "This blind looks like it's been here a while," she commented. "The tarp and all."

"I've been coming here sporadically for the past three weeks—didn't want to spook the elk with too many intrusions. They're used to the carloads of sightseers out on the highway, but not back in here."

"Have you gotten footage of them before?"

"Twice. I hope this'll be the last time." He turned his back on her, crouching as he wedged the tripod against the foliage, evidently centering the camera lens through an opening in the leaves.

She understood without his elaborating that time was

precious to him. He spent every spare minute scrabbling in tide pools and scraping dock pilings for creatures he could dissect, study, film or preserve. So far, he had only sold prepared microscope slides and a few live specimens to Humboldt State, but he was collecting more than he could sell, squirreling away inventory for those orders he was anticipating. The hours he spent building this blind and filming the elk were hours he resented, because the action drew his focus away from his foremost goal: establishing the marine business.

Swinging her flashlight in an arc, Dawnelle found the rifle propped against a split trunk. The orange flight bag she'd carried hung from a branch, while his yellow canvas backpack lay like a deflated balloon nearby. Careful not to bump his arms, she edged closer to Baird and craned around him to see.

His lean fingers were quick and practiced as he manipulated the tripod, leveling the camera. At last he squinted through the lenses, swiveling one then another as he gauged which might be best for his first glimpse of the elk. "Turn off your flashlight," he whispered.

She snapped the switch and set it near the rifle.

"Tim-ber-r-r," he muttered, evidently pleased at the rickety hum he'd produced inside the camera.

Dawnelle thought the scarred equipment grated more like an underpowered car trying to climb Mount Everest than a tool he should rely on to pull him out of a financial bind.

"Where'd you get this equipment?" she asked cautiously, not wanting to insult him.

"From U.C. Berkeley when I was studying film, and some of the stuff I got in Japan. Centuries ago...."

"I thought you studied marine science at Humboldt."

"Partly. I also conducted postgraduate work at a small school affiliated with Stanford, down in Monterey. But before that it was film at Berkeley."

"Why the switch?"

"I left Berkeley when my mother died, came home for the funeral, then ended up in Vietnam with the marines."

"Good Lord!" She tried to add up a young film student and a very nasty stint in the bayous and jungles of Vietnam. "Why'd you do that?"

"Drafted. Anyway, there was no sense training myself to take over the family business. My older brother, Charles, stood to inherit the reins after granddad—that was what the family planned, at any rate. After my mother's funeral I couldn't...put things into perspective, somehow. Couldn't act on anything tangible. A cause, maybe, was what I was looking for. I was glad when the marines drafted me." He laughed shortly. "I don't know what I was thinking. If I couldn't handle tragedy at home, how did I think I could handle so much more of it in Vietnam? Naturally," he added sardonically, checking the field outside, "my two tours of duty over there stiffened my upper lip, as the English say. But they didn't do much for my faith in human decency."

So he hadn't abandoned his grandfather, after all, as Sarah and the Civic Club thought. His brother Charles had, since he'd shunned the lumber company in favor of wheeling and dealing real estate in Las Vegas. Not that she condemned a man for taking up his chosen work, but Baird had once hinted at his brother's frivolous nature.

Interested in the family but unwilling to hurt him with the gossip she'd heard, she returned to the military subject. "Your work in the marines took you to Japan?"

"Only on leave. I was in the thick of battle during most of my two stints, filming the most god-awful hell."

"Did you do well in the service?"

His side-glance seemed to say, *you're just like all the others.* Still, he spoke again. "They wanted to give me a citation for training-film footage of hand-to-hand combat between some men in my unit and the villagers of a hamlet near Hue, if you can imagine such a thing. One day I was told to report to the colonel. His speech was very eloquent, I'll give him that."

"You refused it?"

"I said, 'With all due respect, sir, you know what you can do with the damn thing. Colonel, sir.' "

"What happened?"

"He clamped his jaws. I gave him the sharpest salute of my military career, then turned on my heel and walked out of the tent."

"He allowed that—said nothing?"

"It was a field citation in the first place—nothing that took place at the White House or anything. I was issued a reprimand. They put both documents into my personnel file and left it alone. Hue was under siege—destruction everywhere. They don't quibble in times like that."

"From all I've read, I can see why you were angry about the war."

"Everyone over there was angry. I didn't want a piece

of paper, for crying out loud, to prove I'd done my duty. Anyway," he grunted, fiddling with the tripod, "afterward, when it came time to finish my education, I wanted to study anything but film. I chose marine management." He laughed dryly. "Funny, isn't it? Marine Corps—marine management?"

She touched his sleeve. "Ironic, perhaps. At least you have film to fall back on—temporarily."

"*Very* temporarily. Want to take a quick look through the viewfinder?"

"Love to."

As she leaned toward the mouse-eared camera, she felt his body come around her almost protectively. His chest melded to her shoulders, his beard grazing the crown of her head. He groped along her arm—even through her heavy jacket sensations raced along her skin at turnpike speed—until he found a lever on the tripod. He braced against it.

Forcing concentration, she peered through the eyepiece, then held her breath. Gray gold light played softly across the landscape. A bird, then two, dived across mounds of grass and brush, swooping gracefully.

"The birds are always the first ones awake," she said excitedly.

He shook her shoulder gently. "Lower your voice. The elk should be entering the meadow any time now."

Without thinking, she turned abruptly into the circle of his chest and arms, her lips parted only inches from his.

He inhaled sharply. He seemed to devour every feature of her face: fringe of dark lashes, gentle curve of cheekbone and jaw, silken chestnut hair made lush with the filtered glow of dawn. The hunger in his gaze sent ripples of anticipation through her.

His own face was a glorious portrait in gradient tones, one angular cheek palest china white, planes of forehead and nose a darker shade, the curling hair on his beard and mustache glinting rich chocolate. Shadows masked his deep-set eyes, but a pale blue smoldered within. Unnerved by his smoky passion, she drew a shaky breath.

He kissed her gently, quickly. Leaning toward him, she kissed him back.

He caught her, crushed her against him. "Lass," he said huskily. "God help me, I need you!"

In business or in bed, she wondered, yet did it matter? Perhaps just the fact that he wanted her was enough. It was such a rare exquisite feeling to be held by him.

Suddenly his lips were warm and possessive against hers, igniting her doubts and desire in explosive feeling. Warm moist lips, velvet soft with gentleness—then demanding, hungry, taking every ounce of her breath. Her body filled with aching. Each kiss, each warm whiff of him scorched her.

His hands moved over her back and slid down, cradling her against his hips. Her reaction was unexpectedly urgent and sinuous. *His priorities,* she reminded herself wildly. *His work*. . . . But it was hopeless to try to dwell on such concerns when she was thrust into the fast sparkling vortex of sensation. And when he pressed her closer, expressing his passion rawly, she felt flung onto a long, star-studded trail, heaven-hung and glowing with ancient fire.

Shaken now, she couldn't think why she was here.

She could only plunge deeper into the magnetic field they created between them. Knees trembling, lips and arms drawing him to her, she satisfied his demands with deep undulations of her body. Male-hard flesh yielded, answered her, arched and curved away, molding her to him. Anguished at the restraint of thick clothing, yet thrilled to her core by this ecstasy, she inhaled, exhaled with him, heard him moan—and then felt bereaved as his lips left hers and his body stiffened. Ragged gasps sounded in her ears; tremors racked her limbs. Slowly she opened her eyes.

Baird averted his face—his breath held—concentrating. With a start she realized he was listening, and her heart plummeted. "Oh. . . ."

Suddenly she was thrust away. Baird crouched over the camera. He cursed softly, and the sound was sobering. She reached out to him, fingers trailing lightly from his shoulder to his elbow. Like ice. Unyielding. His attention remained rigidly trained on the faint crackling sounds breaking the stillness of the meadow. She bit back a cry of misery, realizing just in time that he was devoting this moment to his own brand of survival.

Sick with regret that she may have cost him valuable footage, she sank dejectedly to the canvas. *Idiot,* she castigated herself. She shouldn't have convinced him to bring her, not when this day was so important to him. She'd considered only herself, her desire to see the elk and her increasing need to share every moment with him.

She remembered the makeshift partition he'd erected across one half of the glassed-in porch of his home. The Pipe Room, she called it: sawdust and shavings everywhere, knots of briarwood he said he'd bought while he was in prison and learned to carve into pipes. He would try to sell them, he said. Did the man ever rest?

And she'd nearly wasted one of his precious mornings with her intrusive presence. Of course, nobody had forced him to kiss her. She knew that. But she was a distraction. As surely as that halo of light rose through the branches of the blind, she knew he would storm at her—or worse, seal himself off from her again.

Gradually she realized he'd been working. In competition with strident birdcalls, lenses clicked, the light meter tapped gently against the tripod where he'd hastily replaced it and film purred through the advancing mechanism of the camera.

Relief washed through her. She twisted, stared at green leaves, tried to curl comfortably on the chill ground. Maybe she hadn't ruined everything with her endless questions about Vietnam and her foolish move into his arms. But why did regret coil like a reptile in her stomach?

AN HOUR LATER, when Dawnelle had shed her heavy coat because of the rising warmth of the enclosure, Baird turned to her and whispered, "You want to see the elk? They're magnificent."

"Yes!" She grinned, unfolding her cramped legs as quietly as possible. He pulled her up.

Though his features were plainly visible now, she allowed herself only a brief glimpse of his face before averting her eyes. In that split-second appraisal, he seemed intense, as always, but not angry. Elated, she stepped to the camera.

When she looked into the eyepiece, she saw a young buck snapping green shoots from a thimbleberry bush, causing the flowers to dance like white stars. Smaller than an Arabian horse, though thicker through the belly and possessing the slightly dipped neck that reminded her of cattle, the youngster seemed docile. Sleek and quiet. His dark eyes were dewy-moist beneath Hershey-colored oval ears. Chocolate down covered his long muzzle. Already the mantle of brown crept over his flat forehead and along his neck, so that at maturity he'd wear a handsome hood over his coffee-and-cream withers and body. Antler nubs protruded a few inches above that refined head. Dawnelle shivered, awed and intrigued. She watched him snake his pink tongue around a leaf cluster, contentedly pulling it into his mouth.

The yearling's ears flickered as a mature doe, larger and lacking the horn stubs, grazed close by. Even though she possessed the dark underbelly and snout of the buck, this animal's head retained much of the creamy body coloring.

Dawnelle didn't feel Baird's presence close behind her as before, and wanting to share her delight in the elk, she turned to sigh, "Spectacu—"

He raised a cautionary finger to his lips, then gestured toward the eastern side of the blind. "Buck," he mouthed, glancing apprehensively at the rifle in his hands. With obvious stealth, he pried back the firing hammer. He frowned at the metallic click.

Dawnelle paled as she watched him step to the branches and peer through, listening intently. She grew aware of soft snuffling sounds just beyond the leaves.

Dreading that Baird would have to kill one of the lovely creatures she'd just been admiring, she nonetheless recalled television documentaries and haphazard comments warning of the dangers of provoking a mature buck. Her fingers felt like cold sticks curled in her palms. Flattening her hands against her jeans, she crept closer to Baird and tried to see the animal.

Leaves and boughs shook as the elk tossed its head. Dawnelle followed a partially obscured branch of ivory as wide as four, maybe four and a half feet across, at which point the foliage blocked her view. Dark pitted bone extended into numerous pale smooth tines, the points probably rasped thousands of times against trees and other sets of antlers. He was a beauty, and judging by the glimpse she'd got of his shoulder, perhaps as large as a mature quarter horse.

Greenery shivered violently with the bull's increasing ire, rocking the tripod up on two legs. It settled jarringly. Dawnelle cringed, thinking of the loss to Baird if the camera was cracked open, exposing the film to bright light. She reached reflexively for the apparatus, but Baird's hand clamped over her arm. He firmly pulled her back from the trees.

Glancing around in search of a weapon of her own, she seized a gnarled branch about the width of three fingers. When she drew the staff from among green saplings, bark and leaves crackled like the firecrackers she'd once seen on a Fourth of July in Disneyland.

An answering *whoof* sounded from the bull. He thrashed the flimsy barrier, showering them with leaves. Suddenly a bellowing snort. Crashing! Dawnelle screamed and clutched Baird's gun arm. He jerked her behind him, then threw the rifle to his shoulder. She peered around his elbow. The walls of the blind folded inward, revealing the dark striking foreleg of a beast bent on killing them if he could. Another leg and part of a great heaving chest broke through. Then the mighty antlers came crashing in.

A crescent of blue sky hugged that brawny head. Ears flattened, teeth bared, brown eyes circled with flame streaks, the elk half rose on his haunches and swung his brace of antlers directly at Baird. The rifle roared. Elbow, rifle butt—something—kicked her in the chin, and Dawnelle was hurled backward into a thousand painful spears.

CHAPTER EIGHT

SILENCE. The celery scent of crushed leaves. Memories of early summer in a meadow. But today the birds were frightened. As Dawnelle opened her eyes to the lace of greenery above, she felt pain in her jaw and lower back. A hand gently stroked her forehead, smoothing away hair, pulling leaves from the tangled mass.

"Baird?"

"You were only out for a few seconds," he murmured, bending over her. He picked a gray twig from the weave of her burgundy-and-pink sweater. "Where are you hurt? We may not have much time to get out of here."

She struggled to sit up, wincing at the stab she felt in her back. She gave him a weak but grateful smile for his supporting arm.

Baird had green leaves woven into his hair and beard. A ragged tear parted the sleeve of his white jacket. Blood was just beginning to ooze through the fabric. "You're cut!" she said sharply, leaning quickly toward him.

Glancing at his arm in surprise, he grunted agreement. "I don't think it's bad. Can you stand?"

"Give me a hand up, and we'll see."

"Okay?"

"Wait—easy on my back; it's tender.... Yes, fine."

He steadied her until the return of circulation strengthened her legs.

"Where's the elk? Not—did you hit him?"

"Took a big chunk of ivory off one antler and scared the devil out of him. We're lucky he's gun-shy." He scrambled toward the morass of broken saplings, returning with a branching piece of elk horn. After she'd made a face at the danger it represented, he stuffed it into the orange flight bag.

"Souvenir?"

"No," he muttered. "Future stems and display bases for my pipes. Horn is handsome on stained briar. Let's move out."

"What about the tarp?"

"We'll leave it. I may have to come back."

She sighed in commiseration as Baird glanced through the gaping snarl of branches formerly in service as camouflage for his camera. "He's taken the herd out of the meadow, but I wouldn't want to stay here and play roulette with him again." Limping slightly, he came back to Dawnelle. "You all right?"

"I'll make it. What happened to your foot?"

"I haven't the slightest idea. All I remember is that pitchfork of ivory coming at me, and the report of my rifle—then a guilty suspicion that the butt of my rifle put you on your back. Sorry about that—here, get your coat and let's check the clearing again."

They squeezed cautiously through the branches before limping at a half run across the field of wild flowers and grass, and up into the forest. Panting, they charged to a standstill beneath the blackened and jagged hilt of a redwood felled by lightning. Here in the shadows of a tree whose girth rivaled that of the lighthouse, they turned to scout below. Lush and peaceful now, the deserted valley seemed to have forgotten their recent brush with death. Laughing in relief, Dawnelle and Baird pulled each other through blackberry bushes dancing with white blossoms, heading deeper into the woods in search of the landmarks of their trail.

AN HOUR LATER, Miss Mo lavished them with whines and happy lunges as they entered the destruction of Dawnelle's living room. *Advertising Age* looked as if preschoolers had consumed it for lunch, and the braided rug, though still intact, seemed to have armadillos burrowed under it in spots. Draped over the fireplace poker, a powder-blue towel from the bathroom looked suspiciously damp and frayed at one corner. Dawnelle groaned and pushed the dog away. Misinterpreting the move, Miss Mo growled playfully and planted her feet roughly on Dawnelle's jeans.

"Down!" Baird commanded, jerking the dog to a sitting position. "Down!" he commanded for good measure, although Miss Mo's shock took the eagerness out of her.

"Thanks," Dawnelle said simply.

Frustrated and mildly in pain, she stared around her. She was embarrassed about the living room and thought perhaps she should scold Miss Mo, as he'd suggested earlier. But how to begin?

"Show her each object she'd ruined and tell her no," he said, evidently in tune with her thoughts. "Otherwise you'll never break her of her bad habits."

She complied, her back muscles pulling painfully as she bent to show the dog the infractions and to mete out terse noes. When she'd finished the schooling, Baird nodded approvingly. She ordered the dog outside.

As she faced Baird again, he was removing his stained white jacket and hanging it familiarly on the hall tree. "Want one of those ham sandwiches?" she asked, her heart rate beginning to undermine her composure as she wondered why he didn't rush off to some task or other.

He came to stand in front of her, shaking his head. Reaching to her jaw, he turned her face gently to an angle that caught the sunlight from the living room. He shook his head again at the sore area of her chin. "A shame to mar your pretty features with a nasty bruise but it shouldn't last if your circulation is good. Better lay ice to it to reduce the swelling."

Remembering her remorse over their last ill-timed kiss, she gently disengaged herself and wandered to the shell mirror. The lower left side of her jaw bulged in mauve bruising. "First," she decided aloud, exercising her jaws experimentally and finding the discomfort bearable, "I want to take a look at that cut on your arm."

"My thoughts exactly." Appearing disconcertingly close behind her, he grasped her arm and steered her toward the leather chesterfield. "But first *I'm* going to rub liniment into your back—if you've got any. You're wincing with every step."

Crimson rose to her cheeks, and she half turned away from him. It would be torture to feel his hands on her bare flesh. "No need. I'll just take a long hot bath to relax the muscles."

"Nonsense—where's your bathroom? Across from the kitchen, if I recall." With a slight limp he walked to the hall and disappeared. She heard glass clinking and cupboards clapping as he rummaged.

"Under the sink!" she called. "Brown bottle!"

He returned, smiling as he uncapped the jar, a fresh blue towel over his arm. "Uh-uh," he admonished when he saw her dismay. "Strictly business, remember? Off with your sweater and lie stomach down on the towel. Can't have my ace P.R. director calling in sick. I expect we'll have to lot to talk over on this notion of yours about renaming the business—that is, if you don't have visitors tomorrow about six in the evening."

She glanced at the recorder on the end table. "It appears I might. The flag's showing—turn around, will you?"

He handed her the towel, then faced the fireplace. "Did you want to check your messages now?"

"Later," she mumbled, jolting the knot in her back as she pulled off her heavy sweater. She unsnapped her jeans to ease the injured tissues, then glanced over her shoulder at his broad back.

It wasn't primness that made her reluctant to have him put his hands on her. It was having to deal with the emotional havoc he created every time he touched her. She suspected his interest in friendship stemmed either from sexual attraction or loneliness. Neither was enough, not if the result was a casual sexual encounter that left her feeling used again. . . .

He shifted impatiently and leaned against the mantel Dawnelle breathed shakily and looked away. Still wearing the rose T-shirt and her bra, she stretched over the towel, pulling the cotton away from her lower back. She laughed inwardly at his promise to remain detached. It wasn't his control she was worried about—it was her own. How many times could she stand wanting him as badly as this morning and being shoved aside by his priorities?

As she lay on the couch, expectant and nervous, she considered the idea of an affair with Baird. Except for his enigmatic moods, he embodied all things male and sensual she desired in a mate. His lovemaking was varied, inspired, passionate. His life was devoted to achievement and service, as was her own. But no, she thought, suffering a twist of fear. To be loved by such a man only once would be to long for him ever after, as her father had mourned the loss of his wife's affection. The thought startled her. Lost love. Was she so frightened by her parents' empty marriage that she'd thrown up walls to her own happiness? Would she always be attracted to men who couldn't fulfill her?

Across the rug, Baird politely cleared his throat.

"Okay," she said apologetically, pressing her right cheekbone into the towel to still the fine tremble of her nerves. "Please work miracles, because I'm near death's door."

He chuckled. The couch sagged as he wedged his hip beside hers. She felt a brush of fingers, an efficient snap. Her breasts blossomed slightly at their sudden freedom. "Hey!" she objected, feeling awkwardly for the catch on her bra.

"Strictly business," he soothed in a low voice. "Relax...."

After her hand was placed gently near her face and

her tumbling hair smoothed aside, she heard his palms rubbing some of the liniment. She jumped when his first touch warmed her flesh. He began circling her upper muscles, firing her blood with excitement, flooding her face with bright color. She wanted to tell him the injury was lower, but he mesmerized her with his supple fingers. She closed her eyes, beginning to float in a downy space where holding back feeling was impossible, and only the senses mattered. She uttered a tiny moan of ecstasy.

"Good Lord!" he breathed, returning her rudely to reality as he folded back the waistband of her jeans and leggings. He began caressing her wound gently, massaging away the discomfort. "Nasty bruise. No wonder you were bent double with pain."

"Is it purple?"

"Ugly! No, now close your eyes and try not to jump around. I'll go slowly. We'll have you all set for the fish-fry dance next Saturday. Trust me."

She felt a new tremor of excitement "Are—do you dance?"

"A mite. You?"

"Crazy about it, but my tastes are a little strange for this day and age. I did some exhibition ballroom in college. Say—" she angled around to him "—you wouldn't by any chance know how to tango? It's impossible to find partners for the really beautiful dances anymore."

He firmly pushed her back to the couch, then worked her jeans lower on her hips. The feeling his hands evoked was too wanton to permit concentration on his answer.

"The samba, too, although I—"

"What did you say, Baird?"

"I said I like the tango fine, and I used to a get a kick out of those crazy dances that were always coming out of New York. It's been a long time, though. I'm probably pretty rusty by now."

"Are you going to the fish fry?" She took a brave breath. "And the dance?"

He silently stroked her back for a moment. "I guess so, not that it would have been my choice."

Naturally he meant a woman had talked him into it, just as she herself had conned her way into his blind today. Probably Lau. Then she remembered her own date with Ben. She keenly wished things were switched around. When the telephone rang, she stretched quickly for the receiver, answering hollowly. "Trinidad Head Light Station."

"Hi, it's me," Ben's voice said. "You sound as if you need cheering up."

"No, I'm fine." She forced cheer, unwilling to describe her fiasco with the elk right at the moment. "How are the tests coming?"

"Your light station gets a clean bill of health, beautiful—still standing, still reliable, just like you said. Shoptalk aside, dinner was super the other night at the Grove." Ben's tone grew husky. "I'm ready for a replay. How about you? Dinner Wednesday? I really called to ask you if you'd like to head for the Trinidad fish fry about two o'clock on Saturday, but dinner was so great. . . ." His voice faded as Baird's tender caress on her hips disturbed her concentration. "Called to see if you'd say yes," Ben finished.

"Yes to what, Ben?"

Baird's fingers froze on her skin.

"Yes to the hour we go to the fish fry, gorgeous friend who makes me love California. And yes to dinner, too. Say, did you fade off over there? Is it definite, then?"

"You're persistent!" She laughed at his contagious good humor. Then, with sudden decision: "Wednesday, yes—and about the other, two o'clock is fine."

"Great. Glad I caught you. I left you a message this morning. Guess you were out checking the foghorn or something when I called."

"I was out. Well, goodbye, then. . . ."

"Seven on Wednesday?"

"Right," she said, anxious to get off the phone and check Baird's reaction.

"Bye, babe!" She smiled at the endearment and hung up the phone.

The magic of her moment with Baird had been broken. As she craned to look at him, he stood up and capped the jar. All traces of humor and warmth were gone, replaced by the preoccupied "business" expression she'd seen in past weeks. Obviously she wouldn't be struggling against another onslaught of Baird's kisses this afternoon. Relieved but vaguely disappointed, she sat up.

"Friend?" he asked casually, placing the jar on the end table.

"Yes. Ben Fallon. He said the tests he performed out here the day I started cleaning the shed turned out positive. No problem with stability where the rock is concerned." *Only where my feelings for you are concerned,* she thought, rising from the couch, fastening her bra and pulling her shirt straight. "My back feels much better."

He nodded absently.

"Let me take a look at your arm." She moved to his side.

"Oh.... No, I'll get it cleaned up at home. Got to get a move on if I'm going to get those mussels collected for Dr. Warren."

"I've had basic first-aid training," she persisted, frowning at the dried blood on his plaid sleeve.

He gave her a wry look.

"Let me get some water." Ignoring his indifference, she backed away and headed for the kitchen.

In ten minutes she'd cleaned the deep vertical scratch and applied a wrap of gauze. He rolled down his sleeve, retrieved his coat. "Thanks, Miss Nightingale. You have the touch of an angel."

"Think nothing of it." Stepping over a crushed magazine page, she followed him to the front door. "You ought to have a shot, you know. I don't want to show up at your place and find you with lockjaw, frozen stiff over that microscope-camera affair in your lab."

"Video camera. I salvaged it from the San Francisco fiasco. Did I tell you? I'm starting to make videocassettes of living organisms magnified by the microscope."

"No, and you're just changing the subject."

"Better get some ice on that chin," he countered. "By the way, your schedule's getting pretty tight. You sure you can work this week?" There was a thin veil of sarcasm in his tone.

"What—me, put Langston Marine aside?" she

mocked with a grin. "Never! After all, I have my priorities, too!"

The dog wiggled through the door the minute Baird opened it to step outside. He saluted Dawnelle vaguely and left the porch.

Not a word to her about disrupting his film assignment, she thought, marveling at her good luck. And no goodbye kiss, either. Evidently all their tender moments were going to be accidents. She turned reluctantly back to the silence of her cottage.

Dawnelle shamed Miss Mo several times as she picked up the debris in the living room. Once she'd straightened the room, she rewound the tape on her answering machine, listening to the shriek of several messages being run backward.

The first voice was Ben's, laughing self-consciously about being recorded and asking about dinner Wednesday. Sarah had also called. Her sweet voice warped almost to a squeak by electronic distortion, she reminded Dawnelle of the Civic Club meeting Thursday evening.

Sprigs of wild rose clung to the fluted throat of the crystal vase near the recorder. Dawnelle stroked one of the pink blossoms, thinking over the events of the morning at Prairie Creek while she waited for the wail between calls to die out.

Finally a beep announced her last caller. Pencil poised over her message pad, Dawnelle leaned close to adjust the volume. The sound of someone exhaling rasped over the line. *Where had she heard that wet breathy sound before?* Apprehension fluttered along her backbone. Why would someone call simply to breathe on her message tape?

Suddenly a whiny chuckle filled the room, the voice of a man insinuating intimacy. Panic, absurd panic, dampened her skin.

"Forget something?" As the voice wheezed into another malicious soggy laugh, she went cold.

"Maybe we could trade," he crooned, and the point of Dawnelle's pencil cracked under the pressure of her fingers. "Get cozy, you 'n' me...." More excitement in the wheezing. "I'll be seein' you, lighthouse lady—"

His voice ended on a strangled metallic beep.

Immobilized with dread, Dawnelle stood over the machine, listening to the static hiss of the tape as it wound endlessly over the reel. She jumped when she felt a warm presence touch her thigh. Pivoting, she brushed Miss Mo's muzzle with her hand. *Only the dog,* she thought in relief. Thank goodness she had the shepherd for protection! Crouching, ignoring the pull of sore muscles, she snuggled Miss Mo against her.

But black thoughts wormed into her brain—the isolation of the cottage, the potential danger of the precipitous cliffs. Who would threaten her? Who owned that filthy voice?

The dog's impatient squirming refocused Dawnelle's thoughts. Jenkins? Miss Mo's former owner, Paul Jenkins? No. In the two or three minutes while she bought the dog she hadn't given the obese man any clue about where she lived. Nothing but a crank call, she insisted. Some other woman had something going with the caller, that's all. She'd probably dumped him, and Dawnelle had inherited the number after moving to the station. Being the perverted type, the guy had decided not to let the phone number go to waste. Minimizing his losses with—sure, *with a scary little message for me,* she decided grimly, hoping she was right.

Visitors—strangers—had to be considered. Before their arrival, each guest wrote to the Guard for permission to visit, so technically they were "registered" and therefore traceable should any harm befall her. A minor deterrent, she thought, but she was grateful for any small defence.

"Forget something?" The sudsy voice haunted her. What had she forgotten that the creep wanted her to worry about? Drained as she was by the stress of the elk attack, her brush with romance and the eerie phone call, her mind pictured a blank domino. No white dots led her to suspect anyone—unless. . . Jeff? No, impossible. It wasn't Jeff's cultured Boston, chipped-beef voice she'd heard. Even with all the electronic distortion she'd recognize Jeff. Oh, he'd been righteously indignant about her "abandonment" of him during the touchy transition he'd masterminded. But revenge? No. Jeff would ease his false hurt by snuggling under the cape of the boss's daughter. Who, then?

Suddenly she reached for the telephone, dialing frantically. "Ben? Dawnelle. Yes, I know—no, I haven't called to cancel Wednesday. Listen, Ben. I want to play a weird message for you that came over the recorder while I was gone." He made a bad joke about beautiful women getting X-rated phone calls.

"Actually, that's what I was calling about," she said worriedly, reaching to rewind the tape. "Hold on. . . ."

She leaned close and waited until the first raspy breath reached her ears. Shuddering, she went back to Ben.

"This is just a crank call, I'm sure of it," she said without conviction. "But I had to tell someone in case— I mean if— Here, just listen." She held the receiver directly over the spinning cassette, gritting her teeth as the speaker broadcast the ugly chuckle through the room.

CHAPTER NINE

A MENACING GROWL issued through the eight-foot redwood fence. Fighting down fear, Dawnelle firmly took the latch in her fingers.

"Yurok. . . ." She waited while the animal sniffed through the gate planks, identifying her. Why was the dog growling? Always before, he'd greeted her happily and led her straight to Baird. She hadn't seen his truck in the drive, but that wasn't unusual. Unless he intended to leave again, he habitually locked the Ford in his garage. Was he gone? Disappointment speared through her. Ben had been comforting when she'd called him about the telephone threat, had insisted she consider the call a one-time attempt to vent twisted cravings. But for some reason the reassuring effect of his words had faded overnight. All she could think about now was Baird's response, Baird's concern.

Remembering his warning that Yurok would admit only friends to the spacious cliff house, she cleared her mind of the ugly call. She wanted no fear, no bad vibes to rouse the dog's instinct for defense. Hearing a low whine, she pulled open the gate and met Yurok's first inspection with a smiling greeting.

He brushed against her moss-green slacks, controlling his excitement at seeing her. *Miss Mo ought to spend more time around you,* she thought affectionately, patting his shaggy black side. She'd do well to acquire some of that polished manner.

Leaving Yurok outside to guard the acres of timber and seedy lawns rimming the house, she went through the side entrance Baird had instructed her to use. When she reached the landing above his subterranean laboratory, she called out to him. A clock ticked in the living room, but no human voice rang through the house. Perhaps he'd shut himself in his study?

The doorway to the kitchen opened on her right, but she went through to the spacious living room, shaking her head at the layer of dust covering his custom-made redwood furniture. She glanced beyond the glassed-in pipe room and what remained of his porch, briefly relishing the golden evening sky and the sweeping view of the ocean. Baird wasn't working on his pipes, she noted, turning away to call again. Still no answer.

She bent to polish a spot in the six-foot free-form coffee table. She'd never noticed the table had been sliced from the trunk of a redwood and propped in the air by a thick gnarled branch. The piece was very much like its owner, she thought—the polish only visible if you wiped away the grime of the past.

An immense bookcase lined the wall behind the couch. Once Baird must have been fabulously rich. An eighteen-inch pale green jade horse from the Orient held a special position among exotic vases and carvings. A mahogany horse of Etruscan design stood staunchly, saddled, its back flattened to form a small table near the hearth. Faded best-sellers from past years filled two lower shelves. Strangely saddened by the dusty collection, she wandered to the line of fish tanks across the room.

Here was life and vibrancy. She was reassured by the bubbling sound as the filters sent streamers upward past the lazy gaping mouths of fish. A purple sunflower star wrapped its many arms around a gray rock, while in a neighboring tank the wine-red spines of a giant urchin stood guard lest the mammoth star enter his glass domain for a meal. Intrigued though she was by the marine life in the tanks, Dawnelle crossed the living room to the book-lined wall, opening the paneled door to the library.

A window looked out through the woods, and beneath it, Baird's carved desk awaited her. Here, she missed him, missed the familiar link between her brain and his when they worked together. Sighing in disappointment, Dawnelle sat down.

It was always difficult to work in such chaos: pink bills, white letters from educational institutions, a sea of notes, news clippings, useless advertisements. Today was worse than usual. He hadn't even left her the token space swept clear in the center of the desk. She knew Baird was organized; she'd seen the rows of neat, bottled, labeled substances in his lab, the tidy drawers full of sandpaper and grinding tools in his pipe room. But his office! The man needed a mother or a secretary—or both!

What should she concentrate on? He'd planned to discuss the change of company name with her today, and she'd come prepared to suggest several themes on which they might base an ad campaign. Now what? She gazed at the mess before her, suddenly reaching out to remove a taped-up lined yellow sheet from the desk lamp.

Dawnelle:

Sorry to miss you. Had to drive to San Francisco on business. Rough out your ideas on Langston Marine and leave them. I'll be back in touch by Wednesday, and we can talk then. I've arranged for the care of Yurok and the specimens in the tanks. Just remember to shut the gate when you leave.

Baird

The note held a dismissing tone, as if he clearly wanted distance between them. But couldn't he have called? The knowledge that she wouldn't see Baird today settled heavily on her. Then she remembered she'd been out around the station or in town most of the day. Plus she hadn't checked her recorder when she left the cottage to go to work for Baird. He may have called, after all. That thought made checking her messages this evening less distasteful. Somehow, hearing his voice would soften the blow if she had to listen to another crank call. No accounting for the way some people gain comfort, she chided herself.

Still, it was unfortunate she couldn't discuss Langston Marine with its owner. Every delay in her work was a delay to his cash flow. With that thought in mind, she began to sift through the piles of paperwork, looking for a writing tablet.

Nagged by guilt, she read the astronomical figures entered on Baird's bank statements, a sheaf of pale blue sheets she'd unearthed and glanced at by mistake. These were not statements easily put down—at least, not if you'd invested part of yourself in the man whose financial status was revealed.

Unable to believe her eyes, she checked again. He'd written two checks in May, or rather, the bank had, and listed them as automatic transfers—each for $56,000! Curious, she glanced at the attached canceled checks. They were both computer-imprinted to Lienholders and Stockholders Fund, Marine Exports One Inc., dba Baird L. Langston and Veedas Vilkan. Obviously the money was being paid into what remained of Baird's old company. Six other monthly statements exactly duplicated the May figures. Where had he gotten the money?

Carefully she read the deposits listed, two equal amounts adding up to $112,062. She cross-referenced the code letters TT: transfer from trust account. Good Lord, he was paying off old debts with some kind of inheritance, living like a pauper, scrambling around trying to wire together a new business, while his rightful inheritance paid debtors and stockholders! Some quick arithmetic told her the inheritance averaged in excess of one million dollars a year.

Numb from the discovery, she replaced the bank notices beneath a stack of mail he hadn't yet opened. Better find that note pad and get to work.

She was destined to destroy his faith in her, she thought moments later. That is, if he discovered she'd also found and read the letter from C. Cole, private investigator. Hating her deception, she read what amounted to a letter requesting payment for work conducted in the first quarter of the year. In part, paragraph two read, "plus subsequent searches conducted in the general area of Singapore, yielding substantial leads on your subject." Evidently C. Cole would be forced to cease investigative operations immediately if some token amount wasn't forthcoming. Cole suggested they meet to discuss the case.

Vee, she thought, tucking the sterile San Francisco letterhead beneath Baird's electric bill. Cole is looking for Vee, and threatening to stop looking for him if Baird doesn't pay up. A nasty snarl in Baird's life. He wanted revenge. Badly. For a moment Dawnelle felt pride in Baird's mission and indignation toward both Cole and Vee that burned like banked coals.

The feelings were swiftly snuffed out. Baird was becoming her latest humanitarian project, and she could lose him, lose him in this mad manhunt for Vee. Would he die at the hands of his crooked partner in some Asian port, while she sat at his desk helping him earn the money that allowed him to go? The thought angered her, and she flung herself deeper into the chair, wincing at the twist she'd given her back. There was already too much waste in the world, too many damn fine people living in misery because things had gone wrong for them—unlucky breaks, mistakes, people letting them down. Singapore could be Baird's downfall, and he was too fine a man to end up a broken penniless failure. More than any cause she'd joined, she wanted to see Baird succeed, to know he tasted success a second time around. But he had to let go of revenge before it destroyed the inner man.

She'd make him forget lost causes, she resolved, and concentrate solely on Langston Marine. If he labeled her a meddling fool at first, so be it. At least when she stuck by him, he couldn't brand *her* a Judas. And, she thought with the beginnings of a smile, she'd enjoy proving that loyal business associates, especially the female variety, still existed. She wanted his arm around her shoulders, a smile of surprise and respect on his face, when the money rolled in. She'd work for that smile—for his happiness.

Of course Baird might feel her attempt to sidetrack him from Vee constituted the purest ether of disloyalty. But to worry about that was short-range thinking. The real subject was the future. Baird's future. And perhaps...theirs.

She closed her eyes for a moment, imagining his arms slipping around her, his smile of respect darkening to something else, something moody and hungry...a look that even now stirred her blood and heated her flesh.

CHAPTER TEN

"THE VOTE IS UNANIMOUS!" Sarah beamed from her presidential position before the podium. Her yellow-and-salmon print dress rustled as she raised her arm to the audience. "May I present to you our Señorita de la Luz—our very own Lady of the Light, Dawnelle Belanger. I might explain," she added, raising her steel-rimmed glasses the tiniest fraction, heightening suspense, "Dawnelle's sporting a bruise on her chin, the result of a fall while investigating some of our beautiful backcountry around Prairie Creek. I asked her if she'd had to fight off a strapping gent from one of the lumber camps back in there, but she denied it and said, 'Don't you think *he'd* be wearing the bruise?' "

Warm laughter rattled through the cavernous town hall. Amused faces turned toward Dawnelle, wedged into the fourth row of seats. It was mildly embarrassing to be introduced to the Civic Club this way, but so much better than having the real story she'd related to Sarah broadcast around town. She'd been warned again that the subject of Baird Langston was taboo.

"Dawnelle?" Sarah was waving encouragingly. "If you'll come forward for the presentation of your membership certificate?" Her round face lighted up with pride as the enthusiastic applause swept Dawnelle to her side.

"You deserve a bouquet of roses for your tact," Dawnelle whispered as she accepted Sarah's congratulatory squeeze.

"Nonsense!" Sarah thrust crisp parchment into her hand. "The truth is none of their business! Turn around and let them get a good look at you."

Smiling her thanks, Dawnelle turned and inclined her head toward the forty-odd clapping grinning women crowded into metal chairs. Suddenly she felt unreasonably happy that she'd dressed so carefully for her Civic sisters. Her white boat-neck sweater, a fine wool blend, suggested a yachting look in thin horizontal stripes of navy blue, the colors repeated in her low spectator pumps. White baby pleats swirled around her calves as she faced each section of chairs. She laughed softly with genuine pleasure.

Greer Sking, a woman near Sarah's age who ranked second-in-command at the Civic Club, shuttled her immense bulk into speaking range. Stretching out an arm she wrapped Dawnelle in a welcoming hug and leaned close. "We're all mighty glad you're with us, dear girl! Take another bow!"

Sarah's gavel crashed as she sang out, "Meeting dismissed!"

"You're the first real heroine material we've seen in these parts for years," Greer's radio-announcer voice crooned into Dawnelle's ear as the women scraped noisily to their feet. "Glad we grabbed you up before the volunteer fire fighters or the Garden Club or any other local group got ahold of you."

"What do you mean, heroine material?"

"The station, dear girl, the station. You're a woman alone out there, and we're all women in the club. The link should be obvious." Greer ducked her chins, peering at Dawnelle until the younger woman laughingly nodded understanding. Then, tucking her tan purse under an arm that tested the stretch of her mint green knit dress, Greer waved to an approaching group of women and took herself off.

Several members squeezed close to offer congratulations to Dawnelle, but their introductions were cut short when Sarah and another woman with a rather square face bustled into the group. Sarah's smile looked pasted and stiff with contained anger. "Dawnelle," she said with unaccustomed brusqueness, "Grace wanted to meet you. She and her husband own the bait store in town."

Curious about Sarah's clipped introduction, Dawnelle turned to greet the woman who'd stared at her from the lighted doorway of the red shop early last Sunday morning. Instantly she noted the severity of Grace's style. Out of her narrow brown skirt dropped legs much like dock pilings, the shapeless length anchored in spike heels. As Dawnelle gazed into obsidian eyes glittering with chronic suspicion, she felt a warning tingle on her nape. Grace's face had an arrogant toughness, and her blond halo of hair did nothing to soften the look. She seemed agelessly hard.

Despite her instant dislike of the woman, Dawnelle held her eyes, then smiled. "Hello, Grace," she said.

"Miss Belanger." The aloof voice sounded like rain over window glass, a pebbly drone. Grace inclined her head. "Sarah tells me you've gotten to know quite a few folks already. Have you?"

"A comfortable number so far." Dawnelle took a quick reading from Sarah's face. Compressed lips and the slight shake of that gray head warned her to keep silent about Baird. Dawnelle met the stony stare again. "Sarah is my mentor, actually, Grace. She's brought me into your club, invited me to dinner and insisted I spend an evening in town now and then to stave off the possibility of going daft in the wind out there on the Head. Though I don't imagine I'll have a chance to get lonely with so many wonderful friends here at the Civic Club."

"Of course not, dear," Sarah agreed, turning a chilly shoulder to Grace. "We've got the Yurok graveyard we're trying to protect from scalp-hunting archeologists and the Fourth of July festivities to organize." She smiled warmly at Dawnelle. "No chance you'll be lonely when you're up to your elbows in civic projects. And don't think your membership only amounts to that piece of paper you're holding. We're going to make full use of your talents."

"I imagine you were just warming up to your civic duties, then, last Sunday?" Grace asked in a syrupy tone.

Dawnelle's face grew warm. "My civic duties?"

"You'll agree civic responsibility often includes distasteful chores, won't you? You might, for example, have to associate with someone who isn't, let's say, a bosom friend? Then again, no matter how distasteful the person is to *others*, you might stick by him, anyway, mightn't you?"

"What is your point, Grace?" demanded Greer, who

turned back to the group, folding her heavy arms over her midriff, crushing her tan purse. "This isn't one of your courts of inquisition, is it? Because if it is, I've been gone from home three hours, and George and the boys are waiting apple pie on me. Fresh-baked this afternoon."

"No need to jump to conclusions, Greer. I have as much interest in seeing to Miss Belanger's welfare as you or Sarah or anyone."

"Glad to hear it. Just didn't want Dawnelle overwhelmed on her first night by our combined interest in her well-being."

"Grace," Dawnelle interrupted diplomatically, "please call me Dawnelle. I'd feel much less like a new arrival." Grace's smile attempted warmth but came off as a grimace.

A few of the women said goodbye, drifted away, and two others arrived at Dawnelle's right, diffusing the uncomfortable moment. Yet Grace wouldn't permit the diversion. "That Langston man," she mused. "Now, there's one to keep away from."

Dawnelle's face paled. Her palms grew damp.

"We're doing our best, Grace," Greer pointed out with mock patience, panning the tight group of women. "Langston doesn't seem to be contaminating our chaste midst at the moment."

"Troublemaker!" Sarah erupted, glaring at Grace. "I told you it was nothing to worry about. But no, you insist on digging dirt where marble should lie!"

Sarah now had everyone's attention, and her cheeks glowed with sudden embarrassment. She sent Dawnelle an apologetic look. Grace grunted indignantly.

"What dirt?" Greer wanted to know, never one to mince words. "Langston is old news."

"Why," said Grace, tugging her brown skirt, "I was just trying to warn Dawnelle about sticking by distasteful friends. Everyone else has already decided the man *is* deceitful and contaminated!"

"That's spiteful and rude," Dawnelle said levelly, her distaste for the situation carefully controlled.

"But I opened the shop last Sunday morning. Maybe I didn't see what I thought I saw over at the gas station?"

"You saw correctly, I assure you. It's your assumptions I question."

"That's your right, of course. I'm only out to warn you of potential trouble."

"If that was your intent, Grace, I hardly think you'd do it so publicly." Dawnelle felt a light touch on her arm and glanced down into Sarah's worried eyes. "It's all right, Sarah," Dawnelle said softly, choosing her words carefully to protect Sarah's reputation; she *had* tried to avoid this scandal. "Baird Langston is a friend, so I don't mind speaking for him. I've heard that some of your members cast him in a black light, and I feel bad about that."

"Not some of us," Grace pronounced regally. "All."

"He's just...different," Dawnelle countered, bridling. "A loner."

"Criminal."

"You're degrading him without knowing his character. He's living like a caged animal because of views like yours, Grace. His wife and brother deserted him. He's isolated, always working, carving pipes, collecting marine specimens for Humboldt State—does that sound like a common criminal? And he's supposed to have abandoned his grandfather, right? Well, it was his brother, Charles, who was being groomed to take over the family empire, not Baird. It's not fair that everyone condemn him without hearing his side."

She glanced around the group. Mouths had fallen agape; eyes were wide. With a disgusted sigh she held out the parchment to Sarah. "I won't abandon a friend just because of what others think of him, Sarah. I believe he's innocent. You have every right to take back my membership certificate if you think I'll taint the reputation of the Civic Club."

Shaking her head reprovingly, Sarah refused the paper. "Nonsense," she said firmly.

"He rescued a raccoon once." The gravelly voice drew all eyes to the stocky woman between Sarah and Grace. Self-consciously bobbing her steel-gray waves, the woman hugged a thin red sweater to her rounded shoulders, for the hall was chilly and high-ceilinged. She looked to be in her late fifties, a stout, plain-featured woman with round hazel eyes.

"That's very interesting, Genia," said Sarah. "Dawnelle this is Eugenia Forester. She used to work for the Langstons years back. Genia, what's this about a raccoon?"

"We're getting off the track," Grace insisted. "The point is, he's got a prison record."

"The point is," said Sarah, smartly adjusting her glasses, "Genia has a story to tell, and you've already had your say! Genia, go ahead."

Obviously a timid woman despite her grating heavy

voice, Genia peeped around the circle. "Well, like Sarah mentioned, I worked for Mr. Langston. He came up here to get away from the city pressures. Anyway, about the raccoon. I was driving along Mr. Langston's kind of curvy driveway, going down toward the garages, when I saw a little ball of nothing curled up on the side of the gravel. Well, so I parked and took a look. Little old raccoon was lying there, all bunched up and miserable looking. 'Course I didn't want to touch it because—"

"Rabies," Grace interrupted. "They'll give you rabies."

"Well, I wasn't sure about that, so I hurried on to the house and told Mr. Langston. He came out and picked up the animal and brought it into his kitchen. Examined that raccoon as professional as any doctor, see, and found a broken leg. After he put some little flat sticks against the leg and wrapped it in gauze, he drove into Arcata for some pet vitamins and jars of baby food. He kept the animal in a padded box under a lamp. Then he found a shelter that would take over the care while he was back in the city."

Genia took a deep breath and bobbed her head around to see if she still had an audience. Evidently satisfied, she continued in that rough-hewn voice. "He was wrong to leave his grandfather in the lurch, and he got sent to prison for larceny or something, but he'd never hurt anything. Not like that."

"How do you know with a big brute like him?" Grace countered, staring at Dawnelle's chin. "I tell you, Dawnelle's not safe around him."

"Will you let Genia tell her story?" Sarah demanded irritably.

"What's the use? It won't change the facts!"

"Well, I'll just tell the rest." Genia continued to hug her sweater, glancing at Sarah for encouragement. "He was back eight weeks later—just about perfect timing for healing a broken leg, I thought at the time—and he went back to the shelter. I remember he took the Maki woman and her boy with him. The boy was only seven. His father had died the previous winter in the big blow we had—lost at sea, remember, Sarah? Such a shame." She shook her head.

"She ought to keep out of his way, too!" Grace said.

"Who?" said Greer.

"Lau Maki, of course! She's a good mother but she ought to keep that boy away from bad influences."

Dawnelle's heart beat erratically. Ought to? Was this proof that Baird was dating Lau regularly?

"Genia's still got the floor!" Sarah's pretty voice thinned, reminding Dawnelle that she'd better keep her wits about her while the hive was still swarming.

"That's about it," Genia growled softly to the group. "Mr. Langston had Lau and the boy with him when he went off to get the raccoon. They turned it loose in the woods right where I'd found it that first day."

"A touching story, we all agree," Grace immediately announced into the lull. "But what has he done for any of us but bring shame on us by inhabiting that monstrosity of a house right here in our midst? I think we ought to gather a committee to see about banning him from the community!"

"I'm sure if he had the pleasure of meeting you, Grace," Dawnelle couldn't prevent herself from retorting softly, "He'd show you the same pity he showed the raccoon. As to kicking him out of Trinidad, you could broach the idea to him Saturday at the fish fry, but I doubt you'd meet with success. He's quite fervent about earning a living right now. Especially since every penny of his inheritance is currently going to pay off the stockholders and debtors of that company he owned. Debts, I might add, that were created by his ex-partner, who is the real culprit in the matter."

"He claimed such things, of course," Greer stated skeptically. "In those newspaper interviews I read when I followed the story, he said he'd been framed. But everyone says that when they're being roasted. What proof has he offered?"

"That's up to him to discuss, if he chooses." Dawnelle was afraid she'd already revealed more than was decent about Baird's private affairs. Twisting the parchment into a tube, she tapped it nervously against her palm. Her statements would probably condemn her one day. "I will tell you I'm helping him to write a few ads for his marine business," she began, and continued after the shocked breaths had subsided. "Quite by accident I discovered certain...bank transactions. They indicate Baird is shoveling a large inheritance into a trust account for lien holders and stockholders of his old company. Why would he do that if he was guilty?"

"A man as bright as that," said Grace, "can finagle figures to *look* innocent when they are entirely the opposite. I tell you, ladies, he does nothing but disgrace our community."

"I think I'll call him and see if he needs any work done around the house," quiet Genia interposed.

"Unfortunately, I don't think he'll offer you work,"

Dawnelle said. "He's scrimping now—every cent counts. Building up his business is taking everything."

"You say he makes pipes?" Genia asked.

"Yes, beautiful briars. I happen to know he's planning to put elk-horn bits on some of his future designs."

"Then I'll see if I can get him to have the housework done in exchange for one of those pipes. My John is a smoking *fiend*, you know, and really good pipes cost as much as a used car."

Dawnelle smiled brightly at Genia, then swept the group with a quick glance that came to rest on Sarah. "Well, Sarah, it's not too late to call back your membership certificate if you think you'd rather wait a few months. You know my feelings about choosing my own friends."

"I knew your feelings on the subject before I introduced you tonight, dear." She glanced disgustedly at Grace. "No one has the right to judge you by the company you keep. As your friends, we only have the right to express our concern for your welfare. I, for one, have complete faith in your judgment. Greer, do I hear a second?"

"Second. Ladies, let's get the chairs folded and stacked along the wall for Saturday night's dance, and then I'm heading straight for that apple pie!" Though Grace would have liked the last word, the group disbursed under weightier leadership. With a victimized sigh she stalked out of the hall, her heels digging viciously into the pine flooring.

Dawnelle felt the blood return to her tense fingers as she went to the nearest gray metal chair and folded it. Well, her worst fears had been realized. The women knew about her association with Baird, and she'd had to defend him with less than half a clip of ammunition. What they didn't know—that Baird harbored a strong desire for revenge against Vee—was better left unsaid.

Now that she'd met the enemy, and if not conquered then certainly held them off, it occurred to her that she had more to worry about. How long before Baird found out about her "gossip" tonight—especially with at least one of the town's women intending to reenter his life? How long before he surmised that she'd seen his bank statements? She couldn't have him believe she was just another chatterbox. She would have to tell him about this meeting of the Civic Club.

Dawnelle had called distant good-nights to the women, the moist evening had wrapped around her when an old emotion emerged that she recognized. Jealousy. She stopped abruptly two paces from the door of the Fiat. It was a sick emotion, damaging, but, "What about Lau Maki?" she demanded of the chill night. What place did she fill in Baird's life?

CHAPTER ELEVEN

"PERSONALLY, I never liked the old adage 'little girls should be seen and not heard.' Why so pensive, Dawnelle?"

She looked guiltily at Ben. She'd been having difficulty keeping her mind on his conversation, had even forgotten for the moment that he was her date for the fish fry, an event already under way across the parking lot.

They'd had dinner Wednesday, and after Ben's shock over her bruised chin had subsided, they'd enjoyed another evening of laughter and friendly banter. Ben, to her relief, hadn't pressed for physical closeness, not even today. Instead he remained charming, attentive and fun.

In Gatsby style, he wore tucked sand-tone trousers with a ribbed brown sweater tied over his shoulders. A beige dress shirt, the sleeves rolled up, complemented the thick hair falling over his forehead, which was wrinkled in worry.

Seeing him so freshly-scrubbed and utterly appealing in his concern, Dawnelle offered an apologetic smile. "Guess I was off somewhere for a minute, Ben. Sorry."

"Anything you want to discuss?"

"No, not really. Let's just let the sun shine and enjoy ourselves."

He nodded agreement. They walked through the collection of pickups and station wagons, their silence broken only by distant laughter. *You're good for me, Ben,* she thought, glancing apprehensively toward the crowded school yard across the parking lot. *Always positive, never demanding. If only Baird possessed more of your warmth and steadiness. I wouldn't feel so chewed up inside.*

The heel of her white sandal caught the sharp point of a pebble, and when she stumbled Ben's arm came around her waist. He momentarily crushed the wide kelly-green satin belt that matched the delicate trim of her hem and shoulder ruffles. The feminine off-the-shoulder detail lent a summery freshness to the snowy eyelet-cotton dress. Ben squeezed her affectionately, as if to let her know he approved the creamy expanse of skin visible from his taller vantage, and when he finally released her, he murmured, "Sure you don't want to let me carry some of your troubles?"

Again she frowned toward the fish-fry celebration, hoping the icy resentment she felt at Baird's silence this week would thaw in time to prevent her from making a fool of herself in front of Ben. Not a word from the man. At least Baird could have called to acknowledge her notes on Langston Marine! Gripping Ben's arm as if to anchor her emotions, she smiled vaguely at him, deciding in that moment to relate some of her angry feelings. Otherwise she might blow the lid off in the wrong company.

"I'm just a little perturbed about not hearing from that client I mentioned, Ben. He was under such pressure to initiate cash flow for his business, yet he hasn't called about the proposals I left him."

"It still bugs me that I didn't get to be the first client for your new business, you know," he chided, smiling. "I'll expect you to be the first passenger on my charter boat."

"Is that a promise?"

"You got it, my sweet. Nothing would give me more pleasure. About your other client—maybe he didn't make it back to town yet."

"I doubt that. He couldn't afford to stay away this long."

"Who is he? Do I know him?"

"Possibly. He's in the marine-studies field. Baird Langston."

Ben wrinkled his brow, thinking. "No, haven't met the guy. By the way, did you get a chance to ask the Caldwells if they located that contact you mentioned? What was the name—Maki? Lau Maki?"

She cringed inwardly, but forced enthusiasm. "They're working on it. Together they know every man, woman and child in the area. I'll bet you a dance tonight they come up with something."

"You're on! My, oh, my, that would make my day!" She smiled indulgently.

Covered walkways connected a horseshoe of low red buildings curving away from the dusty lot, each set of classrooms banked by a porch that faced a green quad. Through the entry companionway, Dawnelle could see the bright shapes of townsfolk and visitors, their laughter bubbling toward her even before she could identify anyone by sight.

Scanning the haphazard rows of vehicles as they left the lot, Dawnelle finally spotted Baird's beat-up blue

Ford. Her heart pounded dully. *Remember to stay calm.*

"I'm pretty angry at Baird for being rude," she said quickly, before they joined the melee. "If I get nasty, just step on my toe or something, will you? I really shouldn't insult my first client—not if I want to run a public-relations business right here in Trinidad."

"Be glad to keep you in line." He grinned. "But don't expect me to put up with some guy mouthing off to you."

She looked at her date. "No heroics, Ben. Baird and I have a way of getting under each other's skin that most people wouldn't understand. He's...a loner. Resents almost everyone."

"I've met the type." He eased her past a group of noisy youngsters hurling darts at a wall covered in red, yellow and blue balloons, then whispered in her ear, "Leave it to me, kiddo. I'm tact itself when it comes to calming rough water."

She hoped so. But to be on the safe side she began scanning the crowd. She grew convinced that if she saw Baird first she would have time to shield her heart from the sword-thrust of seeing him with another woman.

Worsteds, wools and cottons in simple designs clothed the folk crowded onto the green. Ready smiles deepened the lines of many weathered faces. Baked goods, crafts, cooking pots nestled on card tables beneath the porches facing the quad. Amid the chatter and laughter, the scents of fresh fish, hot donuts and coffee rose like mist from a newly turned spring garden.

Nearby, steam mushroomed from a blue-and-white enamel caldron each time a woman with a dusky complexion lifted the lid. Withdrawing a crusty Dungeness crab with her metal tongs, she set the crustacean on a paper plate and handed it to a lad in blue jeans. In another booth, a bearded young man wiped sweat from his brow, then raised a basket of golden fish fillets from a tank of sizzling oil. He tamped the wire cradle against the cooker before dumping the fish into a tray already heaped with the succulent chunks.

Dawnelle kept up her vigil for the towering figure in jeans and a pale stained jacket. She glimpsed the starched white uniforms of the Coast Guard in a corner spot, a coin-toss concession in another, but no Baird. At last, despite her inner turmoil, the frivolity of the day began to lift her spirits.

"Speaking of Sarah," she laughed now, pointing to a booth just inside the entrance. Wearing a paisley dress in rosy shades that matched her cheeks, Sarah stood behind two pushed-together tables. Beside her, Greer looked constricted in knit slacks and a white top bearing Zorro slashes of black. A white cardboard sign reading, Civic Club. Fish Fry Tickets hung on the wall behind them.

"Shall we?" Ben said, raising his voice over the noise. Dawnelle acquiesced, enjoying the rich texture of the scene.

They stepped into line behind a husky blond man who wore rubber boots with his tweed trousers tucked into the tops, as if even this party couldn't force him to abandon some link with the sea. A small sturdy child clung to his outstretched hand, her flaxen hair swaying below the bow at her waist.

"Swing me!" the child demanded in a high eager voice. "Swing me, daddy! Around and around!"

"Nej, nej." He shook his head, looking regretful. His voice lilted with a Swedish cadence. "Is enough, eh, *lillan*? We stop now before we hit somebody."

"Okay, daddy. But later we'll do it again. Please?"

"*Ja*, we will." The charming pair approached the ticket table. "Over there," Dawnelle heard the child answer her father's inaudible question. A chubby arm lifted, one short finger pointing toward the far left corner. "Near where those men are taking turns going swimming."

Dawnelle followed the child's gesture and got a good glimpse of Henny. Inside a wire-mesh cage that held the sign, Dunk your favorite Councilman—Courtesy of the Chamber of Commerce, Henny's sodden form balanced on a narrow board.

A wiry teenager stepped to the throwing line, then whipped a ball so hard it whistled over the hubbub of the courtyard, cracking smartly against the black bull's-eye. Gaping in surprise, Henny disappeared with a splash. Moments later he reappeared and climbed to the bench above the water tank, taking his place among a lineup of soggy, chuckling fellow councilmen.

"Henny get it again?" someone near Dawnelle asked.

She glanced up to see Sarah smirking out of the side of her mouth. "Yes," Dawnelle answered gaily. "Hi, Sarah. Greer. If you need me to stand in for you while you put Henny in the water, just say the word."

Greer counted out carnival tickets for the Swede while Sarah took his twenty-dollar bill and handed him change. "Already had a go at him and hit one of the spectators instead," Sarah replied with a chuckle. "Greer? You need a break?"

"Shh! Nine, ten, eleven. There you go, young man. Twelve tickets. No, Sarah, I'm fine. Besides, Dawnelle just got here, didn't you, girl?"

"Yes, but I told Ben I might be working with you a while."

"Ben?" said Sarah, running her gaze over Ben, coyly patting her gray curls. "The geologist?"

"I see my reputation precedes me," Ben remarked pleasantly.

Dawnelle quickly made the introductions. Sarah adjusted her glasses to get a better glimpse of Ben's features, then glanced at her booth companion. "I was thinking—that is, Greer and I were thinking, perhaps you'll speak before our Civic Club about those tests you conducted out on the Head?"

"Speak?" Stopping in midsentence, Ben slowly opened his wallet, bought several tickets, then folded it again. "You mean talk to your club?"

Sarah nodded. "About the tests. The girls are very interested in every aspect of the community. You could tell us all about the rock formations out there."

"Girls?"

"The members. I'm the president, and Greer's the vice-president. We'd love to have you. With so many in the audience, you'd stand a darn good chance of finding that fishing job you're looking for."

"Blackmail!" Ben reluctantly handed Sarah a white business card. "I suppose I can't refuse, since you put it that way. I haven't done much speaking, though. You'll tell the ladies to be gentle with me, I hope?" Dawnelle smothered a chuckle. "I suppose you think this is funny—" Ben accused her with pretended resentment.

"Meanwhile," interrupted Sarah, "I had a terrific idea and called someone about getting you set up with a boat. Been trying to get her into the club for years, and I thought maybe introducing the two of you might change her mind about joining us. She said she'd be willing to talk to you but doesn't think she can use you on her own boat."

"I've heard there's a woman in the fleet," Dawnelle said, feeling a tingle of apprehension. She would finally meet Lau. And see Baird with her, no doubt.

"She's been fishing for several years by herself, trying to teach her son the ropes," Sarah explained. "There's a tragic story behind her working the boat, I'll tell you."

"Better leave it untold," Greer admonished, folding her heavy arms over her bosom and sending Sarah a meaningful look. "That girl's suffered enough without you reminding folks of her loss."

"Appreciate this," Ben said to Sarah as Dawnelle looked over her shoulder, trying to glimpse the mantle of flowing black hair and Lau's beautiful face.

"Last time I saw her she was with that man Grace said Dawnelle ought not to call a friend, if you know who I mean," Greer said blithely, selling tickets to a woman standing behind Dawnelle and Ben. "Here you go, Jane—two dollars' worth. Better take double that amount, though. It takes seventy-five cents in tickets just to put Sarah's husband into the water tank."

Dawnelle stood frozen by the wooden table as the transaction took place, overcome by a rush of feelings and memories. Lau Maki. The only name she'd heard in connection with Baird's during the whole time she'd been in Trinidad.

Trying to imagine Lau being strong enough to spend her days raising ten- or twenty-pound salmon over the side rail of a troller, Dawnelle came up with an image of courage. The thought was sobering. She'd envisioned herself as a saint supporting Baird's lonely struggles, befriending a man who abhorred all personal ties except those he'd known in his youth, with men long buried in the loam of the Redwood Coast. Despite the emotional danger to her own life, she'd felt she couldn't desert him or his business, yet she was about to meet another woman who perhaps even more effectively rounded out Baird's solitary existence. After all, Lau Maki had known him for at least a few years.

"I've arranged for the care of Yurok and the specimens in the tanks," he'd written in his note last Monday. Lau? Supporting him in his struggle for revenge? Lau bringing him to a fiesta that celebrated her own livelihood? Dear God, she shouldn't allow this jealousy to warp her. But could she ignore the loving feelings she felt every time Baird held her, kissed her?

"Dawnelle?" Ben touched her elbow. "Sarah offered to take a break and help us look for the woman. She's found a replacement so she can get away for a few minutes." Sarah came around the edge of the table and slipped between Dawnelle and Ben, peering up at her future Civic Club speaker with a charming smile.

As they rounded each cluster of celebrants, Dawnelle's apprehension grew. Silent during the chatter between Ben and Sarah, she attempted to quiet her nerves with reasoned resolutions. She would *not* show her jealousy. She would speak calmly to him, as if it hadn't been the least bit difficult to get through the week without hearing from him. She wouldn't be angry that he hadn't called. She wouldn't hate the woman. She herself was a competent, busy, free woman with a handsome date, and now she was only disrupting Baird's privacy for Ben's sake. She wouldn't—

A pair of large bib overalls briefly caught her attention. The man who wore them lounged against a post several feet away, a smoking crab grasped between his pudgy hands.

She remembered those fat fingers. Jenkins had clutched Miss Mo's chain leash that day in Eureka, snarling when the dog cowered from him, jerking the chain with his puffy hand. He glanced at Dawnelle, and when their eyes met, he snapped the back of the crab, the sound like a rifle shot through the crowd. Steam rose around Jenkins's face, obscuring a vaguely threatening, leering grin.

A warning sounded deep in Dawnelle's brain but remained buried beneath her overpowering worry about Baird and Lau. Disgusted and unnerved, Dawnelle turned away from Jenkins. She'd stay clear of the beastly looking man.

Where were Baird and the woman? The search seemed unending. Would she lose her dignity? Say something stupid? Her feelings and behavior were so unpredictable around Baird. If he verbally put her down in front of Ben and Sarah, she'd...what? Embarrass herself by yelling at him? God, she hated these next few minutes already.

Suddenly he was there, at the edge of a picnic table twenty feet away, holding a beer while he laughed—laughed—with the beautiful dark-haired woman Dawnelle had seen at the post office. Beside her sat a slim boy of about fifteen who had the largest eyes Dawnelle had ever seen on a youth.

Baird was not the woodsman of past weeks, with his thick boots and heavy shirt. He had transformed himself into a man Dawnelle imagined she might encounter around the gaming tables of Monaco or Las Vegas. Beneath his coat, a white turtleneck sweater hugged his powerful neck, and it seemed as if someone had poured pale honey over his skin. His face lightly tanned and glowing with enjoyment, he gestured gracefully with his raised beer.

As Sarah exclaimed over the fact that she'd found the fisherwoman, Dawnelle studied Baird's mustard leather sports coat. *His shoes match it,* she realized absently, focusing on the rich dull glow of his coat. *Do not look at the woman!* It was a beautifully well-cut garment. His shoulders seemed molded in brass. Yes. Brass is cold and hard after the fires cool. Baird of brass. She must remain detached, uncaring, despite her feelings, her crumbling composure. As if to bolster her confidence, the wind came up, fluttering the supple panels of Baird's jacket, the faint flapping sound like a red cape to Dawnelle's quick rage.

Baird set down his beer and stood up, the abrupt movement drawing Dawnelle's gaze to his eyes. She remembered that assessing look, shivered slightly beneath its power. Would he know, just staring at her this way, that she was furious with him? Aware she had brainwashed herself into behaving calmly, she dipped into her reserve, slackened her tight jaw, shuttered the rage. He would not have the satisfaction of knowing he'd hurt her.

As Sarah moved toward the table, the youth rose and disappeared into the noisy crowd. Dawnelle took the opportunity to move close to Ben, yet something prevented her from communicating her turbulent feelings to her date. She glanced at him.

If it were possible to mirror Baird's intense expression, Ben was doing so at this moment. Evidently he was spellbound by the woman sitting with her fingers laced over the tabletop. Her own eyes were riveted on Ben. Brown black pools as lustrous as dark pearls conveyed a message of sexuality entirely natural and unknowing, Dawnelle grudgingly admitted. No wonder Baird spent time with this beauty. Her softness was not weakness but earthy warmth, her look one of honest interest rather than predatory hunger. Dawnelle could not hate her, she knew instinctively. She could only mourn the fact that so exquisite a creature held Baird.

Raising a hand to her mink-soft hair, the woman disturbed the tableau. Sarah greeted the woman and came to her side. But watching the two clasp hands, Dawnelle felt the pull of sorrow. Lau's fingernails were broken, the skin around the nails callused and marred by half-healed cuts. Ah, yes, the fisherwoman.

She wore a sleeveless sheath of navy blue cotton with a white lace collar that heightened the olive tones of her face, her curves revealed but not played up, her chiseled shoulders held back proudly so the fabric draped rather than molded.

During her brief appraisal, Dawnelle missed Sarah's introduction of Ben. Barely in time to avoid appearing rude, she smiled at Lau Maki and was rewarded by a faint smile in return and an offer to shake hands. She grasped Lau's hand firmly and felt the hard calluses, saw the ripple of toned muscle in her satiny forearm.

Then Lau was extending her hand to Ben. He took it eagerly, holding her fingers so long that Lau withdrew. She stood then, turning to Baird, and Dawnelle realized Lau was slightly shorter than her, perhaps five-seven.

Baird's mouth curved slightly as he watched Ben's reaction to Lau. *Strange,* Dawnelle thought. He seemed faintly amused that Ben found Lau attractive.

"This is Baird Langston," Lau said, her voice reminding Dawnelle of wind sighing over the decks of a yawl, modulated and melodic. She turned, her long black hair sweeping against the deep yellow leather jacket. "Baird, this is Sarah Caldwell."

Her mouth held stiffly, Sarah bobbed her head courteously. "We met once at the Grove years ago."

"Yes, I believe we did, Mrs. Caldwell. How is your husband? As busy as in former years?"

"Why, yes, Mr. Langston." Sarah smiled, warming a little toward him. "He's got the post office and his council work. He keeps up, thank you for asking."

From the corner of her eye, Dawnelle could see two women, heads together, gesturing toward her group. Grace stood on the right, again wearing spike heels and looking down her beak nose at Dawnelle and Sarah. Guessing at the comments being exchanged, Dawnelle nodded remotely and turned back to her companions.

"My best regards," Baird was saying. "Henny Caldwell is a very fine man."

"I shall." Sarah beamed, patting her curls. She coughed. "Of course, you know Dawnelle. . . ."

"Hello," Dawnelle greeted him, her anger curbed by the developments of the past few minutes. She could think of nothing else to say.

"Baird told me about your work," Lau began in that enviably soft voice. "You've been very valuable to him."

Wifely comment, Dawnelle thought. "Thank you," she said, "but unless we get moving I'm afraid we'll miss out on the orders Baird's expecting from the universities." She looked guardedly at him. "You did say the professors were already buying supplies for next year's classes?"

"Right. I was hoping we could find a few minutes today to catch up. I'm sorry I didn't get in touch before now."

"And I was hoping to talk with Lau about the fishing trade," Ben said, bestowing his most charming smile on Lau.

"I can't promise you anything, Mr. Fallon," she said. "My son and I have been managing over the years. He's big enough to bring most of the fish aboard now, so I can almost step back from that part of it, finally."

"Someone as lovely as you should get to step back from that harsh life whenever it suits her." Ben grinned. "And please, let's use first names. Forget the Fallon part. It's Ben."

"It's not the difficulty of the work that troubles me," Lau corrected him. She gazed beyond the townsfolk to a wedge of blue ocean visible between the buildings. "Even being out there, I'm defying the code of my people. According to Yurok custom, it is seven years' bad luck to those I love if I break the rules." She looked significantly at Ben. "And I have broken them."

Ben frowned. "I don't understand. What code?"

"In past years, the men of the village took their redwood canoes out past Trinidad Head, twenty-five miles offshore, to hunt sea lions. When they returned from the hunt, they cached their spears in a secret place on the Head, a crevice known only to the men. They did that for a reason. I've had to break ancient tradition, Ben—go on the water and hunt like the men of the old village. I'm the great-granddaughter of the last medicine woman of my people, and I've broken the rules."

"Why did they hide the spears?" asked Dawnelle, intrigued but skeptical about Lau's superstitions.

Without forfeiting pride, the lush brown eyes asked for understanding. "No worse luck could befall a man than to let a woman touch his hunting spear. A woman was not allowed to touch any implement a man used to provide food for his people."

"The women took care of the children and cooked meals?"

"And gathered seaweed. Dried it, dried the surf fish her husband netted and ground acorns into mash for toasted cakes. Baird lives above the beach where my family once did these things. But I've broken the code by teaching my son the skills his father would have taught him, had he lived through his last storm."

"But you had no choice," Dawnelle insisted. "You had to teach him to survive."

"There are those who say my husband's accident could have been prevented. I used to scoff at such things, but. . . ."

"What things, dear?" Sarah asked, drawing close to Lau's elbow.

"Spirits following a person through the woods, whistling at night outside the bedroom window of a child who ends up dying shortly thereafter, because his father broke the code, failed to repay a debt or something. Things like that. Perhaps my husband had a debt to pay for me. Or I for him. . . ."

"Hmm," Sarah said.

"Poppycock!" Baird touched Lau lightly on the arm, catching her attention. "You did nothing but go fishing with your husband, Lau. Couples, entire families do it all the time."

"But, Baird, I might have touched something I shouldn't. How can we ever know now that he is dead? They say my debt is not yet paid!"

Lau's dark eyes glittered when she saw Baird's curt dismissal of her words. Dawnelle and Ben looked at each other in wonder.

"There are those who say I'm bad luck," Lau continued quietly, gazing beyond Baird to the sky, following the path of a white gull. "That anyone connected with me may meet with misfortune. That my son—" She couldn't finish and seemed to change her line of thinking. She looked fiercely at Baird. "You have already met disaster, my old friend. I pray it is finished."

"Nonsense!" Sarah interjected. "Dawnelle says it was his partner's doing! It hasn't a thing to do with you, dear."

Baird's indrawn breath was enough to chill the blood in Dawnelle's veins. A red flush crept to her cheeks. Sarah and her big mouth!

"Well—" Sarah hastily stepped back, evidently realizing she'd embarrassed Dawnelle "—Greer will be needing me. Lau, I was hoping to talk to you about that graveyard project down in the Tsurai village, but I know you promised to meet with Ben just now. Keep in touch, won't you?" Sarah scurried off toward the ticket booth.

Ben looked strangely at Dawnelle, but he had the presence of mind to reserve his questions for later. "Good luck. I don't think I need to step on your toe," he whispered to her as he started toward Lau.

His expression controlled, Baird strode around the end of the table and took Dawnelle's elbow, his mustard jacket flashing dully in the sunlight. "I think we'll have that little discussion now," he said in a voice that brooked no argument. "Lau, I'll see you later. Ben." He nodded and urged Dawnelle away.

"I'm not a cow to be led around by the nose!" Dawnelle objected as they passed under a covered walkway, heading for a lone spruce some distance uphill from the buildings. "Ease up, will you?"

"And I'm not a bit of trash you can toss around the community, fodder for idle minds!"

"If I'd said bad things about you, Baird, I could understand your irritation. You'll notice, however, that Sarah practically blamed your ex-partner. That's a victory, believe me."

"Am I supposed to be moved?"

"You should be grateful, yes! Henny and Sarah have a lot of clout in town. They could do you some good."

They'd gained the shade of the spruce, and he snapped around to glare at her. "I won't tolerate being the subject of gossip! Leave me out of your local coffee klatches!"

"Just as you left me out of your tête-à-têtes with Lau?"

He didn't blink for a long measure. Then his lips curled in a slow smile. "Touché. One of these days I'm going to remember before I open my mouth that you are *not* Suzanne Langston. You are quite a different woman entirely, aren't you, Miss P.R. Director?"

His smile grew warm and disconcerting, and Dawnelle had to tell herself sharply that they still had a great deal to discuss. "I am not Suzanne, nor am I Lau or any other woman. Don't judge me or my actions by anyone else's standards."

"I understand, but you've made a slight error. Lau's standards are quite different from the charades Suzanne used to perform."

The pang of jealousy returned, and Dawnelle jutted her chin into the air. "Would you mind just one personal question, Baird?"

"Perhaps not."

"Are you in love with her?"

"Who?"

"Lau."

"Don't be ridiculous!" He turned away so abruptly she couldn't read the feelings written in his eyes. "Lau and I go way back. Before her husband. Before my wife. She stood by me through everything, even came to see me while I was locked up, which is more than my own brother managed. I owe her a great deal."

Why had he turned away? Because he couldn't admit to loving the beautiful Yurok woman who had remained loyal? Dawnelle forced a normal tone. "How did you meet her?"

"Meet her?" He faced her at last, his expression nostalgic. "It seems as if I've always known her. She's Pete's granddaughter."

"Pete from the Klamath River?"

He nodded. "When I was fourteen and had that accident in the river, Lau was seven. I met her when Pete took me to a brush dance—a kind of ritual meant to exorcize the evil spirits from a sick child—at a village up where the Klamath meets the Trinity River. Many of Pete's family were guests of the village that day, including Lau and her great-grandmother. It was a fine long affair. We stood above a pit with brush in it. Men circled around a child in this pit, dancing, singing their favorite songs, showing off masks and weapons and jewelry of great beauty. Meanwhile the medicine woman worked her healing over the child. Back then, the ceremony really meant something. Now...well, let's just say the tourists get a big kick out of it."

Dawnelle was thinking it would be difficult to replace a friendship steeped in so much tradition. Perhaps Pete had hoped Baird would marry his granddaughter. "What a rich past you've had," she whispered, awed.

"Yes...I've been lucky that way. The history and culture of the Yurok mean a great deal to me, though I do my best to dissuade Lau from that business about bad luck."

"I know what you mean. You think about it too

much, you're apt to bring on the bad luck when it had no intention of heading your way." She chuckled musingly. "I'd been wondering how you named your dog. Such an unusual name. But even after meeting Lau, I'm not sure I've figured it out."

"Actually, I wanted to name Yurok after the Indian Robert Spot, who trained in the ocean south of Luffenholtz before he joined the fighting during World War II. Yurok is a survivor like him. Proud and silent. Strong. But I wanted something a little more original than Spot for a large black shepherd."

"And Lau doesn't mind that you named your dog after her people?"

"Belanger's a French name, isn't it?" he asked, apparently inconsequentially.

"My father's family immigrated from France to Quebec, yes. I was born in northern Maine, where my mother and father farmed during the early years of their marriage."

He seemed pleased with this news. "You're from rural roots, then?"

"Definitely. Not the city slicker you thought, am I?"

"All right!" He laughed. "Do you think your father would be insulted if I named my dog French or Frenchie?"

She smiled. "I guess not."

"There you go. I feel I named Yurok well. Lau has never objected."

She tired of hearing Lau's name so reverently on his lips and shifted to gaze at the ocean, a skirt of blue furled beyond the bosom of the hill.

"Dawnelle...?"

Turning back, she saw, briefly, something of the highland chieftan in him as he stroked pensively at his beard. Proud, silent, strong. He'd described himself.

He guided her deeper into the green glade, then leaned on a prickly branch that angled past her shoulder on toward the sea. "I was out of the country until Thursday," he began, watching her carefully. "I was hoping to talk to you today about the promotion ideas you left me. They're excellent. One in particular appeals to me."

Dawnelle digested this information slowly, hiding her shock and worry while she calmly nodded her head. He'd been in Singapore! Trying to find Vee. What a fool. Chasing the outlaw when his business needed every available second of his time—and all the cash he could possibly lay his hands on.

Like Lau, she studied a point in the sky, then asked wryly, "They giving away plane tickets these days?"

"I didn't hear about it if they were. Why?"

"Oh. . .you've been under a tight budget lately. I thought maybe you had a friend on one of the airlines."

"No such luck, I'm afraid. My advance on the elk footage came in handy."

Shaking her head, she pulled loose needles from the spruce branch. The cost of an overseas ticket would have paid the entire bill on the promo package she planned to put together for him. Would the balance of his film contract be enough to get out the first mailing?

"Dawnelle, you look bothered." He glanced reprovingly at her. "I haven't been on vacation, if that's what you're thinking, seeing this tan of mine. Afraid I'm neglecting my other duties?"

"Actually, yes." Raising her brows, she let her irritation show. "Before this week, all you could do was hustle around collecting specimens, worried about when the ad campaign would hit the streets. Now I wonder how concerned you really are about your company."

"Oh, I'm concerned all right. I spent sixteen hours yesterday making the final selection of universities and writing that letter you recommended—the first phase of your program outline, I believe? I've sent the heads of appropriate departments a personal note telling them to expect more details by early August."

"Early August! That's barely enough time. There's artwork to be designed and type to be set—printing, packaging, the mailing labels to be typed. For that matter, we haven't even decided on an approach! A theme!"

"I looked over your ideas and—"

"From Singapore?" she said angrily, thinking he'd had time for the letters and Lau, but not a spare minute to call her. And then she realized what she'd admitted. He was looking sharply at her. She blushed.

"How did you know I was in Singapore?"

"I...well, I recall you said that...that your ex-partner was spending your money in Hong Kong and Singapore." Glancing at a tuft of weeds on the ground she tried to summon the gumption to tell him about the bank statements she'd found...and talked openly about. Yet their relationship was already so tentative. She mustered enough courage to face him again, and then, seeing his suspicious expression, could only stumble on. "That day on the cliff, remember? When you first mentioned your time in prison? You said Vee was having a high old time on your money or something."

He took hold of her arms, his fingers disconcertingly warm and insistent on her bare flesh. "Why do I get the feeling you know more than you're letting on?"

"You're a fool, Baird. You're wasting your time with revenge!"

"You've been prying!"

"All right!" Her eyes glinting like sunlight off a seething brook, she braced against his chest, her fingers curling into his soft white sweater. "Yes, I know about the investigation, and Singapore, and Vee. You could at least have cleaned up your desk for a change if you wanted to keep something like that secret!"

"You've pawed through my private papers!" He shook her slightly. "On what authority?"

"On the authority of having to work in that mess in your office—alone, I might remind you! Under your orders, I was trying to pull together something tangible on your business while you went off on a wild-goose chase to the Orient!"

"My mistake!" Setting her roughly aside, he dropped his hands from her arms. She rubbed them, watching his mouth curl in derision. "I should have guessed you were no different than the other women I've known!"

"Spare me the laundry list!"

"You're all so concerned with appearances!"

"Do you include Lau in that category?"

"No. She's a damn sight more understanding that any woman I've ever met. Most of you don't want your white gloves tainted with reality!"

"What reality? The only reality I know about is that

you could make Langston Marine a success if you reconsidered your priorities. Focused on the company instead of conducting your own personal manhunt!"

"You say 'Langston Marine' as if you owned the place." He leaned toward her face, his eyes cutting like blue blades. "I warn you, stick to your copy writing and leave the rest of my affairs to me!"

"Copy writing!" Insulted, she clasped her hands together to keep from slapping him. "By your own admission, I'm something more than a copy writer! I've spent millions of other people's money developing campaigns that made them ten times that amount. You'll not get that kind of talent by hiring someone who jams out ad copy for a living. You're paying for my brains and experience, Baird, and if you don't appreciate that fact, I'm wasting my time working for you!"

She drew a shaky breath, suddenly realizing she'd made her point. Tight-lipped, exasperated, he stepped close and searched her face. "Why do you make me so angry all the time?"

"Because you're always insulting me!"

"Look...." Tentatively he raised his hand to touch her, then changed his mind. "I hired a bright woman who knows her stuff, and I've counted myself lucky. Many times. I don't mean to insult you, nor do I intend to fight you. Just...let me run my life and my business."

"But that's my point, Baird. You've got to concentrate on the important things. Stop chasing Vee. Stop alienating the people who can help you get what you want."

"Come off it, Dawnelle. You knew from the start

women meddling in my business irked me more than anything. I'll try to stop putting you in the same category as Suzanne if you'll promise to stick to promotion."

"But I can't understand why you'd risk everything you care about to do God knows what to that criminal in Singapore!"

"He's got my money, Dawnelle, and if I can bring him to trial, the marine business will eventually be back where it was three years ago. Don't you see? Without investment capital it'll take years to get back on top. I've got to find him!"

This last sounded...desperate. It spoke volumes. She remembered, with a twinge of guilt in the knowledge, that he also received a healthy inheritance every month. Surely the trust fund would eventually pay off his debts with capital to spare? "It's more than the money," she stated flatly.

"What do you mean?"

"Something...else. There's some other reason behind this chase. What, I wonder?"

He sighed. "Don't you really see, Dawnelle?"

"I think I'm afraid to even guess."

He chuckled then, softly, and lifted a strand of her hair, letting it flow through his fingers. "Afraid?" he mocked gently. "When neither of us has anything invested?"

She caught her breath sharply. He was repeating the words she'd flung at him in the shed that day. Hearing them again made the lie a tenuous thread, a thread linking hearts afraid to speak other than what was *not* true between them.

"I know only that we can't build trust on lies," she admitted, pausing to let him grasp that she was retracting the lie, asking for his own honesty. "And that something deeper than the need for money drives your search for Vee."

"A man has his pride."

"Ah. Must revenge it, you mean."

"He's got to be stopped, Dawnelle."

Shuddering, she said softly, "Singapore was a dead end, wasn't it?"

"Unfortunately, the trail was cold. He'd disappeared. Just in time, I got the feeling."

"And if you do find him, what if it's too late? What if he's spent every cent?"

"No!" Abruptly Baird paced away to stand with the sunlight glinting off the waves in his hair. "He's too good with figures to be that dumb. Sure, he likes a good party, but he's a genius with money. He leaves shady deals behind him like bread crumbs, and that's what'll lead me to him. Besides, he'll always make more than he spends. That's why I took him into the business at the beginning."

"How'd you find a creep like him?"

"I didn't find him. He found me."

"He applied to you for a job?"

"Hardly any need for that," he said roughly. Moving back to the tree, he propped a hand against the gnarled branch, his wrist just grazing her bare shoulder.

"We were in Nam together. Best buddies. When he wasn't moving heavy artillery and leaping into the hottest frays in the jungle, Vee was running the most extensive black-market system in Southeast Asia. He went to Vietnam with the shirt on his back and came out with two million dollars in cash."

"Then why did you trust him?"

"You trust the men in your unit, that's all. And you know, you think you can reform someone you're close to." She smiled at the irony, but he was too engrossed to catch it.

"After the war I talked him into getting his high-school diploma. Then he went through Stanford's business program. With that kind of education, I thought his shady ways were buried in the past. I'd started Marine Exports during my last year in Monterey, and it was natural to bring him in when he graduated. After all, he was partly the product of my influence. He had a good head for finance, too. I was the front man, the one who went all over the world setting up shop and opening trade. What I didn't count on was his—" Baird looked at her with that bitterness she could easily recognize now "—his honesty."

"You mean his dishonesty, don't you?"

"No, I mean that one little spark of truth...." He turned to gaze over the brow of the hill, his eyes unfocused, his hand raised in a small gesture of futility. "We were split off from our unit once in a particularly nasty skirmish in Nam, working our way around behind a nest of Viet Cong. Vee intended to take them out. Just before we came up on them, I said to him, 'The boys are going to appreciate hell out of what we're doing for them. Their left flank is hanging out there looking damned vulnerable.' Vee looked at me kind of funny and said, 'Buddy, this isn't for the boys. On the other side of those Cong is K-rations, more ammo and a way out of this stink-hole. I never do nothing for nobody but number one. Remember that.' Trouble is, I forgot all about that little piece of honesty during the years we worked together."

Goose bumps rose on Dawnelle's bare shoulders and arms. "God, Baird, let him rot in his own lies. He will eventually, you know. They always do. Don't let him take you with him."

"I have no intention of going with him, Dawnelle." Suddenly his eyes were very bright as they scanned her face. "But I have every intention of helping the law put an end to his clever little games. Singapore officials are coming around, thinking of working with me."

"He might kill you!"

"He might try. Agreed, during the war I usually only carried a side arm along with my cameras. But I've spent years in the woods, hunted a great deal. Vee knows that. And I'm sure he knows where I've spent the past three years. Vee should count on the fact that I can handle myself."

"Do you hear yourself, Baird? Talking about guns? Talking about human beings as if they were lemmings? Let someone else stop Vee. What about Langston Marine?" *What about me,* she wanted to scream, her hands fisted with worry. *My feelings! I don't want to lose you....*

He was smiling a little sadly as he straightened and moved to her side. He slipped his arm casually around her shoulders, making her long to clutch him tightly, as if by sheer force of will she could protect him from his own vengeful folly. His next words killed the notion.

"I have two priorities in my life, Dawnelle: finding Vee and running Langston Marine. You keep to your side of the bargain, and we'll make a go of it. Trust me."

"But the money. How can you afford to pay that investigator, Cole, and still run the business?"

"Worried you might not get paid?"

"I don't need your money!" she snapped, hating to turn away his tentative warmth but vehement about changing his mind. Hands still fisted at her thighs, she studied the silver patterns of pitch oozing from the spruce. "I just don't want to put the best of myself into an operation that stands a good chance of failing."

"It won't fail," he argued, unconsciously tightening his arm, squeezing away her breath for an instant.

"Langston Marine can't exist without its founding father, Baird, and I can hardly carry on in the absence of a man who doesn't trust me!"

"I'm beginning to trust you."

"In a pig's eye!" Yet she felt a quick surge of relief. She turned to him. Her nostrils filled with his spicy scent, and she had to suppress a desire to caress his rugged features. "There's still the matter of money."

"I thought you weren't worried about that, green eyes."

"Not for me, Baird! It takes plenty of cash to support two habits—running a business and financing revenge. The two are at cross-purposes."

"You're testing my patience, Dawnelle." He removed his arm but did not walk away. "I've admitted I need you in the business. I've said I trust you. I've even capitulated about renaming the company. Leave it alone, for crying out loud! Enough is enough!''

Perhaps he was right. He could use some time to think about what she'd said. After all, she'd already influenced some of his decisions, hadn't she? More than she'd hoped. It hurt that he'd admitted needing her only for his company, but anything could happen in the future. For now....

She realized she had unconsciously adopted Ben's turn of phrase, and the thought sent an unexpected pang through her. There would be no future for her and Ben. She wouldn't settle for less than the excitement she felt at this moment, discussing business with Baird Langston, even arguing with him. Should Baird end up spending his life immersed in the Indian culture he loved, side by side with his exquisite Lau, she wouldn't settle for Ben. Because Ben couldn't spark fire in her soul, and fire was what she wanted. She wanted to *feel* each moment with her mate, as she did every second with Baird.

If she didn't marry in the next few years, she would adopt a child, build up the P.R. business, bring the child to work with her part of each day. That would be "settling" to some. But to her it would be a life of paradise compared to the living hell her parents had shared—that sparkless loveless marriage. It would be passionate love or nothing, she resolved, and smiled up at Baird.

"It's going to be Langston Marine, then?"

"Yes, Langston Marine. It takes a lot less time to say or write. You were right. The other name was stuffy. Satisfied?"

She nodded. "And you trust me?"

Silently he nodded.

"Thank you. . . ." She tipped onto her toes and planted a gentle kiss on his cheek. "Perhaps now we'll really get things done!"

CHAPTER TWELVE

HAVING SENT BAIRD back to the party, Dawnelle spent a few minutes speculating on her newly discovered needs in the romance department.

Baird had wind-carved features and a caster's way of turning her insides to molten metal, a smoking, hot-running fire that cooled when he so much as turned away from her. How easily found was the man who never for an instant let you forget you were a woman, a woman who erupted in anger or compassion or desire at his mere word? Did that kind of man turn up more than once in a lifetime? If not, Baird was a rare gem indeed, and she'd better find a way to deal with his volcanic nature...which hid, she suspected, his real feelings for *anyone*.

Turning away from the spruce, beginning to descend the hill toward the red school buildings, Dawnelle found her natural self-confidence resurfacing. Perhaps Baird wasn't romantically involved with the mother of that sloe-eyed youth at the picnic table. Lau had called Baird "my old friend." In fact, had there been even the slightest caress exchanged between the two? No, only words of respect and affection.

He'd denied loving Lau—angrily denied it, for some reason, that was true. If they were friends, that left lots of room for other relationships in his life, she speculated, her attention caught by the muffled shouts of men and children playing baseball at the far end of the school property.

When she turned toward the buildings again, she stopped. Though it was a blurred image, she saw a husky man staggering into a recessed doorway. Surely the school was closed this late in June. No parents streamed in and out of classrooms, viewing children's artwork or math papers. She was the only other person on this side of the grounds. Well, someone was probably trying to avoid the more crowded restrooms near the quad.

But as she neared the school, she saw no sign above the alcove indicating it was a restroom he'd entered. Anyway, those windows stretching along the wall suggested a classroom. Perhaps she ought to at least check to see if someone was breaking into the school. Or maybe he'd staggered slightly because he was ill.

Striding with purpose now, she cut across the lawn to a narrow concrete walk at the back of the structure, letting her heels scrape noisily as she drew near the shadowed entry.

"Looking for your lover boy?" said a slurred, high-pitched male voice. Even before fear could fully register, a hand snapped out and gripped her wrist, dragging her up against a soft protruding paunch.

Panic flew through her stiff body. She shrieked and began to twist, bruising the skin on her arm where thick fingers applied pressure. She glimpsed a bulbous nose, felt brief nausea when sour beery breath warmed her face. The stench of fish mingled with the beer, and the color drained from her face as she recognized him: the man in the bib overalls, the man who'd deliberately cracked the back of that crab while she watched. Jenkins! *Dear God,* she thought in the first seconds of her capture, *will anyone help me?*

"Your lover boy ain't around, so ya might as well give up the thought," the obese man whined, trying to hold her still while he clamped his damp hand over her mouth. "Been waitin' fer ya fer weeks! Purty li'l thang."

Terror sapped the strength from Dawnelle's limbs in the instant it took to realize this was the man who'd left the message on her recorder—the filthy man she'd bought Miss Mo from that day in Eureka! She moaned, suffocated by Jenkins's grip on her mouth. *Fight him! Must get free!* She forced her voice to squeal, the sound dragging over her vocal cords like sandpaper. Wrenching, doubling down, she loosened his grip. But he grappled, locked her throat with his heavy arm.

He chuckled, an awful wheezing sound full of lust and drunkenness. "Skin like cream! Cain't wait to have some of that purty throat."

"How did you find me?" she said hoarsely.

"You're famous, lighthouse lady. I read all about yer fancy past."

Pulling her roughly up against his stomach, her back to him, he rubbed moist lips over her shoulder. *Oh, Baird,* she cried in silent despair, willing him to come back to discuss one last forgotten detail. "Forget something?" The leering question haunted her as she fought against Jenkins's flabby embrace. *Hurt him!* She summoned strength, brought the heel of her pump down hard. The shock of solid concrete momentarily stunned the nerves in her leg.

Jenkins laughed grotesquely and spread his legs. "No ya don't, pumpkin. Just makin' me crazy for ya with tricks like that. Whyn't you come along with me and we'll have us a time right in here! Got the place all ready fer ya." He grunted with the effort of dragging her up against the boards near the door.

Mustn't let him get me into that classroom! Never get free until it's too late!

Jenkins had to loosen his choke-hold in order to pry open the door, and when he did, Dawnelle jabbed sharply with her elbow. Musty breath blew against her turned face as Jenkins took the impact in his ample middle.

"Now, ya didn't fight *him* like this! Ain't gonna shingle ol' Pauly outta what's due him! Hold still now!"

When he slammed his arm against her shoulders, pinning her to rough siding, she screamed again, praying even the tiny wheeze she made would reach around the red building into that bright raucous group on the green. She was beginning to tire, and Jenkins was opening the door! Raggedly summoning strength, Dawnelle yanked herself hard, until she felt his fingers loosen from her face. Instantly she scrambled out of the shadows, panting, groping with shaking fingers along the wall.

"I'll have ya!" he squealed. "I'll have ya yet!"

"Filthy—animal! You won't!"

Run! Her breath whined as she stumbled along the sidewalk toward the corner. She heard Jenkins panting behind her.

"Someone!" she cried. "He's—auw-w-w!" Fingernails bit into her arm. Then the lacy ruffle of her dress drew taut across her chest, effectively checking her flight. She stumbled back. When Jenkins awkwardly pawed her breasts she screamed again. Her anguished cry seemed to mingle with the laughter of three hundred others.

His laugh was a whinny of success. Drawing her against him, he said, "Damn, I'll have ya now!"

"I'll kill you first!" With tremendous effort, she pulled against the fabric that bound her. It tore away, hanging shredded and loose over her shoulder, and she fled again. *Nearly to the corner! Legs rubbery. Got to keep running.*

"Aw, please, pumpkin! We'll trade. Listen—listen, I've got something you want. Listen—WAIT!"

Suddenly Dawnelle knew she'd won. Jenkins wouldn't follow her into the crowded quad. He was whining like a child, warning her about "next time," but she'd won; she was heading for help. Baird! She'd find Baird and ask him to hold Jenkins until the police could take him away.

There was satisfaction in the thought as she rounded the corner—and ran hard into Ben.

"Dawnelle, Baird said you were— My God! What—"

"Ben! Ben, it's him! Help me. Oh, God, he tried to—it's. . . ." Her cheeks were wet. She was blubbering and pointing behind her and huddling into Ben's arms, grateful someone had come, wishing it were Baird, crumbling with the shock of Jenkins touching her.

She was thrust aside with Ben's enraged, "What

man? Dawnelle, who did this to you? Where is he?"

"There," she whispered huskily, jerking her head to indicate the doorway behind her. Realizing Ben was stunned, that he was staring in confusion, she glanced back. The concrete path glittered mockingly in the sun. Jenkins had disappeared.

"WHAT I DON'T UNDERSTAND," Ben said from the corner of the lighthouse, where he and Dawnelle were discussing the events of the afternoon, "is how that swine got up enough nerve to approach the sheriff and accuse you of stealing his dog!"

"I think he had no choice, Ben. He knew I'd lodge an assault complaint against him. I guess he figured if he went to the sheriff and explained that he'd 'politely' tried to demand his animal—that I'd provoked him to the point where he had to defend himself against me—logically the authorities would have to side with him. Psychologically, at least. If I'd found the sheriff first, the opposite would have been the case."

"Your word against his."

"Exactly."

"I still think you should have pressed charges." He came away from the lighthouse to stand on the ledge above the water, his gaze trained on the swells rolling into the cliff. "I have a bad feeling about it, Dawnelle. The things he said to you.... I feel helpless to prevent some—something terribly unpleasant."

She came to him, fighting a momentary sense of vertigo as she glanced down over the rock shelf. "Don't you see? Jenkins has made his accusations, I've made mine. Plus I've sworn I bought Miss Mo for twenty dollars out front of that grocery store in Eureka, and he claims I stole her. Neither of us has eyewitnesses to refute the other's allegations, but Jenkins can't afford to prove my complaint valid by attacking me again. He just wouldn't be that stupid."

"I hope you're right. But what about the dog?" Ben turned and watched as the animal skirted the bluff above the beacon, winding through the bushes in search of small animals and native scents. "Don't you think he'll pay the few bucks it would cost to take you to court? Get her back from you just to get even? He claims she's worth more than six hundred dollars."

Huddling into the red cardigan she'd donned after her recent bath, she shook her head, then recalled the ugly scene Jenkins had staged in the parking lot of the elementary school. She'd been pulling another sweater around her shoulders then, covering the gaping bodice of her dress with Ben's brown pullover while she fought down panic at seeing Jenkins again. He was whining to the grizzled lawman about her illegal deeds.

"But he attacked me, sheriff!" she protested shakily.

"There," whimpered Jenkins. "Didn't I tell you she threatened to blacken my reputation? I'm the wronged party, I tell you!"

But after careful questioning during an interview conducted only a few yards away between the sheriff and Dawnelle, the constable had explained the futility of pressing charges. "We might nail him for breaking into the school," he said, "but not much chance of pinning this assault on him, despite the fact that I believe you. You didn't scratch him, so we'd get no evidence with fingernail scrapings. Your dress is torn, but you're not roughed up. No witnesses. It would be nothing more than a mud-slinging match in court, Miss Belanger. I'm afraid your personal life would be scrutinized with a spyglass, even though such evidence would probably be ruled irrelevant and thrown out of court. Naturally everyone in town here would be, er, uncomfortable about the media coverage."

She'd thought about his advice, and about Sarah and Greer and the Señorita de la Luz name they'd given her, and turned away.

She turned to Ben now and said, "If it came to fighting Jenkins over legal ownership of the dog, I could post an advertisement in the Eureka newspaper—ask people who'd shopped at the store that day to step forward as witnesses. Interview the grocery-store personnel, build a case. It wouldn't be impossible finding witnesses to testify that Jenkins was trying to sell Miss Mo the day I bought her. But something tells me Jenkins is going to let this drop—which is exactly what I want us to do, Ben Fallon. The sheriff kicked him out of town for the duration of the fish fry, and there's an end to it. I'm sick of the subject of that filthy creep!"

"I don't blame you," Ben said, his smooth brow furrowed. "There are certainly better things to discuss. You sure you're feeling up to that dance tonight? We could skip it."

"And keep you from wooing that lovely Maki woman you met today?" She smiled. "I wouldn't want such a black deed on my conscience."

"Wooing her?" Ben dropped an arm around Dawnelle's waist and led her away from the drop-off, toward the boardwalk. "Who said I was *that* interested in Lau

Maki? I just want to talk her into letting me crew on her boat on weekends, that's all."

She gave him a skeptical look. "Liar."

"She is gorgeous, isn't she?"

"Mighty."

"And bright, too." Ben guided Dawnelle up the walk and into the living room. In the hallway, he paused. "Did I tell you she's read everything Shakespeare ever wrote?"

"That so? Seems to me you quoted some of his lines that first day I met you. Misquoted, I should say."

"Mmm. . . . He's the only writer I really got interested in during those Lit classes of my younger days. I wouldn't mind reading a few of his plays again, you know?"

"In that case, will you excuse me?" Dawnelle went into the dining room. A single shelf above the wooden sideboard contained a variety of old books. Pulling out a red volume, she returned to Ben, handed it to him. "Take your time. If Lau is an expert, perhaps she'd like to discuss interpretations with you. I like Shakespeare, but I prefer modern authors."

She wondered if she and Baird would ever set aside conflict long enough just to chat like friends about books, films, music.

"Dawnelle?"

"Mmm?" She turned.

Ben gazed at her with something like longing and concern. "You should have someone looking after you, you know that?"

"I'm not the helpless type, Ben."

"No, not helpless." Setting the book on the back of

the couch, he came to her and trailed an index finger delicately along her cheek. "You're very special to me, Dawnelle. If anything were to happen to you, I'd never forgive myself."

She placed her palm over his hand and held it tightly to her face, emotion rising in her throat. Despite her denial of helplessness, she felt vulnerable. And a little guilty for wishing fervently that it was Baird telling her how special she was.

She shook her head, her eyes revealing how grateful she was that he cared. "You're a truly rare man, Ben," she said gently. "I love your warmth, your sense of humor, your caring. But fate—or perhaps I should more rightly call it God—has a way of dictating things and though we fight our destiny, we're really powerless to turn aside what's meant to be. When it's right for me to have a mate to share my life with, he'll be there. I'll wait."

"Are you in love?"

"I'm not sure." She paused. "What about you? I saw the way you stared holes through Lau today."

He grinned, his playful mood returning. "If you'd stuck around instead of getting yourself dragged off to Langston's cave, you'd have seen me having a devil of a time trying to discuss business with her. I kept getting sidetracked by those gleaming arms and all-knowing eyes. Unfortunately, I think she considers me an overgrown sophomore."

"You're just being humble. But be careful, Ben," Dawnelle warned, wanting to save him misery. "Lau and Baird have known each other for years."

"I know. I was wondering how serious they are."

"That's something we'd both like to know."

Ben's eyes widened in surprise. "You've got to be kidding! Why do I get the feeling the four of us are acting out one of Neil Simon's screenplays?"

"Try a few centuries before Simon, Ben. Everyone knows history repeats itself."

Ben simply stood still, shaking his head.

The tight sensation in Dawnelle's chest had eased. Smiling, she backed a half step away. "Tell you what," she said. "Before I change for the dance, I'm going to make a sandwich and a cup of tea. Would you like something to eat?"

"Sure. Both of us missed out on the goodies at the fish fry. But I just can't get over it. Lau and him and me. . .and you!"

During their meal Ben and Dawnelle developed a pact, unspoken though it was. They would both be testing the fabric of Baird's relationship with Lau.

She left Ben happily thumbing through Shakespeare's writings while Beethoven's "Allegro con Brio" resounded through the small living room. She smiled privately about the record she'd selected—the composer's tribute to the great human struggle was a natural complement to Shakespeare's passionate portrayals. Congratulating herself on clever staging, she went through the hall to climb the stairs.

Tonight, she resolved, entering her bedroom—tonight she'd just see what defences of Baird's she could tear down. If he and Lau were lovers, or in love, the romantic atmosphere of the dance would be one of the best places to see such ties revealed. And the fact that she worked for Baird almost certainly guaranteed she would be dancing with him at some point in the evening She planned to make the most of that encounter.

A ripple of anticipation tickled her spine as she opened the door of her closet to pull out her most seductive dinner dress.

CHAPTER THIRTEEN

SET INTO A LOW HILL, Trinidad's town hall loomed over the street, its peaked roof crisply backlit by a yellow moon. The double doors were thrown open, bathing the porch in lantern light. Drums and guitars thrummed to the rhythmic shuffle of shoe leather on pine flooring.

Ben eased Dawnelle up three steps between teens lounging on handrails and a young couple wrapped in a loose embrace. As they approached the entrance, he slipped an arm protectively around Dawnelle's waist.

"Hi, Ben," said one of the slim young men on their right.

Ben craned to see a jeans-clad figure. "Casey! How come you're not dancing, man?"

"Aw...." The boy glanced toward the shadows bobbing in the internal glow, and Dawnelle saw his chiseled profile, recognized his luminous eyes. Lau's son turned a teasing smile on Ben. "I don't know. Just here to keep an eye on my mom."

"What, no music in your blood tonight?"

"Naw. Plenty of wild stuff going on in there as it is. Somebody's gotta keep a clear head."

"You'd make a heck of a bouncer, Casey. Want me to check on your mom while I'm inside?"

Casey studied Ben for a moment, assessing him silently, his gaze straying shyly over Dawnelle's plunging neckline of black silk. Suddenly, as if she and Ben had passed some kind of test, he grinned. "Yeah, sure, Ben. I'm always bugging her to get out and have some fun, but she usually ignores my good advice. Maybe if you tell her, it'll sink in."

"Will do, Casey. You have fun, too."

It was normal for teens to think parents were stodgy, Dawnelle thought. But something about the way Casey spoke made the light comments ring as a plea. A brief sense of disquiet settled into place beside her other impressions of Lau as Ben nudged Dawnelle and ushered her into the din.

"Before you've charmed the entire Trinidad fleet with that curvaceous figure and those jade-green eyes," Ben teased, his breath disturbing the tendrils feathering down from Dawnelle's chignon, "dance with me."

He brought her into his arms as a slow beat began to pound through the wooden cavern. Gazing at the perimeter tables, where candles cast a red glow over couples as they smoked and laughed and drank, Dawnelle automatically sought Baird's impressive form. She recognized several women from the Civic Club—even spotted Grace in an ice-blue dress, chatting with a male companion who seemed awestruck by the woman's height. She didn't see Baird on this side of the room. She began to long for a glimpse of him even if it meant seeing him with Lau.

Ben stumbled at that moment. Catching her waist with both hands, he mumbled an apology and glanced over her head. *Lau* she wondered, turning slightly. Her heart contracted.

Wearing the navy blue sheath, her hair swaying against Baird's leather sleeve, Lau danced as serenely as a summer tide eddying against a bastion of rock. Baird, looking like a well-dressed giant in the leather jacket and pale antique gold dress slacks, held her close, apparently enjoying the way Lau rested her cheek against his chest. The image made every muscle in Dawnelle's face draw tight. She'd expected to deal with jealousy at seeing the two together again. Yet in spite of the pep talk she'd given herself, her heart did its own strange dance, as erratic as a poorly executed samba.

Ben whirled her once, then settled into a comfortable rocking step that put Dawnelle in full view of the man she'd been watching. This time, Baird was looking at her. He turned his partner so the back of Lau's long hair swayed in full view, while he simply stared. Their souls seemed to lock for a long delicious moment.

She'd planned to stun him with her image tonight, but she was surprised to see him so evidently captivated. Fighting the urge to check her dress for spills or white threads, she sent him a brilliant smile. He answered with a sardonic one of his own, and his gaze lingered. The look made her wish all the more for that moment when he would hold her as he held Lau, but she purposely glanced away.

Perhaps undergoing his own form of envy, Ben sighed and gathered her closer. She glanced at his face. He was frowning slightly. "Am I being as obvious as you?" she chided softly.

"You're right. I've never been the subtle type. How do you manage to look so self-contained and unneedy?"

"Lots of practice." She smiled ruefully at him. "Stringently enforced pretense, Ben designed for self-protection."

Abruptly he whirled her among other couples until Baird and Lau were no longer visible. "I just wouldn't tolerate his hurting you," Ben said with tenderness. "No matter what happens in our respective personal lives, Dawnelle, I'll always feel protective toward you."

Ben had a talent for piercing her heart with unexpected arrows. Had she got a brother back after all the years of loss? She leaned back to study the smooth planes of his face, the shelf of sandy hair so natural and appealing over his brow. No, she decided, meeting his gray blue eyes and letting his compassion wash through her. No—not exactly a replacement for Tommy. She could love Ben in a different way—not with the passion she felt for Baird, but with a kind of undying steadiness.

She smiled and tapped him on the shoulder with her black evening bag. "Ben, I haven't had a deep friendship with a man for years, other than the long-distance relationship I share with my father. I want our friendship, yours and mine. It makes me very happy to hear you say you care."

He studied her speculatively, his eyes narrowed. "You know, beautiful, Langston is going to have a helluva woman when you two quit fencing." She raised one skeptical brow. "I'm serious. As soon as he finds out how you feel about him, it'll be all over but the final vows. Send me an invite, will you?"

She laughed. "I don't admit to being in love with him, Ben. Not entirely. . . yet."

"Irrelevant, my dear Watson. The Fates have decreed that you two get together. I know these things," he pronounced with certainty. "But I'll tell you—" he winked "—dressed as you are tonight, looking all remote and very much like a temporarily retired young volcano. . . if we hadn't had that little chat earlier today, we might have gone on forever trying to make pudding out of hazelnuts."

To that she would not reply. She, too, had once considered more than friendship with Ben.

His chuckles fading away, he rested his cheek against her hair, evidently pondering his theory. "Lau and Baird took the matter out of our hands," she finally murmured against his brown sweater. He didn't answer. She fell silent. The band blended the last note of the song into another slow dance featuring the saxophone, and they continued making small turns in a relatively unpopulated spot.

Temporarily retired volcano. Maybe the image fit. The black dress stressed the ivory of her skin. She possessed a lanky grace and had underscored this spare look by pulling up her hair. The only softness she'd permitted herself were the tendrils feathering around her nape and ears, the hint of an exotic fragrance.

No matter how close she felt to nature, no matter how much she enjoyed tramping through rivers and tide flats, a part of her would always long for the stimulating life of a successful career woman. Not as a steady diet, perhaps. But discussions with people clever enough to earn fortunes would always lure her. She had tasted that life for four years—five if she considered the commercial work she'd conducted in college—and had grown comfortable there. This black silk put her back in that league.

She was merely biding her time until she could build a business that connected with many other businesses, many other lives. She would be influencing the incomes of countless people, and the brainpower she expended to help these clients would eventually push her own income into an increasingly higher range. Significantly, after less than half a year away from the world of money and business, she had devised a scheme that would return her, at least occasionally, to that world she'd escaped.

Inadvertently reminded of her very first client in Trinidad, she let her thoughts drift to a more visceral plane. She lacked facts in trying to decide what bond existed between Lau and Baird. The only thing Dawnelle knew for certain was that the sexual tension between herself and Baird was as alive and healthy as it had ever been. He'd displayed a lingering intensity in his gaze that she'd very carefully planned to provoke.

Not all men appreciated—nor could they handle—the "ice maiden" she was tonight, minus the typical blond hair, of course. It was the look most challenging to the arrogant executives she'd encountered at chic city gatherings. Instinctively she knew Baird would be drawn to her precisely because he so vehemently protested against such high-powered style in a woman. She'd simply turned up the volume, so to speak, on a part of herself normally camouflaged by faded jeans and bulky sweaters. The reality was that both men and women played many roles in courtship, and this role, though she'd never consciously practiced it before, suited her perfectly. Subconsciously, she'd also known that Lau, with all her earthy beauty, would be incapable of achieving the look.

But, Dawnelle cautioned herself, settling comfortably against Ben's warm chest, she must be careful not to read more into Baird's attraction than was actually there. Lighting the match would not launch the rocket. There remained the task of getting the flame to the fuse. Even if she and Baird were attracted, a great crevice still gaped in her plan: on one side, the knowledge that he wanted her: on the other, beckoning like an oasis, the dream of sharing his life.

The thought startled her. Was she even ready to handle a relationship again? Had she healed enough to be strong through the tough moments? She didn't know. She only knew she wanted him, and that she was still vulnerable. She also knew it would take two to provide the explosion to close the gap. Baird must make the next move.

A muscular back edged into Dawnelle's peripheral vision, making her wonder how long she'd been daydreaming. She watched the man's pogo-stick dance style. He ought to stick to fishing, she chuckled silently, finally recognizing the Swede from the fish-fry celebration. Bobbing his head, he whirled rather abruptly, and Dawnelle barely had time to recognize Lau in his arms, her sleek midnight hair flying close to his curly blond mane.

Then Ben spun her through a set of clever steps that ended with her staring straight at a most surprising sight. Baird was dancing with Genia Forester! Of all the wonderful events. It seemed he was capable of making inroads toward acceptance by the locals. Genia would never have been brave enough to ask Baird to dance. Likely for old times' sake, he'd approached her. Dawnelle wondered if the gruff-voiced, stocky woman was asking him about his pipes or about cleaning his home.

Please say yes, she pleaded silently, watching Baird bend solicitously over the upturned pleasant face. Nodding, he chuckled in delight at something Genia said. Again he seemed the international playboy, the man in leather and cashmere who would bend as gracefully over a dice table as over a smiling woman. The subdued light played over his gold coat, lionized him, making him seem the wealthy world traveler of former years. Feeling a quick jolt of jealousy at the evident warmth he bestowed on Genia, Dawnelle reminded herself of the dance she knew would be hers some time during the evening. Her skin tingled at the thought.

"You're gawking, Dawnelle," Ben murmured, rocking into a position that eased the strain on her neck. "It seems we both need to learn a little subtlety." He whirled her a half turn. "Take note of that raving beauty."

"Lau?"

"Uh-huh. You'd think she was having the time of her life with that guy."

"But, Ben," she teased, "they have so much in common—fishing, children."

"You're detestable!"

"What, my halo's slipping so soon in our relationship, dear?" He spun her through five fast turns that stole her breath away. When the music ended, the scenery had changed considerably. She found herself leaning against a table draped in white linen.

"Red, white or beer, honey?" asked a sultry voice behind her.

Startled, Dawnelle whipped around. Ben laughed.

A thick-set redhead plopped two plastic cups on the makeshift bar, then glanced down at Ben. "One more turn, Fred Astaire, and you would've lost me my job. What'll you two have?"

Dawnelle chuckled. "A white wine, please. Lots of ice."

Several other boisterous dancers crowded behind them. Ben had to repeat his order. The redhead poured Dawnelle's wine, then handed Ben a dark bottle of beer. "Want a glass for it?" Ben shook his head and led Dawnelle through the tangle of thirsty dancers.

In moments they stood talking with Sarah and Henny, who sat in the midst of a large group sharing three tables clustered together. Greer introduced her husband; Dawnelle introduced Ben.

Scouting neighboring tables for two extra chairs, Henny said, "Why don't you join us?" Even while he was speaking, Dawnelle felt a slight tension invade the group. A few heads turned; grins faded slightly. Dawnelle followed Henny's stare behind her and saw Genia Forester, her eyes sparkling up at her recent partner. She held a fresh drink in her hand.

Baird's blue eyes gleamed as he inventoried the group. "It's not quite so crowded at my table," he said to Ben. Transferring the magnetic look to Dawnelle, he challenged her softly, "You're both welcome to join us across the hall." Turning, he handed Genia into the only vacant chair.

"It was wonderful," Genia said in her shy gruff voice. "And thank you for the drink."

"The pleasure was mine, Eugenia. I'll let you know about that project you mentioned. John." He nodded to a graying man, Genia's husband, who gestured with his dark pipe. "Henny, good to see you gain. Sarah." Baird turned quizzically to Ben.

Dawnelle and her date looked at each other, a silent agreement passing between them. "Sure." Ben waved, smiling at the entire group. "We'll see all of you again through the evening. Dawnelle?" Never one to pass up an opportunity for chivalry, Ben offered his arm. Though she strolled casually enough at his side, her right shoulder burned from Baird's brief guiding touch. He pointed to a distant table.

The band had deserted the stage for another twenty-minute break, so they crossed the wood floor without difficulty. Yet Dawnelle felt tension begin to twist inside her. It was never easy carrying out her plans where Baird was concerned. Now that he'd made a move, she faced the difficulty of watching Lau and Baird at close range. She wondered if it would be possible to witness an exchange of intimacies between the two without leaping up from the table in agitation.

When they arrived at the table, Lau rose excitedly and wrapped her arms around Baird. Dawnelle's heart skittered. Before everyone, Lau drew his head down and kissed him resoundingly on the lips. Chuckling softly, Baird brought her head to his chest and held her tight. He whispered something in low tones. Lau turned her sculpted face up to his and nodded.

"I'm so glad you talked me into coming here tonight," she said, her happiness palpable. "You were right. I needed to get out and have some fun."

So Baird hadn't been "talked into" bringing Lau to the dance—quite the other way around. The old insecurities settled heavily on Dawnelle's spirits.

Patting her sleek hair, an exquisitely feminine gesture, Lau stepped away from Baird. She turned. "Ben!" She seemed equally excited about seeing him, and Dawnelle could only shake her head in confusion at the woman's mood. "Good to see you again, Ben! And Dawnelle. Come join us."

When the shuffling was complete, Dawnelle was seated opposite Lau, with Baird between them, Ben on her right.

"You were wearing white earlier today," Baird remarked casually, raising a glass of pale liquid to his lips as he looked at Dawnelle's sweetheart neckline with more than casual interest.

Taken by surprise, Dawnelle hesitated over her reply, settling her black purse on the crowded table. "I was wearing white, yes." She sipped her wine.

"Spill something on it, did you?"

"What?"

"You left the fish fry early. I thought perhaps you'd ruined your dress."

A rehash of the incident would be embarrassing, painful. Until now she'd managed to block it out of her mind. She glanced at Ben, but he and Lau were already discussing diesel engines and the hull construction of fishing boats. Studying the nearby tables, she lowered her voice. "You're perceptive, Baird. I did."

"Did what?"

"Ruin my dress."

"How?"

"I tore it."

"Pity. You looked springtime fresh in white. You look predatory in black."

Meeting his bold stare, she smiled sardonically. "Thank you. Let me return the compliment. I'm so used to seeing you looking more...comfortable."

"Actually, I've very happy to take advantage of the opportunity to dress, as you say, comfortably. Soon enough I'll be back to the suit-and-tie routine full-time." She nodded supportively. He was counting on making it big again.

"So how did you ruin that dress? I was hoping to see more of it tonight during our first dance."

Anticipation rippled down her spine again, but the sensation was spoiled by his insistence on knowing about the white dress. Perhaps he'd guessed she was being evasive and was pressing the issue out of curiosity. Perhaps he was subconsciously fighting the sexual challenge her black dress signified. She took another drink. "I was attacked," she replied quietly, wishing Ben weren't so engrossed in Lau's description of her Canadian-style troller.

Baird leaned toward her, the flickering candle highlighting red glints in his beard. "Dawnelle, what did you say?"

The band launched into a slow number that began with a seductive note from the sax player, and she used the interruption to turn away. Thinking to freshen her makeup, she put her drink down, started to her feet. Baird's hand stayed her.

Ben was already rising to lead Lau to the dance floor, so didn't see Dawnelle's wistful look in his direction.

Baird now stood and circled Dawnelle's waist with his arm. "Perhaps we'll have more privacy on the floor," he suggested, his words an intimate rumble in her ear. "Will you dance?"

She nodded. Her special moment with Baird had arrived, but her head was suddenly filled with the ugly memory of Jenkins's hands on her flesh, his lips on her shoulder in a burlesque kiss. She shivered as Baird slid her into position and took the first step.

"Cold?" he murmured. "Or have you begun to resent my touch?"

"No! No, it's not that."

His male body enveloped her as he swept her in graceful turns, swept away the ugliness. This was the feeling she'd missed, imagined. Baird's spicy scent filled her with other memories as he held her against taut, well-defined muscles sheathed in fine wool and leather.

She remembered tasting the slightly salty smoothness of his skin that day in the work shed, remembered wanting more of him then—and later—in that secluded bed of nature crushed by the elk. The images played through her mind, dissolving the ice-maiden facade she'd created in order to attract him. She might have no more of him than this moment once she discovered how he felt about Lau.

He held her close in the masterful style she'd always admired in a dance partner, his leading hand held out gracefully, his guiding hand pressing her breasts and stomach firmly to his body so she could feel every movement. Because his right arm came around her in the classic embrace, his jacket had fallen away. As she relaxed against him, white kittenlike cashmere cushioned her breasts and caressed the side of her face. She felt the pull of his bunching chest muscles when he steadied her through a fast turn.

Curling her hand around his neck, she slid her fingertips into the velvety hair at his nape. The waves wrapped around her fingers like a pelt, and the rich silkiness made something clutch and churn deep inside her. In the semidark, surrounded by laughing murmuring dancers intent on their own pleasures, the flame of desire spread quickly through her. Closing her eyes, she moved with him, quietly overjoyed that he danced superbly.

"Now who's not expressing herself?" chided Baird softly. "What happened to your dress, my lovely green eyes?"

A hot sticky tension held her against him, the kind of half awareness one experiences after a long nap in a warm room. Her concentration had clouded. With effort, she pulled away from his chest and said, "Don't you like the one I'm wearing? You're so concerned about that white one."

"You misunderstand. You make me want to break all my firm resolutions about you, seeing this low-cut black number with the slithering skirt. But I'm curious about the other one. My mind's playing tricks. I thought, back at the table, you said you'd been attacked. I was hearing things, right?"

Reluctantly she shook her head.

He stopped, and she felt other dancers nudge them.

Baird stared gravely at her. "Exactly what happened to you today?"

"I had a run-in with someone. It's over, Baird. I want to forget him."

"Your ex-boss?"

Again she shook her head. "A man named Jenkins."

"What kind of run-in?"

She was safe here, held within his arms, embraced by a man she dreamed of loving. She felt no need for hysterics, and no need for bad memories to turn this moment into one of high drama. "I've already talked to the sheriff about it, Baird. Since there were no witnesses, neither of us has a case."

"What do you mean 'neither' of you?" His eyes glittered dangerously. "What kind of run-in, Dawnelle?" She explained briefly about Miss Mo's registration papers.

"How did he happen to ruin your dress?"

"It was ripped while he was trying to—" She studied the collar of his jacket, then said in a desolate voice, "Rape me."

Suddenly she was brought up hard against his chest. He squeezed her so tightly, her breath escaped in a whoosh. Wincing at the pressure against the lower back muscles she'd thought entirely healed, she protested.

"Your back—I'm sorry. I meant to ask how you were feeling." He held her away and studied her worried expression. "Your bruise is gone, I see. Did he—did you— Dammit, Dawnelle, where was I while you were going through this?"

"I'd sent you back to the party," she explained, understanding his remorse at leaving her alone on that hill. She brushed his tense lips with her fingertips. "He didn't do anything but scare me and tear my dress, Baird. The sheriff hustled him out of town. It's over. I want to forget about it."

Muttering a soft oath, he pulled her protectively close again. He began to move, slowly finding the rhythm of the music, melting her bones as he held her against his undulating hips. After a moment he said, "When we get back to the table, write down that guy's name. His address, too, if you know it."

She stiffened. "Why?"

"I just want to learn as much about this guy as possible—in case there's any more trouble. I don't mean to alarm you."

"It's—it's Paul Jenkins," she stammered. How she resented having to destroy the intimacy of their moments together by discussing so crass an issue as the attack! She attempted an uncaring finale. "But I certainly don't know his address. I only got a quick glimpse of the registration papers that day I bought Miss Mo. Besides, only an imbecile would try for me again after the sheriff took down my side of the story. Jenkins was defending a weak case, and he knew it. He'd had a few beers, that's all, and after seeing the two of us under that spruce tree, he decided to stage a little private party of his own." She laughed uncomfortably.

He slid his hands up her back to press her closer. Closing her eyes, moving gently against him, she felt the longing come rushing back. "It was an act of violence," he said softly, with an underlying ruthlessness. "In the sane light of day I want you to tell me everything you know about him."

The music ended on a wailing note. The twang of an electronic guitar changed the mood. Surprisingly versatile, the small-town band picked up an off-beat version of New Wave. Baird led her into this second dance, swiveling in sexy hip movements. Relieved that further discussion about Jenkins was now impossible, Dawnelle moved rhythmically a few feet away.

Glancing back at the table, she found it empty. Again she wondered about the relationship between Baird and Lau. She cautioned herself one last time not to give her heart away foolishly, then gave herself over to the sensual delight of dancing with Baird.

At the end of their fourth fast dance, Dawnelle's blood raced and perspiration beaded her brow.

Baird bent over her, threading his arm loosely around her waist. He was barely breathing hard, and Dawnelle recalled the time they'd climbed the cliff below his house, that day he'd kissed her for the first time. It seemed he was regaining his wind by tramping the woods and coves on a daily basis.

"Another dance?" He grinned, showing plenty of pearly teeth.

"Drink first," she gasped, miming someone dying of thirst.

"You go rest, then. I've got a special request for the band." Feeling his hand leave her back the moment she'd reached her chair, Dawnelle turned and saw him weaving around couples, heading for the stage. Already she missed his touch.

Her companions drifted back to the table as she sat down, and they all exchanged rowdy greetings. Over the next little while Dawnelle had several dances with men from the Caldwells' table, including Henny. The evening became a carousel of laughing faces, damp palms, shuffling feet—and glances over her shoulder to find Baird smiling down at Lau, then, finally, at Sarah Caldwell. Even Sarah, it seemed, couldn't reject the opportunity of a dance with the brawny marine scientist.

Henny jiggled to a standstill exactly on the last beat of the dance. Grinning proudly, he handed Dawnelle back to her chair. Ben was there, mopping his brow with a napkin and trying not to stare toward the center of the room, where Lau stood chatting with the stocky Swede, waiting for the next song to begin. Frowning, Ben finished his beer.

The band leader made a short speech into the microphone about the next song being dedicated to women who love the dance of love. Polite laughter clattered through the hall.

"Our song, huh?" Ben said from across the table, setting his beer down with a small slap of disgust. "Only trouble is, the objects of our hearts' desire are off dedicating themselves to others!"

"Haven't you danced with Lau but once?"

"Sure—in between races with that blond guy and half the U.S. Coast Guard. C'mon. I'm not sure what the band's got cooked up next, but I think you and I make a helluva second string."

When he rose and extended his hand, she stood up. The band's series of quick beats ended on a familiar suspended sax note. She stopped. Her heart picked up rhythm.

"No, Ben, I'm sorry," she said softly. "If memory serves me, this dance was taken days ago." A smile too ethereal to convey her meaning left Ben gaping with surprise.

She turned. Watching her dance partner, who slipped off his leather jacket as he hurried toward her, she felt emotion well up inside her. "To women who love the dance of love," the announcer had said. The tango was the dance of love, the dance she'd told Baird was her favorite, and he'd remembered. She knew this would be a dance to remember.

His eyes were smoky blue in the smoky room. He said nothing, only flung his jacket carelessly into a chair and pulled her into his arms, already moving to the music.

The thing she loved about the tango was the long languorous beat when the man and the woman dipped low, sliding to the woman's right in a sensuous step that ground their hips inexorably together. No matter that the song really required the blatant blare of a trumpet. The sax player put his heart into it, playing the high quick notes with zest and the extended love note with passion.

To her joy, Baird knew the showy nuances of the tango: the temperamental tricks of anger and jealousy when the partners turned away with a definite snap of heads; the graceful raising of the arms in fanciful turns; and always, always that lingering sidestep.

Halfway through the dance Dawnelle tore her gaze away from Baird's for the coquettish side-glance and saw a nearly deserted dance floor stretching away toward a shadowy circle of faces. The moment struck her as familiar.

During her college days, when she'd performed with the dance-exhibition team, she and her partner had always been the tango soloists. But then, though he'd been an exquisite dancer, her partner had had pocked skin and vacant eyes. Nothing beautiful about him, she recalled, except his ability to execute steps gracefully.

Baird, on the other hand, moved through the tango as if he were performing an exotic love ritual. His eyes grew dark, rich as the first darkness after sunset, and every motion expressed sexuality as a burning need.

She and Baird danced this sensuous unpracticed choreography as if they'd trained together for years. Now he grinned—not a simple grin but a challenge—and she arched her back, playing with him, glancing from beneath the crescent of her raised arm. She gathered the soft folds of her skirt and fanned them, teasing, mocking. Applause fluttered through her concentration. She ignored it, earning praise from Baird in the form of a slightly raised brow.

And then he was seducing her, demanding that she mold to him without the barest hint of distance between his undulating hips and hers. Turning her, he met her with a subtle thrust of his hips. She flowed into him, vaguely aware of the moisture glistening above her parted lips, then aware only that they moved as one body, her black dress curling around his pale slacks, her fingers twined in his dark hair. As his hands splayed over her back just below the waist, he manipulated her body merely by pressing with his thumb or smallest finger. She began to move a split second before he gave her the direction.

They made love as they danced, the music swirling around and through them as if it were the sea the way it sometimes washes among the rocks on a particularly misty night.

They were taking the last steps now, shifting together in that last wide sway. He was bending her supple back, lying over her, his face nearly touching hers, his eyes burning with a strange light. Back, back she bent while the long note sang through her body. And then briefly, enticingly, he kissed her. The note sighed away. Silence enveloped them. Her shallow breathing resulted more from arousal than exhaustion. As he raised her, her body sliding along his to a standing position, she felt first his heaving chest, then a tenseness in his thighs and knew he was as aroused as she.

The room erupted in applause. Hugging her at the waist, Baird stood still for a moment, unreadable emotions playing over his face. Dawnelle wondered how he must feel to have the adulation of so many for so simple an act as a dance. A dance of love, she corrected herself, gliding as if on ice when he escorted her to their table.

From the corner of her eye Dawnelle saw Grace gesticulating toward her, talking rapidly to a group of women. She shrugged off the momentary feeling of disquiet and gave her attention to the clamorous greetings from their companions at the table.

SOMEHOW BEN DREW LAU into a long series of dances. Dawnelle found herself sketching logos for Langston Marine. She used every dry white cocktail napkin she could find.

Following a host of others, two neophyte Guardsmen with pencil mustaches took their turns attempting to interest Dawnelle in a dance, but she politely declined in favor of working head to head with Baird. It wasn't in keeping with the vaguely flamenco evening she'd planned, but she was immensely pleased about the narrowing gap between them.

"The word 'Langston' should lie just above this water line," she said, enjoying the way Baird leaned close to her. "And 'Marine Specimens, Inc.' would naturally fall below the wavy lines that indicate the ocean."

"What about the test-tube or microscope idea? Any way to work them into the design?"

"Microscopes have been used to death. I think it would date the whole image. A laboratory beaker might work, outlined in twenty-percent gray screen behind the water—that might give you the scientific effect you want. But remember we've got to keep it simple. Some of the ads will be run in black and white, and probably you'll want to have your stationery and billing forms printed in one color to keep costs down. Also, a logo shouldn't interfere with the overall theme of a given ad, but should remain strong and easy to recognize. Baird, next week one of us should call on some printing houses—see what kind of artwork each of them produces. I think we want something stylized but not too modern."

"Agreed. Here's a thought. I'll work up a few roughs and show them to you."

"You?"

His eyes glinted with humor. "I'm no slouch just stumbling off the mud flats, Dawny. Who do you think designs my pipes?"

"Why, you of course, but I never imagined— Baird! That could save us several hundred dollars!"

He leaned back in his chair, arms folded as he gave her a speculative look. "Us, huh?"

"Sorry." She blushed. "I got carried away."

"No, no, that's all right. I like dedication. Makes me feel what I'm doing is worthwhile to someone besides myself."

Reaching for his glass and finding it empty, he made an apologetic face. "The well has dried up, lass. I'll go get some refills while you dream up a way to work that lab beaker into the design. Excuse me for five minutes, will you?" He rose, dropped a light kiss on her crown, then headed for the bar across the room.

IT WAS DIFFICULT TO TELL what made her glance up a while later. Perhaps it was the irritating, pebbly drone of Grace's voice. It could even have been a sixth sense that warned her Baird's blood had begun to boil. Dropping her pencil beside her evening bag, Dawnelle scanned the room, the feeling of unease growing stronger.

Their table companions were still dancing. Between the pumping beat of a surfing-era number and the shuffling of hundreds of feet, Dawnelle could not determine whether she had really heard Grace's voice. She continued to peer through the gloom, searching in the direction of the portable bar.

Then from somewhere beyond a group of dancers, she heard Baird's deep rumble. "What exactly did she tell you?"

"Well. . . nothing specific, of course. Except that you have a substantial bank account, which leads one to wonder where it might have come from. . . ."

Grace's voice, Dawnelle realized, feeling the color drain from her cheeks. She strained to hear, to see details. If only that enormous man in the orange-and-black plaid shirt would jostle himself out of the way! It sounded as if Grace was hedging, but that would be her way—her way of destroying a person! Insinuations. Half hints.

Suddenly, during a hushed moment in the music, Dawnelle heard very clearly: "Just asking, Mr. Langston. Really! If what Miss Belanger tells us is true, you have no need to hide behind rudeness! No need whatsoever."

Numbly Dawnelle stood up. What had the woman in ice blue told him? What irrevocable damage had she done to the carefully constructed framework of Dawnelle's relationship with Baird?

He materialized from behind the fat man in plaid. Watching his long stride carry him toward her, she was reminded of the day he strode across the beach in pursuit of Yurok. *No hope now,* she thought, sure her pounding heart must be audible to everyone in the hall. She could clearly see the lines of strain around Baird's mouth, the anger in his expression. On he came, three yards, two, until he reached out to her and dragged her forward. His fingers felt like stiff rope binding her arm. Automatically she placed a protective hand over his, and he jerked away as if she'd struck him.

All detail of the smiling crowd faded. She watched that once-laughing face crumple. Even the golden tan had vanished with his fury. "I'll spare you the accusations," he said harshly, drawing in short choked breaths. "You're fired!"

"No! What did Grace tell you? Baird, for your own good, don't. Please don't do this!"

Abruptly he brushed past her and scooped up the pile of white napkins from the table. He whirled to her, held out his hand, and crushed them. "No evidence!" he snarled. "Nothing left that you can conveniently leak to guttersnipes!"

For a long moment he stared at her. Under that scorching look she broke apart inside, piece by piece. Her dreams were flung away. The image she'd created to lure him melted even in her own eyes, eyes that stung with a salty dampness.

He hated her. Such venom in one look could never exist alongside real love, or the promise of real love she'd hoped, uselessly, he felt. She'd been a tool to him—a diversion, a bright mind—no more. And so another piece of the puzzle fell into place for Dawnelle.

As she stared into the hating blue eyes, she remembered telling herself it was important for her future mate to respect her mind, and he had. It was also essential that a kind of electrical sexual energy pass between them, and she couldn't deny that it had, even now. But what she also required—the new discovery—was that her man know her soul so thoroughly that mistrust would never break them apart. It was a tall order. Looking into her future, she realized there was every chance she would be adopting and raising a child on her own while she built up her P.R. business. Because she wanted that as much as she wanted to make the best use of her commercial skills. But here in front of her was a man who would cheat his children of their right to be nurtured by a trusting parent.

Tears stood in her eyes, but she didn't bother to clear her vision. Her heart ached so. Baird hated her, and he had let her down so completely. A deep shudder passed through her body.

"My business," he said suddenly, bitterly, "is all that's important. I ought to thank you."

"Thank—" she cleared the obstruction in her throat "—thank me for what?"

"For making me realize my work is all that's important—worth my time. That the only one I can trust is myself."

"That's a lonely road."

"But a reliable one, for the most part...if you don't let others get in your way." His shoulders slumped then, and his eyes went dead, opaque. "Bill me for your hours," he concluded dispiritedly. "I'll pay you as soon as I can."

Would he always condemn her? Had she really done this to him? Deepened the disillusion? "There's no need to pay—"

"I said bill me! Your work was good, dammit! If you'd just kept your nose out of my personal life!" He looked away, struggling, she thought, with his lethal anger. Perhaps she still had some chance to explain, to say she'd been forced to defend his reputation.

"Baird, you've misunderstood everything. I wasn't undermining you when I made that speech about you."

"Save it!" His head snapped around, and her slim hope sank. His eyes glittered with renewed fury. "Tell Lau I'm with the boy whenever she's ready to leave!"

"You tell her!" She whirled to grab her purse, stuffing the pencil inside, then spun around to him. The sense of loss washed through her, but doggedly she confronted him. "You tell your precious woman," she ground out. "And don't be too surprised if one day your understanding girl friend walks into someone else's arms. There's only so much anyone can take of your destructive paranoia. You have no heart, no eyes, no soul, Langston. You don't deserve a woman like her, and you certainly—" she choked out this last "—don't deserve me!"

"Who doesn't deserve you?" Ben queried from behind her.

She tore herself away from Baird's condemning blue eyes and whirled for the third time. Ben and Lau stood there, arm in arm, faces animated and flushed from exertion.

The tears threatened to flood down Dawnelle's cheeks, yet she grasped the last shred of her courage and jerked her thumb over her shoulder. "He doesn't! In his typical callous fashion he has misunderstood a benevolent gesture on my part. He wants to storm out of the place like some shell-shocked war vet. Well, I won't give him the satisfaction! Take all the time you want, Ben. Take all night! I'll have plenty to do out there in the car, dreaming up ways to undermine the reputation of my next client. Everyone knows that's the best way to run a public-relations business!"

In the stunned silence that followed, she found some satisfaction in walking past Baird with her head held at an imperious angle. And it wasn't difficult to keep walking—not until she'd gained the porch. From there she fled into the darkness, tears streaming and sobs issuing painfully from her throat.

CHAPTER FOURTEEN

TWO WEEKS LATER, after touring a photographers' club around the station, Dawnelle came indoors to hear Baird's first message on her recorder. It was a simple few sentences—terse flat words. "Let's discuss this awkward silence between us," he began. "Please call me. Let me explain. . . ."

But her heart had hardened. The slight tremble in her knees and the deep ache in her stomach—these were only angry reactions to hearing his rumbling voice again. *Well rid of him.* She'd heard that phrase before, read it somewhere. The logical part of her found solace in repeating the words over and over.

Her depression lasted days longer. She fought it, kept busy.

Baird called again one evening while she was reading, but her sixth sense told her to let the machine take his message. She struggled hard not to answer his quiet plea for a meeting. She knew when she was beaten, though, her heart clamoring in an argument with her common sense. Skulking moodily to bed that night, she listened to the squabble and rustle of chickadees nesting under the rafters, mutely cursing their domestic repartee.

His third call came after she'd painted the picket

fence, while she was soaking paint thinner and exhaustion from her body.

Baird said, "Dawnelle..." with a shadowy regret in his voice. This time she knew, hearing him, that the weeks had dulled her anger. She was left with a longing that could not be doused as easily as she darkened the cottage each night.

So, washcloth clutched tightly to her chest, Dawnelle listened, waiting as Baird cleared his throat. "Expected, hoped you'd call." His voice came faintly to her ears. Her eyes slid closed, and she felt a lowering sadness within. It sounded so very much as though he missed her.

"I was wondering if you'd had further trouble with what's-his-name. Jenkins. And if you're all right. I was wondering that."

No, she wanted to tell him. *I haven't been all right since you—your arms, your lips, your accusations.*

"Oh," he added as if he'd just remembered something important. "Serano. I asked him to lend a hand. Getting pretty busy these days, filling orders from the letters I sent off before the fish fry. Then in a week or two I guess we'll be getting responses from the brochures. Your design ideas look great on paper. But I'd rather be telling you this in person...." His voice drifted.

Suddenly she was sloshing water as she leaped from the tub. Grabbing a towel, she stumbled over Miss Mo and tore down the hallway to answer his call. Serano; he'd hired the graduate student. That was his first big step in returning to the world of the reasonable.

"Have dinner sometime—"

As she reached a dripping hand to the telephone, she heard the warped twang of the message marker, knew he was hanging up even as she lifted the receiver.

"Baird?"

The line hummed.

"Baird!"

A second or two passed with that final-sounding tone in her ear before she realized how close she'd come to opening her heart to him again. *Fool!* She lowered the black receiver. *Ready to open your arms to him, tell him you missed him. Dawnelle, you're a weakling in this game of self-preservation. No backbone. No pride.*

And yet . . . his voice still vibrated in her memory.

How lonely he'd sounded, as empty of joy as she. Tears slipped down her damp cheeks. She went to bed at seven-thirty, remorse and confusion disturbing her sleep.

She grew stronger as the days ticked by. And busier. A group of one hundred fifty geologists tramped through the boulders and brush of the headland, dropping words like "Pleistocene" as casually as if they were toothpaste and having major disagreements over the configuration of the great boulders.

Writers, more photographers and tourists besieged Dawnelle for historical anecdotes. Miss Mo played the energetic guide, the children safe from her nipping jaws as long as they didn't shriek past her nose at a terrific pace. Watching her closely, Dawnelle encouraged a friendly pat for Miss Mo from each child who ventured to the headland. The lighthouse keeper retrieved visitors from patches of poison oak, cautioned them about the dangerous drop-off and added their business cards to her growing collection of contacts. But these new acquaintances did little to ease her longing for one friendly smile from Baird Langston.

He was a kind of stimulant, creeping into her thoughts so that she paused midsentence and forgot what she'd been saying—haunting her nights, making a tranquil evening all but impossible.

Ben complained good-naturedly that since he'd been working on the boat with Lau on Saturdays and Sundays, Dawnelle had grown jealous and withdrawn on their occasional dates. They chuckled about it, but admittedly Dawnelle's laughter lacked its old lighthearted ring.

Ben claimed his relationship with the fisherwoman was one of those "strictly business" deals, but he, too, was sometimes long-faced. Clearly he was falling in love with Lau, but she refused to respond romantically. She was probably in love with Baird, Dawnelle often thought. Ben didn't need the reminder. Airing such views to him would only add to his worries about starting a new career alongside a woman he cared for.

One warm Friday evening in mid-August, Dawnelle arrived home to the jingling of the telephone. She'd been to dinner at the Caldwells and had brought home some smoked salmon for a late snack. It was ten o'clock. Only Ben would call so late. She opened the door, greeted Miss Mo and chased the dog playfully to the recorder. Her station message was already running.

"Hold on a minute," she said breathlessly into the receiver. She tossed the salmon to the end table and clicked off the tape. "Hi! Just made it in time. Thanks for holding."

"Any time," Baird said, and her knees were suddenly strung like rubber bands, loose and unstable. "You're hard to reach," he went on softly.

"I've—been out most every day."

"Summer season been tough?"

"Yes. Yes, I guess it has.... How are you, Baird?"

"You know. Same as you. Busy. Glad to put my feet up at the end of a day."

"Yeah," she laughed, sinking to the couch, staring with an incredulous expression toward the fireplace and bookshelves. She was actually talking to him—not making much sense so far, but, then, neither was he. What did he want?

"Dawnelle, I'm in a bind, and I need your help."

"Sure, what can I—" *Damn. So willing.*

He chuckled. "When you hear what I want, you may not be so anxious to help."

Vee, she thought with distaste. "Not anxious, Baird. It's just my way. Go on...."

"First, I want to say something, Dawnelle." His voice dropped so low he could have been standing behind her, whispering in her ear. "I've called often, left messages. Sometimes I got so fed up with hearing that mechanical metallic version of you, I just hung up. But I have tried to reach you."

"About what?" She held her breath. This conversation was getting very personal.

"You...me. I hated to leave things as they were. Our relationship was good until I climbed all over your case for that Grace incident."

"I thought we didn't have a relationship," she replied softly.

"We did, and I miss it."

"That locked gate outside never stopped you before. I'm surprised you didn't vault it in a single bound if you felt so strongly about our—" she exhaled sharply "—relationship."

"You're still very angry."

"Of course I'm still— I've had my moments of anger."

"And I've had mine. But forcing another confrontation with you at the wrong moment.... I didn't want to chance a permanent rift. For once I wanted to do things right. My temper...." She waited silently, half glad of his discomfort, only half fighting a crazy joy. Finally he continued, "Anyway, the rest of the time I've remembered other things. Good moments, times when we really clicked. I can't believe I'm the only one who felt that."

Fear rushed through her. He wanted her to admit her feelings after all the pain. And what would he do with that knowledge—hurt her worse next time? What next time?

"I can't believe I'm the only one, Dawnelle."

"Baird, I was hurt. Insulted."

"I'm sorry. I *hate* the damage gossip can do. It shouldn't have come between us, and I'm very sorry it did."

"Me, too." A lump was rising in her throat. She couldn't put the words "I love you, Dawnelle" into his mouth, but oh, how she battled the urge to blurt out those words to him. The feeling was foreign, this sudden sweeping love for him.

For a long while she'd managed to avoid the truth

that seemed so unavoidable now—thrashed around that truth like a wave tossed by converging seas. Now her chest constricted with a sharp exquisite pain that cried out for expression.

There was Lau, too. There was the anticipated pain of having Baird back and losing him again. She needed to know what he wanted of her.

"You were going to ask me a favor," she said with difficulty. "How can I help?"

"No. I'd like to come to some kind of understanding about us first. I want you to know, whatever you decide about the other, this personal matter is very important. I've been calling all day, trying to spend time with you to explain things."

Her gaze flicked to the white flag showing through the smoke cover of the recorder.

"I had to call you tonight because I need your help. But most of all—" his voice grew deeper with unexpressed feeling "—Dawnelle, I want to be with you again, see you, talk to you, do I don't know what with you. Just be with you. Damn, I've—I've missed you."

Tears clung to her eyelashes. She sat listening to him struggle with words that put heat and fire and new power in her blood. She'd been feeling she was a butterfly just slipped from its case, yellow wings vulnerable in the first breath of wind. With his words, she was vital again, new and ready for flight.

"Well," Baird said after a moment, "enough said, I suppose. I've called you so often without reaching you, I'm speechless at finally having made the connection."

"Jokes aside," she answered gently, at last wanting

to ease his discomfort with a touch of humor, "you want your P.R. director back on the books."

A laugh came from him in two short syllables.

"Right?" she asked.

"You're forcing the issue, I can see. I had wanted to mend the fence between us first."

"You mean you're actually calling to see if I'll work for you again?"

"Not just for that reason, no. I told you—"

"But to work for you again! You've got to be kidding!"

He sighed. "If you insist, no. I'm not kidding. I need you."

"You need me."

He paused. "Yes."

"To work for you."

"Yes."

"I see. I'm to forget all about your penchant for cruel insults."

"I don't even know you well enough to be sure you're the type to forgive mistakes. Are you....? What do I hear in that silence?" he asked softly a moment later. "Anger or deliberation?"

"A little of both, I guess."

"If you let me come and pick you up, I could bring you back here for an hour or so and explain the setup."

"It's the middle of the night," she pointed out, her heart pumping strangely at the thought of seeing him tonight.

"It's...." She could see the watch he would be consulting, the metal dials and buttons. "Ten-fifteen. I could have you back home by, say, twelve, twelve-thirty. Okay?"

"This is ridiculous."

"I know. The timing is lousy. But I have a flight to catch at nine in the morning."

"Vee," she said flatly.

"Right."

"Baird—"

"Don't, Dawnelle. Some things about me won't change—not right away."

She couldn't know whether he was offering her something more than forgive and forget and let's work together again. She bit her lip. He'd said what he called to say; she could sense that. He was waiting—no push, no plea. It was up to her.

"I shouldn't agree to this, not for anything."

He waited.

"All right," she sighed. "But dammit, Baird, no accusations. Either trust me this time or forget it!"

"Be there in twenty minutes, love. You just made me a happy man." He hung up.

Love.... She stared at the receiver. Then, feeling a sudden burst of energy, she yelled exuberantly and tackled Miss Mo.

As HE STOOD in the yellow glow of her porch light, studying her, blinking at the occasional brilliance of the beacon, neither of them spoke.

He wore a shirt of blue plaid, sleeves cuffed short across smooth brown biceps. He looked very fit, very virile with his beard and powerful torso. Tanned. And, as always, lean-hipped in jeans.

Miss Mo was whining excitedly as she stretched and rubbed against Baird. Yet he could spare the dog no greeting as his gaze roamed the contours of Dawnelle's tall figure. She, too, wore jeans. Fresh from a quick shower, her hair flowing around the silk folds of her forest-green blouse, she filled her starved senses with him.

He moved restlessly. His eyes dark with an emotion that spoke of need, he said thickly, "Give us a hug."

She seemed to fall toward him. His arms enveloped her, squeezing tightly yet lovingly. His beard pressed into her hair.

He uttered a groan, agony and relief indistinguishable in the sound—an echo of her own pleasure and doubt.

She said softly, "Baird."

His hands slid up her back, over her shoulders. Leaning slightly away, Baird slipped his palms against her jaw. For a moment his eyes played an intimate melody with hers. Then he was lifting her hair, letting it cascade through his fingers, leaning close to nuzzle its softness.

He sighed.

She recognized the spicy tobacco on his warm breath, relished the memories it brought. She grew dizzy at the realization that his lips were inches, a hand-span, from her mouth. But his slow penetrating gaze stayed her impulse to kiss him. She began to tremble. When she wet her lips, his eyes followed the movement...and lingered.

A wild electricity snapped alive between them. In the instant when she closed her eyes, lifting her mouth to his, Baird's lips descended.

It was a sensual caress made exotic by the slight tang

of tobacco. Time and anger eddied away. She clung, moved against him, inspired the kiss until she transformed his adulation to passion.

Tightening his arms around her shoulders, he probed with his tongue, gently exploring her teeth. The act of giving way sent a searing heat through her as he went deep into her mouth.

Now his groan, against her lips, expressed sheer hunger. "Dawnelle...."

The word was sweet, evoking a physical need she understood.

"I planned a hug of greeting, just a hug," he murmured, kissing her cheek, her throat. "But how good intentions do get lost! You look so good after all this time!"

"Me, too," she said. "I mean, you, too." Joy sent a bubble of laughter from her throat. She clasped his neck in a tight hug. "Let's not ever have another argument, Baird!"

Pressing her flat against his body, aroused, he said huskily, "How could such feeling ever turn to anger?"

"Do you hear that, Miss Mo?" Shivering slightly as desire rippled through her, Dawnelle turned her cheek against his shoulder to look down at the dog. "Feeling! He said *feeling*!" Miss Mo wagged her tail indulgently and slumped contentedly against the porch post.

Dawnelle leaned far enough out of Baird's embrace to look into his eyes. "Feeling, Baird. You won't deny it, hide it, fifteen minutes from now, will you?"

A shadow of uncertainty clouded his blue gaze. But his voice held wonder as he answered, "How could I refute it, Dawnelle? I don't know how to name what I feel right now, but I can tell you, I wouldn't trade it for all the tea in China."

"Nor for all the shysters in Singapore?"

He chastened her with a frown.

"Sorry." She grinned. "I'll always want you safe and sane in the U.S.A."

"I shouldn't complain." He said this into her hair, for he was hugging her tight against him once more. She gasped at the fierceness of his warmth.

He let her go after a moment, and without consulting her, called Miss Mo to go with them to the Ford.

"The dogs can run free for an hour or so while we work," he replied to her protest. "They've no doubt missed each other, too."

In the dark beyond the porch, with Baird's arm lightly across her shoulders, Dawnelle smiled.

BAIRD DIDN'T STOP TOUCHING HER during the hour they spent checking his inventory of prepared slides, dissection illustrations and video training cassettes. Even when they left the stacks of shipping cartons piled against the walls of his lab, Baird kept her hand tucked in his.

He had smoothed back her hair once, absently, while he explained how to oversee shipments while he was gone. He'd caressed her arm, hugged her shoulders eagerly as he showed her invoices from thirty orders he'd delivered in July. He'd pressed fingertips to her back to guide her to the sink and counters, where Serano would prepare orders for shipment next week.

Each time he touched her, Dawnelle's concentration wavered. Gone was the distant, "strictly business"

Baird of former work sessions. He, too, behaved as if she were a drug—he an addict constantly reassuring himself of her heady presence. Her skin was already burning with awareness as he guided her up the stairs, down the hall and into the living room.

"As you can see. . . ." He paused, indicating a corner of the soft white couch where she might relax. He walked to the wet bar. "I need you. Serano can prepare the orders and package them, get them sent off. All you need to do is open the mail, log the orders and keep Serano organized. He's got the skill of a hunter when I ask him to find a rare marine organism, but he's just about useless with paperwork. Lacks discipline in the business area. That's why I need you."

He glanced over his shoulder at her, his hand poised over the liquor bottles. "Cognac? Amaretto?"

"Cognac will be fine." She smiled, remembering the spot below his house where he'd first offered her the drink.

"Two Cognacs," he murmured, turning to pour from a crystal decanter.

His bar and every expanse of redwood and mahogany in the room gleamed. Gone was the layer of dust she remembered. Eugenia Forester, she had learned from the Civic-Club meeting, was earning that pipe for her husband, after all. The Etruscan horse now served as a cocktail table near Dawnelle's elbow, and a trunk of woven wicker near the fireplace held a spreading Boston fern. The sliding glass door was ajar. The fresh tang of salt, the muffled rush of waves came in to mingle with the bubbling of the fish tanks along the hallway wall.

Glass clinked. Dawnelle glanced toward the bar. She

found Baird standing near the carved horse, a delicate snifter in each large hand. Her eyes traveled to his face.

"God, I'm sorry," he said with a quiet sincerity that pierced her.

"About what?"

"Insulting you with those accusations. That *woman*, that sea gull with the instincts of a scavenger!"

"Grace," she said.

"She told me you described a big savings account I had—that you practically said outright I skimmed the money from Marine Exports, served my time and got out to spend it free and clear."

"I said you were using some kind of inheritance to pay off your stockholders. Though she would admit nothing when I confronted her, I figured she twisted everything."

"Can you understand why I was angry? As angry as I've ever been in my life?"

"No, Baird," she said emphatically. "You gave me no chance to explain—sent me to jail without a trial. You of all people." She forced herself to give him a hard look. "You should have had the decency to ask about my side before deciding my guilt."

He grimaced, handed her the goblet. "Two weeks later I knew that. Genia mentioned that you caused a small scandal in the Civic Club, dragging Grace through an inquisition. It was Genia who set me straight. I felt like a heel, tried to call you." He looked down at her, his eyes both sad and softly eager. "Dawnelle, will you help me, give me time to work out some rough spots in my life?"

She looked at him, trying to see the future he envisioned. Slowly she nodded. "Yes. Yes, I'll help you."

Sighing, he nodded, too.

She wished he'd sit beside her, hold her. She felt the need to draw from his physical strength, to be reassured about her decision.

"Toast number two," he said then, touching his glass to hers. She raised one brow. "To earning a second chance with you."

The glass tilted in her fingers. She righted it, sipped some of the burning liquid, then gazed at her hands. "Chance?"

He moved to the couch and sat down. "Chance," he repeated, looking at her intensely. "I want you in my life. Somehow—any way you'll allow it. If this trip hadn't come up and forced me to talk you into helping me with the business, I'd have tried something else—leaped that fence out at the station, probably. Because I'd tried diplomacy and just about run out of patience."

"You've never been big on patience."

"No."

They drank in silence. She studied his grandfather's shadowy portrait above the stone lintel of the fireplace, the cognac making her stomach warm, her mind racy. Glancing sideways at Baird, she asked, "Why is it so important to...have me in your life?" *You've got Lau,* she wanted to add. *Haven't you? Something's keeping her from Ben.*

Baird took her glass, leaned over to set it with his own on the redwood coffee table. Sinking into the pillow beside her, he angled slightly her way and gave her a warm look that made her heart thud. He was touching her again, she realized, his fingers sending streaks of awareness from her arms to her shoulders and down like hot lead to her stomach.

"Because," he murmured near her lips, "I can't get you out of my system. Believe that I've tried. But I think of you at night, and out on the beaches when I'm collecting and in the afternoons in my lab."

"Guilt?" she said hesitantly, her voice soft with expectation.

"Not guilt. Desire, perhaps. Maybe just missing your smile...." She smiled at him.

"The green of your eyes...." He kissed her lightly on the cheek. "Eyes that are as deep with mystery as the stands of century-old redwoods that are so rare these days. Rare green eyes...."

She met his own mysteriously compelling gaze and swallowed nervously. Something was happening inside her at his melting words, a kind of sinking euphoria.

"I don't know why I missed you," he said, frowning slightly, his eyes riveted on her lips. "I just—" he tentatively touched his lips to hers, sweetly "—need you," he murmured.

The kiss deepened, and Dawnelle fought the fear of surrender for a moment. The velvet cushions cradled her hips, Baird's hands slid down her arms to her waist, and her own need went lurching through her.

"Dawnelle, I want you—" he whispered urgently, his mouth playing over her face, searching for delicate spots beneath her ears, down along her throat "—missed you, my love. Dreamed of you so often, tasted your kisses again and again, wanted you with a terrible ache, pain, need...."

The heat in her stomach stormed now, gathered into a

rolling fireball and sped through her limbs, igniting delicious demons in her hips as his hands gripped her close. Yes. Better to have this moment of surrender than to die missing him, to live a half life of longing.

"I've missed you so," she found herself saying. "Wanted you to call."

"I didn't know...." Groaning softly, he circled her with strong insistent arms, his mouth searching, breath hot against her cheek, until his lips covered hers once more and her mind went winging into a deep blue black senselessness.

She grew molten and supple in his arms. *I love you,* she said silently, minding very much that he didn't return the pledge, but knowing Baird was still struggling to shed his cloak of paranoia. Lau's image came to her once, questions about Lau and the boy and Baird. But Baird's hands were molding to the long lean contours of her hips and waist, and Dawnelle let the fears and uncertainties melt away.

He lifted her until she lay across his lap, her shoulder wedged between one arm and his chest. She gasped softly at the insistence of his desire. Her heart ran like a riptide when his palm slid over her breast. The green silk of her blouse shimmered at his touch. Her creamy skin was sheened with arousal, her lips dark ruby with passion.

"You're beautiful, heart-stoppingly lovely," he whispered, tracing her breast with a fingertip in narrowing circles until her nipple stood taut beneath the silk and the gauzy bra. Following the line of her body along one hip and curving leg, his gaze lingered at the hidden recess between her thighs. "So soft, so seductively feminine...." His gaze went to her face. He leaned to her, kissed her lips, looked into her glowing eyes. "But slowly. We must go slowly. I want your whole body to want me as much as your eyes claim you do."

Grasping his hand, she pressed it to her pounding heart.

"Not enough," he said.

She laughed, a throaty ripple of pleasure. "Is it possible to want you more?"

"You don't know?"

"Not about this—not this *much*, no. This crazy need I feel—this singing like the sea's inside me, all frothy and wild." Her voice faded slightly. "I want you, Baird. I've always wanted you."

He drew a harsh breath and kissed her impatiently, his lips rougher, yet still passionate. Abruptly he withdrew a little. "I want to touch you until you want me more than you've ever wanted anything, ever. As I want you now!"

Gathering her close, he moved her bodily, carrying her, her head over his arm, hair falling free. His mouth roamed over her throat, and through half-closed eyes she saw the light recede. Massive furniture against his bedroom wall blurred past. She clung to him, arms around his neck, shivering when his mouth explored her raised inner arm through the silk. Then a wide bed with carved head and footboard claimed her hips, thighs and back. She sank into a furry comforter.

"A moment. . . ." He left her, his shadow crossing the dim slant of light in the doorway. Clothes rustled. She strained to see him.

Centuries later, it seemed, the pale shape of his male form approached the bed. He paused, looking down at her "Take off your blouse for me, Dawnelle," he said urgently. "Show me your beauty." Already her passion for Baird had far surpassed anything Jeff had aroused in her, and she complied rapidly, shaking fingers freeing the pearl buttons.

He would rush nothing, she mused, sobering slightly. Of course there would be even more now, more than the delight of past excursions into sensuality with Baird. The wait would be worth it, had already been worth it. She had never before been so eager to give herself in a relationship, she thought, watching Baird stare at her.

But this was a different situation requiring new rules of conduct. Her heart and her future were somehow bound to this man. Their coming together would be unforgettable, his lust for revenge a shallow breath compared to their need for each other. Lau would be only a memory to him—ashes after the consuming flames of tonight. She could feel it, the almost heroic quality of their attraction. She knew she would move with him, touch him, please him—knew they would show each other exactly what they wanted. Suddenly she was eager for his lips on her breast. She stirred with mild impatience, her hand hovering over the final loosened button.

"Dawnelle?"

"Why are you still standing there in the dark?" she asked.

He was suddenly beside her, caressing over her clothes. He stopped at her hand, lifted it away. Slowly he parted the flimsy blouse, sliding it seductively from her jeans. He made the act one of excruciating pleasure as the scant light revealed to him the creamy expanse of her skin. Her chest rose and fell, breasts rounded above the lacy black bra, rib cage tapering to a slightly hollow stomach sheathed in fitted, well-worn jeans.

His fingertip touched her lips; she gently tasted the tip before a trail of dampness followed his finger down over her chin. She trembled, felt her breasts peak. He traced beneath her jaw, drew a wavering line down her chest. Swiftly his hand caught one breast. He squeezed gently, then moved to her other breast. Squeezed again.

"Baird!" A moan was released as ecstasy arrowed through her.

"Yes, my love. Slowly. . . ."

His chest was a wide bridge above her, darkness trapped in a triangle of hair, darker still the shade of his beard. She longed for his lips. But the trail of exploration had begun again.

"I don't think I'll have you home by midnight," he murmured. "Not by hours."

Her answer was a soft cry that said it didn't matter.

Leaning over her, his hip a firm wedge against her thigh as he sat on the edge of the bed, Baird ran the tips of his fingers down the spare flesh of her ribs, across her waist, and when he suddenly unsnapped her jeans, she felt the rocochet through her whole being.

She gasped, gripped his hands, stayed them.

"Eager to help?" he teased in a thick contained voice. Her fingers loosened. "I won't rush you, Dawnelle," he soothed. "Slowly with us, only slowly. With great longing. . . ."

He slid her zipper free. Then lips and a beard like angora found the soft depression in the center of her stomach. He kissed her there as he slipped away her blue jeans, his body pressed warmly against her. His breath shortened and hot with desire, he paused one last time to look at her. Then his fingers went to the tiny satin bow between her breasts. He snicked open the fragile clasp, and slid off her blouse and bra and brief black panties. Casting them somewhere beyond the bed, he lowered his lips to her breast. She clung to the dark waves at the back of his head as he drew her inside with his tongue.

In seconds she was quivering beneath his wandering hands, hands slightly rough with calluses, but so good at lingering caresses.... Driven by desire, she gripped his arms, slid her hands to his massive rocky shoulders. She caressed his neck, ears, face, kissed his shoulder when he bent close, then found a male nipple just above her mouth and arched to close her lips over him.

Baird moaned and cradled her head. "Yes," he whispered urgently, and she began to tease the point with her teeth, gently, back and forth, suckling, circling with her tongue, until the nipple grew firm against her lips, and he groaned again. He buried his mouth in her hair as if the agony was too exquisite to bear.

Pulling away at last, his lips closed over hers, his tongue excitedly seeking the moist secrets there. She felt the warmth between her thighs spread like a rippling tide through her body. It was a rising consuming warmth that brought with it the need for action. Their bodies entwined, rolled. His muscular lower half enveloped her legs, held her captive when her body screamed to move.

She was shaking with need when he ended the kiss. Murmuring to soothe her, Baird nibbled her ear while his palm stroked her stomach and legs. Each stroke brought a soft moan and a responsive arch of her hips. Gradually he calmed her, then began again the moist kisses down her body, the probing sensitive intimacies with knowing hands.

"Baird!" she demanded once in agony, but he gently eased the pain of denial, bringing her to the very brink of sanity and guiding her eager hands into an exploration of their own....

Only a few moments later he grasped those hands with such force he frightened her. Thinking she'd hurt him, she cried out in alarm. "It's all right," he replied hoarsely, barely able to speak. "Your hands know me too well now. I nearly...nearly went over the edge... and it's too soon...."

She was suffused with joy at her ability to arouse him, torn between a desire for release from the sweet longing he'd created within her and the glory of transporting him to the brink. So she alternated between the two pleasures, one moment writhing beneath him and murmuring his name; the next, inhaling his smoky-cinnamon scent while she drove him wild with the silky feel of her hair on his skin, or the sensuous play of her hands....

On and on they loved as mellow shafts of dawn slanted in around the curtains. The dim light was balm to Dawnelle's senses, bathing her lover in a haze that blurred the angles of his body and blended the tones of tan skin and dark hair. She once tried to imagine his face without the beard, even searched at the point of his chin and discovered a sight dip there, a cleft. But his soft hair tickled against her neck, and she curled her body beneath him to begin a new journey....

The musk scent and the slightly salty taste of his skin were part of her now, as familiar as the perfume of her own body. And as he stayed her mouth on his hip yet again, crying out for her to stop before it was too late, she smiled and nipped him mischievously on the sensitive muscle she'd found slanting down from his hipbone. He writhed.

"Wild woman," he gasped, sliding her along his body until she was nestled in his arms. "Wild woman, I need you. All of you."

He kissed her searchingly, demandingly, urging her to move with him in the rhythm that was now both familiar and a new excitement, a new promise. His hands roamed hungrily over her breasts—massaging, cupping, rekindling the heat of countless times before.

Rolling above her, Baird slid his lower body against her hips, circled, shifted away, closed again and drew away. Teasing, leading her in sinuous arching motions, he caught her in a wild free moment and inexorably entered her, held, moved away, coupled close and rhythmically brought her higher into ecstasy than she had imagined possible.

But she was not imagining, not thinking. She was only feeling the tremendous heat that swept her, all of her, and brought a damp flush to her skin. Experiencing an incredible oneness with the man she had loved so long, she sought his mouth. She ached to succumb completely to him. Feeling a mighty wave begin to swell inside her, she gripped his moving shoulders.

"Bai-i-rd!" she cried as the wave mounted—and then she was hurled through a cloudy gate and into a soft sinking paradise, where she felt the oneness but knew no conscious thought.

Floating back through the clouds, she began to know her lover's release. His guttural moans came shatteringly to her ears, while his untamed movements and the grip of his hands on her shoulders thrilled her, spurred her to response.

She wrapped her arms, legs around him. Moving with him, aching to give him pleasure, she was again stunned by the lifting heat of that great wave. It carried her high, higher than before—a raging swell that stormed through her until she was so utterly consumed she could only hold on and let the tide hurl both of them toward the sun. . . .

CHAPTER FIFTEEN

GONE IN THE MORNING. How bitterly disappointed she felt at waking to a midmorning sun, with the lethargy of fulfillment clinging to her limbs; to see his pillow askew near the carved headboard, to draw in the lingering scent of him in the stillness of his home. And yet not find the man who'd forever changed her life.

Feeling cheated of the sight of his body naked next to her, she rose and pulled on her clothes. Hadn't she heard the murmurings of love between them last night? Yet who had spoken of love—she or Baird? She knew only that she would live the rest of her life remembering their passion. She would live always with the desire to be his mate.

She found a note on the redwood coffee table, pinned down by keys and a stack of twenty-dollar bills for operating expenses. His words expressed his amazement at the beauty of last night—*please come home safely,* she cried silently—and once more he thanked her for trusting him. Then he wrote:

> Serano picked me up at eight and drove me to the Arcata airport. I left keys to the house and garages and one for the Ford so you and Miss Mo could get home. Serano will pick up the truck later. I didn't

want to wake you. Sleeping, you looked like a beautiful child exhausted after her first day at camp. Will call. Keep your doors and gates locked. Please stay safe.

Baird

Suddenly reminded of her responsibilities at the station, the late hour and the forgotten guests, she raced to collect Miss Mo, pierced to the heart at having to leave behind the possessions, the atmosphere that spoke so eloquently of Baird.

WHEN NO VISITORS toured the station, Dawnelle conducted her outdoor chores wearing a brief green bikini—if the fog didn't obscure the sun. As the days went on, she grew as nut-brown as Baird. Kept busy with tourists, she still spent most of her private hours thinking of him, longing for the moment when her insistent desire to have him back safely in Trinidad would be satisfied.

On Labor Day morning Dawnelle left two families picking blackberries near the chain-link fence and walked back toward the cottage to finish washing a sinkful of lingerie. Miss Mo suddenly growled and came rushing up, slamming into Dawnelle's legs. Curious, she bent to pat the dog, noticing the normally erect silver ears now flattened against her head, the thick tail tucked between her hind legs.

Miss Mo glanced apprehensively toward the center of the headland where the concrete cross commemorated the Spanish explorers. She whined, growled, slunk to the ground. She looked askance at Dawnelle, who reassured herself that the gate was closed. She urged the dog to seek whatever was frightening her, but Miss Mo wouldn't venture into the brush.

That evening there was a wheeze on Dawnelle's telephone tape that reminded her of a pig being squeezed. Jenkins, she knew. No threats by word, just by deed.

As she stood poised by the arm of the chesterfield, listening to the guest itinerary for tomorrow, her numb horror of the man overwhelmed her. She couldn't forget how isolated she was, how very close to the edge of the world she lived. Baird had hinted at his concern in that goodbye note, reminding her to lock gates and doors. She needed no further urging to do so.

SHE HEARD FROM BAIRD only once, on a Sunday night in mid-September. But the conversation was so brief she had time only to tell him the orders were pouring in, and that Serano was doing a marvelous job. Baird sounded exhausted, his voice thin and ragged, his manner preoccupied.

"Been delayed," he said. "You're one in a million, lass. I'll try to call you again when I can get free."

"Baird, when will you be home?"

The line was already disconnected.

No opportunity to ask him what was going on in Singapore. No time to mention Jenkins. No chance to tell him she'd found the Langston Marine checkbook and deposited seventeen thousand in checks he'd received in the mail. No time to tell him she'd used the two hundred dollars he left to buy preserving and packing materials, and then purchased with her own savings the duplicate videotapes needed to fill a huge order from a school district in Florida.

He was taking no chances on a repeat of Vee's betrayal by having either Serano or herself able to countersign his checks. That hurt, hurt badly, but she'd readily put forth her own capital to keep him going. He would pay her back. Still, it worried her that he would stay away beyond the three weeks he'd scheduled, leaving others to run his business. She lay awake nights fearing for his safety, fearing he would never return.

October dawned. Indian summer made the coast vibrant, the sky royal blue behind the dark fist of Trinidad Head, the bay glassy. Insects creaked in the brush. Trinidad's streets were deserted as Dawnelle, having shopped for groceries Saturday night after closing the station, drove toward the headland. As she rested her elbow on the Fiat's window ledge, feeling the breeze on her bare arms and lifting wisps of her upswept hair, she glanced toward the harbor parking lot.

Impulsively she swerved into the dusty area near Ben's five-year-old green Chevrolet. He was stowing buckets into the trunk. In a lighthearted mood Dawnelle jammed on the brakes, sending a roll of paper towels bouncing to the floorboards, and leaped from her car. Tiptoeing up behind him, she said loudly, "Ben!" and when he turned with a grunt of surprise, she flung her arms around his neck.

"Ben, I haven't seen you for days!"

"Hey, beautiful," he laughed, hugging her. "If you don't mind a few fish scales, I sure don't mind a hug!"

She pulled back and grinned at him. "It's so good to see a familiar face."

"Been stuck at the station or over at Langston's for weeks, huh? The life of a talented woman!" Chuckling, he ducked around the trunk and peered toward the shadowed passenger window. "Got a sec to say hi to Dawnelle?" he called.

Ben turned back as Dawnelle glanced into the darkness, searching for the woman she always connected more with Baird than Ben.

"I was going to call you," Ben said, catching her attention. "Lau has some news."

"Oh? What's up?"

Then Lau was leaning into the circle of gold from the weak trunk light, and Dawnelle drew a soft breath. The other woman was smiling, saying hello, her long hair billowing around her exotic eyes and dark luminous skin. *Lovely,* Dawnelle admitted to herself, returning the greeting—even with her figure lost in a bulky stained army surplus coat.

"How's the fishing?" Dawnelle asked, stepping slightly away from Ben, because Lau's gaze had flicked over the two of them, registering a brief question. The last thing she wanted was to put a rift of jealousy between Ben and Lau. "Season good so far?"

"Surprisingly good." Again Lau's eyes settled briefly on Ben before returning to Dawnelle. "Sometimes I think my luck has changed. Ben's...making things easier on the weekends." She smiled teasingly at him. "When he's not all tangled up in the gear."

"Hey," he protested, waving toward the water. "How was I supposed to know you were going to troll off a point of land that had about fourteen different riptides running in opposite directions? Especially right when I was trying to shake loose that shark that grabbed the bait. Huh, skipper?"

Lau smiled.

Dawnelle said, "How about a drink at the Grove to

settle this controversy? I could meet you there in, say, half an hour? I've got to put away my groceries before the frozen vegetables melt."

"Sounds terrific!" Ben agreed. Then he glanced at his shirt. "If you don't mind the smell of fish across the table."

"I order it all the time," Dawnelle returned with a laugh. "Lau?"

She shook her head, glanced away. "Not this time. Casey's waiting at home."

Ben frowned. "He'll wait an hour. Switch lanes for once, Lau. You need the break."

The dark eyes came up in appeal. "You know I can't, Ben. You said you understood."

Ben glanced uncomfortably at Dawnelle, then sighed. "I do. But sometimes I think all you need to do to change the course of your life is to give me—" he coughed "—to let go of the old ways. Let the past die."

"That's asking the impossible," Lau said crisply. "The past has made me who I am." She turned to Dawnelle. "Baird called last night. He sends greetings and asks you to look for his return sometime next week."

Baird called Lau to give me a message? "He called?" she said, low and contained. "He's well? Coming home? But—" *Why did he call you?*

"Said something about working with the government officials in Singapore." Lau tossed back her mane of shining hair. "It's taking more time than he expected, because they're using him to track Vee."

"Any luck so far?" Dawnelle strove to control the shake in her voice.

"Oh, they know where he is now—Vee, I mean. He

runs a plastics-manufacturing operation that he bought for peanuts after he bankrupted the previous owner. Baird has been serving as a consultant to local officials who plan to infiltrate the plastics firm and find evidence of Vee's methods."

"Why the subterfuge? Couldn't they just close down his operation?"

"I don't know. It has something to do with not wanting to shake up other foreign investors who run legitimate businesses employing local labor. It's complicated."

"I thought Langston was gung ho to get his own business liquid," Ben commented as he shut the trunk of the car, bathing them all in darkness. "Dawnelle's running herself ragged trying to keep it operational, even productive, and Langston's off playing cops and robbers overseas. Doesn't make a lick of sense to me."

"I don't mind the work," Dawnelle said. "I just hope he's got plenty of backup when they finally go after Vee."

She felt Ben's hand on her arm. "Langston looks as if he can take care of himself," he said softly.

"But he's had a run of bad luck," Lau insisted, her voice floating through the darkness.

"What's that supposed to mean?" Dawnelle asked quickly, alarmed.

"Nothing...just that some things are beyond our control."

Dawnelle didn't want to recognize the concern hidden beneath that calmly delivered line.

"Lau...." Ben's voice chided gently. His hand left Dawnelle's arm, and she suspected he'd reached toward Lau. She heard the scratch of canvas—Lau's green coat, perhaps. "Can I change your mind about that drink?"

"I'm sorry," came the woman's calm denial. "I told you, Ben. It'd just be inviting trouble."

"I don't feel much like one, either," Dawnelle said. "Think I'll just. . . catch up on my rest. Sunday's a busy day with Serano."

"Dawnelle?" It was Lau's mellow voice.

"Yes, thanks for the message, Lau. I—I was expecting to hear from him any day now."

"Of course. He said he'd call if there was another delay."

Call you or me, Dawnelle wanted to say bitterly. She turned toward her car. "Thanks. You two take care."

She was inside the Fiat in two strides. When she engaged the ignition, spreading the bright glow of her headlights over the parking lot, she saw Ben leading Lau toward the passenger door of his Chevrolet. Dawnelle frowned. Baird had spent one of his precious phone calls on Lau. He was working under cover, that was why he couldn't keep in regular touch, but he'd called Lau, not her. And she knew more about Baird's Singapore activities than he'd ever confided to Dawnelle. That might imply that Baird was the "trouble" Lau expected if she and Ben went out for a drink.

As Dawnelle circled and drove past them, she saw Ben leaning into the open window, his head very close to Lau's. They weren't kissing—Ben had confided in her that Lau still kept him at arm's length—but Dawnelle wished to the depths of her soul they were. And not just for Ben's sake.

GREEN SATIN lay in waves against the crimson blanket, firelight streaking up the folds of the dressing gown as

Dawnelle bent toward the heat. Her hair was still damp, the floral scent of shampoo still aromatic as she ran her fingers through the chestnut tangles. Miss Mo lifted her head from the corner of the blanket, watching her mistress.

Laughing quietly, Dawnelle sprawled to reach the shepherd. She gently scrubbed the dog's chin, and with a languorous sigh, Miss Mo stretched flat and closed her eyes.

"Spoiled," Dawnelle chided softly, drawing her fingers through the silver fur. "And no kind of a watchdog, either. Letting those kids climb all over you last week. Letting Baird in that time he brought the fish. Dad says he's relieved you're here, but he doesn't know what a pushover you are, does he?"

Miss Mo's tail curled, the barest hint that she'd heard.

" 'Silver cub,' Baird called you that night. Huh! You look more like a raccoon with that black mask you're getting." Grabbing the dark muzzle, Dawnelle playfully pried it open to look at the sharp teeth. "Alligator!"

Roused finally, Miss Mo grasped Dawnelle's teasing hand in her jaws, making awr-r-ring sounds as she gently played tug-of-war.

Wrestling absently, feeling restless herself, Dawnelle turned to watch the fire.

It's Wednesday, she thought, *and still he hasn't come home. You'll have white hairs in place of the black, Miss Mo, when he finally gets here.*

Miss Mo dropped Dawnelle's hand rather abruptly and issued a short high yip. Dawnelle glanced around.

Surging to her feet, the shepherd stood looking toward the kitchen, then the empty dining room. And then, tail wagging, ears pricked eagerly, she raced to the front door. She skidded to a stop, barked once, a shrill greeting, and stood waiting expectantly.

Baird, Dawnelle wondered, aware that her hair straggled around her shoulders, uncombed, and that she wore the clinging robe. Had Miss Mo recognized his truck? His stride? Perhaps it was Ben. Or perhaps Miss Mo had got so used to visitors she no longer feared strangers, even at eleven o'clock at night?

The picket gate creaked—it still needed oil—and a brisk tred moved up the walk. "Dawnelle?" Baird's voice thundered from outside. "It's me, Baird. Don't be alarmed."

Dawnelle gave a small gasp of relief and anticipation. Rising, she ran to the door and flung it wide. A chilly breeze flipped at her gown. Miss Mo rushed into the lamplight of the porch, groaning and whining, seeking Baird's hand, rubbing against him as he caressed her.

"Surely you didn't come all this way," Dawnelle mocked her own words of last June, "just to scratch my dog silly."

"Matter of fact I didn't. . . ." Straightening, Baird now stared at Dawnelle, his mouth slack with amazement. "My God!" he said.

"What?" Dawnelle searched her body, raised a hand to her hair. Then, seeing the burning light in his eyes, she faltered, "What's. . . wrong?"

"It's just—I've thought about you, missed you all these weeks. You're tanned. Thinner. So much better in real life. Ah, Dawny. Lass. Give us a hug!"

She came to the haven he created when he held out his arms. And it was different this time, familiar, yet more exciting for the precious memories she carried. She heard him mutter softly, a coming-home kind of sound as his great arms pressed her against his brown cotton T-shirt. She could smell soap and a hint of masculine cologne. He'd just showered. His hair was damp and cold.

"Why didn't you call me to pick you up at the airport?" she asked. "What happened in Singapore—I suppose you'll have to go back again? Serano has just about run out of packing materials, too, for the second time, and we've—"

He laughed heartily, the belly laugh of a big man. His chest jarred against her cheek. "That's my green eyes," he chuckled, at last holding her at arm's length. "Don't invite a guy in or anything. Give him the third degree before he sets foot inside." His eyes twinkled.

Her cheeks burned, and she backed away, her smile sheepish. "I was just glad to see you," she said, mildly defensive. Reaching for his hand, she drew him inside. Miss Mo squeezed through, creating a momentary traffic jam before the door was closed against the crisp night.

"You can hardly blame me," she continued as Baird's eyes strayed to the red blanket spread before the fire. "I mean, you were supposed to be home weeks ago. Weeks...."

But his dark, dark blue gaze returned to Dawnelle, silencing her. His gaze traveled over the rise of her breasts, the shimmering satin molded to her narrow waist, and back to her face.

"You have no idea," he said, his voice husky, "what this secluded cottage scene, the fireplace, the one lamp burning, your clothes.... No idea what they do to me. Dawnelle...you're not wearing anything under that gorgeous satin grape skin...are you?"

Mesmerized by his tone, she silently shook her head.

Her answer seemed to tip him over a ledge into a free-fall zone where control was impossible. As suddenly as he'd arrived this night, Baird swept her into his arms and kissed her with such passion, she went weak in a glorying reveling way that was both madness and perfect sanity. Every marble-cold resolution she'd erected against this moment came crashing to earth. The rubble lay scattered, and she didn't care.

But when the kiss ended and she realized he was aroused, she pulled back slightly, remembering all her unanswered questions. "Shouldn't we...talk or something?" she said shakily.

He touched her cheek, longing evident in the lingering caress he made of that touch. Glancing toward the fire, the blanket, he said, "It'll be difficult. I suppose we could try."

The serious doubt in his voice tickled her. She laughed. "We'll do more than try. C'mon." She led him to the fire.

Taking a steadying breath, he stood beside her, too close, forcing her to concentrate very hard on raising the strands of her hair to the drying heat. She did not look at him. They must talk.

She began lightly. "Lau was worried about you last week."

"How about you?" His smile was baiting.

"Aren't *we* smug?"

"No, seriously." He circled a casual arm around her waist, nuzzled her hair. "Did the lighthouse lady of Trinidad Bay set out a flare or two for me?"

She slipped away, laughing, pretending great determination about drying her hair, covering her erratic feelings as best she could. "How could anyone miss a demanding opinionated man like you?"

"You just said Lau—"

"Was worried," she interrupted emphatically. "Worried and missing are different. Why did you call her from Singapore, anyway? I mean," she added quickly, disappointed in her tactless question, "surely you were worried about how Langston Marine was getting on."

"With you in charge?" Baird gave her a reproachful look. "You think I'm crazy? I didn't want to chance disrupting that tremendous momentum you obviously had going over at my place."

"Yeah?" She grinned.

"Definitely. The lab is in better shape than when I left."

She nodded, agreeing.

"The books are more orderly than I keep them. I'll be able to pay you well for your efforts."

"Thanks. It was nothing."

"Sure. That's what they all say. But the orders have been pouring in, haven't they? Due in large part to you, your ideas, your hard work."

Now she shrugged, her gaze skittering around the room. This much praise from Baird Langston was rare, high stratosphere. It made her feel strangely humble. "I need to comb my hair," she said, stepping away.

"I'm coming with you." He caught her hand.

She stopped. "That's bold."

"I know. Familiarity breeds. . . boldness. But I don't want to risk your changing out of that beautiful green number. It does things to me."

Smiling softly, she pulled her loose collar closed and led him to the bathroom. The two of them barely fit into the space between the sink and the tub. Too intimate, she decided, grabbing her comb and pushing him backward out of the room. Besides, they had to talk.

Miss Mo was standing by the front door when they returned. Baird let her outside to run while Dawnelle went to the dying fire and combed her hair. The dark mass was nearly dry, fluffy with electricity, and as Baird advanced, she remembered the way she'd teased him by draping her hair across his chest. She'd driven him wild....

"So what else did you want to talk about?" he asked, straightening her collar. He paused, hands resting lightly against her breasts.

"I'm sure you have news," she said, fighting the awareness that urged her to wrap her arms around him.

"I'll be here several weeks. Plenty of time to catch up." He draped her collar wide to reveal more cleavage.

She dropped the comb then. His eyes moved to her face. His expression forbade her to pick it up.

"Singapore," she said—sentences were impossible. "Langston Marine, Lau...."

"I've set up a small trained staff to infiltrate Vee's plastics company—all with government sanction this time. My business is in great shape, thanks to you and Serano. And Lau? Since Casey's illness last December, Lau's nerves have been as brittle as pond ice after the first freeze. She thinks another tragedy is hanging over her head. That's why I keep tabs on her. How's that for a quick rundown?"

"Great," she replied absently, preoccupied with guilt for the jealous darts she'd thrown, mentally at least, at Lau. The woman evidently had serious problems. Did Ben realize it? She'd seen so little of him lately.

"Dawnelle?"

She looked at him again.

Baird was smiling faintly. "Any other items for discussion before we adjourn the meeting in favor of a proper homecoming?"

Difficult as it was, this next had to be asked. She plunged. "What about you and me, Baird? What are your feelings about us?"

"In relation to what? I missed you like mad. I'm crazy about you, and I'm afraid tonight I have a one-track mind. It's worse now, you know...since that night, the night before I went overseas."

He'd evaded the real question, and she feared she couldn't send him home. She'd planned to, those many nights when she'd wrestled with having an affair with him. Fearing his eventual betrayal, she'd decided to give him an ultimatum: talk seriously of commitment, or eliminate the sleeping-together part of their relationship. Not to tease him or to make him pay for her love, but to put some badly needed weather strip around her emotions. She felt, sometimes, as vulnerable as he insisted Lau felt. But was Baird ready for commitment? Did he even love her?

His hand slid beneath the back of her collar. He began massaging, rubbing the slinky fabric over her skin, melting her resolve. "Anything else?" he prompted softly.

The tone went deep into her, a satin blade. She looked into his eyes but couldn't form the questions again. Just this one night. One last time of loving....

"In that case," he said, assuming the subject was closed and scarcely hiding his eagerness, "I'd like to make proper restitution for all you've done for me."

Wanting a diversion, wanting more answers, fighting

the tingle at the back of her neck, she asked a little desperately, "Would you like me to turn on some music? Serve you some tea?"

"Actually," he said seriously, "now that I have my lady lighthouse keeper with me, everything is perfect as it is."

"Charmer. I thought you were a man who preferred solitude."

"Usually."

"Are you saying there's something different about tonight?"

"Could be. As you know, I have my own canine companion. My own fireplace."

"That leaves me. You don't have me in that huge house of yours."

"Timber-r-r," he said softly. "I don't have you."

And the moment for answers passed out of reach. She watched him leave her, snap off the light by the blue lounge chair. Next, shuttling her delicately aside, he built the fire to a crackling blaze that threw waving forms like primitive dancers on the walls. Turning his back to the flames, he stood gazing at her.

A tightness gripped her stomach and thighs.

"My heart rate would explode a stethoscope," he said, a hoarse whisper from his shadowed form. "I want you so badly."

She stared at him, running her eyes over his long legs and wondering, without his close-fitting shirt and jeans, what the fire would reveal of his body. The light caught in the down on his arms, outlining the prominent muscles in gold. Except for a line of blue encasing his legs, everything else about him was dark—a dark-skinned laird of the highlands warming his hands by the fire before loving his woman. She shivered, yet she watched him boldly, knowing he could see the green lights in her eyes.

He bent in front of her, his lips poised invitingly close to hers. His dusky eyes asked something of her; she felt her own lips part. All the dark nights of longing...the fragile moments when her mind was free to remember....

She invited him with her eyes, invited him to kiss her and knew something singularly lonely was flung away with the look.

"Dawnelle...." The deep blue of his gaze drew her into his arms. Her eyes widened at the shock of coming full against him, feeling every rippling muscle as he embraced her. He was still aroused, she realized with a mixture of embarrassment and excitement.

Holding her quietly for a moment, he let her relax and become familiar with the places their bodies molded. And when she stood pliantly enclosed in his arms, her hands resting on his shoulders, he kissed her lingeringly. It was a sweet kiss that flamed quickly into passion. Her uncertainties forgotten, she began to feel the iron press of his hips against hers; began to respond with slow undulations, part need and part seduction.

Even as she arched back, eyes closed, willingly letting his lips travel down the taut skin of her throat to that valley of softness between her breasts, she knew she needed him. Purely by instinct. As she needed to breathe. As a woman needs the only man she has ever deeply loved.

"Can't sleep for dreaming of you," he was saying.

The low rasp spurred her to grasp his face with her hands. She fused their lips in a wild moving kiss, remembering the great wave in that night of love; the wave that had become a symbol of her nights and her future. *What are we,* she asked silently. *Ships colliding in a storm, or the sea itself?* The sea—billions upon billions of particles clinging together in a world-wandering tide, weathering storms, lying in sunny shallow bays, giving life, always giving life. Always together. One.

Baird's kiss wandered to her earlobe, where his teeth and lips and tongue made her shiver with pleasure. His breathing coming faster, he nibbled her skin until she began to shudder. Slowly he kissed his way over her jaw toward her mouth. Anticipating his next caress, she turned her head, eager to feel his mouth full on her own.

He laughed huskily, met her lips, pulled away. "I take it the missing business isn't one-sided."

"No," she said urgently, "No, I've missed you, too." She tried to wrap her arms around his neck to pull him back, but he laughed again and stepped away.

He stripped off his shirt and dropped it on the floor. When he'd kicked off his leather loafers and set aside his socks, his smoky gaze captured hers, making it difficult to satisfy her curiosity about his body.

Yet she did look; at last she stood watching the firelight flicker over bronzed pectoral muscles. The dark hair on his chest flamed reddish, tapering out of sight beneath his jeans. Veins traced over lean forearms, and biceps cut sharply by hard work bulged as he drew a casual hand to his hip.

She wanted to put her mouth around one of his dark breast points, and perhaps he guessed her fantasy, for the peak rose slightly. Her gaze traveled down.

As if following her visual exploration, his hands appeared at the snap of his jeans. An efficient "pop" had the clasp undone; an inch more of the dark hair curled tantalizingly from behind the zipper.

Perspiration moistened her upper lip now; a damp warmth suffused her thighs. The tension of waiting grew nearly unbearable. That first time, he'd said he would make her want him more....

He hung a thumb nonchalantly, teasingly, in his waistband. The act prompted her to glance hungrily at his face, her heart drumming into her throat.

Lips parted slightly in a delicious smile, Baird stood before her a moment longer, his magnificent body cast in browns and golds. "Now I know why your eyes are green," he murmured, coming close and putting both hands at the belt of her gown.

"Why?" She could barely speak.

"Greed."

A small laugh burst from her.

"So you don't deny it?" The belt slipped free, and her gown parted.

"I...could deny nothing now. I could deny you nothing you wanted."

"That's good, my greedy goddess. For I'm as greedy as you...."

As the satin slid away, she closed her eyes. Warmth from the fire wrapped around her. She stood three-quarters turned from the bright heat, knew her body was outlined for him. She stood proudly, her back straight, her breasts taut and rising with shallow breathing, one hip tilted in the classic model's pose.

"Goddess," she heard him mutter softly. Just as she languidly opened her eyes, she felt the first touch of his hands on her naked flesh, reverently searching the narrow dip between ribcage and hip, straying to just below her breasts. Something proud and uninhibited possessed her to close her eyes again and arch her body, chin tipped, back bent in a graceful dancer's dip.

Baird's arm came around her waist. As he lowered her to the blanket, he teased the delicate nerves of her throat with light kisses. She felt the soft red wool cushion her hip—then felt his lips close over her breast in the most sudden and erotic kiss she had ever known. Her breath escaped. She lay draped over his supporting arm like some exotic flower while his moist mouth tasted her.

Removing his arm from beneath her, his tongue encircling and arousing her nipple, he swayed. She heard the purr of his zipper. He was leaning away from her now, standing. Through a haze of eroticism she saw him reveal his body to her. With the moving flames as a backdrop, she took in his form, narrow-hipped as she remembered, with strong thighs and curving calves that would have been the pride of any kilted highlander.

But this man was not kilted, and her gaze returned to the deep shadow between his thighs, where flickering light revealed the pale glow of full arousal. Still he stood back from her, and as she watched the fire glow carve from the darkness an angular musclar buttock, she knew he must be taking a lusty look at her own body, curving against the crimson bed.

Then with a guttural love sound, Baird was lying with her, kissing her, and their bodies began a dance as wild and sinuous as the fire shadows on the walls. Heat buoyed Dawnelle's senses, making each touch of his velvet skin a half touch, a knowing invasion of secret pleasure spots. It was as if he couldn't touch other than with awe. His caresses were as light as hers, and she knew no greater ecstasy. They were matched in passion, equal in sensitivity. Yet both grew as bold as adventurers in discovering new ways to delight each other's senses.

The feather touches became more insistent; the twining of their bodies more ecstatic and finally more rhythmic. Baird's skin was sleek now with heat and moisture. His lips demanded, his hands molded, slid, ravished with an eagerness and hunger that thrilled her.

He joined with her, a gentle, sure, powerful act of possession, and she welcomed him. Her cry of longing earned his husky response, "Yes, my beauty, my love. So long...since we loved. This pleasure is...ours."

Again Dawnelle called out, a haunting sound that meant only urgency, and with the inward vision of a sweeping tide, the awareness of a great tension, she arched and dove and sank with her lover.

When the wave came—a swift, lunging, mercifully consuming euphoria—she heard the brief glad cry of Baird's own unleashed passion. The wave that was hers was also his, the pleasure mingled, the swift uprise and explosion, theirs.

CHAPTER SIXTEEN

AS OCTOBER GREW DAMP AND COLD, Dawnelle felt herself slipping away from the resolutions she'd made to seek Baird's commitment. She'd never been happier—waking in his arms, tramping the coastline in search of marine specimens, working with him and Serano at the cliff house. But there were scary moments when she saw ahead to years of casual splendor—no children, no joint tenancy, just years of emotional bliss—and she the only one fully committed to the relationship.

For Baird was also seeing Lau.

Twice when Dawnelle was home alone because Baird "already had plans for the evening," Ben called. Casey had mentioned to Ben—"Tonight's Uncle Baird's night to visit"—and Ben had disclosed the news, suspecting Dawnelle was worried but anxious to reassure her.

"Say, Dawnelle," Ben said over the telephone during their second catch-up conversation, "you want to know what they do when they get together these nights?"

"Ben, no please."

"No kidding. They talk about books."

"Books! Books, Ben? How do you know?"

"Casey let it slip last Sunday when we were scrubbing the fish slime off the decks. Besides, Lau's whole living room is full of books—two walls of them. I saw them one morning this summer when I came by to pick her up and she was fixing Casey's breakfast. Books stacked by a reading chair, boxes of them lining the hall. Incredible. She once wanted to be a research scientist. She told me that, you know, the way one might say, 'I wanted to go trout fishing last week.' "

"My God, Ben. She fishes for a living!"

"Tell me something I don't know."

Shocked, Dawnelle stared at the coals glowing in the fireplace. "What prevented her from pursuing her goal?"

"The family was against it. They wanted her to marry, have kids. I was disgusted when I heard that. All those brains going to waste. I mean, can't women do both? And then her husband dying tragically. She says Langston understands all that. . . ."

Dawnelle drew a tight breath, let it out slowly. "Do you think it's more than understanding, Ben? Between Lau and Baird?"

"No—that is, I'll bet it's just friendship. But Lau's so complicated. So secretive."

"Then why are you so crazy about her?"

His tone grew serious. "I get short of oxygen just standing next to her. And she's a helluva good mother to Casey, too. If all that loyalty ever got aimed in my direction, I'd probably keel over from the force of it."

Beauty, brains, loyalty, courage—how could any man resist Lau? Sighing, Dawnelle turned the conversation to fishing, letting Ben tell her about Lau's fanaticism with safety aboard the boat.

His only qualm in their early days together, he said, had been taking orders from a woman. But he'd soon learned someone had to run the boat, make decisions that might someday save their lives. "What do I know about boat safety?" He laughed. "Me, a dirt farmer from the Midwest?"

"Dirt farmer or not, you've got it good. This is exactly the life you wanted."

"Yeah.... And I think Lau will trust me enough to confide in me one of these days...."

His optimism was admirable. When Dawnelle and Ben concluded the call, she realized his hopes about Lau weren't dimmed in the slightest by "Uncle Baird's visits." Dawnelle, on the other hand, sat brooding before the fire, a cup of tea in her hand. Push had finally come to shove. She must talk to Baird.

BAIRD WAS MASTERFUL at avoiding personal issues. She tried several times in the next month to open discussions about their feelings, but twice he circled back to business topics. The last time, he'd grabbed her in a laughing hug, swung her around, and grinned enchantingly. "What is it you want of me, green eyes? Isn't it enough that we get along so well?" He'd quelled her answer with a kiss, a warm, clinging kiss that sent them to a place where only sensual hungers were fulfilled.

The next morning, disgusted with her easy capitulation, she'd announced that she planned to serve him dinner that night. They would "settle things." Her tone had brooked no argument. He scowled at her but hadn't asked for an explanation.

He arrived at the cottage at eight o'clock. Hair up, a hint of crisp perfume wafting around her, she allowed a quick squeeze and a peck on the cheek—which she'd diverted from her lips—then seated him at the candlelit kitchen table. She served him wine.

Despite her preparations and resolve, throughout the meal Dawnelle was edgy. Baird attempted his usual loving manner and casual conversation, but she knew he sensed a showdown.

What are your intentions, Baird, she thought, pushing roast beef and cooling mashed potatoes into a heap on her plate. She could hear how prissy the words would sound. She could imagine his surprise, his smooth attempt to hide dismay. He'd already expressed uncertainty about his feelings, but she didn't know if that was because of Lau, or because he feared commitment. Yet every soft word in the dark, every hungry caress, every laugh, sigh and lingering look from him spoke of his love. Why couldn't he say the words?

She closed her eyes, took a deep breath and was about to speak when Baird set down his wineglass and cleared his throat. His lips, tinted with California burgundy, looked regretful.

"I'm afraid I have bad news," he said, brushing his mouth with his napkin and setting the cloth aside. He pushed back his chair, leaned his elbows on the table, looked at her. "Well—" he shrugged "—bad news and good. I'm expecting to be called overseas again any day."

She groaned involuntarily.

"Mmm." He nodded. "Vee is very close to being arrested and extradited to the States for trial."

She rose, deflated, already feeling the pain of his absence. "That's. . . wonderful." She was unable to muster the joy she knew he expected. "How soon?"

"A week maybe."

"Thanksgiving."

"Then, or just after."

She turned from the table, heading out of the room, wondering if she had the courage to push the personal issue now. Another roadblock, another delay, while her insides churned with uncertainty.

"You forgot your wine, Dawnelle."

She stopped at the door, turned. "Us, Baird," she said softly, her throat sore from pent-up emotion. "We never talked about us."

He stood up. "Aren't you pleased about Vee? Only eight months, Dawnelle. How about that for a drag-net?"

He came around the table and reached for her, but she turned and walked swiftly to the living room. She began to pace agitatedly before the fire, hardly aware that she was clenching her hands, twisting them together. Something was wrong between them. A nameless thing still stood in the way of his feelings. He was so sensitive when they made love, yet he lacked sensitivity in the most crucial area of their relationship: verbal communication. For weeks he had refused to see her distress. Or to seek its cause.

Stalking her for a few steps, he abruptly caught her wrist. "Dawnelle, I can't just forget all that's happened to me. I know that's what you want, but I can't promise you rose gardens when I'm still climbing out of the briar patch."

"How do you know what I want?" she flared, jerking her arm free. His words stung her, his assumptions, and she accused him bitterly, "You sound like Lau."

"What kind of crack is that?"

"Lau." She waved. "She says she can't let go of the past because it made her who she is today. She's mired in it. Maybe that's what you want—someone to share your past, wallow in it with you so you don't have to make anything sure and good of your future."

His skin reddened with suppressed anger. "I'm not 'wallowing' in the past, dammit. I'm trying to rectify the damage that's been done and go on from there. You expect miracles in less than a year."

She faced him, hands still clenched. "Not miracles, Baird. Courage."

"Do you think it's easy traipsing around the tropics looking for that crook?" His voice was rising, rising, filling the room. "Do you think I like it, Dawnelle? Give me a break!"

"I think you like it, yes," she returned, incensed by his argumentative tone. "You're playing war games because you're damned scared of starting over in the business world. In the real world."

"I've started over!" he said, the words almost a curse.

"Yes, and look at how dedicated you are to making Langston Marine go. Serano gets your orders out, and I play bookkeeper while you spend months overseas—months, if you add up the weeks! I think you're scared you'll be taken to the cleaners again. You're not giving your company the attention it needs to grow. Instead, you're chasing tigers who have no intention of being cornered. That citation you refused in the marines?" she challenged, her fist under his nose. "You're earning it now. This time you'll take it, won't you? You'll put that extradition in your file like a citation for bravery. Well, the war's over, Baird—long over—and Vee's too high a price to pay for losing your soul. Maybe your life."

"I have to try, Dawnelle," he said, grasping her hand. "We'll bust him, I can feel it. We're so close now. So close—"

She snatched her hand away. "Meanwhile I'm a convenient way station between Vee and Langston Marine. For how long, Baird? How long will you expect me to wait for you to come to terms with your future?"

"Give me time, Dawnelle. Indictment, trial—they're just around the corner. All we lack is final proof, a confession."

"And if you don't get it from him? Perhaps until next year?" She was disgusted with the circles that always led back to the past. Jeff's blond good looks wavered before her. She was used again, thrown aside after valuable time invested. She looked at Baird leaning toward her with intensity. Baird. The man who meant more to her than anyone ever had. Suddenly she knew a falling sensation—sinking; drowning in the years of waiting. She would be gray. Too old for motherhood. Used again and again by men who saw their own needs first.

"No," she choked, twisting her hands once more. "No!"

She looked more desperately at him, saw his face pale, saw the crescents of tension around his mouth. Still the words she longed to hear would not be spoken. So only survival mattered. "I'll continue to fill in for you when you need me," she said hoarsely over the constriction in her throat. "I won't run out on you. But

Baird—" her hardness was sudden, surprising even herself, and it tore her like glass inside "—don't ask me to be your mistress!"

"For God's *sake*, Dawnelle, don't do this!"

"Baird." She gripped his arm. "I've been chasing you. All these months, even after the dance when we were apart, my mind still chased you, wanted you. Me—" she struck her chest "—the woman who came to Trinidad to heal, to gather herself for a fresh life. And I found you— God—" she laughed bitterly "—how right the psychologists are when they say you repeat mistakes in relationships, repeat them over and over until you face and correct some error inside yourself. Well, you're my error, Baird."

"Dawnelle, let me—"

"No! I'm correcting the error tonight. I want it back. I want back that part of me that I gave to you in that bed of yours. I want to be completely my own woman again—not partly yours." Heart pounding painfully, she drew a long irregular breath. Distractedly she walked to the chesterfield. Without facing him, she concluded softly, "Don't ask me to sleep with you again, Baird."

Silence met her words, and she turned to look at him.

She nearly cried out. He stood glaring at her, breathing heavily, hands fisted as tightly as that day in the forest at Luffenholtz when he'd told her of Suzanne's betrayal.

"I knew you would do this," he said tersely. "I always knew."

He strode to the door, jerked it open and slammed it mightily behind him.

HE CALLED AT TEN O'CLOCK. She'd barely composed herself from hard bitter crying. "I needed to get out," he said, the regret so thick in his voice, he sounded ill.

The silence built for a minute before she said gently, "I know. You need time."

"Yes. Time." His laugh was empty. "I didn't realize I was hurting you. I guess. . . I guess I was, but you just kind of go along on a cloud when things are good. You know, Dawny? They were good. . . ."

She closed her eyes, felt the tears bead on her lashes and did not try to stop them.

"Just need a few days," he said vaguely. "Think things out."

"This is crazy," she replied huskily, her head swinging from side to side and the tears gathering, running unchecked down her cheeks. "When we have so much. . . ."

"My greedy green eyes. Just. . . a little time." He sighed unsteadily. "I'll keep in touch."

"Baird!"

"I'll call. Dawnelle, you're right. You know me, said some things I'm just now looking at. I just need to. . . sort things out, get them straight. Give me that, will you?"

"Yes," she said in a small voice.

"All right. Good." He repeated more firmly, "Good. I'll be here a few days, then, if you need anything. Remember to keep your doors and gates locked, huh? I'll call before I leave."

"I'll be there working for you—" The tightness in her throat overwhelmed her, and she held her breath to keep from sobbing.

A long silence. "I'll call you." He hung up.

She wept bent over, the black receiver clutched against her, and what came of the weeping was a washing away of agony and doubt, a resurgence of hope. He cared. She was certain he loved her. And now she didn't need the words, but he needed the time to realize it, too.

CHAPTER SEVENTEEN

THE HORN MOANED and the world wrapped around her in a cool white shroud, increasing her sense of isolation as she stood on the railed lookout of the lighthouse. The entire coast was socked in. Moody and still as a cemetery. Shaking off morbid thoughts, Dawnelle scanned the bluff. She could barely see the red roof and white walls of the tiny old bell house set high into the south rim, its clapboards quaking every twenty seconds or so with the throaty call of the fog signal.

She couldn't see the water or Pilot Rock a mile south, so thick was the fog. She glanced beneath her. Bunched around the base of the light, orange flowers on lacy stalks looked as if they were waving behind frosted glass. The lily of the valley and the profusion of pink wild roses were gone now, but the spicy scent of brush and stunted pines mingled with the salt that always hung in the air on still days. Poison oak, a mature red blush staining its clustered leaves, peeped from crevices twenty feet from the swath she'd cleared around the lighthouse.

She found herself more and more frequently steeping her senses in the beauty of the headland. Like the addict she was, she needed the balm of sea and rocks and greenery to erase those persistent longings for Baird.

Five days since that talk on the telephone. Long days. She'd been so sure he'd quickly realize his love for her and call again. Nothing so far. Her brief certainty about his feelings had begun to waver.

No visitors to sidetrack her loneliness. No spirit for the endless chores she should get done. Henny and Sarah had gone to Sacramento to see their daughter and grandkids, and Ben had already flown home to see his family. Maybe Baird was gone, too. Maybe she'd misjudged the emotion in his voice that final night. She couldn't remember when she'd had so many questions and suffered so much over the answers. Had he broken off their relationship completely and gone to Singapore without calling? Or would he be sharing Thanksgiving with Lau? Would Baird wear a leather jacket and cashmere sweater, carve the turkey, smile at Lau, kid around with Casey? The image bit sharply into her. She turned to duck through the door of the lamp housing, went below to lock up.

She should have invited her father out to the light station for Thanksgiving, but she knew why she hadn't. André Belanger had strict standards when it came to sleeping with someone you weren't married to. She loved him, respected his feelings, couldn't flaunt her life-style in his face. And she had been so expectant about a reunion with Baird.

She ought to drive home to see her father. Yes. Pick up the turkey she'd ordered weeks ago and freeze it for another day—no. The freezer was full of blackberries and steelhead trout. Better ask the grocer to keep the bird frozen.

Well, she'd decide on an itinerary while in town doing

errands—a quick bath, a fast run into town, and maybe tonight she'd bake that blackberry pie she'd planned. Then she just might drive all the way to central California and present it to her father. It was nonsense to feel like the gray sky was lowering around her. Enticed by the thought of a family reunion, she'd fight the doldrums all the way to the Shasta-Trinity National Recreation Area!

THE QUICK BATH evolved into a leisurely one, while the sky darkened and the wind blew up, silencing the foghorn.

An hour later, Dawnelle tugged her fitted Western plaid shirt straight and tucked it into her jeans. She glanced into the mirror over the bathroom sink. The blouse was a green-and-black tartan accented with a thin line of canary, its scalloped shoulder detail piped in matching yellow. Her eyes shone richly green in the subdued light, full of specular highlights that betrayed her rising excitement about tomorrow's trip. No makeup, she decided. The rich tones of the blouse would frame her face with plenty of color. Quickly she swept tortoiseshell combs into her hair, pulling scant wisps around her temples and ears, brushing the chestnut lengths into waves behind the combs.

Heading for the kitchen, she paused to listen. A frantic scratching against the front door. She groaned inwardly. Poor Miss Mo—locked out all this while!

Dawnelle hurried to the door and pulled it open. Miss Mo bounded into the hallway, then circled around Dawnelle's legs, clearly restraining herself from leaping bodily into her mistress's arms. The silver fur was glistening with moisture. A beautiful animal, Dawnelle appraised, grateful for the thousandth time that Miss Mo seemed so happy living with her. And now, so trusting. Most evenings lately, they'd spent curled in front of the fireplace, Miss Mo's head on her lap, Dawnelle reading and idly stroking the satiny fur behind the dog's ears. The bond between them grew steadily stronger as the seasons in Trinidad slipped by.

Praising the animal for her newly acquired manners, Dawnelle led her into the kitchen, where she opened canned dog food and fed her. "Eat well," she advised her ravenous pet, "because tomorrow you may be carsick. It's a long drive to dad's place."

Dawnelle scooped up a black nylon bag containing her checkbook and personal items, took her keys from the rack near the door and went out.

ON THE DRIVE HOME from the store, Dawnelle gripped the ebony wheel and peered hard through the windshield. The wind had died again, and the world had turned white as a snowstorm in the headlights of her car. Visibility was thirty feet maximum. Moisture-laden bushes draped over the narrow lane, clutching at the Fiat, scraping eerily along the paint. It would be a relief to cozy up by the fire with Miss Mo on this night, a night that reminded her of old Vincent Price movies featuring screams from the catacombs. She shivered and braked for the stop at the perimeter gate, drove through and locked up.

As she parked by the big boulder and stepped from the car, both arms full of groceries, the fog alert blared. The sound sent a shiver down her spine. A buoy tinkled faintly. Far below, the ocean seemed to rush at the cliff, pounding against the rock and slithering away, thundering in, hissing away....

She knew her way to the cottage as well as she knew any pathway, but it still felt as if she were walking on the very lip of the earth; she could almost believe the globe was flat. She thought she heard a yelp from Miss Mo—one of her high-pitched greetings—as she moved carefully along the gravel path.

The lighthouse sent its beam through the thick mist, blinding her momentarily. She staggered through the picket gate.

Then, one foot on the porch, she stopped—afraid. The cottage door was ajar.

"Miss Mo?" she queried into the dimly lighted interior.

Had she slammed the door so hard on her way out that it had popped open? No. She'd forgotten to lock it.... Swallowing a feeling of trepidation, she pushed against the heavy structure. It fell wide.

"Lady Mo?" A throaty growl came from somewhere toward the back of the house, and then a high yelp.

Dawnelle stepped into the hall. The air in the room was warm from the oil furnace, leaving a heaviness like cheap perfume on her skin. A strange stillness pervaded.

Her heart worked in deep, slowly paced thuds, pumping adrenaline. Only silence, yet something was very out of place in the tiny cottage. Her nerves, she thought, gripping her keys tightly in her palm. Too much mental stress and no food in her stomach. Miss Mo was probably having one of those chase dreams she suffered after a particularly grueling day on the hills.

The foghorn moaned. Dawnelle jumped, watched the lighthouse beam swing across the living room. The blue easy chair was skewed, as if the dog had plunged into it at that rocketing speed that characterized her play. Where *was* she?

Turning, she closed the door, then called again, "Miss Mo. . . ."

She thought she heard an answering whine from the dog. Worried that the shepherd had hurt herself playing, Dawnelle hurried down the hall. She saw the animal's silver back and black-tipped tail lying just inside the kitchen door, the front of her body hidden behind the wall.

Dawnelle leaned into the doorway to rouse the dog. "There you are, you crazy—"

Fingers caught her wrist, holding her when she pulled sharply away.

"Baird, is this your idea of a jo—"

She gasped in terror. Jenkins stepped out from behind the door, his bulk encased in stained coveralls and a thin white undershirt, his flabby face shining with perspiration.

"No!"

"Here I am fer sure, pumpkin!" He grinned, stretching to step over Miss Mo. The animal suddenly came alive beneath the obese form, snarling and snapping at his blue legging. She lunged, grappled with his leg, but the worn material tore away as Jenkins kicked at the dog's head. His black boot landed squarely on her jaw, knocking a gleaming canine tooth free, sending it scratching across the floor. Miss Mo yelped in pain. Blood trickled down her jaw, and she kept on yipping as

Dawnelle sank the nails of her free hand into Jenkins's thick wrist. He slapped her hand away.

With a terrible sinking regret, she realized she'd forgotten about Jenkins—had even forgotten to relate the Labor Day incident to Baird or Ben. "Act of violence"—Baird's angry growl the night he'd danced with her at the town hall. No crowds milled around the corner now, drinking beer and playing games of chance. Even if she lifted her voice in the most terrified scream, no strong male friend was within range. Jenkins was bent on making good his threats, and she was alone.

He was breathing heavily from the effort of holding her still, but she knew well how powerful he was, despite his considerable weight. Grinning maniacally, he tried to pull her close. A scream wrenched from her, a long agonized cry of terror. She tried to yank away.

Jenkins wheezed into his familar laugh. "Scream all ya want, darlin'. It'll do ya no good out here. Planned this for months, ya know. Had me a dry run on Labor Day, just to make sure it would all work."

"Wh—what do you want?"

"You, darlin', that's what I want." He laughed heartily. "Lookee here what I got fer ya if you're real nice." He probed in a pocket of his coveralls and came up with a crumpled white paper. He held it in front of her: Miss Mo's registration. Stuffing it away, he said, "She's worth a bunch more'n you paid. You're gonna pay extry for every pound of that bitch."

From the corner of her eye Dawnelle watched Miss Mo circle behind the giant, hackles raised, lips curled back and tongue running ceaselessly over the bloody gums. She limped but still stalked with the menace of a timber wolf, eyes glittering.

Suddenly Dawnelle felt the bite of metal in her captive hand. The keys. Had she locked the door when she came in? No! *Get to the door.* Could Jenkins be conned? He was standing astride in the kitchen doorway, one beefy arm extended to hold her wrist, the other fisted, as if he was waiting for her next move. The tough question was, could she control her terror long enough to coax him into the living room? She took a deep shaky breath, then let it out in a pretense of resignation.

"All right," she said flatly. *Too harsh. Soften your voice.* "All right, let's get this over with."

Jenkins giggled. Soon enough he sobered, though, eyes narrowed. "Hey, what's yer angle?" He jiggled her wrist as if to make her come to life, and the ripple he set off in his middle nearly turned Dawnelle's stomach. "Where's all that steam you had cooked up last time?"

"Last time I was wearing my prettiest dress," she said, looking away. "I—I didn't want to ruin it."

"It was real purty." He jerked his head over his shoulder and Dawnelle couldn't stop the gasp that escaped. Her lacy lingerie lay scattered across the kitchen, hanging on chairs and counters, her black slip torn up the middle and spread on the floor. A wail came from her before she closed her lips over the sound. She stood staring, trembling with chills. "I got some sexy things for ya to try on for me, right here in the kitchen," Jenkins wheedled. "You got real nice things, ain'tcha?"

She gaped. He shook her. "Ain'tcha?"

"Yes—yes. Nice things."

"Well, now. You said some real mean things to me,

remember that? Called me names and things." He jerked her hard. "You remember?"

"I—I remember!"

"Now watch yer tone with me, lady. And apologize! You say you're sorry!"

"I said mean things." Her voice rose, and Miss Mo growled. A warning. The dog would attack. Dawnelle wondered if that would compromise her plans. "I'm sorry, sorry I said those things."

"That's more like it. Now get on over here and put on that rosy-lookin' little bitty top." He gave her arm a powerful tug, dragging her against his stomach. The beery breath poured over her face.

She rebelled, struggled. "Wait!" she breathed. "Let's go—"

She heard a welling growl that gained force as a train gains speed. Then she felt a jolt, heard Jenkins cry out. Cursing, he twisted abruptly. Keeping a grip on her wrist, he brought his other fist down on the crown of Miss Mo's head so hard the crack echoed through the room. Miss Mo grunted but kept her teeth sunk into his leg.

A fiery-red blaze of anger obliterated all logic. Dawnelle raked her attacker's sagging cheek, struck his shoulder, drew back to strike again. "Stop! You'll kill her!"

"Damn right I will." He swung his foot, trying to loosen Miss Mo's clamp on his flesh. In the process he nearly fell, and the anticipated horror of being dragged down with him had Dawnelle fighting to keep him upright. Her fingers sank into the sponge rubber of his side. She yanked away in disgust.

"Don't—just please don't hit her any more. Let me put her outside." She swallowed. "We'll be. . .alone."

"Yeaah. . .I see whatcha mean. Git this bitch off'n my leg, then, and do it quick." She bent away, but he jerked her back. "And no fancy moves, woman. You ain't gonna chisel ol' Pauly outta his rights this time. Ain't no lover boy gonna come ahuntin' you up!"

She nodded mutely, barely able to keep her relief from showing. She would let the dog out—and then run. She had the car keys, could perhaps grab the lighthouse keys on her way out, giving herself more options. It might take some doing, but with the fog, and knowing the station, and having the long legs and lithe body Jenkins lacked....

"Miss Mo," she pleaded, having difficulty dissuading the animal. "Easy.... Come here, girl."

The hackles on the dog's neck began to flatten. The gloom outside the cottage beckoned. Dawnelle wiped her eyes with the back of her hand. "Now, Miss Mo," she crooned shakily, "ease up."

Brushing her hand over the animal's battered head, she kept speaking gently, all the love and compassion she felt for the brave dog coming through in smooth tones. Miss Mo rolled her eyes and began to loosen her grip.

"Don't move," Dawnelle cautioned Jenkins. "She's letting go."

"Stupid bitch better! I'll kill her after this!"

"If you move, we'll be back where we started. These young teeth could rip out your throat if you fell." She sensed Jenkins going calm under the power of her prediction.

Eventually she collected Miss Mo against her legs and began coaxing her from the kitchen, all the while aware that Jenkins lumbered behind them. He was muttering. "Should have killed that bitch when my old lady brought it home! Pawnin' it off wasn't good enough, just like it prob'ly won't do the job with my old lady. Damn bitch!"

"Where is your family?" Dawnelle queried, trying to keep his mind occupied. "Eureka? Arcata?"

"Fat cow lives up the hill, lordin' it over the rest of us in the valley."

"You're divorced, then?"

"Don't she wish! Think you women got somethin' special a man has ta beg for. You gonna learn who begs for a change. And never you mind about that guy you been hangin' around with. He ain't gonna save ya. He don't scare me. You just git that bitch outta my sight. Git movin'!"

She lurched forward, driven by his rough shove. "All right!" She closed her eyes briefly. Baird. So much to regret now that it was too late. Her accusations, the fact that she'd abandoned Baird exactly as Suzanne had abandoned him—not for the same reasons, but giving him that ultimatum had as good as ended the relationship. Greedy fool, she was. Refusing to give him time to grow.

With another shove, Jenkins jarred her loose from recriminations. "All right, all right, Jenkins! I didn't know you knew Langston, that's all."

"Don't. But I seen him around ya. You gonna play with me all night if I want—no bastard with a beard gonna do nuthin' about it. Prob'ly thank me for warmin' ya up some. That picture in the paper made you out a cold female." He giggled as she moved away. "I'm takin' it on myself to change your ways."

Nearly to the door, her heart clamoring like a great machine against her ribs, she repeatedly drew deep breaths to increase the oxygen in her blood, preparing for flight. Gripping Miss Mo's silver collar, she put her hand on the doorknob.

Jenkins immediately bit his damp fingers into the meager flesh of her shoulder. She went still. Miss Mo tried to whirl at the new threat, but Dawnelle held her away with a knee.

"Jenkins," she said with a contrived lift in her voice. "Jenkins, I can neither open the door nor let the dog out with you holding me so tightly."

"Quit fiddly-foolin' around and open it!" Wheezing with excitement, he struck her head.

Black and blue and shards of white careered inside her skull. Stunned, she wavered, then clawed at the door for support. Her fingers slipped away from the chain collar. Vaguely, she felt Miss Mo swerve and attack, the terrible growls racketing through her numb brain. She heard Jenkins's gasp of outrage and pain.

Then, like a river flowing through the pain and terror, the image of cool fog and dark hiding places came to her. She shook her head. *Move,* her common sense urged. *Run!*

Focusing on the black doorknob, she turned it, pulled, felt the rush of moist air. Her head snapped up. Reaching for the lighthouse keys, she yanked them off the rack and darted across the threshold.

She heard Jenkins's angry grunt, a shrill anguished yelp, a thud. Chancing a backward glance, she glimpsed the dog, down and wriggling on her front porch, then the oncoming monolith, Jenkins. His cheek showed angry welts from her nails.

But the glance cost her too much. She tripped, grappled in the thick night, fell forward. Her car keys went hurtling through the mist. She sprawled in the wet grass. Yet she felt no pain—only an urgency to rise, to escape the man caught like a bat in the sweeping beam of the lighthouse. The lighthouse! No time to find the car keys; it would have to be the lighthouse now.

Even as she scrambled to stand, hands reached toward her, circled her waist, lifted her. She screamed, twisted, felt the buttons of her blouse rip away. Soft fumbling hands caught a scrap of material at her shoulder.

"Let me go!"

"No—no you don't," Jenkins panted, attempting to reel her in with his flimsy hold on her sleeve. "Get back here!"

With her footing firm once more, Dawnelle bolted. The sleeve tore away as she staggered down the boardwalk toward the beacon. She must get inside, lock the cast-iron door. The walls were more than twelve inches of solid concrete, tapering walls someone as heavy as Jenkins could never scale. If he broke through the ground-floor window, she would hit him with the huge crescent wrench kept handy to jar loose the points of the foghorn. And if he got the stepladder and gained the catwalk, she'd hear him in time to escape back to the cottage—phone the police, phone Baird.

How terrible she felt about accusing him of fearing success, thinking only of himself. Jenkins. Sick, perverse, brutal Jenkins! *Hard to see through the fog. Got to keep moving. Phone Baird. Watch your step... Boardwalk slick with dew.... Hold onto the fence. Can't see; light too strong. Jenkins, oh, God, Jenkins coming closer! How, how can he move so fast?*

She veered right, groped along the cold wet stone, felt the damp fingers of grass and flowers imbedded in the wall. Ceaselessly, blindly, she ran her hands ahead of her, taking great lungsful of the salty air. It tasted like tide flats. Jenkins again—slithering, stamping down the boardwalk a few feet back, cursing the fog. She praised it, praised the foghorn and the dark. A few feet more.

But the light blinded her again. She paused, disoriented. Jenkins came on, the vibrations of his steps on the walk rattling Dawnelle's thighs.

She began to mutter softly. "Ten feet, nine—black, so black. Poor Miss Mo. Can't see. Jenkins. Pig! Filth! Come on, find the door!"

Where was the lighthouse—worse, the edge of the cliff? If she had to fight him, scramble around in the black seconds between cycles of the light, one of them might go over, over to terrible death either from the rocks or the water. The water, nearly two hundred feet down. A person could live thirty minutes in that water, she'd heard—but only wearing one of those orange dry-dive suits.

Breathing hard, she ducked across the wooden path to the concrete pad supporting the lighthouse. Ten feet through the night....slide the key into the lock, pull the door open, bolt it behind her. Hands feeling through the dark, key at the ready, Dawnelle slid her feet carefully over the bumpy concrete. "Here! God—thank God!"

Suddenly, behind her, she heard a growl so filled with

blood lust she froze against the rough concrete of the light. Miss Mo!

The animal connected with her prey, for Jenkins cried out. A scrape, a dull thud, thud. Silence. He was down, and the dog began making horrendous wailing growls, her nails scratching on the concrete. When the light splayed through the white mist, Dawnelle groaned with horror.

Jenkins had tumbled backward and struck his head. One booted foot was propped on the boardwalk. Both arms were flung out.

He's dead, she thought wildly, her relief swept away by the knowledge that a man lay lifeless only a few feet from the beacon that had saved lives for one hundred and fourteen years. The irony mocked her. *Must get an ambulance,* she reasoned, then laughed shrilly. She kept laughing, the sound mingling with the subdued growls of her dog and the moan of the fog signal.

The beam swung around. Her stomach churning, she glanced away. A damp furry body swept past her knees. Bending to wrap the dog close, Dawnelle felt the laughter ebb as dry panting sobs racked her. Miss Mo whined and licked her hand.

Slowly Dawnelle straightened, clinging to the dog's chain. *Must get help. Baird, help me!* She stumbled forward. Stopped. Waited for the strobe. One step, wait for the strobe. Two, wait again.

Three feet from Jenkins, she hesitated. What if he wasn't dead? What if he reached out for her just as she stepped past? Cold. God, she was cold. Shivering. *Think! Wait for the light, move left, run to the boardwalk.* Holding the chain, she skirted Jenkins, then let the dog guide her quickly down the walk.

The mist had drifted into the cottage. She could see it swirling in the dim light. Jenkins might revive, stumble off the edge. *No, can't think of that.* She locked the door behind her, then let go of the dog and rushed to the telephone. She fumbled for the receiver, left it dangling, dialed.

Please, she pleaded. *Be home. Help me!*

A faint voice made her grasp the receiver again. "Baird! Must talk—sorry. I'm sorry, please help me! He's out there dead. Maybe not dead. You must come—forgive me—" She was crying, swallowing hard, full of relief at hearing his voice, losing control, shaking, needing him....

"Dawnelle!" he thundered. "What in hell are you saying? I can't—"

"Jenkins!" she screamed. "Baird! You must come! He's hurt, dead. I don't know!"

"Where?"

"Here! At the light! Oh, Baird, don't be angry now. Please, I need you. He might come back, don't you understand? Help me!"

"Yes, of course. Have you called the—?"

She strove to hear him, but she was crying too hard She put her hand into her mouth, bit down. Moaned. "Overload," she muttered. "System overload. Killed him—Señorita de la Luz! Miss Mo, here puppy. Here...."

The fog alert was hurting her head. Baird wouldn't help her—yelling, still very angry—and she couldn't help Jenkins. He was dead. She felt damp fur beneath her hand. Miss Mo. Miss Mo would always help her. Dropping the receiver, ignoring the ranting distant voice of the man she loved, she crumpled to the floor, crooning softly about the animal's wounds. Vaguely she felt something uncomfortable beneath her hip. She groped. The fireplace poker. If Jenkins rose from the dead and came for her again, she would use the poker.

"Brave doggie," she crooned, folding the dog onto her lap, laying the poker against her thigh. "Poor Miss Mo, all beaten and bloody and worn out. So worn out. So worn. . . ."

THE POUNDING CONTINUED for an indeterminate time. And the shouts. Funny, the voice sounded deep and familiar. She must have been napping, dreaming.

Miss Mo yipped, groaned, pulled away. Dawnelle watched the animal struggle painfully to her feet, her muzzle lifted in a high yodel.

Loud raps rattled the front door. Jenkins! While the signal moaned, panic raced through her. She clutched the poker. As she rose, her body protested: her head, her side—everywhere. Her mind was a jumble of scenes from past hours, but her senses sharpened. Soundlessly she moved to the door, the poker raised. Someone jimmied the latch, and her respiration increased to shallow panting. The dog rushed, barking, against the wood.

"Dawnelle, unlock the door!"

There was no mistaking that bellowing command. He'd come to help her! Covering herself with the remains of her blouse, fumbling in her haste, Dawnelle managed to turn the latch and swing open the door. Half afraid she hadn't really heard him, she peered cautiously outside.

Baird pulled her forward into his arms, surprising her with his urgency, filling her with such relief and joy, she sank against him. Her legs felt numb.

"Baird, I'm so sorry for the accusations!" He shushed her, squeezed her, hurting her tender side, but she barely minded. The poker slid to the porch.

"Mr. Langston." Someone coughed from the walkway. "Er, Miss Belanger?"

They broke apart, turned. Baird put his arm protectively around Dawnelle's shoulders. She felt the warmth of his fingers against flesh that should have been covered by her missing sleeve.

The grizzled sheriff stood just inside the gate, staring up at them, his flashlight making a pool of yellow light on the grass.

"Sheriff—how?" She turned to Baird.

"I phoned them," he said. "We've been here about ten minutes, surrounding the place. They just finished taking Jenkins back to the wagon in the parking lot. A medic is tending him."

Her eyes widened, and Baird read the question she couldn't form. "Concussion. Some flesh wounds. Bad but not fatal, unfortunately."

"Baird, really—"

"Miss Belanger," interrupted the sheriff, "one of my boys will be back in a minute or two and we can get the facts. That is, if you're all right? Do you need medical attention?" She shook her head. "In that case, I'm afraid we should do it now, before the evidence gets... cold."

Her face lost color. Beseechingly, she looked at Baird. "If we could wait. I—I'm a little shaky, not feeling very strong. Perhaps tomorrow....?"

"He's right, Dawnelle. Tonight is best. If you'd like, I'll go with you."

"Go? Where?"

"To Westhaven, Miss Belanger," the lawman supplied. "I'm sorry to take you out after this, but we've got lab and interview facilities there. You'll want to make a statement."

"Yes. Yes, I suppose." She turned toward the cottage, then swung around. "You and your deputy will want to look at the house, I guess." She gestured uncomfortably. "The kitchen. He—he—"

Baird slid his white jacket around her shoulders, hurried her through the door. "She'll get changed, sheriff," he said over his shoulder. "Give us five minutes. We'll be inside when you're ready."

The ordeal lasted into the night: fingerprints, scrapings from beneath her nails, photographs of the strewn lingerie, the dog's injuries. Statements were signed. There would be a hearing sometime in December, a trial in all likelihood, but Dawnelle couldn't think of those details. She was drained of emotion and completely white when Baird brought her back to the cottage.

Before leaving, the medics had checked Miss Mo and found her sound, despite superficial injuries and the missing tooth. The dog was sleeping by the hearth. Baird had changed the message on Dawnelle's telephone recorder to announce that the station was closed to visitors until Monday morning. The Coast Guard had been notified, explanations made. A veteran of such matters, Baird carefully ensured Dawnelle wouldn't have to face media interviews until her nerves had healed. There remained only the task of clearing away the evidence of Jenkins's presence. She couldn't face such a task in the morning, alone. She would clean up the place now.

With Baird following her closely, Dawnelle made her way to the kitchen doorway. Swallowing, she flipped on the light. The torn black slip seemed to leap at her. The cherry camisole swirled, the blue and white and pink lingerie came to life, dancing mockingly. Her emotions surging, she gasped. The events, the rubbery hands, the wheezing threats began to fire at her from all directions like gunshots rending her flesh, burning through her mind. She began to slip into the terror again. Doubling over, she uttered a long anguished wail. Hands gripped her shoulders. She screamed, fought, pounded Jenkins with her fists. He struck her, caught her before she fell, and the black and blue shards once more hurtled through her head.

When her vision cleared, Baird's rugged face was above hers, inches away. His startling blue eyes were compassionate, concerned. His fingers were locked over the ocean-green silk of her sleeves as if he were afraid she might run away if he let go.

"Baird," she sighed, tears blurring his image. Raising her hands to the beloved face, she reassured herself with the soft scratch of his beard, the strength of his jaw beneath her fingertips. "Please don't leave me now. Don't. . . leave me!"

Slowly he drew her close, wrapped her tightly against his chest. She could feel his heart thudding beneath his thin brown T-shirt. *Life.* She nestled her cheek directly over the heartbeat. *Life, envelop me. For now.*

THE ANSWERING-MACHINE MESSAGE clicked on. Baird's low timbre filled the room as he advised callers the light station was closed until Monday morning. Dawnelle roused from her reading of a book on whales. He'd made that message to give her time to let her nerves simmer down. By this windy Saturday afternoon, after three days and his constant attention, the ugly memories of Jenkins had begun to recede.

Baird had encouraged her to talk about the terror, but she'd gone over it once, then not mentioned it again. Her mind wouldn't accept the events of Wednesday night, nor had she been inclined to talk of any deep emotional problem. She'd read, listened to soothing classical music and talked with Baird for hours about her childhood. And she had begun to heal.

Tonight she and Baird were planning a belated Thanksgiving dinner. Already the roasting hen smelled delicious. As she listened to the message, knowing she wouldn't answer unless it was Baird, she began to think of broaching the subject of their relationship again. He'd been so tender and attentive. Surely he was ready. The beep sounded. She waited.

"Dawnelle, it's Baird. Please pick up the phone."

"Baird, hi! I'm glad it's you and not some dedicated newshound!"

"Hey, you sound healthy and happy. Had many calls?"

"One. Just one, which I didn't answer. Listen, I was going to call you and ask if you'd like to bring Yurok over. With me in the kitchen all day, Miss Mo needs a buddy."

"Ahh." He paused. "That's why I'm calling, Dawnelle. Something's come up."

"Is he hurt? Yurok?"

"No, nothing like that. It's Vee, Dawnelle. I've got

my break at last. I'm leaving tonight, flying out of San Francisco tomorrow morning with one of Cole's associates."

A tightness encircled her throat. Swallowing, she said softly, "You're not coming by."

"I'm sorry." He sounded truly contrite. "I was looking forward to holding you, sharing that lovely dinner with you."

"Supper," she corrected, dazed and hurting. "Sarah says it's supper."

"I'm really sorry, Dawny. Will you save me something from your feast and let me bring over a bottle of wine Thursday or Friday?"

"White meat or dark? Oh, Baird! Are you still intent on going? If it's all over but taking him into custody, why not let the police handle it?"

"You don't know Vee as I do. After all this effort, I'm not going to see him slip away because one of the gendarmes had a fight with his wife and can't keep his mind on the job."

"But you'll have a fortune in a few years. Why do you persist in risking your life?"

"Dawnelle, stop. Serano's coming by in an hour to take over for me here. I'll explain that you may want to come by, give him a hand or something, in case you get the blues? I'll try to call you tomorrow, late in the evening if that's all right."

She was nodding, anguish stealing her power of speech. She'd been certain they could come to some kind of understanding tonight. And now Vee again.

"Is it all right?" he said more firmly. "Dawnelle, will

you be okay tonight? I could call Lau, ask her to stop by—"

"No!" Lau comfort her? They could spend a few hours discussing the man they loved—the same man! "No, thanks," she said more gently. "Baird, I'm fine—just missing you in my typical greedy way. Please be careful, will you?"

"That's my girl," he said more heartily. "Is the turkey nearly done?"

"Yes, another hour or so."

"Will you save me a drumstick? I'm crazy about legs, in case you've forgotten."

She smiled wistfully. "I haven't forgotten. How could I? We're wonderful together."

Listening to the hum of electricity for a long moment, she wondered why he didn't agree with her. Finally he said, "Take care, Dawny. Keep remembering the good things. Remember how strong you are."

"Yes."

"Better make the most of this short hiatus, then." His intimate tone suggested they'd have some catching up to do when he returned. "I'm coming to see you the moment I get home."

She murmured agreement, and then he was saying goodbye and she was left with the black receiver and the echo of his deep voice.

Reluctantly she hung up. Tears watered her eyes, yet she forced herself to open the novel *Sounding*, find the line about the female whale that read, "She should abandon the aging bull here, and quickly. She could not."

While every nerve in her body cried out for Baird's

safety, Dawnelle knew her circumstances didn't parallel the plight of that heroic whale who saved her mate. Now was not the time to rescue Baird, and he was not an aging bull past the strength or will to live. He was still virile and strong, still fueled by revenge, still facing his most demanding battle. Instinct told her Baird must finish with Vee before deciding his future with a mate. She only prayed it was she, not Lau—the woman whose name had come so easily to his lips—who would welcome him home.

CHAPTER EIGHTEEN

In the past twenty-four hours Trinidad fishermen had lost two boats to wind and hellish high seas. Twenty-seven other operators remained on board, engines and pumps running, riding it out to save their boats.

The devilish sea had driven straight in from the south in a sudden gale, pounding over Pilot Rock and Prisoner Rock and into the bay, dashing skiffs to kindling, dragging the anchors of more sturdy craft until the fragile hulls pitched dangerously close to other boats. Nature, in her wisdom, had found and struck Trinidad Bay's only weak point—its vulnerability to southern storms.

Dawnelle had been calling the Coast Guard and the harbor regularly for reports. The latest news from the harbor was that things were fairly calm, but another storm would sweep up the coast at the end of the week, about the time Baird was due home. Unable to concentrate on the brochure she was designing for the Smoke House, Dawnelle paced her cottage by the hour, powerless to help as wind and heavy seas destroyed those fishing boats.

She'd had nightmares of Jenkins. Alone for long hours, she'd drawn too many parallels between her struggle with him and the brutal power of the storm. Physically she felt lucky, as lucky as the boats that survived the storm. But her emotions, when she remembered the terror, were as dashed as the craft that had been beaten to the bottom of the bay.

Now she stretched out on the chesterfield, listening to the wind sigh around the house; setting her mind to the one recent event that could bring a smile to her lips. Baird had called last night.

Stuffing her pillow beneath her head, she ran over the conversation again, savoring Baird's familiar low timbre, amused at the attention to essentials that always characterized his phone calls. After assuring him she'd barely lost sleep over Jenkins—*let Baird come back because he loves me,* she'd decided, *not because his protective instincts are aroused*—he'd brought her up to date.

Vee's extradition had been held up. Evidently Vee's girl friend, a lonely undernourished local who was carrying his child, had threatened suicide if her lover was taken away. Baird had convinced Dawnelle he was seeing to the girl's welfare before pressuring authorities about Vee. When Dawnelle offered to meet his return flight into Arcata, he admitted he was uncertain of the day he would arrive, adding that he might not be able to call again while he was overseas. She smothered an urge to ask if he'd called Lau.

Before concluding the call, he'd told her he'd hired a fence company to repair the chain-link section Jenkins had destroyed. She'd protested about the expense, but the Coast Guard, Baird argued, would have tied up the effort for weeks while requisitions were processed. "I want you safe and waiting for me when I get back," he'd said with authority. Then he'd grown tender and said he missed her.

Would he be saying these things if he loved someone else, she wondered. If only there was a way to know and end the uncertainty. Sighing, weary from a sleepless night, Dawnelle glanced at Miss Mo curled on the rug below her, then closed her eyes. She would sleep. Maybe before the next storm broke, Baird would be rapping on the front door, setting down the bottle of wine, taking her in his arms....

"DAWNELLE, I SWEAR, every time I leave you alone for more than an hour you get into trouble!"

"Ben!" She laughed groggily, holding the receiver to her ear. She rubbed sleep from her eyes and looked outside. An unsure sun glimmered on grass that seemed trodden by heavy boots. "Welcome home," she said, coming fully awake. "How's your family?"

"Wonderful. Are you all right, for crying out loud? The Arcata paper—this nonsense about an attempted rape—for God's sake, Dawnelle, it's a helluva way to start Monday morning at the office!"

"Calm down, Ben. You know me. Invincible. Hardly a scratch on me—" she glanced at a pale bruise on her wrist, shivered at the reminder of Jenkins "—and... and Jenkins nearly died. Does that sound like I can't handle myself?"

"It says you were hysterical when you called Langston for help. 'Langston, a thirty-five-year-old marine scientist from Trinidad,'" he read aloud from the news account, "'called the sheriff's department and joined in a search of the light station, which resulted in the apprehension—' It says you were fleeing for your life when Jenkins was attacked by your dog. That he—Good Lord! I don't know what I want to do worse, stomp over to that hospital and put Jenkins out of his misery or come over to your place and pin a medal on you for bravery! On top of everything else that's happened, I come home to find my best friend fleeing for her life! What I really should do is clean out my desk."

"Ben, what is it?" Concerned because he was jumping from one subject to the next without any kind of logical transition, she said abruptly, "Something else is wrong."

"Everything is wrong!"

"Tell me. What's troubling you?"

"Lau," he said, sounding relieved to express his thoughts. "She had to weather that storm without my help, and I feel like a useless gadabout! In addition, the rudder on the troller has been badly damaged. We're having it worked on right now."

"I'm sorry to hear that. I know you were hoping to do some bottom fishing or something this winter. It'll set you back, won't it?"

"I don't know. We won't know how bad the damage is until tonight. I'm going down to the harbor as soon as I pack up here."

"Pack up?"

"Yes. I gave them notice before I went back home. Dawnelle, I'm not just going to work for her. Lau and I are going into partnership. I've put aside the charter-boat idea for now. We'll be getting in the new fishing gear any day and hope to make our first trip as soon as it's installed."

"Ben, that's wonderful! Then things aren't as distant between you two as you last thought."

"Only in the romantic sense," he said dryly. After a moment his natural enthusiasm resurfaced in a warm chuckle. "But I'm not letting that temporary setback get me down. Say, listen, Dawnelle. You are okay, aren't you? I mean, Langston is out of town, I understand, but if he gave you a hand with Jenkins, it must mean he's pretty solidly back in your life?"

"Yes—or I should say, maybe. Too early to tell—Well, I'm doing great, Ben, not to worry. Good luck with the repairs, and stop in when you get a chance."

"Will do, beautiful. Keep your doors locked, will you? Besides the happy feeling I get when I talk to you, knowing you is giving me an early crop of gray hair."

Dawnelle's throaty laugh died immediately after she hung up the phone. There it was again, the old jealousy over Baird and Lau, the stone in her stomach and the insecurities in her heart. Wandering to the cottage door, she opened it and stood for a long while gazing at the calm Pacific.

On Thursday morning, after days of answering calls from everyone but Baird—feeling she'd explained her good health to the entire town of Trinidad by now—she again stood on the porch.

The ocean was beginning to roughen, the sporadic whitecaps glinting beneath a weak sun. The wind gusted up to fifteen knots, laying the red stems and green leaves of her begonias flat against the foundation of the house, pulling her flowing hair back, then whipping it into her eyes.

According to Henny, this storm was going to be a "lalapalooza." He'd asked if she wanted to spend a day or two in town with him and Sarah, but she'd refused. Baird wouldn't know where to find her when he finally arrived home, and besides, she still held the title of keeper. Lady of the Light.

Feeling chilled, she returned to the cottage to warm her hands at the fire. Miss Mo was running the hills again, hunting with those liquid brown eyes trained ahead and that wet black nose lifted to the wild salty air. Ten minutes ago she'd heard the dog's shrill bark above the house, up on the bluffs. The familiar yodel had brought a crawling memory of Jenkins to mind, and Dawnelle had gone to look outside as if to reassure herself he wasn't lurking.

Disgusted with the turn of her thoughts, Dawnelle went upstairs and changed into her warmest flannel nightgown, then came back to the chesterfield to read and await the dog's return.

MISS MO'S PIERCING BARK woke her from a light doze, although with the wind shrieking and the rain driving against the dark windows, Dawnelle wondered how she'd heard a mere bark.

Rubbing her eyes, she went to the door, twisted the knob. The portal sprang in at her from the force of the wind, spraying her gown with a fine mist of rain. The wet dog bounded into the hall with more than her usual momentum.

Some spark of intuition drew Dawnelle's glance to the horizon framed by the posts of the tiny porch. It was nothing, she decided, beginning to press closed the heavy door. But it came at her again—a tick of brightness—from somewhere out in that moaning darkness on the water. As the lighthouse beam swept over the sea, she followed its glare into the slanting rain. Blinded, she waited through a second revolution.

The light went out, the sea moaned in an ebony mass, and she was left with a warning prickle on her nape.

Visibility was nil. She couldn't see Pilot Rock almost due south, or Prisoner Rock just east of the Head at the entrance to the harbor. No fool would be out in this weather, anyway, she told herself. Every skipper in the area would be inside the mouth by now, running the engines to keep his craft from going aground.

In a southern storm, a boat trying to gain the harbor would be driven against the base of the cliffs. The locals knew this, knew the tide line was a minefield of submerged islets and rock rubble. Yet these flitting thoughts didn't ease Dawnelle's worry that some poor skipper was peering through the same storm, praying his craft would escape destruction.

Thinking of Ben and Lau fighting the winds and thrashing seas inside the bay, possibly having problems with the rudder they'd just repaired, Dawnelle firmly shut the door. She must call the harbor master, check on the fleet. She moved to the telephone. And she would call the Coast Guard, ask if they'd had a distress call from a small craft just off Trinidad Head. She hadn't called them lately, but then the wind had blown to fierce strength during her short nap. Previously there had been no reason to call.

Picking up the black receiver, she dialed. Only after the fifth digit did she take the receiver away from her ear and look at it questioningly. She jiggled the connection button. With a sudden jerky movement she slammed the telephone down, then picked it up again and frantically rattled the button. It couldn't be dead!

But even as the beacon's beam rolled through the softly lighted living room, she felt total isolation wrap around her—total separation. No television to watch human faces act out their daily trials. No telephone to connect her to caring friends. No help if Jen— But no, Jenkins was still hospitalized, wasn't he?

A rumbling thunder shook the walls, jarred the floor beneath her bare feet. The living room was blanched with lightning. She gulped air, gripped the curving arm of the chesterfield and set the silent receiver back into its cradle. *Calm down, Dawnelle. You have choices. You can take the dog and drive to the Caldwells, or to Baird's and hope someone left the side door unlocked. Or you can remain at your post—powerless to do much of anything, true, but you'd be here in case—*

Turning to the moist dark window behind the davenport, she cupped her hands around her eyes and peered outside. Had there been a boat out there a few minutes ago? Had she imagined the pinprick of light? She could see nothing but the swish of jack-pine boughs down over the hill, whenever the beacon circled. Sliding into the cushions, Dawnelle tapped her fingertips on the cracked leather as she tried to decide what to do.

Her idea of the role she would play in helping the Coast Guard rescue someone was rather vague. She'd read many accounts, both tragic and successful, of light-station rescues, but none of them seemed to apply to her situation. The Trinidad fleet was seasoned at fighting battles in that southerly exposed shark tank in the bay; they wouldn't be risking the storm outside. Why was she here then? To paint aging fences and polish the glass of the lantern? A maintenance crew could do that. No, of course. She was here to clang that crescent wrench against the fog-signal box if it got stuck in alert. Or to call the Guard if the auxiliary batteries failed to keep the light going in a storm. She couldn't call them now, could she? The blasted phone was dead.

Hugging her shoulders because the whining of the wind and the drumming of the rain were beginning to unnerve her, she rose, paced the rug, frowned at the licking ritual Miss Mo was conducting by the fire. She cursed the silent telephone, which yesterday she'd cursed for ringing ceaselessly.

Why was Baird still away—not lying injured in some alley, surely. Not back in town and too busy to get in touch with her, a repeat of last June. She should have called his house instead of waiting for his arrival like the dutiful trusting lover she was. If only he were home... she could drive over and ask him to come back with her, keep vigil through the ranting storm. God, she missed him. If only she could hear him reminding her about how strong she was. Strong, Baird? Her knees were trembling.

Captain Harrington wouldn't have left his post, she thought, wringing chilled hands as she remembered her discussion with Henny. She wouldn't leave, either. If Harrington and his family had weathered decades of storms here during years when the horse and buggy wore deep ruts into the gravel service road, she could stay put through one bad storm.

Horse and buggy.... Something about that ancient mode of transport made her memory struggle. Old, outdated, versus new, efficient. Horse...telephone! *My God*, she thought in sudden horror as reason overtook memory. She looked helplessly at her useless telephone, then turned and gazed at the fireplace, seeing beyond the cottage to the shack high on the bluff—the remote transceiver placed there to receive and relay distress calls. If her phone was dead, that meant all lines in the area were probably down—and any boat in distress wouldn't be able to contact the rescue unit in McKinleyville.

Suddenly she was hurrying toward her bedroom to pull on warm clothes. First, she would grab the binoculars and climb out onto the catwalk of the lighthouse, get a good look at the sea. If a boat was lost out there, she'd decide later what to do about it.

CHAPTER NINETEEN

LIGHTED BY THE PIERCING BEAM of the beacon, the boat looked like a child's toy, poised with its stern awash and its white prow hovering over the empty belly of a wave. The light circled around; the troller disappeared. The rain became a slanting screen of gray.

Her heart thudding, Dawnelle braced her foot against the iron rail of the catwalk and tried to pinpoint the position of the craft. Old and heavy, the binoculars were difficult to keep steady, the lenses wide and easily clouded. She adjusted her yellow slicker higher around the lenses to keep out the rain. A sudden gust whipped the edge of her coat painfully across her cheek, staggering her. Her head struck the glass of the lantern, and the impact dazed her.

The earth and sea seemed forged by a demon spirit—angry, howling, oblivious to human concerns or bodily comfort. Lightning jagged across the southern sky. The wind gusted over the bluff and thrust cold and curious into her clothing, plastering her hat brim flat against her skull, stinging her face with driven rain.

Shaking her head to clear her vision and her senses, she lifted the binoculars to her eyes and searched again for the doomed boat. Out there somewhere. Out there the skipper was peering through his wheelhouse windows, arms aching from fighting the wheel as the sea tossed his boat around like a scrap of bark, his heart probably pulsing in his throat. *I must fix his location,* she thought. *Pinpoint familiar landmarks.* She must be able to tell the Coast Guard where he was headed in this gale.

"Work, fingers!" she grumbled, trying to ratchet the focus ring. The light came around, glanced off a pearly crescent wobbling in foam and went on, but Dawnelle fixed the object with her glass. Deep in a trough, the small fishing boat took a punishing wave broadside. "Hang in there, skipper," she whispered. "You've got to be a tough old goat to be out there in the first place."

The craft tipped so Dawnelle could see the glistening wooden deck as the lightning flashed. Twin trolling poles pricked through the gray black squall. The hull glowed in a pool of brightness spilling from the wheelhouse, its red running light flickering eerily. The boat shot straight ahead, whirled strangely and ducked beneath another southerly driven crawler. Dawnelle's heart surged, dived, twisted with the troller, beating irregularly in her chest.

With a groan of desperation she shook the binoculars, raised them again. A crackling bolt split the sky. She cried out as it faded; heard her cry flung into the darkness. She had fixed their position.

There! She saw it again, just this side of the black hump called Pilot Rock—a glowing daub, lurching perilously. Doomed. Swallowing, Dawnelle uttered a prayer.

Rushing for help would prove useless, she realized now. The troller was far too close to danger. In fifteen or twenty minutes that wildly bobbing hull would be driven aground on Trinidad Head. No good to waste a trip to town. Perhaps all of Trinidad was without telephone service.

The realization that she would watch someone die weakened her morale. She sagged and let the gale push her against the glass. She struck her fist against the rough concrete lamp housing, struck again and again until the pain sent a stream of pure reason to her brain.

The rope, she thought suddenly, already turning, burrowing through the low door of the lamp housing. All that rope coiled in the work shed, waiting to lower her down to survivors.

Both bulbs were burning in the light because visibility was so poor, but she barely felt the sear of heat as she careered around the revolving beacon. She slid rapidly down the stairs. Miss Mo greeted her at basement level and followed her to the north wall, whining anxiously.

Hanging the binoculars on the accustomed peg, Dawnelle grabbed a loaded flare gun and a spare cartridge, then led the dog outside. Using Miss Mo as an anchor, she battled the wind all the way to the shed.

HER ARMS ACHED with the exertion of moving the wheelbarrow over vines and brush. It was heaped with rope, flashlights, a canvas duffel bag full of blankets and a life ring. She'd also slipped a first-aid kit around her neck and wrapped fifty feet of nylon cord around her torso to use as a lifeline. Miss Mo zigzagged in front of her, sometimes whipped sideways, often glancing back to make certain Dawnelle was stumbling behind her.

Finally a gray stump near the rim of the bluff came into view, its familiar collar and leash of rotted rope caught in the glow of Dawnelle's light. She propped up one of the flashlights, illuminating the stump and surrounding area.

The thought of lowering herself down into the black abyss on her left unnerved her, made her cold fingers tremble. Refusing to glance in that direction, she summoned up the image of her brother: his eyes pleading for her to hurry, his small hands reaching....

Miss Mo hovered near her side, dripping rain and panting hot steamy breaths on Dawnelle's hands as she tied a string of industrial flashlights to the stump. She aimed the lenses seaward and snapped them on. The collection made a remarkably bright glow, she congratulated herself. Especially since the rain was abating.

Raising her hand to shield her eyes, Dawnelle scanned the water. It seemed the boat had held its position. Anchored, she decided. Probably to repair some crucially damaged gear, the skipper had anchored just north of Pilot. Scant protection.

Light from the wheelhouse briefly outlined a tiny human form. "One man on deck," she muttered, unloading the coiled rope and tying one end to the stump. "One man on deck, so another must be at the controls."

She dug the flare gun from her pocket, held it with the barrel pointing toward the ground. Would her signal only make matters worse? Confuse the crew? No. If the skipper knew the phone lines were dead, he at least might take some comfort from knowing he'd been spotted. Maybe he'd even see the new glow from her flashlights, a further warning of these dangerous cliffs. A slim chance, but slim chances were precisely what all of them were dealing with tonight.

Aiming the gun into the buffeting wind, she fired. Gray smoke puffed around the barrel as it recoiled, jerking her hand. A sparkling orange signal shot over the ocean toward Pilot Rock. Its range was one thousand feet, probably cut short by the strong gusts. The cometlike spark died out far short of the troller, so Dawnelle figured the boat's offshore distance at slightly less than half a mile.

When the ocean was dark again except for the pitching craft, she loaded her final cartridge. She would send the last flare up when she was down near the waterline, to guide them to her or to light the rocks as they drove past the Head and into the bay.

Stowing the gun, she hurriedly tied the duffel bag filled with blankets to the trailing end of the rope. Next, she dumped the barrowful of rope over the bluff and stood listening to it slither away into the darkness. She shivered involuntarily and turned to the dog. *I wish you were Baird,* she thought as she hugged the muddy animal close. Whining, Miss Mo ran a pink tongue over Dawnelle's cheek.

"Now," she said, teeth gritted as she shoved away the fear. "Go now or you'll never do it." Pulling away, feeling rain trickle down the back of her neck, she shone her flashlight over the precipice.

Thunder rumbled overhead, followed immediately by a sustained bolt of lightning that illuminated the entire bluff. Far below, great boulders the size of Baird's Ford tumbled to the waterline. She wiped the rain out of her eyes, then glanced worriedly toward the dog. "Stay," she commanded. "Lady Mo, stay!" Miss Mo obediently flattened herself on the ground near the stump.

"Good. That's. . .fine." Reluctantly Dawnelle turned and grasped the rope. Silently she descended over the edge.

Miss Mo immediately appeared above her. She began racing back and forth on the wet bank, barking shrilly. "Stay!" Dawnelle grunted, afraid the wind might sweep the dog over the edge. "Stay—there!"

Moving hand over hand down the rope, her body buffeted, knees bruised, she tried to keep up her courage, tried not to think of the pit below. The serpent wind cleverly found her even when she huddled, gasping, in a sheltered crevice to unravel kinks in the rope. It buffeted and pressed her, sucked at her sou'wester, bullied and tormented her until it seemed to tire of the bullying and howled away down the bluff. She went on, refusing to give in to the sting in her tiring muscles, stubbornly ignoring her rapidly shortening breath.

Reeling in the gale, she once caught a glimpse of the troller, still some distance off, its cabin lights burning through the gloom. But it was approaching. The engine thrummed sporadically. Contrasted with the moaning wind and crackling thunder, the boat seemed to growl with determination. Perhaps the vessel would make it past the Head and into Trinidad Bay. Perhaps.

Below, the waves ground into the rocks with increasing fury, and as each wave pounded home Dawnelle cringed and closed her eyes. Hell was a cold, night-surging ocean spewing fury onto a two-hundred-foot bluff. And a woman alone.

Suddenly a giant breaker struck the wall. As base-drum thunder rose from the depths, Dawnelle clung intuitively to a chunk of rock. The cold sea churned around her hips and then fell back, dragging her off the wall and leaving her dangling free. The quick rattling pace of her heart nearly choked her. She gasped, whimpered in fear and scrambled up to her perch.

With shaking fingers she pulled her flashlight from her pocket and investigated the territory beneath her. Twenty feet below, the duffel bag lay in a wet lump near the edge of a shelf. The shelf gleamed evilly, rivulets of seawater draining over its lip like the drool of a rabid wolf. The image did nothing to still her shivering, but she forced herself to consider the relative safety of basing herself on that ledge.

Perhaps five yards across, this lower table was only a few feet above the huge boulders that tumbled to the waterline. There wasn't much of a beach, but if the troller stove in nearby, the crew might at least wash close enough to crawl onto one of those rocks. She could attach the old gray life ring to her nylon line, and it would reach just beyond the surf. That ledge would be her goal, she decided grimly. To go any lower would mean being sucked into hell.

Suddenly she felt a tug on the rope, a jerk decidedly different from the whipping motion created by the wind. Automatically she leaned out to scan the upper reaches of the bluff. She was stunned to see the distance she'd gone. A faint glow, like the diffused impression of headlights around a bend, marked her flashlights tied in a string, but ledges kept them from being directly in her vision. A great loneliness swept through her then. She was lost even to the troller's sight, hidden behind a shoulder of rock that reminded her of the folded wing of a gull. She heard Miss Mo barking faintly and took courage from the familiar sound.

Growing anxious to spot the boat, she began edging toward a down-slanting crevice choked with branches and debris. Again the rope tugged in her hand. It wasn't a tug from below, as if the waves were pulling at the duffel bag, but a definite jerk from above. She began to feel more than the chill of her soaked jeans and tennis shoes. She began to feel fear trickle down her spine, like the rain that leaked through her clothing. The rope began to jiggle rhythmically, as it had done when she descended, and her mind pawed through the possibilities. Was someone joining the rescue? Or...Jenkins? Jenkins! He was far too heavy to scale these cliffs, she told herself, far too awkward and fat. *But he's strong,* an inner voice chided. *Remember?*

Panicked, she doused the light. The darkness was even more terrifying. She began scrambling toward the crevice, uncoiling the nylon rope from her torso to free herself of the weight. Stumbling, she slid, kicked a shin painfully against a rock. Clamping her teeth over the pain, she crept forward. She must hide. She must... hide?

Abruptly she was struck by the ridiculousness of being attacked by Jenkins as she tried to aid a boat in distress. Perversely amused, she giggled. She felt possessed of superhuman qualities. Jenkins here, indeed! He was hospitalized.

Her heart rate slowed slightly, until she heard a voice calling topside. She looked up. A man poised for a moment in the dull luminescence of the lights above, his lower body fused with the shadowed rocks. Not Jenkins, but Baird!

"Baird!" she shouted, his name drowned out by a drumming wave. "Baird, oh, Baird, you're home!"

Hope and elation surging within, she flicked on her flashlight and shone it on his descending form.

A muffled chugging came from far down the shoreline. Distractedly she glanced over her shoulder toward the water. She could see no troller cutting its white prow through that angry sea, but she could hear the craft approaching as if through a long tunnel, its diesel engine laboring against steep mountains of water.

Baird slid the last few feet to her rock perch, sending pebbles and sticks rattling down around his boots. He pulled a small red flashlight from his pocket and cast the beam over her.

Dawnelle stood with the rain dripping from her hat brim to her shoulders, her gaze locked with his, her heart so light the cares of her mission lifted away.

"Did you bring the wine?" she shouted above the storm.

A brief smile lighted his eyes. And then he stepped to her and hugged her hard, as if the wind had flung them together. Her raincoat crackled against his muddy bomber jacket. She clung to him.

"You're wet," he called loudly in her ear.

"Soaked!"

"Crazy woman!"

"I thought you were Jenkins!"

"Jenkins?"

She looked up with a foolish grin. Nodded. The fear had stayed with her since Jenkins. She only realized how heavy the burden had been now that it was suddenly gone.

Raising her voice above the storm, she asked, "How did you find me?"

"I couldn't get you by phone. When I arrived at the cottage and found you gone, I searched, saw your flashlights. Miss Mo is topside, going crazy. I saw the troller, put it all together."

As if of the same mind, they glanced toward the water. The chugging of the diesel had grown louder, its distress echoing off the walls of the bluff. A glow wavered beyond the gull wing of rock.

"They've got to land here," she shouted. "No other place!"

He nodded, dashed his light around, picking out the nylon lifeline strewn across the rocks, the duffel bag on the ledge below.

"Blankets," she called, pointing. "And a life ring for that line." Then she drew forth the flare gun. It gleamed in Baird's light.

"I'll go down below and get the line ready," he said hoarsely. He indicated the hump of rock that hid the troller. "Get a look. Let them know we're here!"

She started away, but suddenly felt herself dragging back and turned against him. Before she could focus on his face, his lips closed over her mouth, cold and wet, yet alive with feeling. His hand grazed her breast as he reached up and around her shoulders, pressing her closer. His beard felt like a cool compress on her rain-lashed face, and his lips—warm, now, and hungry—infused her with warmth. Just as abruptly, he moved her away.

Lips parted, lashes heavy with rain, Dawnelle gazed at him, letting all her relief and hope and love express itself in the look. He nodded slightly as if saying he understood. Buoyed by a current of joy, she turned and began scrambling up the rock.

As she reached the gritty apex of the promontory, she saw the lights of the troller spilling over the heaving sea a few hundred yards south. *Fernline* was a compact beamy craft slung low in the water, barreling straight at the bluff. With her white prow cleaving the trough, her stern rode high. The remarkable thing was that her trolling poles were lowered, as if engaged in a day's work of salmon fishing. A growl emanated from the belly of the boat. Then her engine began a throaty rattle, and she receded slightly into the trough of another wave. The skipper was reversing his boat for all she was worth.

Dawnelle began calling to the crew, waving her flashlight in the excitement of seeing them so close. Someone appeared to starboard of the wheelhouse, clinging to the housing as he stared in her direction. "Here!" she screamed, trying to be heard above the wind and surf, stretching to her full height to be seen.

She grasped the rock with the tenacity of a crab while she cocked the lever on the flare gun, took aim and fired. Smoke burned her eyes but quickly dissipated in the wet wind. The emergency light drove high into the wind, sputtering orange-and-gold sparks. It hovered slightly over the water, then arced back toward the bluff, its brilliant glare casting everything in white-and-black relief.

The troller surged nose-in toward Trinidad Head, drifting closer with each crawler despite the backward pull of the engine, until Dawnelle saw clearly that the human figure braced outside the wheelhouse was wearing a bright orange survival suit. Excitedly she raised her arms above her head, hoping the man would see her. Instead he disappeared inside the wheelhouse. Her disappointment was keen.

Suddenly a large wave caught against the rounded stern. The water crashed over the deck, running free as black oil, clipping gear and flinging it overboard, spewing it onto the beach. Spray drenched Dawnelle. She knuckled her eyes.

The engine gurgled, and Dawnelle barely had a second to realize the man had saved himself by ducking inside. Then the stern spun around, exposing the entire port side to the rocks. The red light glittered through the slackening rain. Following the ruby gleam, Dawnelle knew the cold grip of a premonition. Even with her limited knowledge of boating, she realized the troller would crumble against the steep shore. She swayed willy-nilly in the water, mindless, helpless against the broad, powerful oncoming waves.

Where was Baird? He must see what to do! As the thought formed and Dawnelle turned, white-faced, to search for him, she saw him dragging himself and the life ring out of a swirling pool of water. He was twenty feet below the shelf, evidently knocked down by the huge wave.

The sight shocked her into action. Sliding and scrambling, feeling a prick of pain in her right palm as she descended, she fought her way toward the shelf. He'd been pulled out by the wave, and she'd nearly lost him! Her mind rebelled at the idea—now, when he'd come back to her, when he'd understood with one look that she loved him, needed him. Leaping from a boulder, her heart in her throat, she landed in a sprawl and was up again, snatching the descent rope, feeling for the knot where Baird had connected the nylon cord. Finally! She jerked it around her hand, felt it bite into her flesh.

When she looked down at him, she barely had time to scream a warning. He ducked between two rocks as a wave poured over him. As the wave sucked away, the rope pulled taut. Suddenly the life ring bobbed free, out on the water.

"Baird!" she screamed, scrambling over the ledge, dragging in lengths of line.

Praying for his safety, she shone her flashlight on the rocks until she found him, stumbling from his niche, a dark stain draining from his thigh. She found his face. His teeth were clenched in pain. Crossing another great round boulder, she squatted and dangled the line to him, urging him to take it, to hurry.

He dragged himself to her side and was gasping for breath, when a sharp crack cut the night. Dawnelle and Baird glanced around. Beneath an overhang, they caught a glimpse of white prow, a moaning keening length of hull as it ground into the boulders. The word *Fernline* began to warp even as they watched.

Baird seemed to lurch with the impact. A hoarse cry broke from him. When Dawnelle splayed her light over him, his wet face appeared contorted with horror. She bent to him. "Lau!" she heard him mutter. "Lau!"

He was leaving her, awkwardly stumbling to his feet. But Dawnelle was held in place on the damp slick boulder, immobilized with shock. Lau.

And Ben, she remembered then. Wasn't he riding out the storm in the harbor? Surely Lau wouldn't have dragged him to sea in such weather! Ben, green country boy when it came to boats and seafarers' ways. Laughing, caring Ben, who'd castigated himself for letting Lau weather the first storm of the season alone.

Feeling more pain than she ever had in her life, Dawnelle scurried off the rock in pursuit of Baird. *Be grateful you're not alone in this,* she told herself, scraping together her courage. *And keep your head cool,* she thought, worried about his rash behavior. He might try to do something heroic for the lovely Indian woman, and then she, Dawnelle, would never forgive herself. After all, he'd scaled this cliff in the first place to give her a hand.

She hurried toward the sickly churn of the engine, toward the drizzle-shrouded play of lights on the rocks. Ducking beneath the overhang, she glanced down the steep grade of boulders. A soft wail escaped her. It was terrible to watch a boat destroyed, almost as if it possessed life and was giving it up grudgingly. She saw the *Fernline* lifted, carried forward, thrown against the rocks. It sounded like a skyscraper crashing to earth. Taut planking moaned and snapped, rigging clanged, the old diesel gurgled like a drenched locomotive. A trolling pole arced in a moon crescent as the tip burrowed into a crevice. Then, as the boat creaked off the rocks and listed to seaward, the pole snapped straight and settled against a boulder.

Two bright orange shapes, flabby-looking in the air-filled suits, struggled on deck, and Dawnelle knew a battle raged between Ben and Lau. Who would go out along the lowered pole first? Was Lau claiming her rights as skipper, demanding to leave last?

Baird had seen the struggle, too. His hoarse cry wavered on the wind, and as one orange figure began scrambling along the lowered pole, Baird crawled onto a large, egg-shaped rock above the tip of the pole. He stretched over the edge of the black granite, bridging the gap between pole and solid footing. Dawnelle, fearing he would be swept away, rushed forward, losing sight of him as she dipped between two rocks.

Car-o-o-oom! A tremendous grating reached her ears as she clawed and panted her way to the summit of a boulder and peered over.

A breaker had thrust the *Fernline* forward, grinding her hull and raising the escape pole high over Baird's prone form. The orange figure grappled above him. Dawnelle glimpsed a white fearful face—Ben—and then Ben was flung into the rocks.

The pole came smashing into the rock supporting Baird, sweeping him into the water. "For the love of God!" Dawnelle choked. "Baird, noo!"

But he was halfway to the boat when she reached Ben. She clung to her friend's damp spongy sleeve for a moment, read the despair in his pale face. She lurched after Baird, her only thought to bring him back before he was killed. Ben dragged her from the edge, held her captive. She struggled, called again and again to Baird, then heard the thunder of another wave as it drove into the *Fernline*.

The strike left Dawnelle rigid and staring. She saw the boat lift almost gently with the swell. She saw Baird's sodden bomber jacket balloon with water, saw his body flail, turn toward her. She read a kind of terrible determination in his expression. He seemed to see her for an instant—only her—like that young face so long ago. That pleading face. He opened his mouth, snapping it closed as the water rushed up around him, closed over him. He slipped from her sight.

An orange shape glowed for an instant on the tilting deck of the *Fernline*. Lau, her features stiff with fear, clung to the hilt of the trolling pole. Dawnelle barely heard the piercing call from that deck, or the answering shout from Ben, but she felt Ben's hands drop away from her arms. The pole glided along her shoulder, pushed her aside, scraping and splintering in its rude journey.

Then...silence, except for the swish of receding water. And the hollow thud of her heart.

An energy from within drove her to the edge of the egg-shaped rock. She slid down into the tide, her flashlight banging against the rock as she waded awkwardly in a foot of muck. *Climb over that boulder,* her mind ran on. *Jump down. Jump down lower. Watch the slippery stuff. Keep the light playing over the rocks. Look for him. Bring him back.*

She started to cry, felt great salty tears well, blind, blend with the light drizzle. But part of the strength within her was native common sense, and her common sense told her to hurry. Viciously she ground at her eyes with the back of her hand. She stumbled, caught herself on a log spiked with barnacles. Whimpering at the pain, she crawled on.

Something light grazed her head. She looked up to see Lau clinging to the pole as she dangled a line to Dawnelle. The soft female voice directed her. "To the right. Go right, Dawnelle. Here, take this rope. Tie it around him. Hurry!" The soft voice faded in a series of grunts as Lau pulled herself to safety.

Dawnelle scooped at the line with fingers shaking from cold and burrowed around a sharp wedge of rock. In a few seconds Lau would be topside, anchoring the rope somehow, taking up the slack when the next wave hit. Ironic. Baird had tried to save *her*.

"Hurry," Lau had said. *Save my man,* Dawnelle read into the urgent command.

Under the stress of the monumental task, Dawnelle's mind burned with scattered frantic thoughts. Without Baird, without at least knowing his energy lighted some corner of the world.... Hopeless thought! She heard his deep voice commanding her to stop meddling in his affairs, watched the firelight cavorting on his skin as they made love, saw the vibrancy of his drive in business. Life without Baird? Wickless and waxless, a flame dying at a dark window. Better to know that he loved Lau than to know the sea claimed that vital spark.

There! A boot. She scrambled to it, picked it up and flung it away. Two feet farther on, ambient light from the *Fernline* glowed on human flesh. She jammed her flashlight into her pocket. Then she was crouching over Baird's still form, shuddering at the wash of blood around his jaw. He was cradled in a crack that stretched away darkly beneath him. He seemed to sleep as she heaved his arms above his head. With superhuman strength she pulled his torso, so that he slumped upright. An eyelid flickered.

"Baird, wake up!" she commanded, wrapping the deck line around his chest and tying it securely. She slapped his face, bit her lip and slapped him smartly again. "Help me! Wake up!"

He groaned. A roaring came from behind them.

Frantically Dawnelle circled her arms around him and clung to the sharp lip of rock. He stirred. She directed him to be still. "Hold your breath. A wave is going to hit. Hold your breath, do you hear?"

When the water struck, icy liquid pounded over her shoulders, filling her eyes and ears, pulling her fingers from their clasp on the rock, lifting her and the man beneath her. Holding her breath, eyes closed, she snuggled so tightly against him she felt welded to his chest. His arms came around her in what seemed an instinctive reaction to the cold invasion of the sea.

Surge somersaulted them, dragged them over rocks, peppered them with sand, pebbles, seaweed. Water poured over their bodies, clutching at their soaked clothing, ripping the hat from her head, brushing through her long hair with greedy fingers. Her lungs began to burn.

Some part of Baird's body rammed into a rock; she felt the impact and the jerking away of his arms. The rope sawed beneath her coat, tightening around Baird. They bumped into something, settled. The world roared. That meant air bubbles and sand, not deep seas.

The water pulled more greedily at her face, trying to force her to breathe lethal seas. Her brain was dulling rapidly now. Feeling close to death, feeling visited in her head by strange notions about God and love and sacrifice and justice, feeling regret for her father and for the golden years of old age, she suddenly breathed.

It was air she breathed. It was coughing she heard and convulsive movements she felt beneath her body. She sneezed raised her sodden head. A brightness pierced her eyes. She squinted, heard voices.

"Help us." She knew her voice croaked in a whisper. She tried again. "He's hurt. Help—"

She rolled over, away from her burden, her lover. But she was moved by a power greater than her own. She felt something lift her, drag her a short distance, press her body into the gritty bed under her face. "No!" she rasped, wiggling. "Him!"

Reason told her human hands pressed into her back, and that they were attempting to force water from her lungs. Her lungs were fine, since she'd kept the sea from them. Baird. Baird needed help. He'd been bleeding, choking.

Wearily she twisted away from the ministering hands, pushed them clear of her body. The effort cost her, for every movement was sluggish and difficult. But she had to make them understand. "Him," she said urgently, nodding toward her left side. "Help... him."

"Hush now, Dawnelle," said a quiet male voice. "We're taking care of him."

Breathing shallowly, she lay back and let the gentle hands smooth her hair, unbutton her coat, lift something away that had been binding her throat. Her numb flesh began to feel rain. It felt warm, deliciously warm.

"The debt is paid," someone said.

Dawnelle thought she'd heard that silky voice before.

"What do you mean 'the debt is paid'?" said Ben.

"When we lost the rudder," said the lovely voice. Lau. "And when we couldn't raise the Coast Guard—the radio antenna must have corroded with salt or something—I began to remember the old legends. It's the seventh year. He— Baird and Dawnelle have paid the final debt. They can ask no more of me."

"I hope you're right." Silence. "You were foolish back there—you know that. I'd have choked some sense into you if I'd thought I could get to you before you went over the side."

"I couldn't—" a small gasp of restrained emotion

"—couldn't lose you. Not after so many others. Not you, too."

"Never again, Lau. Never. I've earned my stripes tonight, and from now on I won't be taking orders. Understood?"

"The debt is paid. The spirits have avenged themselves...."

His answer was a skeptical grunt. "Here—let's get Dawnelle moved first. Easy."

Dawnelle was carried somewhere, and it seemed much later when she heard Ben's slightly out-of-breath question, "What other forces did you mean back there, Lau? Out on the water, you yelled something about spears. I got the feeling your grandfather was showing you where to land the boat."

Lau chuckled softly. "There may be hope for you yet, Ben Fallon. Baird and Dawnelle sent up a flare, remember? That light sailed right on through my head, figuratively speaking—reminded me of the men of the old Tsurai village heaving their spears at the sea lions, then hiding the weapons out here on the Head so no woman could touch them. When the anchor chain gave way, I knew we'd head for this beach. It was like a sign leading the way."

"The flare?"

"Uh-huh."

"So you really believe the old myths?"

"They're not myths!" Dawnelle had grown groggy, but Lau's sharp reply drew her back from the gray fog. "These two paid for my error. It shouldn't have been them. I should have paid."

"Haven't you, Lau?"

"But not the way they did."

"Your boat. They took your boat, your living. You paid, I tell you."

A soft laugh came to Dawnelle's ears. She strained to hear it, strangely lulled. "So you begin to believe?" said the laughing voice. "You believe my people's tales of revenge. The spirit's revenge?"

"I begin to believe—a little."

"Then perhaps we can be together." The pretty voice was shy now. "If you believe at all."

"Lau...."

Silence.

"Lau, with the *Fernline* gone...we could look around, you know, as I said before, look around for a charter boat. I don't have a job to go back to, and you...."

Dawnelle's concentration faded. When she revived, Ben was talking about his savings, and Lau was saying she'd think over his offer. A rustle to Dawnelle's left prompted her to undertake the painful task of moving her head. Focusing with extreme will, she saw slim dark hands working to remove Baird's jacket. Lau's hands would heal him. Dawnelle giggled. But the sound was alien even to her own ears, and she lay back and let the darkness and wind and rain and roaring enter her mind.

CHAPTER TWENTY

WHEN SHE AWAKENED, she heard surf thrashing in the distance. And a crackling sound, as if twigs were snapping underfoot. A full moon played among clouds in the dark sky, but the image made no sense to a mind troubled by nightmarish dreams, dreams of terror and sadness and death. She sighed unconsciously. Her mind was hazy. Reality eluded her. A heaviness seemed to press around her, yet the warmth accompanying that weight comforted her. She felt safe, and didn't know why.

A stiff breeze reeking of salt and crushed seaweed swept over nearby boulders, bringing vague memories of struggle. Real or imagined? Fighting to gain full consciousness, she began to concentrate on her own body. A slight nausea rose and fell in her stomach. The ill feeling could be tied to the dream, she decided, and thus was likely to be short-lived. Feeling soreness in her muscles, she shifted slightly. She hurt everywhere—arms, legs, torso. Her hands were uncomfortably cold. She raised one of them, wincing at the pull in her biceps, and was surprised to see the orange sleeve of a survival suit. She remembered Lau had worn this suit. It was part of the nightmare. Lau had put it on Dawnelle, or someone had.

Prompted by this small nugget of reasoning, Dawnelle glanced beyond the rim of granite sheltering her. Halfway up a sloping rock, a silent figure slumped by a low spitting campfire. Lau. Her beautiful face, quiet in sleep, was lighted dimly by the coals and flames. Hair as soft as ebony mink flowed over her blanket-shrouded shoulders. Driftwood lay in a loose pile nearby, and jeans and shoes were scattered over the boulder. Dawnelle's white first-aid kit tilted against the sleeve of her crumpled yellow slicker.

Gradually Dawnelle grew aware of the soft sound of breathing, and simultaneously, of a vague concern. The heaviness across her stomach shifted, moved up over her hand, cold as it lay on her chest. At once the mysterious worry and the weight seemed to culminate in a vivid fear. Baird. He'd been hurt, nearly drowned. Startled by the images that seemed now to be reality, she made a sudden convulsive movement and turned toward the warmth at her back.

Baird looked at her through sleep-drowsed eyes. His arm automatically slipped around her, pulling her close. Reflected firelight revealed a gash, crudely cleaned and patched by Band-Aids in places where his skin had been scraped raw by the rocks. The silver moonlight also revealed a gentle half smile on his lips as he closed his eyes again.

She was stunned as she nestled along the length of him, stunned and relieved to the very core of her being. Mutely she watched as he shrugged a red blanket high around both of them, covering his massive chest only partly clothed in a survival suit. Ben's suit, she knew instantly. She'd been groggily aware when someone dragged her own body over bumpy ground. Stripped and dressed again, she'd evidently been wrapped in blankets with Baird to conserve body heat. Ben was absent from the campfire. No doubt he'd gone for help.

Dawnelle searched urgently through the pockets of light and dark dappling the man beside her. Ben's suit was far too small for Baird. The sleeves were tied around his naked chest. The press of Baird's warm, half-naked body against her stomach stirred a buried emotion: desire, and that strange sadness. Reluctant to investigate the origin of her feelings, she resumed her inventory of other facts and impressions.

She felt an overwhelming gratefulness toward Lau and Ben, tinged with compassion for the loss of their boat. A shred of resentment accompanied these gentle feelings, however. Baird, she supposed, was in love with Lau, but Lau was evidently planning to encourage Ben's affection.

Dawnelle couldn't help but be elated at the knowledge that Ben would finally have the woman he loved, and that Lau might be out of Baird's reach. Baird would suffer when he found out, though, and that realization hurt her. He'd been rejected by so many people in his life—wife, brother Charles, Vee—even his grandfather when he returned to the lumber business. Lau's desertion would seal his trusting side forever behind a wall of pain.

Wanting to savor every intimate moment that remained between them, she nestled closer, until she could see the firelight revealed Baird's face more clearly. The gash extended from his ear deep into his beard. A thrill came to her then. After the swelling receded and the ugly redness faded, he would have to shave, exposing his face to her for the first time. It would be a lean face, she guessed. The twin arches of his forehead would seem even more intellectual without the beard; the cleft she'd discovered in his chin when they made love would lend some vulnerability to that otherwise craggy terrain. Sleep already softened his usual ruggedness, and she longed to run her fingers over the familiar features. His dark lashes fringed out over prominent cheekbones. His mouth, wide and traced with that burgundy line, had a look of sensuous need about it.

An answering need within her welled to the surface and broke free in a quiet urgent manner. Perhaps for the last time, she reached out, touched his forehead, closed her eyes.

"Dawnelle?"

Her eyes flew open. She jerked her hand away. Baird regarded her with surprise, the dusky blue of his eyes barely discernible beneath sleepy lids. "How are you?" he asked huskily, beginning to tuck the blanket around her back—in doing so, pressing her stomach against his own, lacing her pain with longing. "Hmm. . . ." He frowned, reached to his jaw. "Feels like a redwood crashed into my face."

"Timber-r-r," she teased softly. "You got that cut from trying to bodysurf in the middle of a south blow—in November, no less."

"Funny girl." He pulled her closer, closed his eyes with a weary-sounding sigh.

"Vee," she said. "Where's Vee?"

"San Francisco," he murmured, eyes still closed. He

sounded content. "Behind bars . . . trial sometime this spring. He's going to pay . . . me back."

"Pay you?"

"The money. Money. . . ."

It was over. Vee, locked up and prepared to pay Baird back, probably to prove he should be treated leniently by the courts. Dawnelle sighed. Jenkins in the hands of the law; Vee out of the picture. Now, only Lau.

As Baird's hips fell intimately over hers, Dawnelle felt the strain of sexual awareness mount. She closed her eyes in melancholy regret. When Lau rejected Baird, if she did, it would be natural for him to try to heal his pain with another woman—especially with another woman who'd willingly slept with him and who'd pleased him sexually. But his greedy, green-eyed lover would not be there for him, she resolved. If it killed her, she would reject him. Or could she? Would it be possible to turn away this man who brought life to her soul?

The question urged her eyes open. Awake and aware, Baird regarded her with an inexplicable tenderness. "Dawnelle, I've got to talk to you. Something's eating at me, and I feel a powerful need to get it off my chest. Are you feeling up to a speech?"

Averting her face, staring at the black underside of the granite overhang, she nodded. He would tell her now, she thought, anguished, beyond speech. While the woman he loved slept not ten feet away.

"I was just thinking how beautiful your nose is, dusted with diamonds of sand." She looked at him, a quick questioning look. He gently brushed away the sand. "A ski-jump nose, all perky and tipped up."

In spite of her inner turmoil, she smiled. He bent over

her, his shadow blanketing her face. He kissed the tip of her nose.

She drew her head quickly aside to look at Lau sleeping, all softly languorous. Baird glanced in the same direction. "Our duenna," he whispered. "You're safe from any liberties I'm inclined to take."

That was a strange thing to say, she thought, and looked up at him. His lips grazed hers. Then they were full on her mouth, tentative and gentle. Savoring. Roaming with inquisitive seduction. His chest pressed against her breasts, sending tingling warmth through her sore muscles, obliterating the ache of exhaustion. She felt shocked in some fundamental part of her soul, shocked enough to push him an inch or two away. Her breath fanned rapidly across his hovering face.

"I wanted to talk," he said, his voice strained. "But I see you're feeling frisky, and the memories that stirs make me feel kind of crazy inside. I wish to God we were alone."

Shaken, she caught her breath in a short gasp.

"Don't look so surprised, green eyes. What do you imagine I've been thinking about since I left you?"

Impossible as it seemed, he was telling her the things she'd gone to sleep dreaming about every night this week. Ideas began to float freely in her mind, like pieces of a poorly matched jigsaw puzzle. Did he want her, not Lau? But he'd nearly killed himself for that sleeping beauty. Had she, Dawnelle, mistaken childhood loyalty and friendship for love? Guilt ridden and half afraid to hope again, she met his shadowed gaze.

"What were you going to make a speech about, anyway?" Her voice tight with tension, she lay back and glanced involuntarily at Lau. "I'd like to hear... what was on your mind."

He laughed. "My head is so full of things I want to say, they're apt to tumble out and make no sense."

"Try one thing and the rest will follow."

"All right. I owe you an apology, a thank-you and an explanation."

She forced herself to remain calm—not daring to hope, not chancing despair. She nodded encouragement.

"To start with, you're one of the most courageous women who graces today's world. I feel ashamed of the opinions I harbored against you even as late as this afternoon."

"Opinions? About what?"

"Your basic character."

"What about it?"

"I misjudged your capacity for loyalty."

"Loyal—you mean when you went on this last trip you still didn't trust me?"

"Right."

Half resenting his admission, she let out her breath in a whoosh. "What changed your mind?"

"Tonight. The fact that you were willing to risk your life for me. The fact, actually, that you risked your life for all of us—Ben, Lau and me."

It was a warm honest statement. She could feel the rise of pleasure it gave her, yet she could feel Lau's presence ghosting the joy, putting an end mark to the stolen moments shared beneath the crimson blanket. "How did you know I went down the beach after you?" she asked, keeping her voice light.

"Your face. In all that water, I saw your face once—by light from the *Fernline*, I think."

The velvety voice rolled like Polynesian waves over her waiting ears, conjuring up the moment she had clutched him close to the maelstrom of water, making it seem a distant sunny afterthought mildly imagined from the lee of a south Seas bay. She had had that image before, aeons ago, when a fire crackled at her back and the man with the velvet voice had been her Scots laird, awakening her, fulfilling her rising passion.

He laughed, a mildly ironic sound, ending her pleasant drift into memory. "I told myself it was ridiculous, of course, seeing your face. You were just haunting me again. It was Lau with me in the water. She'd been knocked out, fallen overboard, and I'd somehow miraculously found her."

"No." With a small, impatient wave, Dawnelle cut short his explanation. "Lau didn't fall overboard."

"I know. When I came to, Ben was just leaving for a hike up the cliff. He filled me in, assured me, too, that he would put Miss Mo safely in the cottage. I went to sleep wrapped up with you, feeling very amazed that you'd put your life on the line for me."

"But you did the same for Lau."

"It's not *your* ability to trust that's in question, Dawnelle. It's me who has the big problem in that department."

"So this is a talk about trust. Your ability to trust. But I don't see—" Uncertain what he was driving at but suddenly reaching the limits of emotional endurance, she blurted out, "Do you love her? Lau?"

"I owe Lau a great debt for her loyalty. When she

visited me several times in prison, making it clear she had faith in my innocence, she gave me a hope that survived—if feebly—all the years I dealt with Vee's betrayal and Suzanne's arrogance. She was the only other person besides Pete, her grandfather, who never let me down."

"Then, Baird...I guess I'm not quite certain how you misjudged me, as you call it. What point are you making?"

"Wait a minute...." Reaching down along his leg, he lifted the limb gingerly, moved it slightly. An involuntary groan came from him as he straightened.

Dawnelle glanced quickly along the angular line of his hip. "Where are you hurt?"

"My right foot is killing me. They wrapped it, I think—broken, or maybe sprained. The thigh of the same leg is gashed from that swim I took when you were setting the flare." He leaned close, ran his fingertips over her face. "You're pretty scratched up yourself. Anything really sore?"

"Everything. But nothing serious." She pulled the orange hood from her head, rubbed a tender spot on her damp scalp. "I'm sorry you hurt so much. Want me to take a look at the wrapping?"

He shook his head. "Under the circumstances I'm lucky, thanks to you. Anyhow...." Propping himself up on an elbow, he settled so he could look over at her, his expression suddenly bleak. His gaze wrenched something painful inside her. When he spoke, his tone was flat, with a self-derisive quality that left her desolate. "I didn't consciously view my father's death and my grandfather's return to the business as betrayals until the trial and prison term. Things just kind of snapped inside me then. I added my whole life up during those years, and the sum total was that I was alone. Except for Lau."

"Your wife left you, I know," she said carefully, realizing this moment of revelation was as rare for Baird as oxygen in the statosphere.

"I hadn't loved my wife in years," he said. "But I felt abandoned by her all the same. Things get to be a habit sometimes, like a handy kitchen knife. Heavy stuff, huh?" Evidently to relax his serious mood, he jabbed playfully at her a couple of times. She chuckled in relief and ducked away.

"Then I met you."

Sobering instantly, she gave him a mocking frown. "I remember precisely how you reacted."

"That's the part I'm red-faced about." He took her hand, studied it minutely for evidence of sand or scratches. She shivered, but he seemed not to notice. Lifting her hand, he grazed her palm with his lips, then spoke with a rumble of emotion: "You're a hell of a woman, Dawny, and I've been an ass to cheapen you with comparisons to a status-conscious grande dame. Or to attribute to your character flaws I created entirely in my own mind."

Unnerved by the warmth in his voice, she quipped, "Flaws? This courageous perfect woman has a flaw? You're kidding me!"

"Charming. You're so charming I think I'll enroll in your charm school."

"'Charming' usually means you can wrap anyone you want around your little finger. I failed with you, remember?"

His chuckle was dry and self-deprecating—that pall of seriousness again. "I think a psychiatrist would tell me *I* was creating failure in our relationship. From the day I met you. I wouldn't have believed five months ago that I was so jaded about people's loyalties. But I believe it now. I created a flaw in your character—disloyalty—that doesn't exist."

"I've always wondered why you fired me back in June. . . ."

"I sent you away from me, don't you see? Using some paranoid delusion about privacy, I fired you for sticking up for my reputation in public. Fear, I guess. I truly believed you would eventually let me down."

"Like Vee." Some vague suspicion made her add, "Like Suzanne."

"Yes."

"You said something to me once in the woods near your house. . . . I reminded you of Suzanne. Even though you said there was a difference in my eyes, I got the feeling when you looked at me, you saw her. Why did you compare us?"

"Your background, which I knew from the news account. She put together business deals that left the small guys flopping in the dust when it was over. Ruthless."

"My track record doesn't even come close to that," she said reproachfully.

"Everything about you was heading you down the same path—or so I thought. Even your picture in that newspaper article—hair pulled up tight, face serious and remote. You were Suzanne all over again."

Inwardly she shuddered. She'd dressed all wrong at the fish-fry dance, she knew now. The white ruffly dress had been particularly appealing to him. She'd looked all summery and natural. But that black number and pulled-back hair, the remote sophisticated look—it had practically flaunted Suzanne in his face: hard, ruthless, disloyal wife. "If Suzanne was so smart," she said sarcastically, hating what the woman had done to Baird, "why didn't she watch Vee's activities a little closer? She should have been able to save you all that grief. If she was so smart."

"In the early years, she might have. When we met—I was crewing on her father's yacht one summer and fell in love with her icy wit—Vee happened to be there. She hated him instantly. Years later I took him into the business as a partner, and after that she refused to set foot inside my headquarters. Marine laboratories weren't her style, anyhow. She liked clean things—silver, electronics."

His gaze drifted to the fire, and she knew he was remembering. In a moment she said, "Do you expect me to change, Baird? I'll always have a little of the city in me. A little of the 'corporate.'"

"No. I know you're part of both worlds," he said with mild impatience. "That gutsy business side of you...it was just a red flag, that's all. I feared succumbing to you so completely that I'd leave myself open to betrayal. The truth is, I was driving myself crazy. My paranoia was always warring with my gut feelings about you."

Warmth filled her. On a disbelieving key she asked, "Are you saying things are different now?"

"Absolutely. You demonstrated your loyalty—love, if you will—tonight."

Baird assumed since she had put her life in jeopardy

to save him, she must love him. She remembered drawing the same conclusions about him when he went after Lau. Tragedy seemed to be playing a symbolic role.

"But if you'd survived without my help?" she insisted.

"I might still be uncertain about your loyalty to me, although your coming down this cliff to help the crew of the *Fernline* would have had me up nights for months, wondering why the act touched me so deeply. In any event, the first night we made love, things changed. I couldn't get enough of you.... And in the morning, I was shaken by my own feelings. That long stint in Singapore allowed me to get control of them again. I determined to take the relationship lightly from then on. I was damned unfair to you, I realize, being evasive and distant when you had every right to know what was going on inside me. I'm sorry. I just wasn't capable of letting go. Of trusting."

"Did you expect me to go for that forever, Baird? Share your bed but not your heart?"

He shook his head. "I know you were borderline. When I returned to the States today, I intended to ask you to go for a trial relationship. I might even have convinced you to go along with it—just on the sheer force of my being so crazy about you. Eh, green eyes? How's that for ego?"

She laughed but said nothing. The words were encouraging. But he'd always been unpredictable.

"Anyway," he added quietly, brushing her cold cheek with his lips, caressing her for a moment with his beard, "ultimately I may have lost you, driven you away with all that trust and loyalty business. It's frightening to think what it could still cost me to learn the truth about myself."

A hot flush crept over her skin. She could scarcely believe what he was telling her—that he cared, that he was crazy about her. Yet uncertainty lingered in his voice. She became impatient to know the end of his story. "What are you saying to me, Baird?"

"Haven't you figured out what I'm trying to say about *us*, Dawny?"

"Not exactly. I guess I need to hear it all."

"God!" He suddenly looked at the rocks, the fire and its sleeping vigilant. "I saw those green eyes of yours at night, and I cursed you for haunting me. In my dreams, you'd walk across the room from me, and I'd cringe inside with the fear you'd never turn back to me. Or you'd be melting in my arms, and every time I let you go I was afraid you'd leave for good. I could never rid myself of your image, the memory of you."

As she settled a hand on his shoulder, her rebuke came softly. "You seemed to do well enough without me for all those weeks this summer."

"Singapore was a haven for me in many ways. There, I could at least feed one of my compulsions."

"Revenge."

"Justice," he corrected. "Singapore did something else, too."

"The money?"

"How did you guess. After Vee's trial I'll be a millionaire again, Dawnelle." His voice came distantly, and she noted he watched the fire. "In five, I'll be a millionaire many times over. Langston Marine is going worldwide."

He's back to the singular, she thought apprehensively. "That's nice," she said.

"Hmm." He lay back and was silent for a moment. Presently he asked in a deliberately matter-of-fact tone, "Do you think Miss Mo would like Yurok around full-time?"

Her heart soared like a rocket jettisoned into space. With the greatest restraint she'd ever employed in her life, she brought her hands above her head, folded them beneath her damp hair and said quietly, "What did you have in mind?"

"A merger."

"A merger. Funny, I seem to have a sudden blockage in the logic side of my brain. What do you mean by that?"

He raised up and looked at her, a silly grin crooking his mouth. "I mean, angel, they'd make a cute couple. Their kids'll be beautiful."

"Re—" Coughing delicately, she composed herself. "Really. Are you proposing I give my canine protector to you? Or are you planning to make me a gift of yours?"

"I plan to keep all three of you."

"Three?" Suddenly the game was up. Her composure exploded in an anxious breath. "Oh, Baird, what are you suggesting?"

"Not suggesting—proposing."

"What?"

"Marriage."

She swallowed. Dawnelle Belanger Langston. Lots of *l*'s. She wondered how her father would take the news and thought he might be thrilled. He'd be wonderful with grandkids. Happy beyond reason, she reached to the familiar whorl in Baird's beard, touched him lovingly. She slipped her hand behind his neck, caressed the brown waves falling over her fingers.

His mouth hovered lower, lips parted. "Be my wife, Dawnelle. Trust me to love you always. If your love can overcome my fears about betrayal, my love for you can overcome anything that stands in the way of our happiness." He kissed her gently. Kissed her again. "Do you care about me enough to marry me, Dawny?"

"I love you, Baird."

He pulled back in surprise. "And here I was, bluffing my way through! I was afraid I'd worn out any feeling you might have for me. Why didn't you speak up instead of letting me ramble on endlessly?"

"You never asked."

"Minx. I'm asking now. Will you marry me?"

"Yes, Baird, and besides, it was rather nice to hear you go on about my character, and how I haunted you, and how much you loved our making love. Women like romantic drama. And since you *are* asking, there's another thing, Baird—" She couldn't seem to stop the flood of responses. The words rushed on and on, propelled by a wildly beating heart, inspired by the amused impatient face of her future husband. "The other thing is, I really want children—do you?—a boy and a girl, at least. And I'd love Miss Mo to have one litter of puppies. Wouldn't it be fun to see little Yuroks rolling around the hearth, all fluffy and dark? And, Baird, after my stint at the lighthouse, which I intend to finish, I'm set on keeping my finger in the P.R. pie, just part-time of course. I really enjoy helping people make a go of their businesses. Speaking of which, I have this marvelous idea for promoting those pipes of yours—''

His lips descended, stemming the tide of words.

Like a nervous bride, Dawnelle tentatively slipped her arms around him, withdrew, then clasped him in an eager embrace, her heart thudding as his lips sealed their new trust.

She thought she heard the distant roar of a helicopter, perhaps sensed a bright play of searchlights shining from above. But her eyes were closed tightly. She wondered, therefore, if the roar hadn't come from her own heart, and the light from some joyous source within her soul.

rude
ligne
cage
maladie
sable

ABOUT THE AUTHOR

"I was raised by my trapper-pilot father and a gentle mom who remembers walking four miles through waist-high snow to buy milk for her children." So says author Louella Nelson, whose first Superromance, *Sentinel at Dawn*, celebrates the outdoors and vital, loving people.

Her background is as varied as that of her heroine, Dawnelle Belanger, a public-relations executive turned lighthouse keeper. Louella grew up in Alaska, Hawaii, Arizona, Mexico. Her recent years have been spent in Southern California, where she is a magazine editor and mother to fourteen-year-old Stacee. While vacationing in Trinidad, California, she met with Ralph Hunter, grandson of one of the town's first lighthouse keepers, who provided much of the little-known lore that characterizes her story.

Apart from her love of rural life, only one other element runs more purely and wildly through the author's nature and her fiction: her own "vein of gold," romance. Louella's next Superromance will take the reader to Alaska to observe "fishpuller" Colleen Conaughy in action. . . on all fronts.